The Wild Earth's Nobility

SWALLOW PRESS BOOKS BY FRANK WATERS

The Lizard Woman (1930, reprinted 1994)
Midas of the Rockies (1937)
People of the Valley (1941)
The Man Who Killed the Deer (1942)
The Colorado (1946)
The Yogi of Cockroach Court (1947, 1972)
Masked Gods: Navaho and Pueblo Ceremonialism (1950)
The Woman at Otowi Crossing (1966)
Pumpkin Seed Point (1969)
Pike's Peak (1971; reissued 2002 as individual volumes):
    The Wild Earth's Nobility
    Below Grass Roots
    The Dust within the Rock
To Possess the Land (1973)
Mexico Mystique: The Coming Sixth World of Consciousness (1975)
Mountain Dialogues (1981)
Flight from Fiesta (1987)
Brave Are My People (1998)
A Frank Waters Reader: A Southwestern Life in Writing (2000)

ALSO AVAILABLE

A Sunrise Brighter Still: The Visionary Novels of Frank Waters, by
    Alexander Blackburn (1991)
Frank Waters: Man and Mystic, ed. Vine Deloria, Jr. (1993)

The Wild Earth's Nobility

Book I of the Pikes Peak trilogy

Frank Waters

With a Foreword by Joe Gordon

SWALLOW PRESS/OHIO UNIVERSITY PRESS

ATHENS

Swallow Press/Ohio University Press, Athens, Ohio 45701
©1971 by Frank Waters
Foreword ©2002 by Joe Gordon
Printed in the United States of America
All rights reserved. Published 2002

Swallow Press/Ohio University Press books are printed on acid-free paper ∞ ™

10 09 08 07 06 05 04 03 02   5 4 3 2 1

This volume reproduces the text of *The Wild Earth's Nobility* as it appeared in
Frank Waters's 1971 edition of *Pike's Peak*.

LIBRARY OF CONGRESS CATALOGING-IN-PUBLICATION DATA

Waters, Frank, 1902–
    The wild earth's nobility / Frank Waters.
        p. cm. — (Book I of the Pikes Peak trilogy)
    ISBN 0-8040-1047-1 (pbk.: alk. paper)
        1. Gold mines and mining—Fiction. 2. Colorado—Fiction. I. Title.

PS3545.A82 W45 2002
813'.52—dc21

                                                                2002021756

CONTENTS

Foreword

This is a story about the West, the day-to-day reality of the men and women who came to a frontier town to build homes and businesses and to raise families. It is not the formulaic, mythic West of cowboys and Indians, although Native American perspectives about the land are an important part of Waters's story. Such adventurous stories reside on the surface of Western experience, and are the stuff of the "western" as traditionally understood by outsiders. This is the story of the West as told from the inside by a writer who was born and raised in Colorado, who experienced first-hand its land and people. This insider's vision makes all the difference, and gives Frank Waters's story its realism, poignancy, and verisimilitude.

Joseph Dozier, Waters's grandfather, arrived in Colorado Springs, a frontier railroad town at the foot of Pikes Peak, "America's Mountain," in 1872, a year after the town was founded by General William Jackson Palmer. Dozier was a successful building contractor, and many of his buildings stand in Colorado Springs today, including the house at 435 East Bijou Street, where Waters was born July 25, 1902—the same year that Winfield Scott Stratton, the "Midas of the Rockies," died. Waters grew up in Colorado Springs, attended Central High School, and dropped out of Colorado College after his junior year in 1924. He left home shortly afterward. Real people, places, and dates are the historical-autobiographical basis of this story, the physical and imaginative places of Waters's story of the West. He didn't even change the names of people and places, except for his family—Dozier to Rogier—but there is no mistaking whom he is describing.

After leaving Colorado Springs, Waters worked at various jobs in Wyoming and California, traveled extensively in Mexico, and along the way became a writer. He visited the Pikes Peak region often in the mid-1930s. By that time he'd written two novels and published one, both set on the border between the United States and Mexico. He also was writing a new novel that would become the first of three in the Pikes (Waters used the possessive form—Pike's) Peak trilogy—*The Wild Earth's Nobility* (1935). The 1930s were important years in Waters's creative life. He was going back to his roots, rethinking his past, and formulating themes that he would develop more fully in his later work. He spent more than a year in the Pikes Peak region, in Colorado Springs and the mining towns of Victor and Cripple Creek, Colorado, where as a boy he'd worked in his grand-father's mines. His return is analogous to that of another Westerner, Mark Twain, who rediscovered his past, the deep pool of his imaginative center, in the small river town of Hannibal, Missouri. Pikes Peak, the mountain just west of Colorado Springs, became Waters's Mississippi River. His next three books focus on the "Matter of the Mountain." *Below Grass Roots* (1937) and *The Dust within the Rock* (1940) continue the story begun in *The Wild Earth's Nobility. Midas of the Rockies* (1937), while not directly a part of the Pikes Peak trilogy, is closely related. It is the biogra-phy of Winfield Scott Stratton, the richest and most spectacularly success-ful of all the miners in the Pikes Peak region, and a friend and sometime business partner of Waters's grandfather, Joseph Dozier.

The three novels that make up the Pikes Peak trilogy can be read in-dividually, for each book is a complete story, each focusing on a different generation of Rogier family history; however, all are related by the central, tragic story of the rise and fall of Joseph Rogier, and the impact of his life on his family. Of growing interest in the story is the life of March Cable, Rogier's grandson, who is the semi-autobiographical representation of Frank Waters himself. Read successively, the books provide a panoramic overview of the history of the American West, especially of the mining in-dustry during the late nineteenth and early twentieth centuries.

By 1960 all three books of the trilogy were out of print. Waters felt the story too important to be forgotten, and began an extensive redaction of the books, sharpening their focus, eliminating interesting but peripheral characters and scenes, and, in general, constricting the plot. In all he cut 800 pages. The result was a single volume, 743 pages long, divided into three sections that were titled after the original trilogy, but were more tightly structured, less rambling. *Pike's Peak: A Family Saga* was pub-lished in 1971. A reprint appeared in 1987, its title modified to *Pike's Peak: A Mining Saga*. Nothing else was changed, and the book remains in print today.

This new edition provides another interesting episode in the history of the publication of Waters's story, for it returns to the original three-volume format, but by replicating the redacted version that appeared in 1971. This allows the reader the benefit of Waters's own editorial judg-ment as found in the single-volume edition of 1971 without the awkward-ness of balancing a 743-page book.

Central to all Frank Waters's writing is his understanding of and commitment to the land, what he calls his "sense-of-place." Pikes Peak, the 14,110-foot batholith rising west of Colorado Springs, dominates the geography of the region today much as it did when Waters was growing up. This explains why the mountain overshadows the three novels in the Pikes Peak trilogy. Joseph Rogier is mysteriously drawn to settle within its shadow. Its meaning and silent power haunt him throughout *The Wild Earth's Nobility,* even as he struggles to succeed in a frontier town still visited by roaming bands of Plains Indians. The mountain is always there "from the depths of dreamless sleep to the horizon of wakeful consciousness." Rogier builds a successful construction business, maintains a household full of relatives, and raises his children. Then gold is discovered in Cripple Creek, just over the mountain.

At first, Rogier resists the temptation to join the miners, to probe the mountain's depths. However, when *Below Grass Roots* opens he is deeply involved in mining; he is not interested in gold primarily, but in knowledge—a need to understand himself by unraveling the secret of Pikes Peak. On one level, this novel includes some of the most detailed and descriptive passages about hard-rock mining in Western literature. On the human level, it is the story, not often told, of those who failed. Rogier's mission to find the heart of the mountain becomes an obsession and ends in financial disaster. The family's dreams of wealth turn to dust in the dry holes drilled in the solid granite of Pikes Peak. Family members find an escape only at the Sweet Water Trading Post on the Navajo Reservation. At various times, Ona, Rogier's eldest daughter, her husband, Jonathan Cable, and her son, March, discover a new world: an environment, a way of life, totally different from that of Pikes Peak.

When *The Dust within the Rock* opens, the family is barely surviving. Rogier is a broken man, and though he lives until the end of the book, he is no longer central to the events of the novel. The story turns to his grandson March, a deeply troubled and alienated young man. March loves his grandfather, but is embarrassed by his failure, and resents the snobbishness of the millionaires who did strike it rich, and who abandoned Rogier and his family. Most important, March is struggling to find his own understanding of the mountain, his own sense-of-place. He drops out of college and leaves home. For several years he wanders the Southwest and Mexico, returning to Colorado Springs only after he learns of his grandfather's death. At the end of the novel, March, like his grandfather before him, stands contemplating Pikes Peak. "Toward it he began his long and resolute journey."

Frank Waters's story of the West is rich in history, the details of life of the people on the frontier. It is, as Waters tells us, the saga of a family and of the most important industry in the early West—mining. Pikes Peak, the great mountain to the west, becomes a symbol of all Western land. In the end the reader must stand with March contemplating that mountain and ask: What is my responsibility to the land? How shall I inhabit it?

JOE GORDON

BOOK ONE

The Wild Earth's Nobility

PART I

SILVER

1

In the dusk it loomed before him now as it had the first time he had glimpsed it from the broad and muddy Arkansas far out on the buffalo plains below: like something risen from the depths of dreamless sleep to the horizon of wakeful consciousness, without clear outline yet embodying the substance of a hope and meaning that seemed strangely familiar as it was vague. Even its discoverer, Zebulon Pike, had first mistaken it for a cloud floating rootless above the upturned blue horizon — a great snowy peak too high for any man to climb. Yet many after him had tried to measure its fatal fascination. Rogier himself had vaguely intended to continue with the caravan on that wide-beaten trail, already called old, down toward Santa Fe. But like thousands of fools from the little towns along the Missouri a decade before, their wagon sheets emblazoned with the ridiculous slogan "Pike's Peak or Bust," he had been drawn toward it like a helpless moth to a flame. Not by the illusion of gold, that perpetual Pike's Peak Bust of greedy mankind, but by a single snowy peak. No more than that.

So he had turned north with a few other wagons to crawl up the Fontaine-qui-Bouille to the new little settlement at its foot. The barren stretch of plains kept breaking in tawny waves against the blue mountain wall as ineffectually as time. Still the peak loomed higher every day, its snowcap flushing pink at dawn, its majestic slopes shining like polished silver in the moonlight, its seamy crags baring teeth to every storm. If it had a single shape or meaning he had not yet found it. At once mystifying and alluring, beautiful and terrifying, it still held him here like a mammoth lodestone whose secret and ineffable power he had no will to resist.

"HEE-YAH!"

The sharp guttural cry roused Rogier from his reverie in the shadow of the porch where his heavy square-built body lounged motionless in a chair, his gaze enmeshed in the vast web of twilight translucent between the row of cottonwoods and the enigmatic face of the peak before him. The cry flashed like lightning across his somber mood, illuminating a crawl of figures along the creek. With it sounded the slip of hoofs upon the stones. Sharply outlined, a horse reared on its haunches, one forefoot knocking at the sky. He could see the slim body of its rider, the single lash of a brutal arm. Then making the leap, Indian and horse cleared the slippery bank to the right of a group of laboring squaws and disappeared beyond the trees as if the night had opened to their call.

Joseph Rogier tipped his chair down to all four legs and leaned forward. A band of Blue Cloud Arapahoes was crawling past to its encampment down the creek. It was not yet too dark to make out the heavily laden squaws and the ponies drawing still more dunnage lashed to spruce tepee poles dragging on the ground. The confused murmur of their voices washed up to him on the breeze with occasionally the neigh of a horse and the cry of a child. The papooses never made a sound. Bound on cradleboards strapped to their mothers' backs, they might have been little mummies embalmed in their casts.

For days such bands had been passing by. Arapahoes and Cheyennes from out on the Great Plains, making for the mouth of the canyon at the foot of the high peak where every fall they gathered to drop offerings in the sacred springs, and to trade with the mountain Utes. There was seldom trouble except when too much whiskey got around, recalling to young bucks the difference between their tribes. Then the school and court house bells began to ring.

People farther out than Rogier could hear them in the thin, rarefied air, gentle mellow notes breaking against the somber mountain wall; and hearing, men and women and children went to stay in the courthouse until the Indians had passed by.

Rogier knew everyone enjoyed the occasion; it made them feel they were pioneers in a Wild West that was no more. Women gossiping over their sewing and basket lunches. Children playing "Cowboy and Indian" on the grass and stealing to ambush behind the lilacs. Young men forever cleaning rifles and hanging open-mouthed upon the words of old men (past thirty) come from the Civil War. Their interminable talk of the Union Saved and the Great American Empire so accentuated Rogier's deep sense of exile that he never went in, himself. A Southerner of French Huguenot descent, born an aristocrat and an individualist, he abhorred their crude provincialism and at the same time suffered his lack of their proclaimed nationalism.

His father had borne all the graces and vices that a South Carolina gentleman was expected to bear during the decades preceding the Civil War. Daniel Lee Rogier owned a large rice plantation upriver from Charleston, maintained a gentlemanly acquaintance with his wife and three sons that was naturally and charmingly noncommittal, and lavished his caresses and outspoken admiration upon his horses and hunting dogs. With the death of his wife he left his youngest son Joseph, a child of eight, to be reared in the Negro quarters and dedicated himself wholly to his career of rum and debt.

His success as a drunkard and an ineffectual planter was soon complete. It was aided by his best friend and closest neighbor, Dr. Lascelles, to whom he pledged the extent of his plantation as security for his conniving oldest son's alleged gambling debts. With the changing wisdom of successive generations men live by the single code necessary for their type of existence; and their catchwords are State, Church, Fame, Courage, or Six Per Cent. Daniel Lee Rogier with others of his time subscribed his life to Honor as the light illuminating his every deed. It was the first thing in his mind that morning when a house servant opened his study doors to a group of lawyers and creditors and went to fetch the rum. Rogier took one glance at the face of Dr. Lascelles and knew that they had come to escort him down the road to ruin. Rising from his desk, he turned to look out the open window upon his spacious rice paddies extending beyond the outhouses and slave quarters to the river.

"A divine mornin', gentlemen," he observed quietly.

The preliminaries were delicately brief. One of the men took a sip of excellent Southern rum and looked up from the sheaf of papers. "Dr. Lascelles advises us of the considerable extent to which you have pledged security for equally large obligations, Mr. Rogier"

"He has my word, suh."

"You wish to contest the regrettable action necessary?"

"You have my word, suh!"

A short silence filled the room. Dr. Lascelles drew an easy breath. Rogier remained standing.

"Then you will be prepared to conclude arrangements, Mr. Rogier?"

He bowed. It was as if all his weaknesses, his life of charming uselessness fell from him with that needless, foolish gesture. As though a man lived a long life of emptiness, like a lonely monk walking his cloisters, awaiting the one moment of fulfillment and knowing the sound of his call.

The vultures moved in quickly. The boy Joseph was ten years old when the Rogier plantation on its estuary, with all the black children of its soil, the white-porticoed house, kitchen, slave quarters, carriage house, stables, and blacksmith shop, passed out of his father's hands at a word and a gesture that had taken generations to make casual. At his father's death soon afterward, he was bound out by his oldest brother to learn the carpenter trade in Roanoke, Virginia, and went there in a tow shirt. He always remembered that tow shirt and others like it. Not for seven years did he have a coat of his own to cover them. It was homespun for him by a widow with a lame daughter his own age. The girl with a club foot taught him to read and write, then kissed him and sent him to Maryland for his first job.

In Baltimore he worked fourteen hours a day in a carpenter shop, and during his two years there squeezed in three months' schooling. With an aptitude for arithmetic, he evolved a method of his own for making computations on a steel square. When Civil War broke out, Rogier ran away to avoid conscription by either side.

It was perhaps then it suddenly struck him — a strange conviction of his solitary exile upon an insubstantial world fraught with fleshly folly and the fraility of human knowledge. If for the first time in his life he felt both the elation and the disturbing falsity of his complete individual freedom, he also found himself with nothing to love nor strive for, no allegiance to any creed or land, no star to guide him across the empty earth.

At St. Joseph, Missouri he got off the train. It was night and he was ill. His hands, his knees trembled. Every few moments as he walked along the drab, dark streets beside the river he stopped and sat down upon his carpet bag to wipe the sweat from his face. Three squares farther on he came to a boarding house with a lamp burning in the window. He knocked and a woman let him in. Next morning he could not get up. That afternoon the woman told him he had the fever and dragged him up into the attic. For days he lay on a pallet of quilts and blankets spread on the floor. At intervals the woman handed water and food up through the trap door. Only in mid-afternoon when all the boarders were gone and the children were playing outside did she crawl up the ladder to his room.

"Well, young fella, still takin' youah naps reg'lar-like?" she would inquire; and then with a chuckle, "Thank Gawd, suh, youah quiet enough, and not a sign of anything ketchin' on the place! Now s'posin' you turn over for a wash. Ovah you do, suh!"

There was something about Rogier's sickness infinitely repugnant to him. It was as if a stealthy fate had struck him down as he had emerged into the brilliance of his freedom; a shameful affliction that condemned him to lonely darkness. And the woman, Mrs. White, was its accomplice. Yet he listened for her footsteps like a lover awaiting his mistress, and received her with the same bright eyes and silent tongue. Only when it was over between them, the doctoring, washing, and cleaning, and she settled back in her blue gingham that had regained its faded color wherever water had splashed, did he feel at ease.

Mrs. White was a slight, little-boned woman from Louisville, Kentucky whose father, Captain De Vinney, had been one of the oldest steamboat captains on the Mississippi. Her first husband had been a wealthy furniture dealer who outfitted boats plying on the river. A short time after he had died from drinking too much sour wine at a boat christening, his warehouse burned. Mrs. White gave the insurance money to her son Ansil to take to her brother-in-law in New Orleans to invest for her. The lad got off the boat there too late at night to catch the ferry to his uncle's home in Algiers, and went to a hotel. Put into a room out of which had just been carried a sick man, he caught yellow fever and died before his uncle learned of his whereabouts. "Leastways, that's what my brother-in-law says. The money was never found," she explained in her casual matter-of-fact voice that betrayed a profound and unmoved knowledge of mankind. With her two remaining children, both girls, she had moved to St. Jo and married Mr. White; and when he had run off to the war, she had opened her boarding house.

"He never said what State he was goin' to fight for, and I ain't heard from him yet. What side do you belong on, North or South, suh?"

Rogier was propped up against the wall in a posture of indefinable aloofness that involuntarily had brought the "suh" to her lips despite his threadbare clothes and coarse hands. "I reckon I just don't rightly belong anywhere, Mrs. White," he said quietly.

He seldom broke his noncommittal silence. Only once he asked briefly, "I wonder why you've been doing so much for me?"

A woman so inured to the vicissitudes of a troublesome existence that human tragedies took on the aspect of mere daily faults, so naturally responsive with a sympathy which was wordless because it was involuntary, Mrs. White seemed surprised at his allegation of kindness. She turned on her knees before the trap-door opening to face him. "I reckon it's because it ain't in you to ask no he'p or expect any, suh."

Upon his recovery Rogier obtained work with a construction firm. A few months later Mr. Powell, the architect and builder, had come to the house to see him. It was evening and Rogier, the last boarder to come in, was eating alone at the table. Mrs. White, quick to meet the astounding occasion of employer coming to employee, hurried into the parlor to light the twisted glass chimney lamps. But Mr. Powell walked directly into the dining room. Rogier rose and shook hands. Then he sat down and continued eating. Mr. Powell sat down beside him and began to talk. The building was not progressing. There were delays and more delays. Something had got into the men. He had to have somebody who could take over the whole thing and keep it going. A firm hand and a head for construction. He had thought of Rogier—he had a way with the men. Finishing supper, Rogier crossed his fork and knife on the plate. "Beginning tomorrow morning I'll see that things get along, Mr. Powell," he said.

A couple of years later Mrs. White's husband showed up. At the close of the war he had wandered down into Mexico where he had been imprisoned for a year. Returning home, he suffered so badly with his maggot-infested feet he could hardly walk. For hours he sat with his feet under the pump to ease the pain. Eventually a friend, a wagonmaker by trade, offered him work in the next county. All the family, Mr. and Mrs. White and her two daughters, Molly and Martha, with Rogier and the other boarders, gathered in the parlor to discuss the impending change.

"I don't know about the girls," began Mrs. White. "As fuh as Molly goes, she's way past schoolin' anyhow. But take Martha now —" Rogier interrupted. "Don't worry about her," he said in his quiet persuasive voice. "You're going to leave Martha here with me. I know a house that'll suit us first rate."

A month later when the Whites left, Rogier married Mrs. White's youngest daughter, Martha. She was a small wiry girl, sixteen years old, and deaf in one ear from an early attack of brain fever. Her habit of listening with her head turned, and the omnipresent string of black beads around her throat — a reminder of the rosaries worn by the Sisters of the Sacred Heart Convent where she had gone to school — accentuated her pose of early maturity. What drew Rogier to her was a mystery neither of them knew. But what held him, even after the birth of two daughters, was the nervous force that surcharged her small body and her great capacity for simply living, both of which she devoted to him.

Old for his age, Rogier accepted his family with equanimity and responsibility, and only to himself admitted the rank heresy of the continuing conviction of his secret exile on a still strange and lonely earth. It was this that had led him across the plains to the high snowy beacon that had suddenly loomed up before him like an etiolated projection of his own hidden longing.

Darkness now had obscured both the Peak and the last straggle of Indians. Rogier got up from his chair on the porch and went inside. In the big square kitchen he lit a lamp, and stirred up a supper of cold porridge with fresh wild raspberries and cream. Then, as he had done every night for two weeks, he settled down to read Martha's last letter. The news had thoroughly penetrated every fiber of his thoughts. She and their two girls, Ona and Sally Lee, were on their way to join him. With them was coming Martha's older sister, Molly, and her two boys, Bob and Hiney, to rejoin her husband, Tom Hines. They were all coming on the new railroad and they hoped everything would be ready for them. Martha as usual had addressed her scrawled note to him with "B. N." — "Big Nigger." The nickname made him smile. He took it as a compliment, remembering the only friends he had known as a child, those great black men who were children yet, maintaining their childlike dignity and divine human sympathy.

As he sat there, waiting with patient anticipation for the morrow when their train was due, he heard hoofbeats outside. The rider jumped off, threw back the door, and stalked inside. It was Tom Hines, young, lean, excited, carrying a rifle in the crook of his left arm.

"Hi, Joe! Haven't forgot what tomorrow is, have you?"

"No, Tom. The house is all ready for them."

"So's mine! Hope they're on the train all right." He was one of those men who never quite succeed in growing up and who appear at their best when affecting boyish enthusiasm — a role that was always changing with new ventures. "I'll bet Molly and the kids will be glad to see me!" His eyes were bright, his face flushed, as he still stood there with his rifle.

"What's the gun for, Tom?" asked Rogier quietly. "Been out hunting?"

With the question Tom changed into another role. "Indians! Never saw so many as this time. There's goin' to be trouble sure and I aim to protect my family. I've never got me a Redskin yet, but this time I'm goin' to!"

"They're peaceful people when they're let alone. Won't you sit awhile?"

"No Joe. I'll meet you at the depot tomorrow, eh? I just rode by now to see if I could get a five from you. Somethin' to celebrate our first night on. Sure, I've got flour and salt and lard, all that, but you know—''

Rogier got up and from a cookie jar took out a five-dollar bill. Tom almost grabbed it from his hand in his eagerness to get away. Rogier from the door watched him swing on his broomtail mare and gallop away. Then again he sat down on his chair on the porch.

Down the creek at the crossing of the Big Ditch a faint glowing pink marked the Indian encampment. In nights past Rogier had walked down there to watch the stomp dancing. Flamelight and pulsing drum; they created a world into which leaped strong lean figures naked to the waist and with that in their faces he never saw elsewhere. A simple and peaceful people, contrary to hotbloods like Tom and his kind; strange only to intruding whites like himself because of all America's many breeds and races they alone were an inalienable part of this vast and naked rock-ribbed earth.

What its rhythm was, the meaning of its hidden spirit, they alone somehow mirrored it as had that rider making the leap an hour before. The black silhouette of horse and rider, the eerie cry, remained burnt into his mind. Rogier did not know why. No more than why the earliest recollection of a child is not the great event but only the queer turning of a single phrase, like the odd disquieting remembrance of the gesture of a loved woman's hand long after she has faded from his mind. He only knew that he could never erase that instant's picture from his memory. The wild rearing horse and its slim rider, arm upraised, exultant in the night. The upright feather stuck into his hair—a single feathered plume descended to him who wore it, not defiantly as men flaunt the faded cockades of their decadent heritage, but proudly, like the everlasting insignia of the wild earth's nobility.

The disturbing sense of beauty in the night was echoed by the throb of the far-off drums. In the luminous purity of the moonlight he could make out again the pale, silvery sheen of the great peak. It too seemed to throb in unison with the pulse beat of the drums, with the living land itself.

2

Near eight o'clock next morning on the depot platform in Denver City, two Englishmen stood discussing the toy train drawn up at the siding before them. It was the Denver and Rio Grande narrow-gauge, projected to run between Denver and Mexico City. The diminutive locomotive was appropriately named *Montezuma* and the two passenger coaches *Denver* and *El Paso*. The undertone of pride in the two men's voices had some justification. Most of the capital required for construction of the initial seventy-six miles of line to Colorado Springs had been raised in London and the rails had been bought in England. Still they argued over a curve of two chains radius, a gradient of one in ninety-two, and whether the train would run or not. The toot of a whistle and the ting-a-ling of a bell that reminded them of "Muffins all hot!" in London, stopped their conjectures. They knocked out their pipes and sauntered toward the "baby railroad."

Down the platform behind them hurried two women weighed down with carpet bags, bundles and lunch baskets, and four children. "Go on! Can't you hurry none?" the smaller woman cried to her two young girls. Her short straight mouth bit off the words in exasperation as though they were another bit of black ribbon dangling from her rusty black bonnet.

"Yeah; go on, boys. Quit bothering your cousins," the older woman called easily to the two boys loafing along beside the two girls. It was a drawl that belonged to her large body, wide-featured face, and air of genial, tolerant strength.

Arriving at the coach, Mrs. Rogier inquired breathlessly, "Is this our train?" The conductor took a chew of tobacco with deliberate concern. "Well, Ma'am, it belongs to the D & RG."

Mrs. Rogier dropped her carpetbag. "Why, of all the —"

"Get on, Martha," Sister Molly's deep voice interrupted, as she hoisted the bags up the steps. Then turning with a grin to the conductor, "Tell us when we get to Colorado Springs, won't you, Mister?"

"Sure," he called back. "We don't go no farther."

The coach was an odd little car with a seat on one side to accommodate one person and one on the other side large enough for two, the seats alternating so that the car could keep its balance. The two girls, Ona and Sally Lee, each took a single seat. Molly Hines' two boys, quarreling over who should sit next to the window, crawled into the double seat across from Sally Lee.

"You just settle yourselves down quick!" Sister Molly flung at them. "Bob, you quit figitin' around. And Hiney, you quit ticklin' Sally Lee with your toes before I step on 'em!"

The two women sat across the aisle from Ona with all the luggage. At the first jerk of the train as it pulled out of the depot, Mrs. Rogier began rearranging and restacking the carpetbags, bundles, and baskets. Imperious and inflexible as one enlightened by the sense of command, she assumed toward her sister an unconscious attitude of unwarranted superiority. Sister Molly, carelessly unconcerned, watched her with tolerant humor, wondering why a man like Joseph Rogier had ever married such a fussy woman. Still it was quite evident that Mrs. Rogier often wondered why Sister Molly had married a man like Tom Hines.

Her few years in southern Missouri, terrible with human mockery, had made Molly a woman. The Whites were neighbors to a bunch of Union soldier outlaws headed by Jessie James and Cole Younger. One day they brought in an old man to shoot at sunrise.

Molly played cards with a Union officer to save his life while the old man sat praying on a cracker box. Molly won, she was sure, because the next day was her birthday. All the outlaws got up early next morning, laughing and talking as they led the old man over the hill. Happy and excited, Molly cooked a gingerbread birthday cake for them. A few hours later the men returned with the old man's body and ordered White to make a coffin.

A short time later Molly married a man named Henry who took her to Kansas City on a wedding trip. After dinner a few evenings later he went out of the hotel to buy a cigar. He never came back.

Soon afterward she married Tom Hines. He was a handsome man who staggered through life blind and smiling; weak without seeming ineffective, likeable because of his faults, and always busy at cross-purposes. With their marriage Sister Molly's life opened into full flower. It was as if all her life she had walked at the edge of a vast chasm of frustration and silent despair. And then, with one divining look of love, she saw in Tom Hines the miasmic nobility, the divine promise of all human life, and dedicated her own to its preservation.

"God, I do love him," she murmured as though he were already close enough to whisper.

"I suppose you do," Mrs. Rogier answered. "I only hope he's got the house finished for you. It's been long enough."

She folded her small hands together in a complacent gesture that showed she had no doubt about her own home. Nor did Sister Molly. Rogier would have his house done, his business started. And then, in a sudden hot rush, came the feeling she didn't care about anything if Tom were there waiting.

"Tom ought to get along better out here," observed Mrs. Rogier.

Sister Molly knew what she meant and was truly grateful. "And don't think Tom ain't either. He thinks everything of Joe, the way he brought him out and helpin' him get started. And Tom's goin' to get along. I just know it, Martha!" Her large coarse face assumed a mask of faith and courage to cover the secret contradiction that had instantly replaced her words.

"I hope so. We all got to start a new life. We got to be somebody!"

The indomitable ambition of the little woman seemed so futilely set against the wall of mountains rising into view that Sister Molly turned her face away.

It had been a long and tiresome trip on the Kansas Pacific to Denver where they had changed trains. Herds of thousands of buffalo, stray remnants of the tens, the hundreds of thousands being killed off. Bunches of graceful, leaping antelope. Prairie-dog towns counted off on the children's fingers. But always the same flat and endless plain. Sister Molly could see no beauty in its empty, arid waste; in the tumbleweeds rolling across the land as if of their own momentum; in the steadily receding horizon. The crude towns where they stopped to eat seemed brutal and unreal. Men, men everywhere. And always eating. Buffalo tongue, buffalo hump, antelope steak, beefsteak. Always men and meat. "We're in Colorado now," a man told her, sniffing out the open window. "It don't look no different, but it's got the feel. Kinda cold. And the wind." Then one sunrise she awakened to see the far, faint rise of mountains. Forbiddingly unreal, they kept rising to block their path at Denver.

Now on the little narrow-gauge they were crawling south along the eastern side of that great blue wall; creeping across grassy slopes between huge cliffs, past castellated rocks of red sandstone, white limestone, and blue shale half-hidden by groves of pine like the ruins of ancient castles in another world called old because it was so much newer. Colorado, the land of colored rock. And then at last Pike's Peak, white and shining, rising more than 14,000 feet above tidewater. The coach was silent as if a blast of wind from its summit had frozen every voice.

A sudden childish shout aroused the coach. "Indians! Hiney, here they are!" He and the two girls rushed across the aisle to stare out the window with Bob. A few men on the coach turned their heads briefly, then sank back to their pipes. Outside, the long line of Indians straggled on. At the end of the column struggled small ponies dragging dunnage lashed to tepee poles, accompanied by squaws carrying their papooses on their backs. Ahead of them were the older men, beclouded in dust, beset with dogs and flies, and enveloped in a dreary aura of weariness. Only at the front of the column a few young bucks yelled and lashed their ponies into a short run beside the coach as the train rolled past.

"Reckon we'll be gettin' in soon. Are your things ready?" asked Mrs. Rogier with her unavoidable assurance.

A queer feeling swept down upon Sister Molly. She could not tear her gaze from the massive peak. Its lower slopes smokily clothed in pine, it reached out like a shadow falling on the plain. "Oh, my God! I hope he's here!" she whispered in a hoarse voice.

He was there on the platform to sweep her into his arms for a hearty hug the instant they got off the train. Beside him stood Rogier to greet his own family with equal affection but less demonstrativeness. At last the hugs and kisses, the excited shouts, were over. Rogier led them to a carriage he had hired for the occasion.

"How can we afford it? Sure it didn't cost too much?" asked Mrs. Rogier sharply.

"Get in. Get in!" He settled in the front seat, taking the reins and lighting a cigar while Tom stowed in the luggage. Then Tom got in beside him, holding his rifle between his knees.

"We're goin' to show you the town first!" announced Tom proudly as they drove off.

The new town had an incomparably beautiful setting. It was located on the flat plain only six miles east of the foot of Pike's Peak. Here at the mouths of its yawning canyons and Ute Pass leading through the mountains bubbled the many iron and soda springs to which the Indians, since time immemorial, had made pilgrimage. Already a small resort was growing up there, named Manitou after the Indians' Great Spirit.

"We won't go over there now. The Indians are gatherin' and they might be trouble," explained Tom, patting his rifle. "Unless of course we do somethin' about it!" Taking it up from between his knees, he sighted along the barrel to a spot about halfway between Manitou and town. That's where Colorado City is – the first capital of Colorado before Denver. Oh, you got lots to see, all right, just as soon as I get me a team and buggy."

Rogier drove slowly up the low hill behind the railroad depot and past a hotel of two stories, covered by a mansard roof with five dormer windows, and with a spacious veranda in front. "That's General Palmer's Colorado Springs Hotel," continued Tom. "He's the one that started Colorado Springs here and built the Denver and

Rio Grande. Rich as all get out, him and all his English cronies. Look there!" He pointed to the ladies sitting on the veranda and then to an English nursemaid strolling behind an English dogcart out in front. "Blasted Britishers all of them! That's why us folks call the town Little London."

"I don't see why," muttered Mrs. Rogier

"It takes a lot of money to build a town and railroad, and most all of it was raised in England," said Rogier quietly. "So naturally there's quite an English colony here. I don't know but what they're doin' a good job. They're quite likely to make the town into a real spa, the Saratoga of the West. It's a new country. There's plenty of room for all of us."

"But I want to see Indians!" yelled Bob.

There were many to see now, as Rogier drove slowly down spaciously wide Pike's Peak Avenue fronting the hotel and the great peak rising behind it. The dusty street was lined with small stores, leather, harness, and butcher shops, riding horses and teams snubbed to hitching racks. Big Indian bucks idled from door to door. Blanketed squaws sat on every corner with their buffalo robes spread out for sale. Little London! What an anomaly it was, this tidy English colony set in the midst of the crude American West!

"It's growin' fast. We'll get along here first rate," said Rogier quietly, whipping up his team to turn northward towards the outskirts of town.

The sun was sinking behind the mountains when he drew up at the Hines' place. It reminded the girl Ona of an old tramp man she once had seen sitting and smiling beside the dusty road. Small and ungainly, its clapboards stuck out every which-a-way. Weeds and sunflowers grew high everywhere around it. Even the flat roof of the kitchen was covered with earth and sprouted a wild growth of oats.

"Wait'll I light the lamp so's you can see it better!" Tom jumped out, ran inside, and came back to help Sister Molly out of the carriage. All the others trooped in behind them. The light of the lamp in the kitchen revealed a stack of unwashed dishes on the iron cookstove, and the unmade beds in the room beyond. Catching Mrs. Rogier's quick look, Tom laughed. "Why, I was so excited about seein' Molly and the boys this mornin' I never bothered about them dishes and covers!" He wrapped his arms about Molly

"It ain't nothin' but a pioneer's home, but you can bet your bottom dollar we're going to have us a house as big and fancy as them Englishmen!"

"I don't care, Tom! This one's fine. Jes' so's we can all be together!"

"That we are, right now, and we're going to celebrate!"

On the kitchen table sat a bottle of Three Star Hennessy surrounded by three small boxes of candy. The candy he hurriedly gave to Molly and the two boys, then opened the bottle of whiskey.

"We're not goin' to stay," Mrs. Rogier said resolutely. "Molly's got the dishes and beds to do, supper to cook, and things to settle. So've I when I get home."

"Oh stay, Martha. We're all here together for the first time to start a new life. I'll rustle up somethin'."

"I want to go home. I'm hungry," wailed little Sally Lee in a petulant voice.

"I'll have a drink with Tom before we go," said Rogier. "How about it, Molly?"

Pleased and excited, she set out three glasses. "Open your candy now, boys, and pass it around."

Tom took his drink down neat and quick, and poured himself another. "Here's to my wife and kids, and you all too! It's goin' to be a great life. Here's to it!"

Rogier smiled gently and set down his empty glass. Then catching Mrs. Rogier's sharp glance, he rose to his feet. "Well, I've got three more of the family to settle in a new house, too. We'll see you in the mornin'."

Tom and Molly, arms around each other, watched the carriage drive away.

3

Ona always remembered their first house. It sat alone in the prairie north of the end of Tejon Street. Built like a Maltese cross, as her mother always said, it had a long narrow room sticking out on each side of the big square kitchen, a porch to the south, and a storeroom with a big cellar underneath, to the north. Seen from the creek where she played among the cottonwoods, the house seemed bigger than it was. Especially at dusk when the sun, dropping behind the mountains, brought on a swift pale night without twilight. Then the house seemed even bigger, the sharp edges of its ramshackle outline, its sloping roof, blurred like fresh inked lines into the dark. On summer nights the yellow radiance of the lamp trickled out of the open doorway and lay liquiscent in queerly shaped puddles on the porch. On cold winter nights the lamp sat in the window, small and white, like a silver stud on a bridle strap. It was only when seen from the other side, a tiny speck against the great purple mountains, that the house appeared for what it really was.

Every day Ona and her mother walked to town, stopping by the Hines' place to pick up Sister Molly. It was only a couple of miles or so and on the way they passed the College Reservation,

a big piece of land bought by government scrip and set aside for
a college.

"Joe's biddin' on the first building, Cutler Academy," Mrs.
Rogier said proudly. "My! A college already!"

"He's gettin' a good start, contractin' so soon," Sister Molly
agreed.

Mrs. Rogier nodded her black bonnet curtly. "Since Joe's so
busy he can't use our six acres and has offered them to Tom to work
with his; I don't see why Tom don't."

"Oh, Tom's pretty busy too, he's gone all day long. Besides, he
ain't cut out for farmin'; he likes to be around people. Next spring he
says he's goin' out on a huntin' trip. He was talkin' to two men who
have been out on the plains since last December and have just come
in. They brought in more than 600 buffalo, wolf, and antelope hides;
and they got $2 apiece for them."

"Well, he'll get more lonesome than he would farmin'," observed Mrs. Rogier drily.

In town Ona lagged behind. There was so much to see, all of it
different. The hotel, its cool veranda crowded with Easterners and
Britishers wearing such nice clean clothes and giving off an air of
opulence and comfort. And across from it, Sample's Boarding
House. The long narrow building with its rooms each opening upon
the long wooden porch was the rendezvous of all the teamsters,
miners, traders, and riff-raff of the town. Teams and wagons of all
descriptions, from a buckboard to an old covered wagon, stood out
in front. As Ona passed by she could see the porch floor strewn with
whips, spurs, saddles, and other gear.

Of all the stores she liked the butcher shops best. In front of
every one hung marbled carcasses of deer, antelope, bear, and
buffalo. These markets were the favorite lounging places of the
Indians. Early in the morning the squaws would arrive and unstrap
their papooses from their backs, leaning the cradle boards with their
little living mummies against the wall. There were old men wrapped
in blankets and a queer dignity; young bucks strutting back and
forth. Despite Tom's constant preaching against them, they didn't
look very mean or dangerous to Ona; just kind of dirty and lazy.

Wherever she went she was aware of the mountains. They
seemed so close you could walk to them to play. From Cheyenne

Mountain and the Devil's Horn to the south, they extended to Cameron's Cone and Pike's Peak with the Bottomless Pit between, and then northward in an unbroken wall as far as she could see. Pike's Peak was the highest. You could tell that by a line drawn across it. Below the line the peak was dark with pine and spruce and cedar; above it, the peak rose bare and white. Timberline. That's what it was called.

But Ona liked the prairies and plains too. Early one morning soon after their arrival she took all the children out for a picnic: little Sally Lee, Bob and Hiney, and the Siegerfries girl Marion. The Siegerfries family lived on two of Tom's mortgaged six acres. Marion brought along their old blind mule. It was good she did, for if Sally Lee or Hiney became tired they could ride on her; besides she could carry their lunch of bread and butter with jam, apples, pickles, and pie.

They walked down the creek to the long irrigation ditch called the Big Ditch, where the Indians always camped on their way to the mountains. Then they straggled eastward toward a low range of wooded bluffs out on the prairie. Austin Bluffs was split by a gunsight notch called Templeton's Gap. It was a great lightning and storm center, Marion said. Last year there had been a cloudburst over it. The water came down with such great force that it gouged a great hole in the earth, causing the mud to roll out in balls ranging in size from that of a walnut to a squash, all hard as if they had been baked in an oven.

"That's where we'll go! To get us some of them mud balls!" everybody decided.

So now they all walked faster, laughing and throwing stones, beside the plodding blind mule. The bundle of lunch tied to a rope looped around the mule was continually sliding down and hanging under her belly.

"Let her hang," said Bob practically. "It can't balance on her backbone nohow." He and Marion walked together now, leading the mule. They were great friends although with her starched sunbonnet she topped him several inches. Hiney and Sally Lee kept close together too, leaving Ona alone. She always felt alone, no matter how many people were around. It was an awful feeling sometimes, when just for an instant you imagined you were dead and invisible, walking with them like a ghost, or spying on them through the keyhole of a dark closed-up room. She would be glad to grow up and not feel that way then.

Still it was good to be out on the prairies, watching the buffalo or gramma grass waving in the wind, and seeing bright clumps of purple lupines and bluebells, crimson Indian paintbrush, wild yucca, onions, and locoweed. Prairie dogs barked from their mounds. Plump meadow larks sang deliriously, ignoring a hawk that hung as if suspended from the cloudless sky. A rabbit ran out from a bush. Innumerable horny toads crawled through the warm sand, some with yellow bellies which caused warts.

"Hurry up! Come on!" shouted Marion. "We've found a red-ant hill!"

When Ona reached them, Bob was on his knees frantically digging into a large pebbly mound. Ona knew what he was after — garnets. She liked to think of the big red ants bringing the flinty blood-red stones up from way down in the ground to build into their hills, and the Indians coming along later to dig them out and sell them in town. Her mother had bought her a little jar of them. To carry all they were going to find here, the children ate up the pickles in their big jar. But digging was hard without a shovel, and the big red ants swarmed bitingly over their legs. So they gave it up, and tied bunches of wildflowers into the rope around the old mule, making a garland of red, white, and blue.

Farther on they ate their lunch although it was hardly mid-morning. Then Bob, who had wandered off, started to yell and wave his arms. They all jumped up and ran to him.

"I've cornered a rattler!" he yelled. "Hiney, you turn over that big stone with Ona. And when he comes out, Marion, you keep pushing his head down with a stick while I grab him by the tail! Don't hurt him none!"

The snake was really big and beautiful with six or seven rattles. Bob carried him by the tail while Marion kept pushing down his head with a stick. Ona led the blind, garlanded mule with Sally Lee and Hiney mounted on her back.

It was then they heard the indistinct sound of hoofbeats. "Do like the Indians do!" commanded Bob authoritatively. "Lay down and put your ear to the ground!"

Obediently Ona sprawled down, ear to the ground. Then look-

ing up from this ludicrous posture of strained attention, she saw two
mounted horsemen galloping toward them over a far rise. The men
were upon them in a jiffy, flinging off their panting horses, grabbing
Hiney and Sally Lee off the old mule to put on their own mounts.

"Leggo that snake, you kids! Now come on, all of you! There's
no time to be lost!"

An overwhelming presentiment of evil, like a black choking
pall from the cloudless sky, caught up Ona. In it they hurried home.
One horseman carrying Sally Lee and leading the old mule. The
other horseman carrying Hiney and lashing the mule with a whip.
Ona, Marion, and Bob took turns riding her double while the other
trotted behind. Ona was sorry for her. "She's old and blind, and
can't see where she's goin'. Quit beatin' her so hard!"

"None of your back talk now!" the man said, lashing the old
mule again. "You oughta be glad we're savin' you from bein'
scalped! Come on, I say!"

Even before they reached home, Ona could hear the courthouse
bells ringing in town. Tom and Sister Molly were waiting for them
with Mrs. Rogier in front of the house. Tom rushed forward, gun in
hand, to take the two smaller children out of the saddles.

"You got the news?" asked one of the horsemen. "It was
Charlie, the herd boy. Scalped on Mount Washington."

"I'm takin' 'em all in to town right now!" answered Tom, patting his rifle. "Don't you worry no more about us!"

Charlie was one of the town herd boys, twelve or fourteen years
old maybe, about Ona's own age. Every morning he would collect a
number of families' cows to drive out to pasture, bringing them back
each night. It seemed impossible that the lazy Indians she'd seen
loafing in town had scalped him on Mount Washington, a low hill on
the prairie just southeast of town. Tom wasted no words on an
explanation of how it may have happened. He was in a raging hurry
to escort them all to safety in the courthouse.

"Git your stuff together and let's get goin'! We'll go by the
Siegerfries place, and then right to town. There's no tellin' when the
whole band of murderin' Redskins will sweep by!"

Despite the black cloud of evil still surrounding her, Ona could
detect the pleasurable air of excitement he exuded. She was surprised that her mother seemed immune to it. "You all go ahead," she
told Tom stubbornly. "Me and the two girls are goin' to wait here for
Joe."

"He's in town waitin' to protect all the gatherin' citizens! Listen to them bells!"

"Protectin' all them Eastern and English ladies drinkin' tea in the hotel? No! If there's any protectin' to do, Joe had better come home and do it!"

"Martha's right," said Sister Molly. "Maybe it's a false alarm anyway."

"You come on! When we see Joe we'll send him back."

Ona watched them go, the four Hines and Marion, with a feeling of abandon tinctured with a curious admiration for her mother's stubborn independence.

Whatever Mrs. Rogier thought, she kept it to herself. She fixed lunch and after it was eaten put the two girls to work on household chores. While they were still busy with these in mid-afternoon, a shrill eerie cry was heard. Both Mrs. Rogier and Ona knew instantly what it was. The Indians were less than a mile away; there was no time nor way to flee to town. Quickly Mrs. Rogier closed the windows, barred the doors, and hurried the two girls with bread and candles down into the cellar.

Looking out the window over which Mrs. Rogier was hanging a blanket, they both could see the band of Indians crossing the creek at the cottonwoods and riding toward the house. The older men jogged along leisurely, sleepy in the warm sunshine. Behind them followed the long ungainly file of laden ponies and overloaded squaws splashing at the creek. Then a dozen young braves on barebacked ponies swept up to gallop around the house, yelling with arms upraised and then crouching low or hanging to the sides of their mounts. It was a brave show though none of the squaws nor their sleepy elders appeared to notice them. They only succeeded in raising the dogs in cry. Down in the dark cellar the noise was ominously fearful, the high pitched yells broken into a staccato by palms clapped to mouths, the thunder of hoofs and the dust sifting through the window, the barking of dogs. Ona raised up the corner of the blanket to look out.

"Ona!" Mrs. Rogier called out low and sharp, and when the girl did not answer slapped her on the cheek. As she flinched, Ona clumsily yanked down the blanket from the window. Instantly Mrs. Rogier pulled her down to lie on the floor. She did not even scold, they were so still. But the hoofbeats stopped, and suddenly as out of a dream, a red-brown face grinned in the window. There sounded blows upon the door and the east window tinkled into pieces. Mrs. Rogier closed her straight short mouth and covered up Sally Lee with a blanket. "Stop that whimperin' and go to sleep!" Then she marched upstairs with Ona cringing at her heels.

The house was filling with Indians. Even the old men were dismounting to crowd into the big kitchen behind the young ones, leaving the squaws massed outside the door. To Ona they looked like the ones she had seen so often in town, old dark wrinkled faces impassively staring out from the striped blankets, sharp young faces grimacing with devilish delight as they threw out shiny new kettles and fresh scrubbed pots to the waiting squaws. Mrs. Rogier stood straight and still with indignation, her head cocked to one side, apprehensively listening for Sally Lee.

The young bucks now discovered the feather bed in the next room. Whooping in positive enjoyment, they wrestled on it, stripped it of blankets, slit it with their knives, and threw handfuls of feathers swirling through the house. Through all this their wrinkled elders stood in a corner, weary, sleepy, and disinterested, as if they had seen it an incalculable number of times. Two of them kept munching apples.

The young braves had opened the flour bin. They demanded pancakes. For an hour Mrs. Rogier stood over the red-hot stove, growing whiter with anger every minute as she ladled up cakes to the savage horde. They knew what hotcakes were, all right, thought Ona. Drowned in syrup, covered with handsful of sugar! When her food was all gone, and with it most of her pots and pans, Mrs. Rogier could stand no more. Little and thin, she flailed at the savages with thin arms. The Indians laughed and hollered, thrusting her down upon a chair. Whenever she tried to stand up, they thrust her down again. Then imagining she heard a whimper from Sally Lee downstairs, her imagination gave way. She sat weeping stonily, wiping the tears from her red-lidded eyes. Ona, holding her hand, remained standing beside her as if petrified, a small stone image in calico set up stiffly among the warm-colored bodies guttering among themselves like splendid beasts at play. Something about her indomitable silence and stony face impressed the council of old men in the corner. They silently held the gaze of their sharp black eyes upon her.

It was then that Ona noticed him for the first time, as he moved toward her. He was a young man, tall and straight as an arrow but powerfully built. He was naked to the waist and she could see the sharp outline of his muscular breasts. His face, with its Roman nose and high cheekbones, glowed rose-red. His hair was straight and coarse and black, like the mane of a horse, and his eyes were piercing black. Stooping slightly, he caught her up like a feather and swung her sideways so that another young brave could catch her by the arms. He then grasped her by the ankles and the two of them began swinging her toward the hot stove. Closer. Closer. Suddenly, with one hand, he pulled up her calico dress and on the next slow swing pressed her naked bottom against the hot iron of the stove. It all happened instantly and at once. She could feel the sharp pain of the burn on her right buttock, the faint odor of singeing white flesh; and at the same time the steady fixed stare of his black eyes into her own, a stare that seemed to penetrate so deep into her that for instant they became one.

Then they set her on her feet, the shorter young Indian still holding her by the wrists. Ona didn't notice her mother writhing on her chair in the grip of other Indians. Nor did she pay any attention to the steady stare of the old men in the corner, muttering appreciatively because she hadn't cried out. She stood looking vaguely at the young brave who had burned her, aware only of the sharp pain of her burned behind creeping down like a slow glow to her crotch, and feeling a warm trickle down the inner side of one leg.

The short Indian holding her wrists gave a sudden jerk and grunted, "Hagh!" He wanted to swing her against the stove again till she hollered. But the tall one, still looking at her, pushed him back till he released her arms. She went back to stand beside her mother and to stare back at him. That sharp, rose-brown face with its slightly flaring nostrils and piercing black eyes had something about it she would never understand nor ever forget; a look at once more repellently wild and curiously intimate than anything she had ever known. The warm trickle down her leg scared her. She didn't know what it meant either.

4

Rogier, sitting in the little board shanty he used for an office downtown, had heard the report of the herd boy's scalping that morning. It was a tragic occurrence of course, but also an unfortunate incident to which he did not attribute the pealing importance of the courthouse bells. The time had passed when they might have signalled a disastrous Indian uprising.

Some twenty years earlier the great peace treaty of 1851 drawn at Fort Laramie had apportioned the mountains and plains among the different tribes for as long as the grass should grow. All the buffalo plains west from Kansas and Nebraska to the Rocky Mountains, and south from the Platte to the Arkansas, had been granted to the Cheyennes and Arapahoes. To the Sioux went the land north of the Platte, and to the Kiowas and Comanches the sere plains south of the Arkansas. The high front range of the Rockies and the mountains west remained to the Utes. The Pike's Peak Rush of 1858, with thousands of white gold-seekers pouring in to found Denver, had proved the treaty false. The finishing touch had come in the election year of 1864 when a rabid ex-elder of the Methodist Episcopal Church running for election as a delegate to Congress,

John M. Chivington, had attacked a peaceful village of Cheyennes and Arapahoes at Sand Creek, not far east, with four mounted companies of Colorado Volunteers. Most of the some five hundred people in the village were women and children. Chivington's massacre of them was almost complete. He returned jubilantly to Denver, parading his troops down the street with their bloody scalps and exhibiting captive children in a carnival. Indicted by a Congressional committee but not punished for the crime, Chivington nevertheless had broken the power of the Plains tribes.

The mountain Utes, Rogier knew, were faring little better. In 1868 the federal government had reserved for them a great section of some 15,000,000 acres in southwestern Colorado, but with the rumors of gold in the region was already taking steps to recover it. Immemorial custom was still strong. Bands of Utes kept coming down the mountains every year to pitch their smoke-gray lodges near the new little resort of Manitou growing up around their tribal medicinal springs; and to join them for trade straggled in stray bands of Cheyennes and Arapahoes. They were quiet and abject enough, these broken remnants of once great tribes, unless disreputable saloon keepers in Colorado City sneaked them a few bottles of whiskey. The commotion they caused was disagreeable enough, but far exceeded by the importance given it.

This was what had happened that morning. For days the encampment had been breaking up; and one small band, urged on by firewater, had run off a few head of stock on its way out of town and then had cruelly and tragically scalped the herder Charlie. Looking out the window, Rogier could see the street emptying of people, the Indians vanishing like wraiths to escape retribution and the white residents fleeing to the courthouse when the bells began to peal their warning. It was quite noticeable that the Colorado Springs Hotel was not evacuated nor barricaded against assault; the ladies on the veranda simply removed inside to continue their games of whist and bézique. So Rogiér, discounting the alarm, had remained in his office. He had work to do.

Early that afternoon, more annoyed than alarmed by the emptiness of the street, he walked down to the courthouse. A crowd of people had assembled on the lawn, all pervaded with a growing air of excitement. Several outlying ranchers had come in with reports that the fleeing bands of Indians had committed depredations of all sorts, running off stock, breaking up wagons, and shooting through the windows. There was no telling when more people, like the herd boy, would be killed.

In the crowd Rogier saw Tom hurrying from group to group with his rifle. In a moment he came up to Rogier. A flush of excitement illumined his clear tanned face. His blue eyes glowed. The men were dividing into two parties, he announced; one to pursue the Indians and the other to stay here at home to protect the women and children. "Come on. Where's your gun? You're goin', aint you, Joe?" he demanded, looming up straight and tall.

Before Rogier could answer, Molly and her two boys came up. "Where's Martha and the girls? You brought 'em down here, didn't you Joe?"

"Why no, Molly. I haven't been home. I had to finish some figurin' on that south wall."

"My God, man!" exclaimed Tom. "They're home waitin' for you to come and protect them after we saved the girls from bein' scalped by that bunch that killed Charlie!"

A worried frown flitted over Rogier's face as he listened to Sister Molly. "I'll go right on up." Then noticing her face bent to her husband's worn-out boots, he added, "First, though, let's see about some new boots, Tom. You can't ride off this way."

"Naw!" laughed Tom self-consciously. He had been talking for several weeks about a new pair of boots "the minute I draw five aces."

"Tom! Don't be stubborn. You can pay Joe back in no time. And please be careful. Don't forget me and the boys, Tom."

Rogier turned away from the look in Sister Molly's eyes with the forlorn hope that someday Tom might see how priceless was his possession. Tom followed him across the street for a new pair of boots. And then, because he was Tom, they bought a bottle of Hennessy in case of a rattlesnake bite or something. Now a bugle was blowing for the men to form. Mounting every available horse and bearing every conceivable kind of weapon, the avengers of small Charlie wheeled into line. At its head Lieutenant Crestmore, an ex-officer in the British Navy, waved aloft a bright saber, his most cherished possession. Behind him rode five members of the English colony in the red-coated attire in which they rode to hounds after coyotes on the plains — Tanzt breeches, Busvine habits, and tailored English riding boots. Tom, brown-faced and smiling, waved back from his borrowed piebald, the finest and bravest gentleman of them all.

Rogier clumped home as quickly as possible on a left-over, swaybacked livery nag. The crowd of Indians massed around the house revealed, to his shame, his neglect of his family. He swung off his nag with a tense square-cut face, pushed through the crowd of squaws, and stalked into the kitchen.

"Joe!" Mrs. Rogier, with red-rimmed eyes, was squirming on a chair beside the hot stove. Ona was standing beside her, holding her hand and facing the two young bucks who had just seared her bottom. Against the wall stood a group of old men.

"You're all right, Martha," Rogier answered almost curtly, walking up to her and giving her a pat on the shoulder. Then he moved close to the stove and its convenient poker. Unbuttoning his coat and leaning an arm on the mantel, he faced the old men with a steady stare.

The afternoon was warm and all the Indians were full of food; they looked torpid and bored. The short young buck, however, wanted a little more fun. He advanced a step, took Ona by the wrists, and waited for the slim one to grab her legs. The latter did not move; he was still caught in Ona's mesmerized stare. Rogier slowly took down his arm from the mantelpiece, then suddenly reached out and caught the short buck by the wrist. As the Indian released Ona and straightened, Rogier stooped and twisted, lifting the Indian off his feet. Then with a half-turn of his wide workman's shoulders he flung the Indian out the door. It was a neat display of strength, but Mrs. Rogier heard and saw the rip of his coat under the armpits. A murmurous chorus of grunts from the old men filled the room. Rogier stood still, his right hand dangling against his leg inches from the iron poker.

The young Indian hit the ground outside in a sprawl and rebounded to his feet instantly. As he approached the doorway the old men broke out into noisy talk, pointing to the lacerated flesh where his arm had been torn by a nail. There was an instant of ominous stillness, like a deep pool nurturing a geyser of trouble. It was abruptly broken by the tall young buck still curiously held immobile by the rapt stare of the young girl in front of him. He pivoted about on mocassined feet, gave a high pitched yell, and strode out the door, giving the other Indian a derisive push on the chest. The old men turned and walked out behind him, followed by other young bucks tumbling everything on the floor that remained erect. The squaws outside scattered in all directions, and in a few minutes the whole band was straggling off.

Mrs. Rogier shut up her sniffle as quickly as if she had been on a stage and the curtain had rung down, and gave Rogier a sharply accusing look before running down to the cellar after Sally Lee. "Well! It's about time you were gettin' home! You might have known something like this was goin' to happen with all them Indians passin' by!"

When she came back up the stairs Rogier gave her a consoling hug. "I'm sorry, Martha, but no harm's been done."

"No harm!" She pointed tragically at the tumbled down furniture bestrewn with flour and salt and feathers. "All my new pots and pans gone. The feather bed ruined. Flour bin emptied. Not a speck of food left in the house. And Ona! They burned her against the stove. Right on her bare behind. Look here!"

Scooping up a handful of lard from a tumbled can she hastened over to Ona and lifted her calico dress. The girl stood helplessly still, looking down with a shamefaced and uncomprehending stare at the sparse trickle of blood down her leg. Mrs. Rogier, upon seeing it, let out a scream of pity and rage. Flinging down the girl's upraised skirt, and grabbing her in a tight motherly embrace, she gave vent at last to all her fright and indignation. "Her first blood-lettin'! Those red devils scared her into it! Because you wouldn't come home to protect your family like Tom!"

Rogier listened quietly to her impassioned tirade; and when she finally released Ona, he put his hand gently on her head. "Every girl has to learn about this thing, Ona. You're not hurt. I'm only sorry you were scared."

"I wasn't real scared when they burned me. I knew I wasn't goin' to be scalped. It was just —" Her voice dwindled off into silence. She could not explain to anyone the strange fusion of feelings in that mysterious moment: the searing pain on the right side of her bottom, the warm glow in her crotch, the knifing stare of those wild but intimate eyes — the wildness and the fear, the sweetness and sudden familiarity, all of it mixed together all at once.

That evening Sigerfries brought over Sister Molly and her two boys in his wagon. The scare was over now that the fighting party was pursuing the Indians, and most of the townspeople had gone home from the courthouse, leaving only the outlying ranchers to stay all night. "I just had to come. I worried all day about you," said Sister Molly surveying the torn-up house. "It's a good thing I did. There's plenty of work for all of us."

"There's no bed to sleep on, nothin' to cook, and nothin' to cook it in. Oh, I'm glad you came!" Mrs. Rogier began to sniffle, recounting all their misfortunes.

"My dad's goin' to shoot himself an Indian! That's where he went!" proclaimed Bob.

"I hope not," Rogier said quietly. "One killing's enough."

"You get to work now sweepin' this floor!" ordered Sister Molly. "Come on. Let's all pitch in."

Worn out at last, they had a few scraps for supper and all went to bed on the floor. Sister Molly lay sleepless in the darkness. "I reckon I'm worryin' about Tom," she said as if to herself. "Oh, I hope nothin' happens to him!"

"Nothing's goin' to happen to anybody," came Rogier's quiet voice. "It's all over. Isn't it, Ona?"

Ona, her burned bottom rubbed with lard, was asleep and dreaming a dream that had no meaning at all.

Late the next day Tom returned home with the avenging party. His breath smelled of whiskey, he was tired and in a bad mood. Leaning his gun in the corner, he went to bed supperless without saying a word about the expedition. Rogier learned from others what had happened. The party had ridden out on the plains, following the retreating band of Indians. There was no one qualified to track them, and going had been slow with all the livery stable nags. Nevertheless about dusk the party had come upon a band of Indians making camp. Some of the men wanted to attack at once. The others held back. They were tired and hungry after their long day's ride, and night was coming on. Besides, they argued, how did they know this was the band which had murdered the herd boy?

Lieutenant Crestmore ended the argument by riding with a few men to the encampment for a parley. The Indians disclaimed any knowledge of the scalping. "They're lying. Indians always lie," he was advised by one of his staff. "Tell 'em we're goin' to punish them anyway!"

The lieutenant delivered his ultimatum. The Indians must give up the man who had killed the boy by daybreak or they would be attacked. He then rode back and ordered camp pitched for the night. The men gathered grass and chips for fires and cooked supper. Afterwards they sat cleaning their rifles and revolvers, and talking over the cavalry tactics they would use. "But it looks like they're goin' to turn over our man," said one. "You don't see any war dance goin' on around their fires or hear any war-whoops, do you?"

"That's all right too!" said another. "We'll march him back to the courthouse and have a public hangin' on the lawn!"

The night dragged by, the men watching the steadily burning Indian fires with mounting excitement. Promptly at the first light of day the bugle sounded. The men saddled and mounted, and under Lieutenant Crestmore the column split into two detachments to surround the Indian camp. The column gradually closed in, then waited for the lieutenant and his aides in their red coats to receive the decision of the Indians to fight or to deliver their prisoner. Crestmore rode back with discomfiting news. There wasn't an Indian in the camp. During the night one Indian had remained to keep the fires burning, and the rest had fled. Grumbling, out of sorts, and without provisions for a long chase, the column had turned back home.

5

Late next spring came the opportunity Rogier had been waiting for. It opened the door of his shanty in the person of a slimly built young man of twenty-five with mild blue eyes and a diffident manner. "Doin' all right, Joe?" he asked, squatting on a chair in front of Rogier's drawing table.

Rogier grinned. "I'm biddin' on the Academy. Suppose you are too, Stratton. Somebody's got to get it if it isn't you." Older, stockily built and more mature, he did not look like a man facing his ex-employer.

Young Winfield Scott Stratton had come out West from Jeffersonville, Indiana shortly before Rogier and set up shop as a carpenter, contractor, and builder. A jim-dandy carpenter, he had no trouble landing jobs in the booming new settlement. He put in the woodwork on the new stone Episcopal church and built several first-class houses including one bought by W.S. Jackson for his bride, Helen Hunt. Rogier, arriving in town stone broke, had worked for him as a journeyman carpenter. The two men got along as well as could be expected from their difference in temperaments. Stratton was moody, unpredictable, and hot tempered. In an instant his mild blue eyes would flame blue fire, and his diffident manner would erupt into a volcano of thrashing fists. He had quarreled and broken off with two previous partners and Rogier was glad to set up in business for himself as soon as he got on his feet. Stratton, owing him a hundred dollars in back wages, remained friendly and often dropped by for a talk.

This morning he came to the point immediately. "No, I'm not biddin' on the Academy. No more building for me. I'm off to Baker's Park."

The look on Rogier's face betrayed his shocked amazement. Ten or twelve years before, a man named John Baker had heard from Navajos that there was gold in the San Juan mountains of southwestern Colorado, one of the wildest regions in America. Gathering a group of men, Baker worked northward from New Mexico into a tiny valley walled by lofty peaks and watered by the Animas River. Although almost all the men perished, it was reliably reported they had picked rubies and garnets off the ground; and D.C. Collier of Central City staked his reputation as a noted geologist that the region would prove to be the most extensive diamond field in the world.

Such wild tales had not been forgotten. The government had abrogated its treaty with Ouray, the Ute chief, throwing the region wide open. More and more prospectors kept climbing over Stony Pass and down through Cunningham Gulch. With the discovery of the Little Giant silver lode in Arrestra Gulch the rush began. Towns were building up — Silverton, Howardsville, Eureka — and the country was now swarming with men. One of them had just come to Colorado Springs to offer the opportunity of a lifetime — a wonderful claim just filed and ready to be worked, the Yretaba Silver Lode in Cunningham Gulch. Within a few days several prominent men in town began to form a company to work the Yretaba. This was the venture on which Stratton was itching to embark.

"You'd sell out your contracting business, an enterprisin' and successful young fellow like you, to run off on a wild goose chase like this?" asked Rogier.

"It's not a wild goose chase, Joe. When I was a kid in Indiana I heard of gold on Pike's Peak. Right then I could see it plain as day, like a dream in broad daylight. A big snowy peak and on it gold nuggets big as walnuts waitin' to be picked up! That's why I came here, Joe. Something tells me I'm going to hit it. Big!"

That great and lofty peak, the beacon for a generation of men with all their foolhardy hopes. "The Pike's Peak Bust! It should have warned you, Stratton."

"I've sold my two lots and I'm still short of the $3,000 for my share. What do you say, Joe? You can take over my office, the whole business. $1,500."

"Well, building is my line, and I'm not interested in gold, silver, mining, nothin' like that." He opened his strong box and taking out a packet of bank notes laid them on the table in front of Stratton. "This is all the cash I've got. $500. I could give you a note for $1,000."

"Good enough, Joe. I can raise the rest of the cash on your note. Now, do you want papers, option and so on?"

Rogier grinned. "I reckon our word's as good as paper."

A few days later Stratton left for the San Juans to make his fortune. Rogier moved into his vacated office on Pike's Peak Avenue. It was an excellent location: a big room with an open skylight on the top floor of one of the few two-story buildings in town. On the glass pane of the door was now painted:

JOSEPH ROGIER
Contractor and Builder

It had taken him some time to decide upon the lettering. The simplicity of the sparse wording, the solid forcefulness of the black Roman letters, pleased him; they gave the feeling he wanted them to express.

Now on his first morning in the office, he ambled around like a bear in a new den accustoming himself for a long winter. On the shelf along the wall he had placed the few books he had collected: arithmetics, engineering handbooks on structural design and stresses and strains, a number of geologies, and with these several books on various religions which Mrs. Rogier had been glad to see removed from the house. On the opposite wall was thumb-tacked a plat of the Colorado Springs Settlement. The names of the cross streets south of Pike's Peak Avenue bore Spanish names from the earliest influence south of the settlement: Huerfano, Cucharas, Vermejo, Moreno. Those to the north had been taken from the

French trapper element: Bijou, St. Vrain, Cache la Poudre. The principal north and south avenues — Wahsatch, Nevada, Cascade — were named for mountain ranges. Rogier regarded with ironic amusement the effort to perpetuate the memory of those *coureurs des bois* and *conquistadores* who had entered these fabled Shining Mountains to rape their treasures of beaver and gold. The day of the Spanish and the French had forever passed. Now the English and Americans had come, so cocksure of their permanence they had made haste to name some streets after mountains before the ranges were trampled under foot and forgotten. As if that high peak out the window would not outlive their own dust and memory, a mute witness of their own greedy and inauspicious lives. Yes, dom it! It was a great land, long as time and wide as the imagination, with the rhythm of its own being. Always conscious of a sense of uplift, Rogier looked down as if from great height upon the slow evolution of his kind from their cenozoic ooze. He could see them crawling upon the slimy land, slinking into the steamy jungle as he had seen men vanishing into the half-light of the Carolina swamps, then emerging slowly out upon the wide grassy lowlands of the Mississippi basin. Always westward and upward until they stood at last upon this great arid plateau fronted by lofty mountains raised like a pulpit before which they could shout their everlasting queries at the empty sky above. This was the end of their hegira. Not a land new and raw to be molded at their will, but one so old it had outlived the forests imbedded in the limestone cliffs just west of town. A land to be lived with, not conquered.

Rogier was brought up short at his drafting board. Spread out on it was a blueprint of the first school building proposed for the College Reservation. Cutler Academy. English Gothic, of course, and to be constructed of gray stone. And imposingly big and durable building, and for a college too. The foresight of its planners humbled him, he was so conscious of his own lack of education. Straddling the high stool before the drafting board, he slid his coarse, calloused thumb up and down a T-square of hand-polished bird's eye maple he had brought from Maryland. He held one end of it down on the board, lifted the other to test its supple strength, and then released it to whack resoundingly on the dusty yellow paper. Dom it! Whatever was to go inside the Academy or to come out, he was the man to build its walls.

An hour or more later he was interrupted by a woman's step sounding outside the door and the rap of her knuckles against the door. Martha! It was so unlike her to come to town to see him that Rogier smiled with pleasure as he opened the door.

"Why, mornin' Molly!" he said in surprise upon seeing it was she.

"Mornin' Joe," she answered dully, standing big, gaunt, and hollow-eyed before him with a bunch of bluebells dangling in her hand.

"Come in, Molly," he said kindly. "It's nice of you to come down to see the place. I thought it might be Martha."

Listlessly she scuffed into the room, laying the flowers upon his desk. "I fetched 'em for your new office." Rogier, aware that she knew his dislike of picked flowers yet appreciating her gesture, acknowledged the gift with his silence. It was obvious she was in trouble. The wrinkles in her faded gingham dress showed it had been slept in. Her black hair, caught at the back, was uncombed and strands of it kept falling over her face. Pushing them back from her dull eyes, she slumped down on a chair.

"What's the trouble, Molly? Bob?"

Her oldest boy Bob was like Tom, always running away from home and playing with firearms. That winter he had shot himself twice with Tom's rifle, once through the hand and the last time in the head while looking down the barrel. The doctor's probing had extracted the ball, and the accident had ended the prized ownership of Tom's rifle. He was his mother's obvious favorite, but Sister Molly said nothing.

"Hiney — Hiney's gettin' along all right, isn't he, Molly?"

A slight, straight-haired little lad, eleven years old, he went about with a shy grin and an amazing self-assurance. With the printing of the region's first newspaper, Hiney had obtained the job of delivering copies along the route to Colorado City and Manitou by horseback. Some time ago he had been thrown and was brought home with a slight concussion. Although he had recovered, he occasionally still suffered its effects.

"No, Joe. But it's Tom." Sister Molly paused and raised her chin resolutely. "Yesterday mornin' Hiney got another one of them spells. Couldn't remember nothin' at all, even who he was. The doctor always said there was nothin' much to do when he got that way but use the medicine and to come after him. So I give Tom all the money in the house to get some more medicine and bring home the doctor. He ain't come home yet!"

"I'm sure nothing serious has happened to him."

Sister Molly's slumped body stiffened under the wrinkled gingham as if she were calling forth all her strength to staunchly uphold a new and devastating conviction. "That's the trouble, Joe. I know nothin's happened to Tom." For an instant she lowered her glance as if in acknowledgment of his shamefulness. It was but a last momentary flinching from the truth, and when she raised her eyes Rogier could feel the force of conviction. "It's been comin' a long time, like I knew it would but couldn't believe until I gave Tom that money. It was two silver dollars in a pickle jar put up on the the top shelf — bein' saved for a rainy day. Tom never knew it was there till I climbed up after it and put it in his hand and told him to hurry. And then the way he looked at me, Joe, I knew! I tell you I knew we was done!"

Her voice rang out clear and strong with all the conviction of a pent-up truth. "I kept thinkin' of it all afternoon when I sat there beside Hiney with his wet face. Tom didn't come back. Bob wasn't around either. So when the herd boy brought our cow back, I sent him after the doctor. Pretty soon the doctor left, sayin' Hiney would be all right. Then Bob came and ate some bread and ham and went to bed. That's all there was to eat. Tom never bothered whether there was much or nothin' to eat in the house. I thought of lots of other things too, after I blew out the lamp. A night's a long time, Joe, when you sit lookin' out the window at the prairies empty in the moonlight and thinkin' just one thing. And all the time things fittin' together like pieces of wood in a puzzle."

She stared past Rogier on his stool and out into the morning sunlight as if seeing painted on the cloudless sky the completed tangram of her fate. "I ain't never complained, or I ain't whinin' now," her eyes came back to him unafraid," 'cause a woman don't want much. But she's got to have a man who'll stick by her and see things through. And I never have. Never! And neither has Mom. In all our family, clear through, we been standin' all we can bear. I'm done! I love Tom, but I tell you, Joe, so help me God, I know we're done!"

Rogier unstraddled his legs and got off his high stool. "You're upset, Molly. Tuckered out and worried sick. Go home and rest. I'm goin' over to Colorado City to see a man. I'll keep a lookout for Tom. Here." He gave her a random handful of silver dollars. "On your way home buy the little tike somethin' from Martha and the girls."

"Joe!" She stood up, rattling the coins in her hand. "Be square with me. That's why I come. Not for these!"

Rogier gave her a keen gray glance that cut through her pride. "You should have been born a Rogier," he said curtly. "If I hadn't been, I'd have thanked your mother for savin' my life."

He moved toward the door. Sister Molly stood still until he looked around. "Joe, what'll I do?"

"What can you do?" he answered her bluntly and simply, with all honesty in his steady gaze and held back the open door to let her pass.

Colorado City, strung out along the creek bottoms midway between Little London and Manitou at the base of the peak, was the sort of place Tom was sure to be. A convenient stop to water horses and men, its short and crowded streets gave an illusion of bustling importance deriving from the fact that while saloons were barred in the plains town, here almost every building swung open its half-doors to any thirsty stranger's push. Tom was not in Jake Becker's saloon nor in either of the two large beer gardens. Rogier continued his search, turning down on one of the side streets leading to the creek. It was an unsavory area of wooden shanties and Rogier sauntered along the cowpaths between saloons. The hitching rack in front of Levy's was lined solid with teams so he pushed open the doors.

In the middle of the floor four teamsters were rolling dice on top of a table; one of them had his arm upraised in the hierophantic attitude of opportuning the favor of his fate. The long mahogany bar was spotted with men exchanging news and drinks. A group of women, their cheeks rosy with paint, noted Rogier's arrival and stood up at mechanical attention with set, stiff smiles. Rogier dismissed their invitations with a quick glance. He had caught sight of Tom lounging dejectedly at a corner table off to his right. Casually Rogier turned his back and strolled to the bar.

He had not finished his drink before Tom got up and ambled toward him. Rogier watched him in the mirror. For an instant Tom stood beside him, his sober red eyes carrying the look of a whipped dog. Then he laid his hand on Rogier's shoulder.

Rogier set down his glass and turned around slowly. "Oh, hello, Tom."

"What you doin' down here, Joe?'"

"Over to see a man and dropped in to hear all the news. Have a drink — my own brand?" Without waiting for an answer he called to the bartender, "A raw lemonade with a dash of sherry."

Tom shuffled his feet, his quick eyes apprehensive of derision in the faces in the mirror. Then picking up his glass, he followed Rogier to a table at the window. For a time he floundered around on his chair trying to get settled. Finally giving up the attempt, he sat up straight. "Damnit to hell! I'm all in! I wasn't home last night!"

His mere statement of one night's absence appeared to have no effect upon the man before him. It sounded so weak and foolish to his own ears that he made haste to supplement it. "No! And by God I oughta been. I was supposed to have gone right back with some medicine for Hiney yesterday afternoon. And I ain't been back since. What do you think of that?"

Rogier lit a cigar without answering him. Tom continued more slowly now. "I left word at the doctor's office and went out to get some medicine. It was our last two dollars, but hell! — a man can't go home without takin' a sick kid somethin' more than medicine. Can he? I thought I'd take him a real whip like he'd been wantin'. One that a Mexican had over at Sample's Boardin' House, braided leather with a silver handle. Well, when I got there and started playin' for it, my luck just turned cold on me. Those damn Mex playin' cards did the trick. With all them *espadas, oros* and *copas* you never know what you're doin'." He leaned forward, both hands on the table. "I didn't quit till I was cleaned cold. Every time that damn greaser slapped down a greasy card hollerin' out, '*Suerte, Senor!*' I thought of Hiney sufferin' and waitin' for his dad to bring him somethin'. So I slapped down mine too, every time. The damn luck! You can't beat it. I was so ashamed I couldn't go home. So I sat here all night. And I owe four dollars for drinks."

Outside, two curs tangled in the street, their yaps and snarls sounding clamorous applause through the open windows. There was a sudden sound of whips and curses, and all was still again.

"Hiney got over his spell. I saw Molly this mornin'," Rogier said quietly.

Tom contracted suddenly, like a turtle drawing within his shell. "Did she say anything about me?"

"She seemed worried, wonderin' what had happened to you."

Tom struggled with his remorse and heroically overcame it. "I reckon. She's always worryin' about me." He grinned, feeling better. "And I'll bet she is mad as a wet hen!"

"She wasn't, but if I were you I'd be gettin' back." Rogier stood up. "Want a ride?"

Tom settled back as though a spasmodic pain had ripped him up the belly. "Sit down a minute before we go. Maybe you can kind of straighten out things in my mind."

Rogier sat down again, steeling himself against Tom's words.

"What the hells' wrong with me, Joe? That makes me stay out like last night when I was worryin' about bein' home, and everything else? I'm just as good as anybody else. I can throw any man my size as many times as he can throw me. I ain't nasty nice like Perkins in the bank, and I ain't overly mean either. Everybody likes me and I don't hold a grudge long myself. But I don't seem to get along. What's the matter with me, Joe?"

Rogier sat still, his face giving an air of flinty indifference as it did whenever he was deeply affected.

"Even Molly is beginnin' to look at me funny, Joe. Like I was no good. Christ! I try hard enough. Why, they ain't a thing in town I ain't tried, but nothin' appeals to me overly much. That's what's worryin' me. Unless —

"Yes?"

"Luck!" Tom's voice rang out suddenly clear and sharp, as though the secret of men's souls, the hidden key to their success or failure, had been revealed to him in an instant flash. "Luck's been savin' me from bein' a carpenter, a blacksmith, a trapper and Indian trader, a banker, a business man, all those dull jobs. This whole damn world is bein' spun around by God like a roulette wheel. He don't have anything to do with which slot the ball falls into. It's luck that picks the slot. And it's been savin' me one!''

"And which one is that, Tom?"

Tom leaned forward. "You remember hearin' some float was picked up by a fellow herding cattle in Wet Mountain Valley flankin' the east wall of the Sangre de Cristos not more'n a hundred miles south of here? Nobody did anything about it till a prospector finally sunk his pick into the hill it come from. Chloride of silver, rich enough to eat! The Humbolt and Pocahontas were opened on the spot, and in the last six months three hundred thousand dollars have been pulled out. Rosita, their camp, already is a town of 2,000 people, with two hotels, a brewery, and a cheese factory. A fellow just told me so. These mountains are full of silver, Joe. That's what luck's savin' for me. To hit a bonanza. And I'm going to name her the 'Molly Hines'!''

How quickly his mood changed. He was like quicksilver himself. "Well, let's be takin' home," said Rogier wearily, rising to go.

Sister Molly was waiting in front of the door when they approached. After a few hours' sleep and in a fresh gingham dress, she seemed like herself again.

"I'm just stoppin to ask about Hiney," said Rogier.

"Sleepin' like a little log."

A tacit agreement of understanding was signed in their glance. Each of them knew the other would never refer to their morning's talk. Tom stood grinning with embarrassment, ready to fling his arms around Molly with a laugh or to snap back surlily, at either provocation.

"So long, Tom."

Rogier went home for supper. Afterwards the girls played quietly while Mrs. Rogier, pregnant again, read from her Big Book. Rogier could not get settled. All the talk, talk, talk of the day had driven him to the deep need of solitude. To let the disconcerting news and conjectures evaporate and leave their residual truth for him to weigh with clearer thought. "I've got to go down town for a while." he said kindly. "I won't be gone too late."

In his office he did not light the lamp but sat at the open window, staring out into the moonlight. How diaphanous, how phosphorescent it was, with the strange alchemy of turning green, blue, or lilac all it touched. Not of the light of living day nor of the darkness of night, but containing something of them both. More penetrating and more inescapable than light itself because it had no direct source, but emanated from everywhere. The high peak looming up at the end of the street shone with a silvery incandescence like the moon itself, mysteriously silver, casting over all the shadowed town, over himself, the same moon-madness. That's what it was, this lure of silver in the Uncompahgres, the Sangre de Cristos, the San Juans, in all the ranges of these high Rockies, a queer moon-madness. Rogier could not blame Stratton, Tom nor all the thousands of men for succumbing to its strange malady. Even he, alone and troubled, could recognize with some misgivings the uncontrollable quickening of his blood at the rumors of the new strikes.

6

Early in July the men who had gone down to the San Juan region returned with the report that the Yretaba Silver Lode foisted upon them was a worthless claim. Yet so entrancing were the deep gulches dotted with camps and claims they were raising money to buy into other claims. the Ouray, Rocky Mountain Chief, and Silver Wing.

Two weeks later Stratton pushed open the door of Rogier's office. He had lost his hat and his long hair was uncombed. His wornout boots were tied with string. His torn shirt and overalls were damp. "I just got in, but I was so dirty I stopped to wash my clothes in the creek," he explained diffidently. "We busted, you know."

"So I heard. Well, maybe it's just as well you got it out of your system, Stratton. Now how about some new clothes and a good hot meal? Then we'll talk about your gettin' back into business."

"I told you I was done when I left here, Joe! The Yretaba was no good, but you should see the silver showin's down there. My God, man! The King Solomon Mountain is so seamed with mineral veins they can be seen two miles away. Everybody calls Begole's discovery the Mineral Farm, and what a farm it is! Rich veins spread out over forty acres! There's a hill black with oxide of manganese they call the Nigger Baby. Full of lead carbonates rich in silver. And in the Uncompahgre range more towns are springing up. Ouray, Telluride, Ophir, Rico. Silver, Joe! That's for me. No more buildin'!"

"Think it over on a night's sleep," cautioned Rogier, giving him some money. "We'll talk about it tomorrow."

The next day Stratton returned still insistent. He soon raised a new grubstake and took off with an old freighter over Ute Pass and up Chalk Creek toward the head of the Arkansas. Here below Granite, fronting the Sawatch Range, another new strike had been reported and Stratton intended to be in on the ground floor.

Rogier ignored the growing excitement; he was too busy. A recognized builder now in a fast growing town, he was finishing the School for the Deaf and Blind, laying foundations for the Academy, and preparing estimates for a new two-story Courthouse on the corner of Nevada and Kiowa.

That fall Mrs. Rogier gave birth to their third daughter, Mary Ann, and settled down to a hard winter. Smothering the earth with a fresh and flocculent whiteness the instant a roof edge or tree tip emerged to view, clinging with tenacious and icy fingers upon its helpless prey, the winter could not be shaken off. Each morning the sun rose scowling, but like the scowl of a man without the inward fire of righteous anger it became placid, without the warmth of conviction, and retreated redly between the great snowy peaks. The mountains reared silver above the prairies like a wall of ice shutting off a white and frozen sea. Herds of antelope gathered from the plains outside the town. Deer came down from the mountains and were to be found in anybody's back yard. Seven grizzly bears were killed above Manitou.

Even Tom tired of the easy slaughter long before his shed was filled with frozen meat. All morning he loafed in the saloons at Colorado City or stood watching the gambling in Sample's Boarding House. At home he sat glowering at Sister Molly, shrewder-tongued than himself, and thus quick to turn his plaints at everything against himself. Bitter and vindictive, they worried at each other's minds and spirits like wolves tearing at a carcass. Tom was loud and swore profusely, beating at her with the crude clubs of many thwarted ambitions. She, with a fine-spun web of pride torn at every sally, hid her hurts and punctured his noisy arguments with the swift sting of a harsh truth.

Their only relief was their evening visit with the Rogiers. Usually they brought along Siegerfries with his wife and daughter, Marion. Ona was glad of the latter's company. Fulfilling the curse laid upon the eldest daughters of large families, she was kept busy all day doing housework, taking care of Sally Lee, and helping to tend Mary Ann.

Siegerfries was a small man with thin reddish brown hair that was never combed. Nevertheless he gave the impression of a man of good family who had known better days at home in New York. He was educated and his speech was precise. Mrs. Siegerfries and her daughter Marion were regarded by Mrs. Rogier as "common." They both always wore sunbonnets, evidently Mrs. Siegerfries' only conception of women's head-gear. Even now in winter they came in with calico sunbonnets wrapped to their heads with long wool scarfs.

The three men usually grouped together on one side of the stove. Siegerfries, a geologist, talked about the silver strikes calmly enough but with quick puffs at his pipe.

"The Saguache, the Uncompahgre, the San Juans, the Sangre de Cristos! Almost every range following down the course of the Continental Divide. I've never heard of anything like it! The whole mountain chain seems to be full of silver."

"Have you heard of the new booms in Wet Mountain Valley?" asked Tom. "A fellow named Ed Bassick wandered north of Rosita a little ways and sat down to take some sand out of his shoe. It happened to be an ant hill he was sittin' on. So, when the ants stung him in the pants he jumped up and lit into the hill with his pick, strikin' silver ore runnin' 150 ounces to the ton. That was the beginnin' of the new town, Querida. But that ain't half of it!" He hitched his chair closer. "Another Rosita fellow called Edwards hiked west a bit to a high cliff, knocked off a chunk, and had it assayed. It was full of silver and the ground around it was covered with pure horn silver. That's the Silver Cliff you're hearin' about now. It's got nearly 10,000 people, ten miles of streets, two banks, seven hotels — the third largest city in Colorado already!"

"And what about Rosita you were so excited about?" asked Rogier.

"Oh, everybody moved to Silver Cliff where the showin' was better."

Rogier chuckled. "Here today, gone tomorrow."

"I don't care!" exclaimed Tom. "I'd like to go down there and pick me out a claim while the pickin's good!"

Siegerfries turned toward him an amused stare. "Humm. All you have to do is put down your discovery shaft ten feet and do a hundred dollars worth of work every year. Five hundred dollars' worth of work will get you a patent. Maybe it'll be a mine worth developing and maybe it won't. Humph!" He spit at the woodpile.

"Too many Yretabas?" asked Rogiér quietly.

"That's the point," agreed Siegerfries. "Too many men staking out too many claims with no knowledge, no money behind them. The mountains are full of silver. No question about that. But when you find it, what then? It takes money to get it out of the ground, more money to get the ore to a smelter or to a railroad. No. These first surface showings are only an indication of what's to come. Wait'll a big district is opened up and the money gets in there for development. Then's when the real fortunes will be made."

"Hell!" said Tom. "If I knew as much about it as you, I wouldn't be grubbin' vegetables out of a couple of acres with a blind mule. I'd go and find me a silver lode!"

"The time'll come, but I'm not going to be stampeded yet. Like your friend Stratton." He turned toward Rogier. "Did I tell you he's back in town from Granite already?"

Rogier nodded. "He's working for me as a carpenter. Just long enough to save up a grubstake so he can return to the San Juan region."

Mrs. Rogier on the other side of the stove pricked up her ears at mention of his name. "That disreputable gadfly! Runnin' around with that seventeen-year-old Stewart girl, Zeurah. The whole town's buzzin' about it."

"I hope you don't add to it," said Rogier shortly. "He's a friend of mine and a good carpenter."

"You run your business the way you want to, but don't expect me to associate with people like that." She flounced out of her chair.

"Ona, let's get them sandwiches and cookies out now."

Early in March Rogier hitched up his mares and drove Mrs. Rogier and Ona down to see the site he had picked for the new house they needed. It was a flat expanse of prairie just east of town along Shook's Run. The little creek, with its bed gouged deep by the cloudburst at Templeton's Gap and deeper by the spring freshets, boasted a new plank bridge. The view of town westward was shut off by Bijou Hill. The only building visible was a wooden shack near the stream, in front of which two old men in blood-stained, tattered clothes were unpacking from two decrepit covered wagons carcasses of deer and antelope and strings of duck and geese.

"Stop the buggy this minute!" demanded Mrs. Rogier. "I can't stand the smell!"

Ona too sat holding her nose; forty years later she could still recall the stench of those bloody wagons and old men. The patriarchal Kadles, father and son, were well-known in town. They made their living hunting out on the plains, driving in periodically with filled wagons to peddle their meat from door to door.

While Rogier went to say hello to them, Mrs. Rogier sat in the buggy, her small pointed chin holding the blanket-wrap down to her breast against the wind. She was scandalized, utterly dismayed that Rogier actually intended to build their house on the exact spot where stood the Kadles' shack. Shooks Run! Living along the creek like all the common people farther down, like gypsies!

In a few minutes Rogier came back and they drove off. Evidently he had been thinking about the house a great deal. It would have to be big; they needed lots of room inside and out. The land was large as a city block, providing good pasturage for a horse or two.

"But I don't like it!" Mrs. Rogier interrupted. "I don't like the idea of people sayin' we come from the South End or are livin' along the creek. When people hear either of those two places they don't stop to think what your house looks like or what you do. They know what you are already. Living on the Kadles' campground! We'll be carrying the Kadles' name with us to the grave. Why, the ghosts of those two old men with their bloody clothes and tobacco juice runnin' down their white beards will be stompin' through the house in their smelly boots as long as it stands!"

Rogier snapped out the loose reins at the mares, and in a splatter of mud they flew along the road. He knew she was right. The best families, the old English stock which made up the best portion, were collecting to the north of town. Despite his own inborn aloofness which he recognized as a fault, he recognized the infallibility of his wife's intuition.

"I tell you, Joe," she went on, "we can't take chances in gettin' a right start. Rogier was a good name in South Carolina. Everybody that went up and down the Mississippi knew the De Vinneys. It didn't make any difference whether he drank himself to death. He had a name. Out here it's all new. Nobody knows what kind of families we're from. Especially the English folks. Maybe it's worse because we're from the South. We got to show 'em, Joe."

"Show 'em what?" He drew up the mares at a ditch, and once over, spoke again. "Well, I'll leave it to you. We can't build in the North End till we have more money. The College Reservation is going to encroach on our land and boost taxes. But by trading it now, we can build in Shook's Run." Rogier patted her arm and let the team out again. "I'll promise you this — Ona, you remember too — the minute I make enough money I'll build you the big house up in the North End you want. Meanwhile this one's to be put in your name — it's all yours."

Mrs. Rogier leaned back, folding her gloved hands. "I'll remember that."

"Well, Ona," Rogier asked. "Is it going to do or not?"

"I guess there's not much difference in looks anywhere, right now. But there ought to be some trees and lilac bushes."

Rogier nodded. He was a man difficult to cross, for he never argued; his silence seemed to smother noisy disagreement with its taciturn force. Bound to her father with the common ties of their inherent aloofness, she understood him better than did her mother. Ona was surprised at her mother's opposition. It always seemed strange that there should be so much strength of denial in the frail body sitting beside her. A bundle of nerves, really, elusive as a reed in the wind.

Nevertheless she gained a new respect for her mother through the incident. Mrs. Rogier never said another dissenting thing about the new house. When they got home they found Tom and Sister

Molly waiting, and Mrs. Rogier told them about the decision cheerfully as though she had helped to make the choice.

Tom and Sister Molly, for all their whole-hearted pleasure at
the news, seemed somewhat ill at ease. Tom shuffled about awkwardly, even after Rogier asked him to boss the construction. He
tried to motion Rogier to the back room. Failing this, he put his arm
around Mrs. Rogier and led her off to the kitchen to hear a secret,
laughing loudly. Alone with her, his face straightened instantly. He
wanted to borrow five dollars.

"I got to have it, Martha," he said, pinching her chin. He sat
on the kitchen table swinging his long legs while she went to the
cupboard and came back. "You're a peach. Now remember, it's a
secret. I wouldn't have Molly know for anything."

He kissed her on the cheek and with his arm around her, they
went back into the room. Sister Molly and Rogier had moved away
from the children, and stood by the window talking in low voices.
Sister Molly stopped talking instantly on seeing them, stepping away
from him and concealing her hand in her dress.

Mrs. Rogier wanted them to stay for supper, but Sister Molly,
murmuring vaguely about getting home to the boys before dark,
threw her shawl over her shoulders and stepped out the door. Tom
shuffled after her. The snow was melting and the ragged smears of
water splashed from the wheeltracks lay copper-red, the *colorado*
of the earth itself, stained richer by the setting sun. The long roadway seemed to run with its bleeding life. Sister Molly walked in
front, hurrying as if from the scene of a monstrous crime.

"What the hell's the rush?" grumbled Tom. "From what you
said comin' over I didn't think you'd be rushin' back to your happy
peaceful home."

"Well, you're always in a hurry to leave. Why shouldn't I be the
one to hurry home?"

"You should. You appreciate what a beautiful big place it is."

"It's the best home my husband can provide for me. If he
doesn't care enough to stop a leak in the roof after being asked for a
month, should I blame it on the house?"

"Christ! You make me tired!" said Tom. "I just been waitin' to
see how long it would take you to sing that song again. I've only
heard it forty times."

Sister Molly increased her pace. Tom kept at her heels, growling. "Oh, I'll fix the damn roof before it falls in, all right. And before Martha gets her new house, too. Or else you'll be shoutin' to all the town about your own leaky roof."

Sister Molly looked around and smiled. "Jealous, Tom?"

He leapt apace with her in one stride and caught her by the arm. "Goddamn, don't you ever say I'm jealous of Joe, or I'll knock your words down your throat, wife or no wife. He's the best friend I ever had and he deserves all he'll ever get and more too."

Sister Molly stopped in the snow and took his hand off her arm. "That'll do, Tom. We think the same about Joe." Then suddenly she grabbed his arm and ran it under hers. They started walking. "Don't let's quarrel any more today, Tom. I'm almost sick from thinkin' what we've said to each other all day. And, oh Tom," she pleaded, "please let's be sensible. Forget about Joe and Martha's new house. Think of us. What are we comin' to? What are we goin' to do now?"

"You're just worryin' yourself sick over nothin'," Tom reassured her. "The kids are growin' up and we're all healthy. I ain't made a killin' and struck it rich, but I been workin' enough to make a livin', ain't I?"

"No. You haven't," answered Sister Molly, "Can't you realize that? Don't you know what we've been eating all this time?"

"Hell, yes!" laughed Tom. "I'm so sick of raspberry jam and frozen venison I could holler!"

Sister Molly's face set. "I'll tell you what we've been eating. We been eating up those six acres Joe got for you. First the mortgage on two acres to Siegerfries, then two more, and now the loan on the last piece our own house is settin' on. What'll we do when it's gone? That's all I ask. Just stop long enough to realize you're a grown man who hasn't supported a wife and two children." Her voice lowered. "I love you, Tom. I don't want much. But you must give us some kind of a living the same as any other man. I'm sick of borrowing money. And I had to borrow some from Joe to buy our supper tonight. There wasn't even any pancake flour left."

Tom turned to her with surprise. A grin spread over his face. "Well, I'll be damned! How much did you get?"

"Five dollars."

"Just what I got from Martha," muttered Tom, holding out a

gold piece on his palm.

Sister Molly stopped and stared at the coin. A dark rush of blood swept to her cheeks, and then receding, left her face pale grey in the flush of evening. Her eyes narrowing, she struck his hand with a quick blow that jumped the coin away into the snow.

Tom stood immovable, his hand still outstretched as if in a magnificent gesture of pardon or mutely imploring forgiveness. His jaw dropped as he stood listening to Sister Molly. She kept on talking; and her voice, low and even, cut at him like a whip wielded not in the frenzy of sudden anger, but with the precision of a cruel judgment coolly meted out. His arm dropped to his side. He stood there, big and clumsy, mouth open, like a man crumbling inside.

She suddenly stopped; a low sob broke from her. She dropped to her knees, hands outflung in the snow searching for the gold-piece, sobbing bitterly. "Never. Never. I'll never forgive you as long as I live!"

Tom bent slowly, as if fearful of tumbling in an empty heap, and dropped to his knees beside her. He lit matches; and their thin bright glow lit up the dusky snow patch, revealed to him the pallid grayness of her wet cheeks, her tight tense mouth. Then, burning his fingers, they each went out, and he lit another without taking his eyes from Sister Molly.

She finally found the coin. Without a word she rose and walked home in silence. Tom slushed in the mud beside her. At the door, turning to face him, she placed the gold-piece in his hand.

"Here's your money, Tom," she said quietly. "I'll not depend on you to bring home anything to eat. Go on over to Colorado City and get drunk, and bring back your excuses tomorrow."

Without a word Tom walked away. Sister Molly turned her back; she did not watch him go.

7

At last it was spring. As if with a cataclysmic shake the great peaks threw off the winter snow and reared heads and shoulders high, free and rock-naked, like immense beasts awakened with new life. The shake started one of the region's worst landslides. A quarter-mile wide, it swept down the Cone gathering trees and rocks. Suddenly the cliffs gave way. With a belching roar the turbulent stream leapt out into the clear sunshine and fell upon the pine and spruce slopes below. An angry brown torrent, it cut through the blue-clad forest like a flow of molasses and spilled into the canyon, damming up the stream with a mountain of timber and rock. Men could hear it miles away; they could see the gash from out on the plains. And as though heralded by the slide, as if born of the catastrophe with the land writhing in mighty travail, the news broke forth from the mountains.

Silver had been discovered in Leadville.

It was not the first discovery in that high region 125 miles west. Some years before, Abe Lee, one of the discouraged Forty-Niners on his way back from California, had christened the area lying at the headwaters of the Arkansas with the name of California Gulch.

Finding gold in his pan, he had jumped to his feet shouting, "I found it! I got it — the hull state of Californy in this goddam pan!"

The yield of three million dollars from the first placer mines, however, had dwindled to paltry thousands and men began to regard the gulch as an area of worthless lead. A black heavy sand cluttered up their sluices till it was almost impossible to separate gold from the gravel, and this trouble was further enhanced by the difficulty of moving out of the way heavy worthless boulders.

It was then a man named W.H. Stevens discovered a supposed lead deposit on the south side of the Gulch, naming it the Iron Mine. Samples from it assayed twenty to forty ounces of silver to the ton, revealing that the heavy sand and huge boulders were composed of a carbonate of lead forming a silver base. Thus spread the reports as more men rushed to the hills and gulches, and brought back more specimens to test. The oxide of iron imparted to one group of ores a red color; chromate of iron a yellow hue; the predominance of silica and lead in others a gray color. But chloride of silver permeated all ores.

The rush got under way. Long mule trains struggled over Ute Pass, breaking the silence with the shouts of the skinners and the pistol cracks of their long rawhide whips. The trail led on through a great mountain valley, once the hunting ground of the Utes and now known as South Park. Here the men could see the high snowy peaks of the Saguache Range, almost three miles high. Twelve glistening silver peaks, like twelve apostles robed in white. And now, gritting their teeth, the men began the steep ascent up Mosquito Pass, that "Highway of Frozen Death," to Leadville, the "Silver City in a Sea of Silver."

Within six months a dense spruce forest was hacked down to make space for the town that looked, as someone described it, like "a Monaco gambling room emptied into a Colorado spruce clearing." The hacked stumps still stuck up in the streets which ran through a clutter of log cabins, board shacks, shanties, and saloons. The first ore had been carted out by ox-teams for shipment to St. Louis. Now a sampling works and blast furnace were established, and more smelters were being built. Money was pouring in — and more was being taken out. The Iron Mine had been sold for $200,000, one share of it being bought by Levi Leiter, partner of

Marshall Field, who was beginning to make millions from it. A storekeeper and the first mayor of the new town, Horace A.W. Tabor, grubstaked two seedy German prospectors with $64.75 worth of groceries. On Fryer Hill the two prospectors, August Rische and Theodore Hook, dug a thirty-foot shaft and struck silver ore which assayed 225 ounces per ton. Naming the mine the Little Pittsburgh, Hook sold his share for $153,000 and Rische sold his for a wad of 262 $1,000 bills. Within a year the mine was capitalized at $20,000,000. Tabor, on his one-third share, began his meteoric flight to wealth and fame, becoming Lieutenant Governor of Colorado that same year and United States Senator within five years. And they were not the only ones. Day after day news of still more strikes, the Chrysolite, Robert E. Lee, Little Johnny, and the Matchless, swept through Colorado to give all men similar dreams, grand, improbable, but by the grace of God not impossible — yet niggardly in comparison to the reality that would shame their wildest imaginings.

The main inlet to that great camp, the narrow wagon road up through Ute Pass was crowded each mile and hour. More than twelve thousand mules and horses crept up, and back the grade. Their eastern terminus and principal supply depot was the settlement on the plains at the foot of Pike's Peak.

Manitou swarmed with crawling wagons like an ant hill alive with a horde of ants. Colorado City blazed with a light that stayed red, and in its flicker mule-skinners, miners, teamsters, prostitutes, and men crossbred to every purpose drank the clock around. Colorado Springs went wild — able to catch breath enough to shout. Day and night the noise kept up, of wagons pulling out for Ute Pass, of men getting ready for the trek. The D & RG couldn't haul goods in fast enough for the stores to empty across their counters. Prices jumped sky high.

Tom went almost crazy with excitement. For days on end he hung around Colorado City, listening to the talk in Jake Becker's place or in Levy's saloon; or else, in Manitou, wandering from wagon to wagon, rejecting the repeated tales of hardship, embroidering the rumors of new discoveries. And then coming home after a three-day absence, unshaven, dirty, and worn-out, he flung himself upon the bed to curse his fate, his own impotence, or the family that tied him to his home.

Siegerfries, although he did not show it, was as excited as Tom. Night after night he sat up studying reports, assays, every topographical map he could get of the Leadville district. From these he meticulously sketched the location of every strike and mine, working out the position of the major lodes and veins.

"Blanket veins," he told Rogier in his office one night when they were alone. "Look here." He spread out his sketches. "They appear in horizontal veins, varying in thickness from a few inches to great chambers forty feet in height, with iron above the ore, capped with trachyte, and covered to a hundred feet with drift."

"You're saying the ore is rich and extensive but expensive to mine?" asked Rogier thoughtfully.

"Exactly. The strikes have been made at surface outcrops. More, much more lies beneath. That's why Eastern money is pouring in to buy up all surface showings and sink to depth. You know what I'm driving at, don't you Joe?"

Rogier nodded.

"It's a boomer, Joe! The big one I've been waiting for. Throw in with me. I've sold out the land I bought from Tom, written home for all the money I can borrow. Be my partner, Joe!"

Long after he had left, Rogier sat in his office fighting for his head. A strange dormant excitement, a desire for something he could not put into words, crept into his veins, pulsed at his temples. Unable to shake it off, he paced the floor and intermittently stared out the window at the inscrutable peak which at once gave shape to his thoughts and masked their meanings. If Siegerfries were touched with the moon-madness that now completely possessed Stratton, Tom, and thousands of other helpless men, he denied the assumption. Siegerfries, cold, analytical, and immune to the possibility of glamor in his trade, was going too. Why not he? For the moment his building contracts, with the first payments for running expenses, the plans for his own new house on Shook's Run, his large family, and the growing dependence on him of Sister Molly and her two boys, all dwindled to insignificance under the appalling proximity of the great boom at Leadville. And yet something held him back. Worn out, he slept on a couch in his office.

Next morning on his way home he stopped off at Siegerfries'

house. It was still early. Marion in her omnipresent sunbonnet was out gathering wood; Mrs. Siegerfries was cooking breakfast; and Siegerfries, when Rogier entered the house, was busy packing his clothes.

"I've made up my mind. I'm not going," he said brusquely.

Siegerfries stood up and brushed back his thin, tousled hair. "I'm sorry, Joe. Keep an eye on my family while I'm gone, will you?"

"I'll do that. Good luck!"

They shook hands and Rogier walked slowly home, feeling the great weight of a repressed desire slowly dissipating within him.

The departure of Siegerfries raised Tom to a pitch of almost uncontrollable frenzy. He refused Rogier's offer to work as construction boss on the new house. Nor could he find time to fix his own roof. He was always over at Colorado City talking to mule-skinners, prospectors, and hopefuls bound for Leadville. When he did come home he would stand at the window pointing at the fold in the mountains through which wound Ute Pass, as if expecting Pikes Peak itself to burst into eruption and roll a flood of molten silver to his feet. Recounting the latest news, his voice grew husky, tremulous, and inarticulate with the vision burning in his mind. "Siegerfries went, didn't he," he would shout again and again. "He ain't crazy, is he? Wait'll he comes back!" These declamations oppressed Sister Molly even worse than his most violent quarrels. But Tom kept waiting for Siegerfries like a disciple awaiting the miraculous return of his chosen prophet. There would be no holding him back then.

Meanwhile, under the clear blue summer skies, rose the ungainly big frame house along Shook's Run. Its original plans Rogier stored away pending a proper site in the North End. For them he substituted hasty sketches as the work went on. His painstaking care and fine craftsmanship were bestowed upon the academy building on the College Reservation. The greater the stones from the quarries, the more carefully they were cut and placed, the more his mind seemed eased, as if they weighed him deep and fast, beyond all possible escape from his chosen work. Only at twilight, when the day's work was done, did he carry in his buggy a box of groceries each for Sister Molly and Mrs. Siegerfries on his way home. The house was finished by winter and the Rogiers moved in. It was an immense house, ungainly as it was, and Mrs. Rogier asked Sister Molly to move in with them. Bob and Hiney clamored to, and Tom assented, but Sister Molly was curt in her refusals. She was getting awfully touchy.

The year went by and another had begun its flight when Siegerfries came back. His wife and daughter were sitting on the broken down front steps with Sister Molly; they were dressed in patched gingham dresses, their shoes tied with twine, and looking mournfully out upon the world under the cowls of their everlasting calico sunbonnets. Sieferfries himself looked worse than a tramp and many years older. After kissing them and telling Sister Molly to bring back all her folks that evening, he laid down on the bed, duffle bag under his head.

That evening they all learned that Siegerfries had struck it rich. He talked little like a man who had plucked the apple of heart's desire, and yet he was going to take his wife and daughter back to his family in New York and build a house up along the Hudson River. He damned the Leadville region like a man who had seen the shooting of men on claims, the hardships, greed, and poverty too well to pay the price again.

"The hell with all that!" shouted Tom. "You hit it, didn't you? Just like I knew you would! Pure silver! What did it look like when you saw it? How much did you get?"

Siegerfries shrugged, then turned to Rogier. After looking over the ground carefully for months, he had staked out a claim in a remote gulch, a mere blind stab at forture. Sinking a discovery shaft through the snow, he had found a showing of silver ore. That spring he had sold it to some speculators for $30,000 without waiting to see if it would turn out good or bad. He had then put all the money into a new mine he had been hired to survey and that was being financed for development. When in one week it produced more than $100,000 in silver, with the prospect of becoming one of the best mines in Leadville, Siegerfries sold out at the first substantial offer for a price that would make him independent the rest of his life. He was never going back. It was a prosy dry tale worthy of the man, and Rogier nodded his approval.

Mrs. Siegerfries and Marion expressed little joy; they lacked the imagination to encompass their good fortune. Siegerfries had met his wife in Kansas on his way West. She was an honest, industrious woman, but uneducated and almost illiterate. Marion, gawky, freckled, and born to poverty, and with barely enough schooling to scrawl an awkward hand, was little better. Now Siegerfries had instilled a new destiny in their minds, "a home on the Hudson," wherever that was.

Mrs. Rogier, Sister Molly, and Ona helped them get ready to leave. On the day before they took the narrow-gauge, Mrs. Siegerfries brought home some new cloth and a roll of lace to make sunbonnets for herself and Marion to wear to New York. Mrs. Rogier was slightly envious and a little puzzled because it had been God's will to bestow this world's wealth not upon members of the blooded aristocracy who might have shown it with more grace, but upon people who after all were common, having no conception of headgear beyond sunbonnets trimmed for the first time with a scrap of lace.

It was left to Sister Molly to bear the brunt of their success. Tom was past all argument and appeal now. It made no difference that he watched men dribbling back down Ute Pass gaunt with hunger and hollow-eyed, broken by the immutable law that levels men to their average that fickle chance might raise one to play a horde of others false. Stone broke as he was, he was determined to go to the promised land.

The break came with an unexpected letter from Mrs. White. Mrs. Rogier was sitting with it in her lap when Rogier came home from work. "It's a letter from Mother. Read it."

Rogier looked at her sharply, noticing the slight flush in her cheeks. "Never mind. What does she say?"

"She's on her way out here."

Rogier nodded complacently. "I'll be glad to see her."

Mrs. Rogier's small foot tapped the floor nervously. "She's coming out here to live with us, and she's bringing brother's little boy Boné with her." She hesitated, never quite sure how he was going to take things. "I guess I didn't tell you I wrote her we'd be glad to take Boné. One more won't make much difference with the three children we got."

"Of course not! I owe your mother much and I was homeless as the little fellow myself."

"Well, I just thought you might be thinkin' it was comin' at a bad time now, but of course it's not as it she were comin' here to live without a cent. She says in her letter — " her fingers began picking at the pages.

"Never mind. What does she say?"

"You remember when my father died Mother gave all the insurance money to Ansil to take downriver to New Orleans, and he died of yellow fever in a hotel there, and the money was never found. Nobody knew whether it was stolen in the hotel or whether his uncle really did get it without saying so. The De Vinneys ended up pretty poor. Even the section of land in Louisville father owned was grabbed and sold for a park."

"I remember!" Rogier said impatiently. "What about your mother?"

"Well anyway some of the stolen money finally turned up. Mother got $500 apiece for me and Sister Molly, and $1,000 apiece for Ansil's and Boné's shares. She's comin' out right away: Sister Molly and I were talkin' about it just before you came."

"Where is she?"

"She left. Said she wished Mother was comin' out here without a dollar. She was terribly upset hearing about her $500. I'd think she'd welcome it like a blessing. You don't suppose Tom — " her voice dribbled away before Rogier's frown.

He sat staring past her with troubled, anxious eyes. Then he rose slowly. "Listen Martha. What Tom and Molly decide to do with their money is no concern of ours. Don't interfere."

Two weeks later the Rogiers and Hines drove down to the depot to meet the two arrivals. Mrs. White got off the train, small, indomitable, and easy-voiced as ever. With her was Boné, a small lad with black hair and blacker eyes. He looked frail and fine-strung as a corded whip and said nothing during the ride home.

Tom and Sister Molly stayed for supper. Bob and Hiney, at the Rogier house since early morning, insisted on spending the night with the girls. So Ona took the children upstairs to bed, leaving Mrs. White with her two daughters and sons-in-law sitting grouped about the lamp on the dining room table. Mrs. White talked at length of her husband who had finally, mercifully died; of the death of Boné's

father; and of his mother who had run away. And then, as out of a
clouded sky, she turned to her daughters a kind smile that reflected a
long life that had held pain, much sorrow, and very little joy, but
never the gaunt emptiness that stared back at her through Sister
Molly's eyes.

"Shuh now," she drawled easily. "I'm pleased to find y'all doin'
fine. Joe heah is gettin' along right smart, and Tom you look healthy
as a lean hound. Molly, how you figurin' on spending youah five
hundred dollahs?"

Tom started erect on his chair as if someone had jerked up his
head by the hair. He flashed a quick look at Sister Molly who sat
looking straight before her without blinking an eye. It was evident to
all that he had not heard of the money before.

Sister Molly broke the silence with a clear calm voice. "Spend-
in' that $500 is goin' to be easy, Mother. But it's taken me a long
time to decide on just what to buy."

"Well anyway, heah it is." Mrs. White gave a packet of bank-
notes to Mrs. Rogier who handed it over to Rogier to keep for her;
another packet, containing Ansil and Boné's share, to Rogier; and
the third packet to Sister Molly who slipped it down the bosom of
her dress. Then Molly rose and put her arms around her mother.
"You don't know what you've done, but you've done it for the best,
Mother."

Tom stood up and pushed back his chair against the wall with a
bang. "I can't stay gossipin' here all night! There's a man waitin' to
see me downtown!" He strode out the door without another word.

Late next morning Sister Molly walked the two boys home. She
sat down on the porch steps, chin on hand, without moving, staring
at the wall of mountains. That afternoon Tom's figure appeared far
down the road. She called the boys and sent them back to Rogier's
on an idle errand, then got up and went inside the house. Drawing
back the curtains she watched Tom slouching rapidly toward her,
swinging his long arms. "Oh God," she breathed piteously, face
upturned to the ceiling, "don't let him be too drunk to know what
I'm goin' to say." At the first angry scratch of his steps on the
gravel, she sat down stiffly at the kitchen table.

It was thus Tom found her when he flung back the door. She
was confronting him with a face as colorless and immobile as if set in

clay. The angry stare in his eyes was extinguished as suddenly as if she had whipped out the blaze with one glance from her own eyes. "Come here, Tom," she said quietly.

He slammed the door behind him as if to break the tension and muttered something about washing up.

"Come here!" she said again, without raising her voice.

He slouched to the table and flopped down in a chair opposite her. Sister Molly drew out from her breast the brown-paper packet and tossed it on the table between them. "Five hundred dollars in bank notes. My share from Mother. There won't be any more."

Tom did not speak nor stir a finger.

"Go ahead and shout," she continued in a level tone. "The boys won't be back for two hours and there's nobody within a mile to hear. You've been thinkin' about it all night, and in Levy's all mornin'."

"I ain't been drinking," he denied surlily.

Sister Molly let it pass. "We got something more important to talk about. Tom, we're going to settle everything right now. Understand? I can't go on like this any more."

Tom settled back, taking off his old felt hat and dropping it on the floor.

"That five hundred is yours, Tom. I ain't keepin' a cent for me and the boys. It's your last chance. You're goin' to take it and make good, or you're never comin' home to us again. She took a deep breath. "You're goin' to Leadville, Tom."

A foolish look of pain crept into Tom's face. It was suddenly replaced by a wide grin. "Molly!" He leapt up to kiss her, to throw his arms around her stiff tense body. She sat quietly without turning her face, as if unaware of his kisses.

"Aw, Molly," he muttered, sitting down again. "I'll make you proud of me. I'll come back from Leadville with ten times that much, easy. I know I'll make a strike — the Molly Hines!"

"You didn't understand," she said coldly. "If you don't make good we're through with you — me and the boys. And because we still love you, and always will, I can't take no chances with you, Tom. You're goin' like I say, or not at all. We'll finish now."

"What's up your sleeve?" he demanded.

Sister Molly raised her voice. "You're more ignorant of mining than I am. You'd rush up there and dig a hole any place the digging was easy or the view was good. You wouldn't know a rock was full of silver if you had the finest specimen in your hand. You been ravin' like a mad man about it for three years, and you haven't bothered to find out anything that might be of use if you ever did go. You're still ignorant."

Tom drew back his hand from the packet that still lay untouched between them. Sister Molly lowered her voice to its even tone and went on.

"Listen. Six months ago that poor old Jew down on Huerfano went up the Leadville with a wagonload of fruit. Hay to feed his horses cost $200 a ton. He paid a dollar to sleep on the floor of a saloon. Even drinking water was bought by the barrel. But he sold every piece of his fruit and came back with enough money to buy himself a house and a little printin' shop downtown. I talked to him."

Tom opened his mouth. "Listen!" said Molly before he could speak. "I can't take no more chances. All I want is for you to make what money you can and come back to us. And this is how. I been down to the corral. Smithy is savin' us a good team of mules for a hundred dollars. You can buy a wagon, an outfit, and a big load of fresh apples, and have just enough to live on while you're gone with the rest of this $500." She picked up the packet and slid the bills out on the table before him.

"Oh, I see!" he ejaculated. "I'm supposed to drive up outside a saloon or on a street corner and get out on a box holdin' up a nice red apple. Shouting like the Kadles with their ducks. Playin' Jacob the Jew!"

"Yes, if necessary."

Tom roared. "What! Me do that? A great big fellow like me who maybe could spot a mine like the Robert E. Lee or the Chrysolite peddlin' apples? Chargin' a dollar apiece like a goddam Jew? They'd laugh me out of camp. Christ! I won't do it!"

"Are you sure?" she asked softly. Receiving no answer, she rose suddenly, overturning the chair. "Then get out! Get out!" she shrieked. "You've been nothing but a shiftless loafer ever since you been here. You've lived up all the land Joe gave you for a fresh start. You've borrowed and begged. And now you expect your wife to borrow to feed you. I won't, I tell you! Before I beg another loaf of bread from my sister, I'll see the boys starve cryin' before my eyes. You're worthless. You're no good. And I hope to God I never lay eyes on you again!"

She flung herself against the wall with outstretched arms and shaking shoulders, gasping for breath, but without a sob. Tom slid back his chair and crouched on its edge in an attitude of arrested flight. With one hand he pulled at his black hair in a futile endeavor to straighten out a kink. "Why sure, Molly," he stammered, "sure I'll go. I — I never knew you felt like this."

Sister Molly pushed herself away from the wall and sank upon the overturned chair which she righted as if it weighed a ton. She pushed back her own hair over her ears, and sat staring with dry fixed eyes across the table at him.

8

It was their last night together, and like their first, they spent it alone.

Bob and Hiney, making believe they were on the trip themselves, took their blankets outside and built a campfire. Sister Molly took them out two potatoes to bake, with bread and jam, and returned to the house. Standing at the window she could see their small forms humped over the tiny fire. The flames lit up the shapes of the sleepy mules tethered to a wheel of the wagon already loaded for the start in the early morning. Gradually the vision built up before her eyes a background of somber cliffs and pines. In the red glow appeared men sitting on the ground or leaning against rocks and wagons, pipes in mouth. Rifles, ore specimens, and liquor bottles passed from hand to hand. Always there was silver: silver ore, silver splinters of moonlight, their silvery words of hope — the moonlight metal ever-present in their thoughts and hers. Then a silvery mist before her eyes hid it all from sight, and Tom was beside her wiping away her tears.

"I love you so much I almost don't want to go, Molly," he

murmured huskily, arm around her waist.

"Oh, I love you so." Her deep tremulous voice welled up with all the anguish of the last few months, and cracking through her last reserve burst forth with a single word that shook him on his feet. "Tom!" It carried all that she could ever say. Turning in his arms, she clasped his head between her palms and bent it toward her. Every feature of his face, the wide careless mouth, the long tanned cheeks with their crescent seams, his dark round eyes, and boyish rumpled hair, she drank in with an eager vision as if to preserve them unaltered in the deep recesses of her lonely mind. And he, sensing their oneness, their perfect union for perhaps the first time in their life together, fell silent and ashamed before the moment's truth. He leaned sideways and blew out the lamp.

They sat together in darkness, looking out the window, then he drew her upon his lap.

"Those are our two kids out there, Molly. Can you believe it? We got two grown boys that'll soon be big enough to lick their dad. But it seems just like we were married this morning." His voice softened. He brushed back the hair from her temples. "And I been loving you all this time, Molly. There'll never be another woman for me."

She knew it. Whatever his many faults, he had given her his only love. She kept silent, running her fingers down his hard corded wrist to his long muscular fingers, firm-fleshed as wrapped steel.

" 'Member the first evening we were married?" he asked. "When we sat up in the hotel lookin' out at the lights and listenin' to the boats comin' up the river? And that little nigger's face what brought us up a bottle of port wine? You said it looked like a full brown moon when you give him a dollar. And say!" He squeezed her more tightly. "I'll bet you won't forget tryin' to get into your nightgown! I thought your fingers were clumsy because of all that wine — or maybe because you were ashamed. Then we lit the lamp and saw it was all sewed up across the bottom. And here we didn't think anybody knew we were goin' to get married. I won't forget that in a hundred years!"

In vivid phantasmagoria a hundred other scenes raced across her memory, too swift to be caught in a net of words. Lying relaxed in his arms she watched the moonlight thin, the night breeze grow colder. After a time even the tiny flames outside ceased writhing and lay curled redly asleep. "It's awful late, Tom. And you've got to be up early. Let's don't be late."

She rose and went outside. The night was still and gray. For a long moment she leaned with bent arms across the wagon-bed, staring at the two boys asleep on the ground. In the shadow of the wagon then she knelt on the cold ground in wordless prayer. She got up stiffly, passed a light hand over the necks of the two mules, and walked back to the house.

Tom was already in bed. She undressed in the darkness and crawled in beside him. Tom put his arm under her head and murmured sleepily in her ear. Then soon, as it comes only to a boy or to the damned, sound sleep came to him. A little while longer and moving in his sleep, he removed his arm, turned from her. Then tears came to her. She lay sobbing bitterly, biting her lips that she might not awaken him. Utterly worn out she finally reached up a hand to his high shoulder as if with the gesture of her lasting benediction, and bent her own wet face to the pillow beside him.

Soon after daybreak Bob and Hiney came in, cold and hungry, preferring their mother's kitchen stove to the trouble of making up their campfire. They found her already awake and dressed, making coffee at the stove. She kissed them as they came in, warmly as though they had been gone a long time, kneeling on the floor with her arms around them both. Then, almost brusquely, she rose and went back to the sink as if dismissing them instantly from her thoughts. They had never seen her more composed, more assured; and warming themselves at the stove, they stood watching her cutting thick slices of bread with unhurried capable hands.

Tom came in the door. "Why, there's ole Zeb Pike and Dan'l Boone!" he exclaimed jocularly. "Don't tell me you're goin' to eat under a roof! And standin' at a stove! Is there a blizzard blowin' outside?"

He was in a hearty, fun-loving mood. He put his arm around Sister Molly; but she, calm and unhurried, only turned her head with a resonant "Mornin', Tom!" and went on slicing bread without missing a stroke.

Before they had finished their bread and coffee the Rogiers pulled in the yard. They were all in a light spring wagon: Mrs. White,

Boné, and the girls sitting on planks laid across the sides behind Rogier and Martha, carrying Mary Ann. "All ready, Tom?" Rogier asked lightly. "Haven't forgotten a thing?"

"No, Joe," Sister Molly answered. "We're all ready the minute Tom hitches up."

"Sure," added Tom. "I'm all set to be gettin' off. I want to get me a place early in the line so there won't be so much dust from all the wagons in front. Come on out and I'll show you how my mules look. I been slickin' them up fine."

When they had gone out with the children, Sister Molly took down the kitchen curtains. They were the only ones remaining; and once down, folded, and placed upon the boxes of household goods, the room looked desolate in the gray light of early morning. Except for a few chairs and the things in the bedroom, all was ready to be moved to the Rogiers. Sister Molly turned for a last look at that crude home built for her simple needs. Mrs. White observed her glance with keen discernment. A woman inured to the faint but troublesome cry of life's appalling lonesomeness, with her own life broken to the fickle faithlessness of men's wayward ambitions, she stood silent with her two daughters as if engrossed in the mystery of her heritage falling with affliction upon but one.

Mrs. Rogier stepped up and put her arm around her sister. "I'm glad we're all going to be together again until Tom comes back." Sister Molly squared her heavy shoulders. Unlike her mother, and without the clinging tenaciousness of her sister, she might be broken but never bent. "Everything's all ready when Joe comes after them. The bed covers are folded up and put on top the mattress, and the breakfast dishes are stacked in the basket on the sink. Shall we be goin'?" She turned, and they followed her out the door.

It was a lovely morning for a ride. The air was dry and cold and exhilarating, so clear that the mountains seemed no more than a mile away. Tom, exultant, gave his mules a free rein. For a half-mile they flew along, the wagon bounding from bump to bump. Sister Molly hung on calmly with a straight face. Only once, hitting a rut with a terrific jolt, she murmured quietly, "I wouldn't bruise up all them apples, Tom. Nobody'll buy the squashy ones."

Rogier, driving behind him, watched Tom's crazy pace with annoyance. The mules would be blown and unfit to make the cruel grade up the Pass at such a rate. Deciding to get in front and force a slower pace, he increased the strides of his mares. There was about him a cold set calmness whenever he began anything he had once made up his mind to do. The mares drew down to the ground and spread their legs. Horses were Rogier's one acknowledged weakness. None of the family knew what he had paid for the team and would not have believed it had they known. Wiry and middle-sized, their looks did not betray their price or its complete justification. But Rogier knew, as did several other men who had tried to buy them with increasingly higher offers. Now, warmed up, the mares ran easily, smoothly, with ears laid back; and the wagon slipped up behind Tom in the swirling dust. Then Rogier lightly flipped the sorrel on the rump with the end of the rein and the mares passed Tom in a pattering flash. Rogier eased them down gradually and kept Tom behind them.

From Colorado City the road was crowded with teams and wagons, with men walking and on horseback. Manitou appeared at the base of the great blue barrier before them as though it had been dropped in a basket and burst open by the ridges of the canyons. Rogier, with Tom behind him, drove slowly up the rocky inclined road to the mouth of the Pass. There they turned off into an open meadow beside the trail, already spotted with a hundred wagons.

While Tom went for his place in line, the three women built a fire and prepared breakfast; the early ride had made them all hungry. Ona, gaining respite, had a moment to look around from the top of a nearby ridge. Incomparably beautiful it all spread out in the thin clear air: the great rocky meadow fringed with red sandstone cliffs; the white-hooded wagons reflecting the bright sunshine under a blue and cloudless sky; the Pass itself, winding narrow and steep above the stream that leapt down white and foaming to the little town below. And rising above them all, tier on tier, the great blue mountains majestic and serene. Ute Pass! Always to her at its sound returned the memory of that roadway as she saw it then. More than any roadway to a trackless sea with its crafts' set sails filling with the breeze, its name spoke to her with the wonder of things far off, sad as if muted by an incalculable distance, like the low voice of thunder echoed by the hills. For like the sea it was a land that slept in time and solitude — a vast realm raised high above the earth, close under the inscrutable eyes of a Heaven that attested the heroism of man's labor, his greed, his faithfulness, or his unfitness to the futile task of its subjection. Ute Pass led up to this domain through the narrow defile of its somber cliffs. A game trail centuries old, the historic pathway of the tribal Utes between mountain and plain, and now wagon wide for the new white breed — old as the hills themselves, it lay dusty in the glitter of the morning sun. And like a disjointed snake drawing its parts miraculously together, the long line of wagons formed round the curve.

Tom came back; he had his place in line. Rogier had gone over after him to satisfy himself that all was ready. There was nothing more to be done; the apples, sound and fresh, had been tied up tightly in gunny sacks to prevent them from rolling about and getting bruised; and over the sacks was thrown a protective tarpaulin lashed down with ropes. There was grain for the mules above timberline, grease for the wagon hubs, and plenty of bacon and blankets for Tom.

All about them as they sat eating, the smoke of other campfires rose unwavering in the still air like soft pillars upholding the vast canopy of the sky. Tom sat cross-legged on the ground, exultant and happy. To Bob and Hiney he was the gay and reckless adventurer of their boyish dreams, and he took every opportunity to strengthen their illusion. Sister Molly sat smiling beside him, staunchly upholding his jokes about the gold pieces to come back inside the gunny sacks. Only Rogier smoking a cigar, seemed to offer in silence the unexpressed faith of them all in one.

The clear trumpet of a bugle brought Tom to his feet, upsetting the coffee pot. Mrs. Rogier rose and stepped up beside him. In his shirt pocket she dropped a five-dollar gold piece wrapped in a piece of brown paper on which was scribbled a verse from the first epistle of John: " — let us not love in word, neither in tongue; but in deed and in truth." Tom laughed and caught up her frail body in one long arm. Then he grapped the children in turn, kissing them roughly and rumpling his boys' hair. "So long ever'body! I'll be seein' you all next spring with a brand new gold piece all around!" He put his arms around his wife. They stood for a long moment in silence before he released her, his eyes wet and shining. Then he turned running, waving one hand awkwardly. Sister Molly watched him go with a calm set face that did not betray the anguishing turmoil tearing at her heart.

Ona wandered back to the high ridge and stood staring fixedly at the long sinuous line of waiting wagons. For a long time it did not move; and then like a snake beginning its crawl, a ripple ran down the train. The first dozen wagons began to move forward. One by one they spread out, moving slowly along the single log railing that marked the edge of the steep precipice falling to the stream below. Against the high mountainside the frequent Conestogas stood out most plainly, their white hooded shapes filing past in the shadowless company of other benign ghosts. Between them heavy deep box wagons rolled cumbersomely behind their eight mules. There were other lighter wagons drawn by only six mules, or even one team like Tom's, but the crack of their skinners' whips echoed just as sharp and loud. And above all their reports, like the incessant shrilling of many insects, whined in a single strident voice the creaking of wagon wheels. It was a difficult grade.

Ona heard a sudden intake of breath beside her, and turned quickly to Sister Molly who had followed her up the draw. Sister Molly was kneeling, bent forward over the rim of rock. With a suppliant gesture of finality she had thrown out an arm. With her other hand she held her breast as if to still in a frenzied clutch the mechanism of pain that rent her. Her face was set in a rigid outline of despair and curious pride. Ona followed the direction of her gaze and out-stretched arm. Tom's light wagon, so small and shallow behind a large ore-box drawn by eight mules, crept up the grade. He sat upright in the exhuberant pride of his quest, waving his whip over his two mouse-mules — brave and foolish and futile, like a toy figure behind a toy team. Behind him the load of apples bumped over the rocks. In that far distance the light load, covered by a square of canvas, suggested a body under a grayish shroud.

Sister Molly breathed deeply again, the gasp of air whistling through her clenched teeth. She followed the hump under its dirty canvas with burning eyes. It was the body of her faith, her hope, her love, the love that giving everything demanded a subsistence that it might give still more. But also it was as if under that jolting tarp lay the corpse of her pride. And with the dull surfeit of her own intuitiveness, Ona watched the pain twisting her tearless cheeks as though Sister Molly sat grieving not for the irrevocable death of her pride, but because Tom believed it yet alive and jolting under the tight ropes that held it down.

At the top of the grade the Pass made a sudden turn around the cliffs. Clearly outlined in the bright glare the wagons seemed to halt a moment on the point. Then, as if admitted one by one through the narrow defile, they vanished suddenly from sight. Tom was almost there, one tiny joint in the gray reptile crawling through the Pass. Sister Molly stood up and grasped Ona by the arm. Curiously at that moment the girl felt as if the woman at her side was bequeathing to her the anguish of giving in bondage to the undying earth a beloved hostage for the preservation of their proud will.

"He's gone. God help me. Tom's gone," Sister Molly murmured helplessly, trying to remember that in the careless beneficence of man's enigmatic faith there always exists the possibility of their wildest, their most undeserved dreams coming true — the last and cruelest jest of all.

And with a last flicker of its gray, disjointed tail, the long reptilian line of wagons slid over the Pass, leaving the mountains like a deep blue curtain veiling their future from sight.

9

The house below Bijou Hill was as anomalous as its builder. Long, narrow, and three stories high, it rose from the flat prairie like an ungainly obelisk. To Ona, who often stared at it from Shook's Run where she went to gather watercress, it looked like a big wooden barn. Two protuberances relieved its stark shape: a small front porch and a balcony jutting out from the front second-story bedroom. The house would look better when provided with a long veranda, a glassed-in kitchen porch, gravelled driveway, and the trees and lilac bushes Rogier was setting out. If it bore the stamp of her father's outer simplicity, it also reminded Ona of the lean narrow faces of the smelly old Kadles, with its slanting roof of thin hair, the clapboard seams down it cheeks, and the long white beard straggling down the front steps.

The interior alone bore the marks of Rogier's taste and craftsmanship. The front hall and parlor were panelled in California hand-rubbed redwood, as were the sliding doors with their shiny brass fittings, and matched by a red brick fireplace. The three rooms on the ground floor — parlor, dining room, and kitchen, with a panelled china closet — were repeated on the second floor. The massive front bedroom with its balcony was also made of solid redwood as were its great bed, bureau, and dressing table. Provided with an open fireplace, three great windows, and clothes closet, this master bedroom was easily the best room in the house and comfortably held Sister Molly and her two boys who slept in an alcove. The middle bedroom was given to Mrs. White, the Rogiers using the back bedroom at the end of the hall, next to the bathroom.

The third floor was given over to Ona and the children. Immense, cold, and gloomy, it was the one area in the house that maintained through the years a passive and careless — and thus indestructible — sense of character. A half-story, its low sloping roof magnified the cavernous aspect of the long front room which extended more than half the length of the house. The only window was placed at the north under the gables, and the thin light diffused through its small panes only accentuated its gelid atmosphere. Here Ona, Sally Lee, and Mary Ann slept in beds pulled close to the fireplace. Boné was given the small second room at the back, with a tiny south window looking out at Cheyenne Mountain. Between these two rooms was a dark landing with carved bannisters that terminated the stairway from the second floor. At the head of the stairs was a narrow west window looking out upon Pikes Peak.

Creeping upstairs to bed so as not to awaken the children, Ona blew out the lamp on the landing and undressed in darkness. She had just got into bed when an arm struck her in the side and a voice ejaculated, "Boo!"

"Boné! What are you doing here?"

The boy moved closer to her and murmured softly, "I like your bed best 'cause I can listen to so many things. Hearin' things is more fun. I bet I can hear more things than you!"

"Be quiet then." Ona pushed his head back upon the pillow. It was true; Boné had a peculiarly acute sense of hearing that made the other children deaf in comparison. His favorite game was to lie on the bank of Shook's Run and count on each finger a rippling sound made by the stream. Then one had to trace it up or down the stream to the particular eddy or shoal of rocks to prove his point. Boné invariably finished first. Unerringly too he could call the exact location whence came the cry of a prairie bird, and he was especially sensitive to voices.

"Who's talkin' now?" he whispered.

"Bob and Hiney are talking to Sister Molly."

"No. I mean downstairs in the parlor."

Ona concentrated with all her will upon the faintest hum of voices two flights down and ventured a guess. "Your grandmother."

The boy squeezed her hand. "Now let's try something else."

"You get to sleep."

"I'll tell you, Ona. The first one who hears a bird gets to poke the other."

For a long time Ona lay listening to the deep silence ebbing in the tiny window.

"Have you heard one yet?" whispered Boné.

"Yes," lied Ona, hoping he would go to sleep.

"You ought to have poked me." Then proud of his own forebearance he boasted, "I heard two, an owl down by the creek, and something in the leaves of the elm. I wondered how long it would take you to hear the owl; he's a long way off."

"What makes the steps squeak, Ona?"

"Ask Daddy. Something about the wood."

"Aunt Martha said it was the Kadles walking around. Who are they?"

Ona pinched his arm reassuringly. It was like her mother to say that, as if she believed the fantastic prophecy or threat that the Kadles would haunt the house built on their land! "Silly!" she told Boné. "The Kadles were two smelly old men with white beards who lived here before Daddy built the house. They're both dead now. You go to sleep now or back you go in your own bed!"

Long after he had gone to sleep Ona lay awake. The hoot of the owl sounded closer and down at the creek she heard the single strident voice of frogs and crickets. Then the night was still. There was only the light breathing of the boy beside her, and at long intervals the queer faint creak as of the Kadles, aged and rheumatic, prowling through the house.

Among the grownups in the parlor downstairs the talk was more disconcerting. As Ona had gone upstairs to bed Mrs. White had observed brusquely, "Looks like she's doin' most of the mothahing and work besides."

"Certainly not!" snapped Mrs. Rogier. "But it's good for her to learn such things."

Mrs. White turned to Rogier. "Too much work and no play for a girl goin' on seventeen, ain't it? She's lookin' peaked. Now music's restful. Why don't you give her some music lessons? If you can't afford a piano, I can. I'm goin' into business."

"Business! At your age! What kind?" demanded Mrs. Rogier.

"The only kind I know. A boahdin' house. I looked at a place today for sale on Cascade. I'll be down to your office tomorrow, Joe, to talk to you about it."

"I don't see any need for that," said Rogier. "We're all comfortable here, aren't we?"

"You can't teach an old dog new tricks," said Mrs. White. "Besides I like to be independent."

Sister Molly did not participate in the conversation. She sat in the corner as she sat outside under the elm all day, one hand at her breast, silently waiting for the weeks, the months, to pass. Thinking now how alike their two lives were: her mother, after three husbands, finishing her life alone, and herself with two husbands just as alone. She tried to think of a reason, a defect in their natures, that might have justified their similar fate. Her mother was honest, faithful, and had worked like a nigger. She too had always been honest with herself. Never in her life had she dodged an issue. It just wasn't in them to squirm and lie for the comfort of the moment. All that either of them had ever wanted was a home, somebody and something to work for. And what had it all come to, she wondered. Loneliness was her only answer. Loneliness! The unutterable cry of every human heart.

"I guess I'll be going up to bed," she said dully, rising and plodding upstairs.

"It's no use askin'," said Mrs. White. "She ain't heard from Tom yet?"

"No!" answered Mrs. Rogier sharply. "I don't know what he's thinking of, staying so long and never writing a word."

To this there was no answer.

There was to Mrs. Rogier something infinitely shocking, repulsively common, about her mother's business venture that menaced on her growing snobbishness now that Rogier was becoming so successful. Taking over Henry Haekel's place next to the livery stable! A rowdy boarding house for teamsters, roustabouts, and no-goods! For all her loyalty to her mother, she resolved never to set foot in the place. One couldn't afford to associate with such people if her husband was to become the town's most popular builder.

She urged him often to go in for the large ornate buildings that were marking Little London's growth as a resort. Two men in town who had struck it rich at Leadville had built an Opera House modelled after the Madison Square Theatre in New York. General Palmer, forced to abandon his railroad route to Mexico, had diverted his tracks west to tap the silver booms in Wet Mountain Valley, and at Leadville, Durango, and Silverton. Now he had just built a great new hotel at the end of Pike's Peak Avenue named The Antlers. Of English design, Queen Anne, its three lower stories were built of stone and the two upper stories of wood; it had gables, turrets, balconies, porches, and a round tower. Mrs. Rogier, taking Rogier to its opening, was even more impressed by its hydraulic elevator, gas lights, massive Gothic furniture, and fine rugs and linen.

"The finest hotel out West! A hundred and one feet high! Oh Daddy, if you could only get a contract for something like this!"

Rogier shook his head. "Let's don't get too big for our boots, Martha. The glass works doesn't look as well, but it'll do." The glass manufacturing plant he had just built in Colorado City was indeed no beauty but it was the largest of its kind in the West, turning out daily 19,000 green-glass bottles to hold Manitou's mineral water. The Antler's foreign air of charm and distinction aroused in him again a shame for his lack of education. Graciousness in architecture as graciousness in character implied the mellow strength of time. It would come, but for the present it was enough to continue constructing simple, stout churches, schools, business blocks, and houses.

If the Silver City in the Sea of Silver had brought to Little London an opera house with a Venetian drop curtain and a resort hotel with blue Wilton carpets, it also had drawn to the swiftly growing English spa a horde of ragamuffins on their way to or back from the mountains. Wagon trains creaking up Ute Pass were being replaced by coaches and narrow-gauge railroads crawling through canyons and over mountain passes, wherever sounded the cry of silver. Still, a straggle of wagons would come down the Pass bearing men ragged and unshaven, in boots split at the seams, demanding a cheap bed as the reward of their fruitless toil. It was a group of these Rogier noticed late that fall on the street corner. Drawing a match across the torso of a wooden Indian at the entrance of the tobacco shop and lighting his cigar, he strolled inside for information.

"Yes, Mr. Rogiér," the man told him, "the last train this fall came down the Pass about noon. The town's full of freighters. The boys will be raisin' hell over in Colorado City tonight, won't they?"

Rogier nodded as he went out. Perhaps Tom had come down with them. It was his last chance before winter set in, and he wouldn't be spending another winter up in Leadville unless something had happened. Walking down the street in the twilight, he paused a moment in front of the old boarding house Mrs. White had taken over. The desicated wooden building needed painting, and the livery stable next door did not add to its appearance. He walked carefully up the steps of the ramshackle porch, avoiding the dunnage bestrewn all over, and went in the door.

Supper was being served. The long dining room table was loaded with food and crowded with men. There was only one woman, a young one, sitting next to Mrs. White's place at the head.

"Howdy, Joe. Set yourself in the parlor and I'll send in some coffee. Weah almost done."

Waiting in the small sitting room, Rogier watched Mrs. White with admiration. He never thought of her as his mother-in-law. He remembered her only as one who once had recalled him to the land of living in an upstairs garret; and he conceded her the homage due one who lived her life always with courage, often with regret, but never with shame. She moved with slow assurance behind the broad bent backs, stopping at the buffet to call out to the girl coming from the kitchen with another loaded tray. Then she sat down beside the young woman at the table. She was not eating, and answered with easy unconcern the rough jests called forth by the omission. She kept them in their place with a natural assumption of unmistakable authority without raising her voice above the drawling nigger-tone they all joked at between themselves. Then she talked quietly to the young woman, diverting her attention from the men in woolen shirts ravenously eating from the coarse dinnerware. A Southern gentle-woman who in her time had done grace to cut glass and silver gleaming in candlelight, she gave off an ineffable sense of good breeding without being aware that it always had been hers; she appeared common and she was never coarse.

In a few moments she rose. "Now boys, there's plenty of pun-kin pie. Y'all just tell Beth what you want." Then she led the young woman into the parlor.

"Joe, I want you to meet Miss Lilly Force. She's just come out West here and is figurin' on givin' music lessons."

Rogier bowed. His quick glance dropped from her black hair with its two-inch streak of premature gray to her small oval face, and then to her olive-tinged, swift-moving hands. He had the instant impression of a young woman sensitive and inexperienced, well-educated, and with more nervous force than she had learned to command.

"Mrs. White has been very considerate to sit through the meals with me. It's so much better than eating in my room." The girl smiled. "And I really don't mind the men, even when they joke. Anyway, it's all what I came out West for. I wanted something different."

Mrs. White gave the girl a key. "Well, I figgah theah's no account fo' you to be scairt while you're learnin' there's nothin' different heah from anywheah. You won't need this key, but take it anyway. They're all good boys. If you'd play them somethin' on that old piano, they'd be fetchin' you shirt buttons to sew on and offerin' to take you to church."

"I certainly shall," answered Miss Force, "and tonight too."

"Well, I got to be goin'. Joe will bring me back early so don't be gettin' figity."

As they walked out Rogier asked her, "You're not staying all night with us, then?"

"Jes' supper, Joe. A supper I don't have to think about gettin' always tastes pretty good. But the reason I wanted you to come by for me tonight was Lily Force." They walked slowly down the street. "Lily's got a lot to her," continued Mrs. White. "She's been over to Europe studyin' music for a year. Her father's a Methodist preacher in Illinois. He sent her. But she jes' had to come West like all the rest of us. Why don't you get her, Joe?"

"Always in a hurry, aren't you?"

"You better be, Joe. Somebody else will be grabbin' her and braggin' about fetchin' a music teacher from Europe. Lily would be jes' the one for Ona and maybe Sally Lee."

"We'll see."

"Anyway I'm goin' to fetch her down to the house some afternoon and have her stay for supper."

"That'll be fine," agreed Rogier.

From the top of Bijou hill they walked slowly down into the prairie lying flat and unbroken toward the straggle of trees along Shook's Run. Behind them rose the mountains, always familiarly near and never unheeded in Rogier's mind.

"Heard about the freighters that come down the Pass today?" asked Mrs. White. "The wagons were full of deer and ducks. The boys fetched me three bucks. I'm savin' one foh Martha till you come foh it in the buggy."

"She'll like that. Did you get any of the men down from Leadville?" he asked casually.

"The big fellah on the end and the red-whiskahed man alongside him. Been a lot of shootin' and jumpin' claims, they say. You can't leave a workin' to go after flour and beans, not unless somebody sits behind with a gun. An' the prices sky high. But I asked about Tom."

"Yes?"

"They nevah even heahed of him," she said casually.

The tall face of the house began to loom up in the darkness like the landmark it was. The place looked better now that its stark outlines were broken by shrubbery, the lilac and the lawn, and Sister Molly's big elm tree transplanted out in front. Again, as every night, Rogier felt a queer inquietude as he approached its shadow spread upon the earth like the dark halo of an invisible crown of pain worn so steadfastly by her who sat beneath it through the days.

Mrs. White moved closer to him and put her hand on his arm. "Joe," she asked in her low deep voice, "what can you be doin' about Tom?"

He bent his head and let down his arm. "Ask God and Sister Molly. It's up to them." He went on up the steps and opened the door before her.

10

As always when she got up, Sister Molly that morning had gone barefooted to the window for a look at the mountains before lighting the fire in the grate. Over them had hung the sign of a storm — a gathering of small clouds, low and puffy in the deep crevice between the Peak and Cameron's Cone. She dressed slowly and awakened the boys. Downstairs they ate breakfast with Rogier and Martha, the first buckwheat cakes of the season. Then Bob and Hiney left with Rogier, and Ona took Boné and the girls to school. Slow and lackadaisical, Sister Molly's gaunt body moved about with Mrs. Rogier doing up the work. At noon Mrs. Rogier left for town. "I'm goin' to ask Mother to come down for dinner tonight. Joe can call for her. You won't mind keepin' an eye on the children, will you?"

Sister Molly nodded. Already the day seemed weary and worn thin. She had hoped it might be warm enough to sit under the elm awhile; but true to the epiphanic clouds above the Peak the afternoon was gray and chill. So she sat in her rocker at the front window, gazing westward at the blue rampart that shut off the world of her conscious thought. Boné, Sally Lee, and Mary Ann came home from school. She could hear them playing up in the third floor.

Late that afternoon the clouds drew back from the sun, and Sister Molly sat staring out upon the gold and copper and brass of the fading Indian Summer.

She suddenly stiffened. Not a movement of her big-boned body was visible under the clean starched gingham; it seemed to have set in a cast of frigid shapelessness. Her face drained to the color of dried clay and hardened without a wrinkle. With effort she closed her eyes as though to beseech the powers of darkness for strength to free her from hopeless immobility. The moment passed. She opened her eyes and got to her feet. Clutching at her heart as though to maintain at precise equilibrium that mechanism of almost unbearable pain, she walked stiffly out of the house.

Under the branches of the elm, and hidden from the house by its trunk, Tom was waiting. She moved slowly to stand before him, unable to speak. Then as though still upholding the oppressive burden of those long months of anxious waiting, she slumped backward against the tree. Tom moved a step forward. "Molly — I'm back!" Sister Molly tore her hot bright eyes from his own. Slowly her gaze lowered from his bearded cheeks to his tattered jacket, down his shapeless trousers to boots covered with mud and split at the seams. He took off his hat, holding it against his leg as if to hide the rent in his trousers, and his uncut hair slid gently down over his eyes. Awkwardly he brushed it back. Yes! Tom was back! Without wagon and mules, even his duffle bag, he had begged his way down the Pass with the wagon train.

A fierce pride of possession burned through her as she stared at his hard rangy body, the thin brown face with its high cheek bones and careless twist to his large mouth. It was Tom. There was nothing — not pride or love, nor herself and the long empty years that stretched so interminably before them — nothing that could change Tom Hines. She opened her lips but could not speak. It all had been said before; there was nothing she could ever say.

Tom made an affectionate jump toward her and reached out a long arm as if dangling his battered hat like a trophy before her. Almost wearily Sister Molly leaned back her head to the elm and closed her eyes. It stopped him quicker than if her hand had struck him on the breast. A foolish look of anger drew his lips back from his gleaming teeth.

Suddenly conscious of the smell of his breath, Molly opened her eyes. She had thought it unlike him not to come swinging home, bursting in the door with a shout as if he owned the world and had it in his pocket like a prize. It was the bar whisky taken all afternoon to work up his courage to come sneaking behind the elm when all but herself were gone. But it had made him remember their last talk together. And it held him there, awkward, silent, and fumbling with his hat, like a shadowless vision ever between them. He remembered! And herself, remembering the worry, the anguish, the vain hopes of days passed, could only think of him drinking bar whisky in Levy's all afternoon instead of coming home to her, whatever had happened. It was the only thing Sister Molly could never have forgiven him, and the look in her eyes brought up a faint flush to his corded throat.

Defiantly he raised his head. "Well — I'm back," he said again.

Sister Molly pushed herself away from the supporting elm with a slight decisive inclination of her head. She stood, as if balanced precariously on stiff legs, one hand resting gently on her breast.

"Well, what're you goin' to say? Ain't you glad to see me?" demanded Tom.

"Yes," she spoke gently; and then as if recalled from a distant past soothing with faded memories to the unbearable contemplation of a world sharp with a living image, she repeated in a fierce whisper, "Yes!"

That was all. There was no surrender in her spoken assent. She stood tall and erect under the branches of the tree, and the last rays of sunlight gleaming through its shadows lit up for an instant her gray tense face. She raised her hand to a branch above. The dry twig snapped off with a sharp report. Tom started slightly. His mouth dropped open as though he had seen mirrored in her eyes a flash of lightning that might have split asunder the tree itself. Sister Molly did not move or speak. As with her hand raised in silent benediction, she watched him with a look of gentle understanding that flooded her whole face. Slowly she let her hand fall. It was as though she drew the curtains of the day dying in silence between them. The sunlight flickered and was gone, leaving the shadows dark and chill about their waiting figures. A sharp breeze ruffled the leaves at their feet; and shuffling suddenly in his boots, Tom turned to look back over his shoulder. When he turned around again, Sister Molly had let her head sink toward the hand still at her breast. As though facing a future so vast and unending that not the swiftest human hurry would ever hasten its interminable procession, she walked slowly toward the house. Tom watched her go with dark appealing eyes and an angry flush in his cheeks. He jammed his hat upon his head. "Goddamn it," he muttered in a low thick voice, his boots shuffling the brittle leaves that, falling gently, obliterated forever the trace of her footsteps underneath the elm.

Sister Molly went straight into the house and up to her room where she sat down facing the window. On the floor above, the children were still playing; she could hear their shouts and scampering feet. Suddenly aware that the need for maintaining her vigil out of the window was irrevocably past, she rose and wandered aimlessly about the big room. She could envision nothing that night or day might surprise her with, nothing that time could bring worth waiting for. Slowly the room began to chill and she lit a fire in the grate. From force of habit, she undressed, hanging her clothes carefully in the closet and throwing over her shoulders an old gray robe. With one hand pinching its buttonless sides together across her breast, she seated herself on a stool before the flames.

A little later Ona arrived and came in the room. "I didn't know you were here till Boné told me. Aren't you feeling well, Sister Molly?" When she did not answer, Ona patted her on the shoulder. "You just stay up here till supper time. Things are all started. I'll call you."

Mrs. Rogier arrived home late and bustled about getting supper. "Ona, you get the girls some mush and honey, and see they get up to bed. Mother's comin' with Daddy for supper. Where's Sister Molly?"

"She's not feelin' so good," answered the girl. "I told her I'd keep everybody quiet."

Going upstairs to change her dress, Mrs. Rogier called in to the front bedroom. "Hope you're feeling all right to come down, Molly. We've got a big supper. Mother's comin' home." She paused a moment, inclining her small head, bird-like, toward the room, but there was no answer.

When Rogier and Mrs. White arrived the house was quiet. Mrs. Rogier kissed her mother, then lit the big lamp in the dining room. "We've got a good supper, Mother. Let's don't wait or it'll spoil."

"Where's Sister Molly?" inquired Rogier.

"She won't be down. She's in bed," answered Ona.

"Reckon I'll run up and see her a minute," said Mrs. White.

They all went upstairs. Sister Molly was in bed, watching the dying flames across the room. Rogier stirred up the fire, and its ruddy glow lent warmth to her cold set face. With visible effort she answered their worried questions in a voice, cold and toneless, that expressed no interest in anything they might find to say.

"Anything happen today?" inquired Mrs. Rogier casually. "Seemed like there was a lot of people on the street uptown. Maybe because I don't get out too much. But I thought somebody might have dropped by."

A quick light flickered in Sister Molly's eyes, perhaps no more than the momentary reflection of an ember that burning through effused a spurt of sparks.

"Nobody except a man that stopped under the elm a minute," said Boné loitering in the doorway. "I heard him out of the window."

Mrs. Rogier turned, quick to remind him of his ready tongue, but he retreated up the third-floor stairs. Sister Molly seemed not to have heard him and even Mrs. White turned casually away. Rogier remained in the room after the women had gone downstairs. He idled about uncomfortably as if waiting for Sister Molly to speak, but she lay quiet, seemingly unaware of his anxious eyes. "Well, I'll be going down I guess," he said reluctantly. "Sure you don't want some supper?"

"Good night, Joe," she said dully.

Rogier closed the door behind him and followed Bone up to the third floor. The boy was already in bed at the head of the stairs. "Well, I didn't know you were sleeping here with Ona," he said, sitting down beside him.

"Just till she comes up. Then we play a bird-game and I go in to my own bed."

"Oh, I see."

"Yes, sir. Sometimes we can hear a long way off."

"Almost as far as the elm tree?"

"Aw, that's easy it's so close!" laughed the boy.

"So you think you really heard a man there this afternoon?"

"Sure. But when I looked out the window here he was standin' behind the tree. All I could see was Sister Molly."

Rogier drew the covers up over the boy. "You're a good one!

You probably heard a woodpecker. Now keep warm. Ona will be up in a few minutes." He rose and went downstairs.

All during dinner and afterward when they sat talking in front of the fire, he kept thinking of Boné's words and Sister Molly. Even while walking home with Mrs. White the thought engrossed him so that he did not speak. Mrs. White herself was silent, puffing from the climb up the hill. Suddenly she gripped his arm. "Don't look around," she said casually, "but get a hand on youah gun."

"You know I've never carried a gun in my life!" he answered sharply. "What's the trouble?"

"There's a man followin' us, Joe."

They crossed out into the middle of the road. "It's all right now," he said. "The lights are beginning to show up. Did you get enough dinner tonight?"

At the door of her boarding house, as she turned to go inside, Mrs. White reminded him to be careful walking home.

"I've got a couple of hours figurin' on that church front to do at the office first. Don't worry. I'll fetch that fine buck home tomorrow."

He kept a sharp eye along the street as he walked toward his office, but not until he stopped in the tobacco shop did he catch a glimpse of the figure behind him. With a cigar between his teeth, unlit, he sauntered out of the store and crossed the corner. He had the feeling that someone was still following behind. As the lights thinned out he increased his pace and swung rapidly along the dark block. At the entrance to his office he quickly stepped inside the doorway and turned around to face the street. Waiting for the steps rapidly approaching, he withdrew his right hand from his coat pocket. Then suddenly rasping into a burst of flame the match in his fingers, he thrust it forward face-high and stepped out upon the walk. The movement was timed exactly; the figure stopped before him with a grunt of surprise that betrayed the sharp smell of bar whisky on his breath. Rogier's quick glance played over the uncouth figure of the man revealed in the glow of his match. Imperturbably he lit his cigar and threw the match away. Still the man did not speak, but stood before him silently waiting.

"Come on upstairs with me, Tom," Rogier said quietly, and Tom slouched in behind him without a word.

11

For two days Sister Molly did not leave her room. Mrs. Rogier, unable to remember when she had been sick before, was worried by her curt refusals of every spoonful of medicine and kept wondering what was wrong with her. For breakfast Ona carried her the bowl of hot milk and fried toast the children called Bear Soup, and at supper sat with her until she ate something of what was brought. Sister Molly did not complain. All day and through the evening she sat in silence staring into the flames, her broad shoulders humped as if under an incalculable and invisible burden that could not quite crush her on the spot.

A light snow fell. And the land, absorbing the small flinty flakes, seemed to drain from the skies the dry gray chill, even the clouds that hung over the peaks. With the recrudescent sun the days turned bright and warm; and the long Indian Summer, mellowed by the touch of snow, glowed rich and golden till the year had almost passed. The good weather robbed Sister Molly of all excuses for sickness and drove her outside again. Yet she acted just the same, listless narcissistically bound up by her thoughts, as if emerging from a long illness that had drained her of interest in any living thing.

Even her two boys, lovingly attendant upon her wishes, moved about as though unnoticed under her dull surfeited look. But never did she return to the elm tree, nor did she ever stand staring out of the window again. When her work was done she went upstairs to her room, sitting in a catatonic stupor till supper time.

The months went by and Sister Molly did not change. An immobility of expression held frigid her broad freckled face. Even her big figure, growing gracious in contour as it thinned, gave an air of impenetrability through which none could divine the cause of her strange malady. Only Rogier knew. Often he made up his mind to talk to her of his meeting with Tom, but as if bound to silence by a casuistical passion for maintaining the integrity of his given word he said nothing.

Only once did Mrs. White voice her anxious surmise. "Somethin' has happened to Molly she won't tell." And she was too shrewd and human to say more. Mrs. Rogier became more worried. "She acts like she was just passing the time away until she died." Terrible phrase! Rogiér's conscience repeated it every night. But they all forebore to talk of Tom.

That winter Mrs. White's boarding house burned down. The hay rack of the livery stable next door caught fire, the flames spreading to the ramshackle building before an alarm could be given. Mrs. White and her boarders were eating supper when they were enveloped in a burst of smoke and rushed out before the entire side wall of the dining room collapsed, bringing down the roof. The fire burned almost everything Mrs. White owned and she moved back into the Rogier's middle bedroom with nothing left but a few clothes still hanging in the closet. The venture had taken all the money remaining from her father's estate.

For the first time since Rogier had known her, she seemed discouraged. Squinting at the memories she recalled, Mrs. White could see no pattern to her life. Yet over and over again there seemed repeated in her life and in Sister Molly's those similar happenings with which fate had marked their days. She remembered a night in her early married life. De Vinney was celebrating the christening of a river steamer. Six darkies had rowed her out to meet him. A hundred gentlemen with their ladies thronged the smooth decks and the salon, or danced sedately to music from Negroes whose eyes and teeth gleamed white in faces sweating black. De Vinney was not present to receive her and help her up the steps, although a dozen gentlemen crowded each other for the honor of her hand. He was at the roulette table in the main salon. From the doorway she saw him there under the brilliant crystals of the chandelier, his face flushed with wine, eyes bright for the whirl of the ivory ball, but not for her. And now, forty years later, she remembered that it was the same boat on which she had sent her son Ansil to New Orleans with all the money from his father's estate. She had believed it had been stolen from him as he lay dying of yellow fever in a hotel room at the end of his journey. But now, strangely after all the years, she seemed to see her son standing in his father's place in the same salon, his own face flushed, hands and heart eager with his father's full patrimony. A man like Tom. The vision passed to bring the memory of that fire long ago, burning the St. Louis warehouses that held her name and wealth. Queer that those flames of fate had followed her through all the years only to take from her at last a place as miserable as Henry Haekel's old boarding house. So Mrs. White sat with Sister Molly, facing a short and impoverished future after a long and malignant past.

Ona sat with them often. Herself big-boned and tall, she had become Sister Molly's constant companion. They never talked, yet the older woman's strange and pitiable infirmity preyed upon her mind. She could not keep away.

Late one afternoon Rogier saw all three of them sitting on the floor staring up at Sister Molly's graven mask of face. The dull bewilderment, the deep compassion in the girl's eyes, brought Rogier up short. For the first time he saw her as other than a child. She was his daughter; she had her own life to live; and he was damned if she wasn't beginning to look and act like both of them — as if all three were of a kind. The truth of that vagrant thought struck and clung quivering in his mind like a spent arrow that had reached its mark. Here she was when all her world should be unfolding with the bloom and fragrance of youth's spring. But instead of horseback rides, mountain picnics, and kisses in the moonlight, she chose to sit and share the insupportable burden of Sister Molly's hidden sorrow. That was no life for a girl. No one could help Sister Molly now. Resentment flooded his mind. This was a miserable house over which hovered like a black cloud a sense of stifling doom. There ought to be noise as in every other house — quarrels and laughter and the empty prattle of happy voices. But here only Boné seemed more than half alive.

Impetuously he called out, "Ona! go down and help your mother," as though work were something she had never known. But that night he told Mrs. Rogier that Ona was to do no more work around the house.

"But who'll take care of the children? And how will the work get done?

"Three grown women ought to be able to cook and sweep the floor," he answered gruffly. "Ona's done more than her share too long. It's time she was learning to play."

As he was getting ready to go back uptown he drew Mrs. White aside. "Whatever became of that music teacher, Lily Force?"

"I reckon she's boahdin' around, tryin' to give lessons."

"Suppose you bring her around. Ona's beginning to look seedy, worrying about things she can't help."

Mrs. White nodded. "This heah house needs a little music. It might keep you home of an evenin'."

Rogier went back to his office and his books without telling her she was probably right.

Stratton showed up at his office again. He looked not only more run-down-at-the-heels, but there was in his eyes the haunted look of a recluse. From Mrs. Rogier's gossip Rogier could understand why. He had married that young seventeen-year-old girl with whom he had been keeping company, Zeurah Stewart, and a few months later had sent her home to Illinois. There she gave birth to a child, a boy whom she claimed was Stratton's conceived before their marriage. Stratton asserted the child was not his and divorced her. To add to this unfortunate affair. it became known that Zeurah shortly after her marriage had received $3,000 from her family's estate which Stratton was believed to have spent on prospect trips. Wild conjectures and embittered gossip had changed the popular young carpenter and builder completely. He had left town to live like a recluse, still searching for silver. Now he was back, broke and friendless.

"I've got three jobs goin', Stratton. I can put you to work on any one of them." Rogier began to describe them, but Stratton interrupted.

"Never mind which. All I want is a good job as a journeyman carpenter to save up a grubstake for spring. Then I'm goin', hear!"

He launched immediately into an account of all the fabulous strikes made in the Sangre de Cristos, the San Juans, the Mosquito and Saguache ranges. He had seen them all, prospected every gulch and canyon, crossed every river, and from his solitary campfires had sprouted a dozen boom camps. Like Aspen on the Roaring Fork! Why, from the Mollie Gibson had been taken a single chunk of silver ore weighing 1,700 pounds and bringing $3,000. But Leadville, he insisted, was the daddy of them all. Tabor had sold the Chrysolite for $500,000. The Matchless was paying him $2,600 a day, and his Little Pittsburgh had brought him $1,000,000 more. What a mine that was! The crews of the Little Pittsburgh had raced those of the Robert E. Lee to determine which mine could produce the most ore in twenty-four hours. The Little Pittsburgh had won, producing $117,500 in silver for the day. Palmer's Denver and Rio Grande Railway had reached Leadville. Ulysses S. Grant was the guest of honor to ride the first train into town. Last year 6,000,000 ounces of silver worth nearly $10,000,000 had been taken out of its mines.

"Did you ever run into or hear of Tom Hines up there?" interrupted Rogier.

Stratton spread his hands emptily. "One man in thirty thousand, in fifty thousand. Who knows how many are up there running around, hunting for work?"

"What did you do to get along?" Rogier asked gently.

"Me? I was lucky. Tabor was building a bank with vaults to store his silver bullion. I got the job of building on top of it a big disc carved and painted like a silver dollar. 'Silver Dollar Tabor'!" He grinned sheepishly and then continued. "You know what he claims? That there's enough silver in these mountains to build a wall of solid silver four feet thick and forty feet high clear across the eastern boundary of Colorado. Colorado, the Silver State! These mountains are full of it, Joe. It makes no difference I haven't made a strike yet. That mountain I dreamed of as a boy is still holding it for me, and I'll recognize it when I see it!"

Yes, he had made the turn. He was wholly committed to his

Again her voice broke and burst forth once more. "But don't you ever be thinkin' I've changed. I'll always be just Tom's."

Before the truth, clear yet indefinable, which found expression in the imperfect connotations of her common words, Rogier bent his head. How unspeakably mysterious is every human soul that it can never be wholly known, seldom approached with perception, and only partly understood with the priceless gift of vision.

Day and night Ona stayed with her, sleeping on a cot beside her bed. It was as if she, of them all, had been chosen to bear with strength and endurance the sinking burden none could support. It was not enough. When Sister Molly died she was buried in the pine-shadowed graveyard south of town. She lay with her head toward Pike's Peak; and the watchers at the funeral remembered how Sister Molly on a wager had scaled its lofty summit in the full strength of her big body—one of the first women to climb the precipitous Ruxton Trail. Now, benign and wrinkled, the Peak stared down upon her final resting place. And standing in the shadow of the enormous pine under which she was buried, none of her family spoke of Tom. Not then or afterward.

That night after the funeral Rogier sat alone in his office, staring out of the window at that high rocky selfhood which alone, of all the living, vibrating entities he had ever known, seemed great and enduring enough to serve as a repository for that human spirit which had escaped at last its small, fleshly and mortal frame.

PART II

GANGUE

1

A death is like a wound in the trunk of a tree; bark, roots, the sap within, all pour forth energy to heal and cover the hurt. So it was with the Rogier family after the death of Sister Molly. For the first time it took on an air of conscious unity, gave off a strength impersonal and fixed. If once its members had been exiles in a new strange land, they now formed one harmonious whole rooted to their earth like a single great pine.

Lamenting the barren outlook from the window, Mrs. Rogier demanded more trees; only the big elm stood between the house and Shook's Run. Rogier went to an old prospector who lived up on Wahsatch. "Maloney, the next time you come down from the mountains bring me a couple of young spruces for our yard. If you need any help I'll loan you a team."

A few weeks later Maloney returned with two half-grown blue spruce with long gnarled roots holding their burden of earth. They were exactly what Rogier wanted. One planted on each side of the walk would relieve the tall three-story face of the house of its gaunt aspect. As he idly kicked the crooked roots, a clump of earth was dislodged and split open on the ground. In it was a piece of rock as big as his two fists, grayish in color with a tinge of purple. A peculiar glint in the cleavage caught Rogier's eyes. Getting out his knife, he began to scrape it.

Calling Maloney off to one side, Rogier showed him the specimen. Maloney hefted it, squinted at it, gouged it with Rogier's knife. "I've done lots of work cause of worse samples," he said tentatively.

"What is it?"

"Could be a showin' of pay dirt."

"You're not sure?"

Maloney's face grew redder under his white hair as he expostulated all he knew. He was an old man, the common type of prospector who really knew little.

"I reckon you'd better take this piece to a good assayer," suggested Rogier. "Do you know of one who can keep his mouth shut? There's no need of going off half-cocked like everybody else."

Two days later the assayer reported that the specimen was an ore he did not know and hence was unable to test properly. Maloney, in Rogier's office, stamped back and forth in front of the window. "If it ain't silver, I'll bet it's gold!"

"Calm down, Maloney," said Rogier. "It's probably a false alarm. But it wouldn't hurt if you went back to where you took out those spruce and looked around. I'll give you a team with a grubstake and some tools."

After the old prospector had left, Rogier found himself unaccountably disturbed . Maloney had brought down the trees from the lower south slope of Pikes Peak. It seemed preposterous to believe that gold could be found there, so close to town, and on the very peak around which men had prospected for years and then gone on to distant ranges. But what if it were? He got up from his stool at the drafting board and began to walk back and forth himself.

For a century the currency system had been based on bimetallism, the unlimited coinage of both gold and silver. Then in the Crime of 1873, as he remembered, the government stopped the coinage of silver dollars and established gold as the standard of value. Five years later silver was discovered in Leadville and the increasing flow of silver from all Colorado began to cast a white shadow over the world at large. All loyal Coloradoans clamored for the right to have coined into dollars all the silver shipped to the mints, and demanded that the ratio of sixteen ounces of silver to one of gold be restored. A compromise was effected in the Bland-Allison Act, directing the purchase of from two to four million dollars worth of silver a year for coinage into dollars. Then, as Rogier knew, the political pot began to boil when Cleveland, opposed to free silver, was elected President in 1884. But the mountains still kept pouring forth a stream of silver — $20,000,000 worth a year now! Something was bound to happen when a country on the gold standard was being flooded with silver.

These considerations were only the surface strata of his perturbation. He kept pacing back and forth as if through a pale white shadow. How strange it was that of all the glistening peaks in every range of these Rockies only this massive mother-beacon for the tide of westward fortune-hunters — this instigator of the Pike's Peak Rush of Fifty-Eight — should have proved barren of its promise. Serene and majestic, beautiful and alluring as it seemed, Rogier knew how cruel it was. It had made fools and vagrants of a generation of men.

Rogier had not succumbed to the lure of silver. A man with ten mouths to feed couldn't afford that touch of moon-madness. Too, he prided himself upon being a rational man. He distrusted moonlight, with all that it always had implied. It had no primary source; it was simply sunlight reflected from a dead planetary body. And silver in turn was but its material reflection in the earth — insubstantial and comparatively worthless as it might prove to be.

But gold! That was something else! The very name held a magic that was unfathomable. Rogier brought up short at the window to stare out again at the enigmatic face of the Peak. What had led him to send Maloney off, hiding his own strange excitement? It wasn't the prospect of getting rich quick, he assured himself. In any case he should have kicked that ore specimen into the hole dug for the spruce. It had caused him only a lot of confounded worry.

Maloney, having exhausted his grubstake, came home disconsolate. He had found no signs on the bottom slope of the talus where he had uprooted the two spruce. As they were young trees, he believed they might have been uprooted and carried down by a landslide. But after packing up the slope and prospecting for days, he had been unable to find the ledge where the specimen had broken off or any trace of ore anywhere.

Rogier felt relieved, and flung himself back into his work with renewed vigor. Lily Force, who had been giving Ona piano lessons, was hunting for a new boarding house. "You come right down here and stay with us," Rogier insisted. "Sally Lee and Mary Ann need some music too." Shortly afterward Mrs. Rogier obtained a maid whom she had met through a peculiar incident.

The two women were kneeling in church one Sunday morning when the services were interrupted by the clanging of bells outside. The congregation kept on praying until the indisputable clamor of men dragging the fire-cart past the church door sounded. Mrs. Rogier raised her head from her arms to meet the gaze of the woman beside her who suddenly shrieked out, "Pray, brethen, let's pray! That's my house burnin'! I left the fire on to cook some beans!"

The woman's name was Lida Peck, and it really was her small shack that burned down. Mrs. Rogier brought her home and persuaded her to stay as a maid. She was enthusiastically religious, attending every church in town. Her yearly vacation of a week she spent attending the Free Methodist Camp Meeting on Fountain Creek outside of town. There would be dozens of tents pitched in a great ring around the rough tables and benches. After a hearty breakfast of wild game, smoked ham, and barbecued beef, the services began. At ten o'clock the songs started, and at three came testimonials from the converted. These daily sessions were attended only by converts and proselytes like Lida Peck. But in the evening people from town would visit; cowboys rode in from the ranches; and later men from the saloons and sporting women from the red-light district in Colorado City wandered over to get religion. They filled the back seats, and becoming hilarious, joined in the shouting. It was all very beautiful and touching to Lida Peck.

This year she conveyed an urgent invitation to the family, as Rogier had good-humoredly donated a tent and some supplies to her cause. With camping space reserved for them, the Rogiers drove over to the meadow between the creek and the red rock walls of the canyon. Mrs. Rogier, peeking out from the frill of her black bonnet, gave a sudden snort of alarm.

"Gypsies. Isn't that a gypsy camp pitched farther down? Right next to where there's a religious meetin' goin' on — even if it is a Shoutin' Methodist Revival. You children stay close to Ona now or they'll be stealin' you away!"

The revival bored Boné. Alone with Ona, he pleaded to spend the silver dollar Rogier had given him with a gypsy woman wearing big rings in her ears. So that evening when the services began they slipped away from the circle of tents and walked to the camp of the gypsies. There were any number of fortune-tellers sitting with their decks of Tarot cards spread out before their fires, or calling from their hooded wagons. Ona was for stopping at any one of them, but Boné walked on toward a thicket of willows.

In a clearing was a dirty canvas-topped schooner backed against a small fire. In it bending forward with her two bare arms crossed over red-stockinged legs, sat a big swart gypsy watching some men playing cards on the ground. "Ona. There she is. Look at the big gold rings in her ears," whispered Boné. "You ask her!"

"No, it's your dollar," she replied. The boy hesitated, then took her by the hand. Walking resolutely up to the gypsy, he laid down his dollar.

The woman grabbed him by the wrist. Rolling out his fingers, she examined both sides of his hand swiftly and intently. Then ringing the silver dollar on the floor of the wagon, she tossed it into the air, catching it in her lap and laughing. "Let a boy with such a hand sing for his own fortune, and not expect it from a gypsy queen with only a piece of silver!"

It had taken not half a minute; and walking back through the darkness Ona tried to console Boné. "These gypsies are sharper than horse-traders and won't be satisfied till they've got every penny on you. But maybe what she said meant more than we heard." Boné trudged beside her silent and sad because the gypsy woman had taken his dollar, not knowing that she had fitted the lasting truth to his long and slender hand.

Ona's own clumsy fingers often reminded her of that enigmatic prophecy. Boné's hands through a few stolen moments each day at the piano were far more adept than hers. Too, he had what Lily Force called perfect pitch. Standing beside Ona at the piano, back turned, he could call out "A", "G", "F-sharp" with astounding precision. Ona blamed Lily Force as well as her mother for the lamentable fact that Boné was not given lessons as well as herself and the two girls.

Though living with the Rogier , in return for which she gave music lessons to them, Lily Force insisted on strict punctuality. At ten o'clock she gave Ona her lesson, and at two o'clock went through the rudiments of music with Sally Lee and Mary Ann. On the evenings Rogier stayed home from work she played for him an hour on the piano. Invariably old Southern songs: "Old Folks at Home," "Old Black Joe," "Maryland, My Maryland." Rogier sat silent, chewing on his cigar. At the end of his favorite piece, "Carry Me Back to Old Virginny", he got up heavily, telling her that for all her technical training she would never know how to play it until she had heard it from Negroes singing.

This endlessly repeated remark infuriated her. She made up for it with her Sunday afternoon concerts to Mrs. Rogier's dinner guests and other invited visitors. It was a display of culture none of them forgot. Lily sat on the piano bench, slender and vivacious, her well-kept hands flitting faultlessly over the keys. Her favorite composer was Mozart, and his perfection of form and style suited her exactly. From time to time she paused to rest, turning to face her listeners. The sun, flooding the room, infused in her olive-tinged cheeks a spot of color like iodine. Her black hair with its two-inch strip of white was never smoother. After she had begun to die it black, the streak took on a greenish hue. No one noticed it, she spoke so prettily of the composers and their compositions. Often she prefaced her remarks with, "When I was in Leipzig" — "In Weimar I saw" — "Well do I remember that crooked little street in Vienna." Mrs. White sat with a smug air of "I-told-you-so," subtly attesting her discovery of Lily Force. Mrs. Rogier was deliriously proud of her and her growing reputation.

Lily Force played, talked on. She was as polyphonic as a Bach fugue. Were music cold and dead as a corpse, she would have excelled as one of its morticians. She knew composition, but not music. She understood the structural design of its skeleton, apprehended with skill the incredible intricacies of its strange texture; but never in her life was she to stand confounded before the profound mystery of the simplest melody. Sincere as her nature allowed, trained well and showing that education handsomely, she was a music expert but not a musician.

This was Ona's music teacher.

Promptly at ten o'clock Lily was always sitting primly at the piano waiting for Ona to come in. This morning, a little late, Ona halted in surprise. "Look here!" said Lily. A newspaper was spread across the piano covering all the music. It was opened at the "Personal" column and Lily's finger was pointing to an advertisement headed "Matrimonial." Lily read it out loud. " 'Wanted: A young blond lady of refinement and education to correspond with a professional, dark-complexioned gentleman with most honorable intentions.' What do you think of that, Ona?"

Ona stared at her with amazement. Lily read these foolish ads every week, but surely she would never dare to take one of them seriously!

"Well," said Lily with a smile, "I answered it anyway. Washington, D.C. it was. By the time he answers I ought to be able to bleach my hair. The pharmacist up on Tejon said it ought to come out well."

Suddenly changing tone, Lily folded up the newspaper and laid it aside. She was no longer frank and engagingly human, but academic, strictly impersonal. "I do wish you would get here on time, Ona. Every moment counts now. In church the other morning your fingers seemed quite stiff. Or were you a little frightened?"

"No," said Ona listlessly. What had it mattered? She merely had substituted for the regular organist to play four hymns.

"You should learn to play well enough to appear in church every Sunday. Then you might attract the attention of some nice young man. At your age you should be going out with one," went on Lily. "What I think the trouble is, is lack of interest in learning fundamentals. Keep on with our study of composition while we're learning to play. Don't you dear?"

"Yes," assented Ona in the same flat tone.

"All right, then. Let's begin."

Following a tedious dissection of the "Blue Danube," Ona started in on her third week's repetition of part of Chopin's Waltz in C-sharp Minor used for finger exercise. Neither of them were aware of Boné's presence in the doorway behind them until he interrupted.

"Why don't you make her play it right? She always gets her finger in the way halfway through and puts in the same wrong note every time. You never do tell her about it, either."

Lily whirled around as though unspun from the string of a top. Compressing her pretty lips she said nothing, but her hand, thrust back toward the piano, struck the keyboard to give out a blatant discord. Boné stood immersed in the sound, oblivious to her anger, and interested only in what his quick ears had detected.

"Don't bother us, Boné," said Ona. "Run out in the kitchen and ask Lida to give you one of her cookies."

Obediently the boy left the room. His small slight figure, with his black hair and blacker eyes, had grown to be the bane of Lily's musical existence. He was immune to her scoldings, unabashed by his daring and childish criticisms, and impregnable against her Sunday afternoon musicales.

Working away, Ona had to smile to herself at the amazing divination of Boné's remark. He would never know how exactly he had guessed her trouble! For the fourth time she flew through those first measures so pliant to her touch and then — she almost winced as her finger again sharped the note he had detected.

"Here," said Lily, "finger it this way." Following the score carefully, and trying to overcome her secret annoyance at Boné's perspicacity, she arched her wrists affectedly and skimmed through the passage.

Outside on the grass under the lilac where he lay munching cookies, Boné looked up at the open window with a childish look of intolerant disgust. Of them all — teacher, pupil, and casual listener, he was the only one in whom music fed a secret and unguessed want. To Lily music was a structure majestic, mysterious, and immense, to be inspected carefully and with caution. Ona liked to hear it and only hoped to learn to play the piano. With Boné it was immeasurably different. His craving for it was as natural as for meat and cookies; and he took it with as little concern. Music revealed to him its secret and subtle truths in audible symbols that all could hear but from which only he could read the meaning; polyphonic, it spoke to him with the wind, the rain upon the roof, the birds in the elm, the ripples of Shook's Run; it was his trumpet, his faith, a secret cancer in his soul, the knotted club for his self-flagellation, and the everlasting solace to his human — and thus lonely — heart. The gift of music was his — and the time was to come when he would offer himself upon its altar as proof of his unswerving devotion.

But now, flat on the grass, he heard through the window the rustle of a newspaper. The lesson was ended; and Lily's voice mused softly, "That's fine, Ona. How long do you think it will take a letter to come from Washington?" Boné rose, and stuffing the last cookie in his mouth moved languidly away.

2

It was Sunday morning and the Rogier family was getting ready for church. Pushed about helplessly, his toes trod on, his cigar knocked awry in his mouth, Rogier retreated to the china closet where seated on a tier of drawers he could watch with safety the confusion before him. Sally Lee and Mary Ann both wanted the same pink ribbon for their hair. In the front room Lily Force called out, "Ona, do you have your music ready?" Whereupon Ona got up from her knees before the two girls and jerked the pink ribbon from their hands to tie up her music — "and let that be a lesson to you both!" Out in the kitchen Lida Peck was finishing the dishes and muttering inculpabilities against all late risers. Her incriminations were softened by frequent looks at her new hat hanging on the cellar door. Bob Hines, already as big as his father, was stooping in front of the buffet mirror to adjust his cravat for the fourth time. "I do wish you'd come with us, Daddy," complained Mrs. Rogier again, hunting a pin for her small bonnet. "It's Palm Sunday." Rogier leaned back against the dark wainscoting listening to the bedlam, attesting with its rising crescendo that the Devil was doing his damndest to frustrate the heavenly design of Sunday morning.

He was no match for Mrs. Rogier. With the perfect composure of seasoned Christian soldiers the family marched out of the house. Rogier walked to the front window where he watched them up the street. Behind the two girls, sedate as white hens in starched muslin fluffing out in back like tail-feathers, followed Ona and Lida Peck. With them was Lily Force. Mrs. Rogier walked primly beside Bob, her hand on his arm. She carried herself erect, head up; and her frail figure garbed in black, with her indomitable, finely chiseled face, expressed all her heart-felt pretensions to Southern aristocracy. Boné loitered in back, straggling along the picket fence with his carved walking stick that Mrs. Rogier, five minutes before, had forbidden him to carry to church. He was discreetly silent, touching only gently with the end of the stick the slats that on week-days he rapped unmercifully with xylophonic glee.

Rogier turned from the window with a reflective puff on his cigar and strolled slowly through the house to the back yard. He had refused to be a deacon lest it might compel him to attend church, declined to act on the School Board because his bids for the school buildings were invariably accepted, and turned down an offer to get into politics without any reason at all. His aloofness created no adverse comment; all who knew him considered it a virtue that he minded strictly to his own business. It proved also to be his weakness. His large family, the prairie land from Bijou Hill to Shook's Run, and two store buildings uptown seemed to have come unbidden but not unwelcome to him. Yet none of them — his family, property, and profession — assuaged the secret conviction of his aloneless.

And the massive mountains rising tier on tier above the flat sunlit prairies refuted any sense of rooted security. He lacked something, he did not know what. Only his books, the evening hour listening to Lily Force at the piano, and the neigh of a horse in one of the stalls, soothed the strange longing that possessed him.

Mrs. White, too poorly for church, came out to sit on the back steps in the sun. She could see him wandering from stall to stall, the hay shed in the corner, the open buggy shed, and along the west side of the enclosure past a second row of stalls newly built and empty. Except for his mares, Lady and Lou — familiarly referred to by the family as Lady-Lou — all of Rogier's teams were draft horses for building work, yet he looked after them like children.

Seeing Mrs. White on the back steps, Rogier carefully closed the gate behind him and sauntered down the walk to sit beside her.

"Hiney ain't up yet," she remarked in a voice that did not conceal the suggestion that the time was nearly eleven o'clock.

"A good sleep won't hurt him any. He has to stay after the play's over to clear things up," answered Rogier, denying the implication of laziness. Hiney was a bright lad, apt at storytelling, and a lover of jokes. He had secured a job as stagehand at the new Opera House built by the two Little Londoners who had struck it rich in Leadville, and he was always coming home with amusing stories. One of Rogier's favorites was Hiney's account of the opening night performance starring Maude Granger in *Camille.* An invited guest asked one of the owners, old Ben, to translate the motto on the Venetian drop curtain, *"Nil sine numine."* Old Ben, who had no idea what it meant, promptly replied, "No sign of a new mine."

"I allow you don't know what I mean," said Mrs. White. "But I ain't told nobody else."

"What do you mean?"

The old woman prodded the toe of her shoe with a broomstraw. "Well, one night las' month I come down the stairs to see a man from the Opera House standin' in the hall with Hiney. 'A prop fell down tonight and give your boy a rap,' he says. 'It didn't hurt him none, but I had to bring him home. He didn't remember the way.' And theah was Hiney grinnin' foolish-like and rubbin' the side of his head wheah the horse kicked him when he was a little tike. He didn't seem to know me, but followed me up to bed."

Rogier sat quietly beside her, one broad forearm resting on his knee. As if to rouse him from his lethargy, Mrs. White spoke sharply. "And that ain't all, Joe. The next mawnin' Hiney got up feelin' fine, but the othah day I saw somethin' else. It was along sundown, time fo' him to be gettin' to work. Yet he was sittin' right heah like a lost coon dog, and didn't remembah nothin' about it. Then in the middle of the evenin' up he starts up and off to the Opera House he goes. Like all of a sudden he'd jes' come to and remembahed all about himself. What do you reckon is wrong?"

"Nothing — probably nothing. He's been watching those actors and actresses so long, and play-acting like them, he's getting absent-minded.

"Go along!" Mrs. White answered testily.

Rogier looked up and grinned; they knew each other beyond the subterfuge of words. Tossing his cigar away, he rose and strolled down the back walk.

"I wouldn't want nothin' to happen to one of Sister Molly's boys," came a voice at his shoulder.

"I'll keep my eye on him" he promised, leaning upon the top of the gate.

Mrs. White stared over the fence. "What's the line of stalls fo' ovah theah? I ain't heahd of no new horses."

"Scrap lumber. Thought I might be needing some new work teams soon."

"Humm. Looks like the back yahd's full of them already. Now I remembah a bay gelding that De Vinney wanted down along the Mississippi. He used to say evah time he come up the rivah he'd give his eye-tooth fo' that horse. Well suh, he did! The day aftah he brought him home, he pitched cleah over his head, rolled into a stump, and come up spittin' that eye-tooth in his hand. A gelding, too. Only a ten-yeah-old niggah boy could do anything with him at all. But them shiny bay flanks of his would look mighty sweet in one of them new stalls, Joe."

Rogier kicked at a pebble on the walk, then ground it under his foot. "There's a race track being built north of town. Up along Monument Creek. They're getting up a Gentlemen's Pleasure and Driving Association to run it. Not that I'd go in for anything like that, but —" He hesitated, then confessed, "I've seen her several times. A sorrel mare just brought here from the east. She's fairly fast."

"A fast horse is fast in any company, Joe."

"Her name's Pet," said Rogier. "Gentle enough for the family to use her in the buggy."

"I wouldn't spoil her," said Mrs. White, watching him closely. He had perked up — considerable, she thought. A minute passed, then she said casually, "It ain't noon yet and the folks are still to church. You wasn't figurin' on goin' out fo' a look at that sorrel mare, was you?"

Rogier grinned: "Dom! You're right! Get your bonnet while I hook up."

She came out to the buggy carefully holding her bonnet in both hands. From it she removed a bottle, took out the cork with her teeth, and wiped off the neck with her long wrinkled fingers. "This heah bottle's been sittin' up in the china closet long enough. Don' you reckon we'd oughta do somethin' about it? De Vinney used to say a drop of brandy nevah spoiled the looks of a good horse."

Rogier waved his hand, grinning at the way she bent the bottle back. After his own turn he set her up in the seat, bonnet and bottle clutched in her lap, and shook Lady-Lou into a trot. She sat at ease as always, the breeze gently brushing her gray hair behind her ears.

"I wish that preachah could see us! A fingah of brandy and a ride behind a fast horse might help them sermons of his some. The smirkin' lil' dandy! Oh Lawdy! give me a good piece of horseflesh to a sermon every day. Don' you, Joe?"

Rogier threw up his head and laughed. "I'm going to buy that sorrel if I have to sell every piece of ground I own!"

Mrs. White was startled at his vehemence. She looked around, face flushed, then murmured complacently, "Sho' enough, Joe. I reckon that's what we're comin' out here for, ain't we?"

The outskirts of town had fallen behind; ahead swept the unbroken surge of prairies. Rogier tightened his grasp on the leather ribbons in his gloved hands, drew back the heads of his mares until their noses pointed at the line of mountains cut into the sky. "How about a little ride? Suppose you can hang on?" Mrs. White shifted her weight, sat on the empty bottle and her bonnet, and stuck out a hand for support. "I been heahin' you say these mares can run, but I ain't nevah see 'em yet!"

Rogier squashed the soft hat on his head, ruffled his sandy mustache. Then suddenly bending forward, he flung out the reins with a slap at Lady-Lou. With a leap the mares shot forward, ears back, and lay down to the road.

Pet was a welcome addition to the Rogier household. The family allowed her to do everything but eat at the table. She was a pretty thing, even-colored and even-tempered, swift and gentle as a rabbit. On week days while Rogier was gone the children often took her over to Manitou after iron and soda water, driving along the creek past thickets of willows, currants, and chokecherries. Sally Lee with her father's knack for handling horses did all the harnessing and driving.

Even Mrs. Rogier approved of the mare. The Little Londoners in the North End were always showing off their smart traps and spiders, their tandems and landaus. The sight of an elegant Park Four roused her to vociferous envy. She watched the wheelers swinging into line behind the two leaders, ebony black, with a crimson plume above each ear. "Gorgeous! And Daddy won't even get us a victoria!"

Rogier didn't give a damn for fancy rigs and tandems and the new Westcott speed wagons tearing along the Sunday streets. Nor could he subscribe to Mrs. Rogier's views. She was a singular woman. Outspoken, courageous to stubbornness, she stood out alone largely because of her false pride. She was dominated by a queer sense of superiority, an unshaken assurance that all the Rogiers had been born to the purple. None of the family could account for it and had long given up trying. But to quiet her, Rogier bought her a coach and horse called Colonel. The horse was slightly locoed but an excellent traveler. Sally Lee was delighted. It was going to be so much fun to care for four horses!

"You won't have any if Pet comes in with a tender mouth again! Were you afraid of her, the way you had to bit her all afternoon?" asked Rogier.

The purchase of a coach to take the family to church gave Rogier a free conscience and free Sunday mornings to take Pet out alone. He had not yet joined the Gentlemen's Pleasure and Driving Association which seemed too sociable for his simple tastes. But as it had leased the Pikes Peak Driving Park for trials of speed, Rogier thought he might see what Pet could do.

Early in the morning he would drive up the hill and turn north on Cascade. It was a wide street graveled smooth as a track. To the railroad north of town Rogier knew it like a line on his palm. When Pet warmed up, he shook her into pace and took out his watch. Then, a mile from the crossing, he let her out. It was a lively stretch. The full blown trees swept by him as on a moving belt. He sat upright, feet braced, head tilted slightly forward and to the left so that his cigar ashes swept past over his shoulder. The wind drove at his face, was parted by his narrowed gray eyes, and eddied about the wrinkles at their ends. Pet ran easily, smooth to the road. The muscles along her back eased and tightened like rubber bands under velvet. He listened to her stride, leaned down to catch a glimpse of her forefeet, and sat back to steal a look at his watch.

At the end of a mile he drew her up slowly. "Why, old girl, you don't mean to tell me you can't do better than 2:40 in this old buggy! We did that well last week!"

Yes, Pet was doing him a lot of good — and he needed a lot of encouragement with all that was going on.

Bob had come to his office one morning for a talk. He wanted to get married and needed Rogier to help him build a house. He was twenty-two, quite love-silly, but had a promising job in a store and was saving every dollar. Rogier helped him draw up his simple plans, and gave him a man and a team to help. Running short of lumber, Bob occasionally stopped at an empty hut on the outskirts of town and pried loose a plank to carry home. In a short time he had completely dismantled the old hut.

A few mornings later the sheriff entered Rogier's office and laid on the table a warrant for Bob's arrest. The boy had stolen the town's pest house. Rogier sent out a crew immediately to build a new pest house, and then finished Bob's house for his bride. It was a joke he never got over. Nor did Mrs. Rogier. The disgrace, the neighbors' laughing comments, and Bob's humiliation upset her for weeks.

And Lily Force! One night at dinner while Lida cleared the table for berries and cream, she looked up with a slight flush tinging her olive cheeks a rich orange. "I must tell you," she laughed with embarrassment. "I'm going to be married! At least I might!" And then, pell-mell, she gushed out the story of the want ad in the "Personal" column of the *Weekly Gazette*, the subsequent letters from the gentleman in Washington, D.C. who wanted to correspond with a light-haired lady of refinement, and the reason for bleaching her hair. Yes! He was coming out to Colorado. Immediately. A Judge Henry, some sort of government man.

Mrs. Rogier gasped. Ona and the children were thrilled. Rogier grinned. "You don't have to take him, Lily, unless you want to. Remember that."

After a half-hour of talking Lily felt better; she had got it out of her system. Mrs. Rogier had taken it better than Lily had expected. She only murmured vaguely, "I do hope, Lily, you and the judge won't repeat this to anyone. It's so — so unusual, you know."

Rogier was more upset than he could betray. Tom, Sister Molly, Bob, Hiney, Ona, failing Mrs. White, and now Lily — what was taking them, one by one, out of their ordered pattern of existence?" Let's have a little music tonight, Lily," he requested as usual. "You might start with a few old Southern tunes if you've a mind to."

Boné flashed Lily a sharp look and strode upstairs. New horses, new husbands — what were they to him? But with Lily gone, he might have more time to play on the piano.

3

Rogier sat on his long-legged stool, head bent over the drafting board. He was copying a page of Roman letters taken from the inscription on the monument to Leonardo Bruni in the church of Santa Croce in Florence. The letters were unusually light-faced, the width of stroke no more than one-tenth the height. Designed by Bernardo Rossellino, they were indeed considered his masterpiece.

Rogier worked hard. His right sleeve was rolled back to allow the free movement of his broad firm hand and muscular forearm across the board. From time to time he stopped to ponder upon the page before him. The force and simplicity, the endurable quality and sense of movement, the beauty of the lettering kept augmenting his admiration. Designed for the utmost ease of expression, of utility, not ornamentation. That was the key to their strength, their beauty. Simple rigid lines on stone.

He had a quick eye for lines, Rogier. The line of a building, the fractures in a stone, the lines of a horse. Yet his eye for line values was really an extraordinary sense of rhythm; a quality that so few men possess, and which an athlete, an artist must have. For some reason he was reminded of a queer incident that had recently happened. One evening at dusk he had gone to the mesa where the Utes were still allowed to encamp several months a year to dance, sing, and drop votive offerings in their sacred medicinal springs at the foot of the Peak. It was an old scene to Rogier. The circle of skin lodges. The orange-red flare of fires. Big-bellied squaws passing with loads of firewood. Bucks sitting around smoking. And a few white onlookers from town, bored to distraction, yet waiting to see the dance. It was for this Rogier himself came: to watch the lines of their naked bodies, the rhythmic steps, the ecstatic faces.

Suddenly he became aware of the beat of a drum. Like the heart of the earth suddenly beating with life. Not with the will to dominate, but softly, unvarying in tone, and insistent. A strange, magnetic rhythm that seemed to pull all within its own field.

Abruptly the big drum beat out stronger. In the same measure without increasing time. But stronger, more insistent and resistless, as if echoing the beat in his breast. One by one the Indians around the fires rose and threw off their blankets, walking within the circle of fires. They didn't walk chest out, belly in, as white men whose living center is in the head and chest. But in a slow shuffle, shoulders relaxed, belly out a little, as men whose center of gravity lies below. The dance step began. Eyes lowered, bodies doubled, they deliberately adjusted the ball of the foot to the ground. Pushing firmly to establish contact so that the earth-power might flow smoothly up their thighs. Then swiftly unbending, flinging up their heads. Lifting their dark faces, the sharp chiseled faces, eyes fixed upward in a blank stare, that the power might spark to the stars above and so complete the circuit to its unending source.

Rogier stirred uneasily. Something in him knew what he did not know. The secret that recoiled from his mind's grasp, that made of him an exile. The primordial power of the earth that must always be propitiated; never conquered, lest the victor be defeated by losing the integrity of his own being. To ally oneself with one's own mother-earth, to be at oneness with its great invisible forces, themselves obeying still greater laws, that one might feel within him the surge of its hidden strength. To seek always this truth of his own nature, acknowledging it above all temporal else. This was the only self-fulfillment, the only true success.

An Indian circling in the ring shouted suddenly. The cry was taken up in turn by those behind him. Then other smaller drums began, quick and reverberant, like the beat of rain. But the big hoarse drum, the belly drum, went on..

Then without warning it stopped. The sudden absence of sound created in Rogier a vacuum, the queer sensation of having descended too swiftly from a great height. His ears seemed to have stopped up; his blood beat at his temples and wrists. He stood foolishly irresolute, feeling lost in the darkness.

At that moment there sounded behind him a quick rustle of leaves in a dry ravine. Rogier stepped back. Believing he saw the form of a man, he spoke sharply, "Stand still!"

It was a boy crawling up out of the wash, Boné. His pale oval face was greenish-white in the moonlight, his lips were trembling. A faint electrical aura of nervous tension enveloped him. Rogier understood why. The beat of the drums, never changing, had worked powerfully upon his plastic childish will. The mesmeric quality of toneless rhythm invoked by the beat of an Indian drum! An ageless sound buried deep within the unconscious, re-emerging dark and mysterious like a dream-flow of things unrecognizable but still of that in us which reaffirms the everlasting mystery of our creation. Boné felt it. He knew! A boy like a violin string responding to the slightest touch. So Rogier had taken him home, his lips speaking comfortingly of common things.

Now, working at his drafting board on a clear spring morning, he methodically sharpened his soft drawing pencils. Placing the knife blade on the pencil and pushing it outward with his broad thumb. Then cupping the shavings and flinging them in a wastebasket. He had the air of seeming very busy. Yet at the moment he had little work on hand. He had just finished a new downtown building to house the *Gazette*. A brick four-story faced with red sandstone, widely pictured and advertised. Not much to look at really, but well constructed and clean-lined, built to last.

Glancing out the open window he noticed a crowd gathering on the corner. Two or three rigs went by at a rush. A queer excitement pervaded the air. Then steps rapidly crunched down the hall. A fist beat upon his door and a voice shouted, "Mr. Rogier! Come on down! They've found it behind the Peak. It's a strike!"

It was Maloney, the old prospector. Rogier accompanied him

downstairs and across the street to the newspaper office where the crowd was collecting. The news was compressed in a brief statement that a rich strike of gold had been made on the southwest slope of Pike's Peak in the Mount Pisgah district.

"That's the area I been workin', Joe!" cried Maloney. " 'Member those spruce! Now they've hit it sure! Gold!"

Once again a queer excitement, a strange foreboding, pervaded Rogier. He could not still it — not with Maloney dinning exhortations in his ears. Nor could he go back to his office to sit and wonder about it all day. "Well, if you're itching to go up there, I'll take you," he grumbled. "Might's well see what all the excitement's about, anyway."

Within an hour they had hitched up Lady-Lou, packed the buggy with blankets and supplies, and driven off. Despite his subterranean tremor of excitement it seemed preposterous to Rogier that gold could have been discovered on Pike's Peak. Why, the Pisgah district was only eighteen miles as the crow flies from the luxurious Antlers Hotel in the Saratoga of the West! But it lay directly behind Pike's Peak and a mile straight up. To reach it one had to spiral around three sides of the Peak, taking the Ute Pass road around it to the north and west as far as the divide, and then turning south. The Pass was crowded with buggies, buckboards, wagons, and groups of straggling men.

"Who made the strike?" Maloney cried to a bunch as they passed.

"Chicken Bill, I hear!" a man shouted back. "He's takin' nuggets out of the ground by the fistful!"

Impossible! thought Rogier, slowing his mares down on the steep grade. Since the Pike's Peak Rush of '58 thousands of men had prospected all around the peak. Not until 1874 had a trace of it been found, when a man named Theodore H. Lowe picked up some float along a crooked stream on the south slope. It was not rich enough to justify digging, and the place had been ignored until a Kentuckian, William H. Womack, had homesteaded a ranch along the stream. The high mountain meadow had good grass for cattle, but the steep-banked stream lamed so many of the animals that it was commonly known as Cripple Creek. A likely cow-pasture in which to find gold!

Reaching the divide, Rogier stopped to rest his mares. They were close to 10,000 feet high, he reckoned, and the whole area spread out in an immense panorama. It was all here, seen from above timberline — all the nobility of the wild and naked earth. A rugged, grassy meadow seamed with gulches and studded with bare, frost-shattered hills rising to an altitude of about 11,000 feet above sea-level. And surging in wave after wave, dark forested ranges rising toward the horizons on the north, west, and south to look down upon the Platte, Leadville, and the tips of the Sangre de Cristos. Only to the east did the mighty Peak itself rise like a wall to break the view. The hour was late and in the flare of the sinking sun its snowcap yellowed to the color of gold.

"Let's get goin'!" urged Maloney.

The road from now on was rough and rutty, the patches of corduroy giving way to bogs of mud. More and more men were strung along it, all heading toward a nipple looming out of the dusk toward the southwest. "Mount Pisgah!" said Maloney. Again he leaned out to shout. "What d'ya hear of Chicken Bill's strike?"

"Never heard of him!" a voice answered. "It's a fella called Butters that sunk a hole into the vein!"

It was dark and cold when they reached the base of Mount Pisgah. The enormous encampment was filled with two thousand men or more tending fires or huddled in tents and blankets. A lot of them were lined up at the back of a wagon where its enterprising owner was selling whisky out of two barrels. Rogier and Maloney pitched camp on the edge of the encampment, Rogier graining his team while Maloney cooked a bite to eat.

"You brought a gun?" asked Maloney.

"I never carry a gun!" replied Rogier.

"Well, I brought one. I figure with all that whisky goin' around, we'd better take turns keepin' watch."

"I'll stay up till midnight," said Rogier. "I wouldn't want anything to happen to my two mares. Then you can wake me if you hear anything."

Neither one of them could sleep. All night the sound of shouting, of still more men arriving, broke the silence of the hills. At daybreak they rushed with everyone over the goldfield, hunting for the site of the new strike. There was nothing: no outcroppings, no workings. There was only one hole about ten feet deep that obviously had been dug months or years before. It was barren of any sign of pay dirt.

"This is where Bútters said he took out those nuggets," a man insisted.

"He salted the damn hole, you fool! Look at it!"

A roar of indignation went up, followed by a roar of anger.

"Where's Butters?"

"Let's hang the son-of-a-bitch!"

But the perpetrator of the hoax could not be found. The Mount Pisgah fiasco was over. "Let's get out of here before the road's jammed," growled Rogier. "I'll hitch up while you stow the dunnage."

The two men drove steadily homeward. "Another Pike's Peak Bust," commented Rogier tersely. Whether he felt relieved or disappointed, he could not tell. But somehow he felt betrayed, either by himself or by that massive Peak rearing above him. It was seldom he saw it from this side and he studied it carefully. From down on the plains its face often seemed feminine and benignant. Here it showed its opposite side, a face masculine, sharp-featured, and cruel. With a start he realized the truth of its dual aspect. This androgynous great mother of mountains who forever watched down upon him with compassion, with menace, or with a strange and neuter aspect of passionless calm. And there swept over him the peculiar oppressive feeling that within the immutable depths of that majestic and enigmatic earth-being still remained hidden the ultimate destiny that was his to seek alone.

4

There was no doubt Rogier's house was haunted. Long before
it had been built, Mrs. Rogier had taken just one look at the two
Kadles who always camped on the spot, and made her prophecy.
"Why, the ghosts of those two old men will be stompin' through the
house in their smelly boots as long as it stands!"

And so they had — the Kadles. Late at night, lying asleep, you
would be awakened by the creaking steps of those two old men
prowling through the house. It was not at all scary to the girls. The
sound came too regularly, night after night, until the Kadles' ghosts
came to be as integral a part of the household as the horses Pet,
Colonel, and Lady-Lou. But it kept them awake. Boné particularly
could not go back to sleep until the Kadles had finished their
nocturnal round of inspection.

Mrs. Rogier raised Cain without avail. The Kadles kept right on
creeping up the third floor stairs. Rogier talked himself into a state of
silent disgust trying to explain that the creaking was caused by a
contraction of the old pine steps. To prove it he removed all the nails
in the steps and replaced them with heavy screws. Two nights later
she awakened him to see if Mrs. White or Lida Peck were walking in

their sleep.

"A nice quiet house! Even the door jambs squeak!" she complained. "Boné told Mary Ann it was one of the Kadles leaning against the wall to hitch up his boots!"

The problem raised the old question of when she was to have her house in the North End. "This is a comfortable place," remonstrated Rogier. "Where would we find stalls and pasture for the horses? But I'll keep it in mind, Marthy. I promise."

To appease her, he did a refinishing job on the house. New furniture and rugs, and carpeting for both the second and third floor stairs. The noise of all the hammering had no more died away than that night up the carpeted stairway squeaked the Kadles investigating all the changes.

It was a very disheartening sound.

But at least the house had been refinished in time for Lily Force's wedding to Judge Henry. Mrs. Rogier so wanted him to think well of them. For at last he had come out to Colorado — a real judge attached to the Mexican minister's staff in Washington, D.C., and immediately becoming sincerely fond of Lily, even to the strip of white running through her hair which she had contritely confessed to bleaching.

This astounding romance — from the want ad in the *Gazette* to Judge Henry's own figure on the piano bench beside Lily — proved conclusively to the girls there might even be a Santa Claus. Mrs. Rogier herself was stunned with amazement, but she was soon won to the urbane and likable presence of Judge Henry. He was a genteel man with Spanish blood, a French childhood, and an American future. Although he was at least fifteen years older than Lily, they made a striking pair: the Judge grave and distinguished looking with black hair and dark complexion, and Lily with her olive-tinged cheeks and vivacious manner.

They left for Washington immediately after the wedding. Lily's departure put an end to Ona's music lessons, as Sister Molly's death had ended her schooldays. Although she had learned to play, her music lessons really had been a nuisance. Save for occasional Sunday mornings when she "officiated" at the church organ, Ona never touched a piano. Nor did Sally Lee; her one interest was hanging around the stalls of Pet, Colonel, and Lady-Lou. Mary Ann did better, occasionally pecking away at the piano in the front room though anyone could see it was more for amusement than from actual interest.

To Mrs. Rogier this was discouraging. Three daughters fated to become fashionable ladies — being Rogier — and not one of them interested in music! It was worse; it was out-and-out backsliding. But Boné, also freed of Lily Force, made hay while his sun was high. He simply couldn't stay away from the piano. He was at the keys every moment that Mrs. Rogier wasn't looking, and plaguing Ona with questions. It was amazing to her the way he soaked up her odd minutes of teaching so completely.

"Go on, Ona! Go on!" he would snap at her. "You said it. Now tell me why!"

There was no denying him. Sooner or later the truth or something they could not distinguish from it, would come out after a wearisome bout between them. It was easier and much more pleasant when Ona related to him the story, the idea, or picture behind the compositions. These had been the human things that had aroused her own imagination, and she remembered many of them vividly from Lily's wordy descriptions; like that of the symphonic poem the boy loved so well.

Boné sat still as death, as though he did not hear her. The vision leaped and remained before his eyes with such vividness he could not speak. A great black flood, viscous and dark, separating man and Hades. And in between, a white and spotless swan unmoving, singing its strange wild song.

Abruptly he rose and slouched out of the room. He walked out in back, through the gate to the stables, and climbed upon the haystack in the barn. Here he lay on his back, staring at the rafters spotted with sunlight overhead, seeing nothing, hearing nothing, but the song of the legendary swan of Tuonela. It revealed to him for the first time the meaning of music. How simple it was! He had heard through its accents the voice of many things speaking with authority to his deepest self. And now he saw in a flash what it meant not only to receive music, but to give it. One saw something: a ship on the sea, people dancing across a castle floor, or the beauty of the night — such a thing as that! — and gave it back in music for all to see and feel. A great accomplishment.

But to feel with profound disturbance something nonexistent yet real as the content of a dream which comes and comes again, indescribable, unspeakable, and impalpable. Like the invocation of an odd strain of melody which ran through him each time he saw the Peak risen above its morning mist like an island floating on a cloud. Like the vision in his mind of Der Schwan von Tuonela. And to give these things in music too, rendering into tangible form the phantoms and the beauties that plagued his secret soul. This was the greatest achievement.

He lay still in the hay, obsessed with his latent power to accomplish the impossible. Just by learning how to weave together those same old notes so long and carelessly misused into the ceaseless fabrics spinning through his mind. This was all he had to know!

School lessons were something else. The evening study hour was an ordeal for the whole family. Lida Peck would clear the dining room table and Sally Lee, Mary Ann, and Boné would gather around the lamp with their books. Mrs. Rogier would sit reading. Then Rogier, lighting a cigar, would offer to help the children with their arithmetic and algebra lessons.

"Now Daddy," Mrs. Rogier reminded him, "please remember to do their problems the way the teacher wants them solved. Not your way."

"Never mind," replied Rogier calmly. "The teacher is only trying to show them how to work problems. I'm trying to teach them to use their heads."

Rogier, feeling keenly his lack of education and at the same time despising the insistence of the teachers at solving all the problems in an orthodox manner, laid out his carpenter's steel square. On this he made his computations in a manner he had worked out alone in lieu of schooling; and though to others as intricate and confusing as a Chinese tangram, it enabled him to figure faster than any rival. But he could never explain its use. Meanwhile the smoke from his cigar rose into a blue cloud, causing the girls to cough and splutter, and their eyes to smart and burn. The evening usually ended in a row. Tired out, the girls went to bed without their lessons. Mrs. Rogier had to write them an excuse pleading "home duties." And more than often Sally Lee brought home her algebra teacher's request that she learn as she was taught and not to attempt improvements on the text-book.

"How about you, Boné? Don't you have any homework to

do?" Rogier would ask him.

"No sir; not tonight!" the boy would answer cheerfully, strolling off the the piano in the front room.

"Boné!"

Obediently he got up from the bench to wander through the house, hands in pockets, urbane, the master of his soul, and then slip upstairs to listen to the night.

When at the end of the school term he brought home a report of failing in his class, and a sealed letter from the professor, Mrs. Rogier was indignant. "Why, I had no idea! Even the letter says how smart he is. 'Exceptionally alert and receptive, but mentally lazy' — see?"

"I wouldn't worry none about that boy," drawled Mrs. White. "He appeahs to me like one of them high-strung horses you can lead to watah but you can't make him drink."

Rogier took the letter back uptown to read. Then he sent a doctor to see the boy, listened to the result of the examination, and promptly forgot the matter. It did not occur to him that he knew the capabilities and imperfections of his workmen and his horses, but not the members of his family.

But that summer Boné surprised them all. It was during the annual Sunflower Carnival when all the covered wagons, traps, and tandems, with Indians, cowboys, and miners trooping behind, paraded through the streets decorated with wildflowers. Boné had written a piece of music for the occasion. A music teacher, a former friend of Lily Force, had helped him with the orchestration and had made arrangements to have it printed. Boné came home thrilled with an armful of sheets. The Cowboy Riders Band of Colorado City was going to play his "Red Rock Garden March" at their night concert!

He was up early next morning to canvas every merchant with his music sheets. He even came to Rogier's office, insisting that he buy a copy, regular price. And during the parade Rogier could see him keeping it apace, selling copies to people bunched along the gutters. That night in Manitou at the pavilion by the iron spring the Cowboy Riders Band played the "Red Rock Garden March." The director, in high boots and higher Stetson, simply shouted out the title and Boné's name, and the band began playing. The piece was very short, but it was a great achievement of which even Mrs.

Rogier was duly proud.

A month later she handed Rogier a letter from the music company. Rogier opened it, glanced carelessly at the sheet inside, and stuffed it into his pocket.

"What is it? About Boné? Do they want him to write another march?" she queried.

"No. Nothing like that. Nothing at all," Rogier answered her carelessly and turned away. The letter enclosed a bill for ninety-three dollars for setting up in print the "Red Rock Garden March," credited with six dollars and forty cents which Boné had realized from his sales.

Ten days after school opened in the fall things came to a head. Mrs. Rogier happened to meet Boné's teacher on the street and she asked when he was going to start school. Mrs. Rogier was dumbfounded. Boné had left the house every morning with Sally Lee and Mary Ann. It was that music teacher friend of Lily's who had lured the boy away! Mrs. Rogier swept up the street holding her skirts high to make the utmost speed. Boné was there at the woman's home. Without a word she took the boy by the hand and marched him down to Rogier's office.

It was a hectic session. Boné denied nothing except that he had lied about going to school. Thin, taut, and white, he sat straight in his chair. "I won't go to school. I can't stand it any more. I hate it." It was all he had to say.

Mrs. Rogier wept.

Rogier sat silent, twiddling with a celluloid triangle while he watched Boné. The lad was stubborn as a mule; he meant what he said. But what was behind it? Indubitably there was something. He stared fixedly at Boné, as though he'd never seen him before. How thin and white he was, and nervously taut as a violin string! His own heavy silence kept pressing down upon woman and boy until Mrs. Rogier, fearful of his rare bursts of temper, cried out, "Daddy!"

Rogier stood up. "I'll think it over. You're both upset. Suppose you go home and we'll talk about it tonight."

After they had gone he sat for an hour, then went out. Boné was in bed when he arrived home. Mrs. Rogier, Mrs. White, and Ona were waiting at the dining room table. "I went to see the doctor again," he spoke without prelude. "The boy's too thin and nervous and highstrung. The doctor believes a year out of school and spent outdoors would help him."

"But what would he do around here, Daddy? It would be just as bad as school."

"Exactly. I though of that when I met the Vrain Girls on the street and walked home with them."

The Vrain Girls had been friends of the family for years. They were old maid sisters who had a house in the south part of town where they lived probably two months of the year. The rest of the time they lived in New Mexico among the Navajos, Lew serving as a government agent and Matie as a missionary. They were small, tanned dark, with graying hair, and their features seemed to be taking on the sharp chiseled aspect of the Indians with whom they already had spent so many unselfish years.

"But what about Boné?" insisted Mrs. Rogier.

"Just this," he said patiently. "The Vrain Girls are getting ready to go back to the Reservation. It was their own suggestion that they take Boné along."

"Livin' with Indians?" inquired Mrs.Rogier incredulously.

"Living with the Girls in a comfortable trading post, getting lots of good food, fresh air, and sunshine."

Next morning Rogier was sitting at the table when Boné came down for breakfast. He looked tired and nervous as he slid into his chair, and kept a wary eye on Rogier as he munched on a piece of toast.

"You look rather peaked, son. Did the Kadles keep you up all night?"

"I slept fine." The boy spoke obstinately, laying down his toast and withdrawing his hands into his lap.

"Well, eat a good breakfast. I'm going to drive Pet out to Templeton's Gap, and thought you might want to go along."

"Yes sir!" Boné relaxed instantly and ate a second piece of toast.

Ona, walking home that afternoon, saw them coming back. Rogier was looking straight ahead. Boné sat still, his eyes fixed on Rogier who turned to him and grinned as he pulled out a cigar. Boné laughed; and Ona knew that the matter was settled. Then Rogier shook up Pet and the buckboard dwindled away from her sight.

5

Time, the ageless and the sexless, the eunuch of all eunuchs. Time, the great builder, the great destroyer, life's great equation sign. The powerful and fickle ambassador of human fate. Time with its vigor and senility, its wisdom and capriciousness, and the infallibility to level with its own mistakes the greatest fruits of its handiwork. Linear flowing time, man's greatest and most persistent illusion in a world whose full-dimensional reality he cannot yet perceive.

Time, dom it! What had it been doing to them all these years? Rogier felt perplexed. Sister Molly had died, Tom had vanished. Boné and Lily Force had gone. Bob Hines was married and moved out of the house. Now Hiney was getting restless too. He arrived home later every night. Mrs. White and Rogier, sharing the secret of his affliction, lay listening for the sound of his cab. What if during another lapse of memory he might — what? The question kept growing in their minds, but Hiney was at the topside of his hour. He was forever regaling the girls with talk of the celebrities he had seen at the Opera House — Lillian Russell, Katherine Kidder, Frederic Ward, Nat Goodwin. One week he imitated Harry Webber from

"Nip and Tuck;" the next, Charlotte Thompson in "Phyllis Den-hor." Barlow and Wilson's Mammoth Minstrels, the cast of George C. Miller's "Fool's Revenge"—his mimicry, like his colored cra-vats, seemed to stop at nothing. No one was surprised when he was asked to substitute as a stagehand for the run of Stanley Wood's opera "Brittle Silver" at the Tabor Grand Opera House in Denver. Think of that! The girls, seeing him off on the train with a new carpet bag and a new cravat flowery with red roses, thought of nothing else.

Held over for "Priscilla," Hiney came home with portentous news. He had not only worked behind the scenes in the Tabor Grand, Denver's million dollar opera house, the most beautiful in the country—in the whole wide world; now he had been offered a steady job, beginning   next month, with a chance to work into the "profession." Tabor's great gesture, designed from the best theaters of London and Vienna, its carpets brought from Belgium, its brocades from France, its woodwork of cherry logs from Japan and mahogany from Honduras. And all of it derived from Colorado silver, Leadville silver, the outpouring silver stream flooding the world.

The "profession" was not quite up the highest social standards, but Mrs. Rogier was impressed. Everyone was delighted save Rogier who was troubled with anxious thoughts. Like his father Tom, Hiney was entranced with bright lights and make-believe, the glitter and tinsel of fame and fortune, with the moonlit gleam of silver. There was no stopping him.

"Hiney," he said, drawing him aside at the railroad depot on the morning he left, "I reckon I haven't paid as much mind to you as I ought to have, all these years. Putting up buildings — I don't know what else or why, son. It's not because I haven't thought of your mother every day since she's been gone, and your father too. I miss them, boy, and I'll miss you too. But remember" — his voice grew stern — "this is still your home! Never forget that, hear? If anything ever happens, come home. Anything! Understand?"

Hiney brushed the cowlick back under his new hat. "Yes sir. I know what you mean. But I only been troubled twice. I guess I just ate the wrong thing both times. I'll remember."

Time! If only time would deal gently with Sister Molly's youngest son!

Meanwhile Rogier let himself be swung in its illusionary flow.

There appeared in the Gazette a news item that pleased Mrs. Rogier immensely:

> Work on the new Lincoln and Garfield school houses in the fourth and second wards respectively, is being actively prosecuted. The rafters are in position on the Lincoln school and already it presents quite an imposing appearance when seen from the foothills west of town.
>
> Work on the Garfield school has been delayed somewhat on account of the limited supply of brick in the market, but the contractor and builder, Mr. Joseph Rogier, expects to have both buildings completed within the time specified in the contract.

In addition to these two schools, Rogier was getting ready to break ground for the construction of the new First Congregational Church. A rambling building of gray stone with a semi-circle of seven pillars upholding a triangular gable with an inset round window of stained glass. Its cost exceeded $35,000. If that triangular gable didn't look too squatty, too mashed-down on its curve of stone columns, it would be well worth the money — for a church.

Every night too he was working up an estimate on a new state institution, the Colorado School for the Deaf and Blind, a huge stone structure that for all his figuring he could not cut down to a less than $80,000 job.

His work did not interfere with his interest in his horses. Pet had produced her first colt, Dorothy, and could not be used. Instead he drove Colonel. Not a bad horse, but still a little loco and lazy. This combination of cussedness Rogiér took out of him on Sunday mornings. Meanwhile he kept hearing about a Maryland horse reputed to be very fast.

The excitement caused by the Mount Pisgah fiasco had died down. William H. Womack had sold his homestead on Cripple Creek; Bennett and Myers, two Denver real estate men, had picked it up for a trifling $7,500 and were running cattle on it. They employed Womack's nephew Bob as a cowboy. He was so careless and erratic, spending most of his time digging for gold, they called him "Crazy Bob." Nevertheless Bennett took a few samples of ore from one of his gopher holes to a pioneer Denver assayer. "There's no use wasting your money for an assay of this stuff, Mr. Bennett," reported the assayer after one look at the float. "There's no gold in it." Womack was not discouraged. He sunk a shaft in Poverty Gulch which he kept working, naming his claim the Chance. Periodically he rode into town, showing samples of ore in the Colorado City saloons. No one was interested. So year after year he relocated his claim without bothering to record it.

Again that winter Stratton came down from the mountains to work a few months for another stake — but not for prospecting this time. He was going to enroll in Professor Lamb's course in mineralogy at The Colorado College, held in Cutler Hall which Rogier had built.

"I've spent too many years chasing Lady Luck," he said straightforwardly. "I don't know anything about ores except hefting a sample in my hand and squinting at it in the sunlight. I'm going to find out!"

For a moment Rogier was surprised at his change in attitude. Stratton looked old and worn; there was the same haunted look in his eyes. Yet something about him, perhaps the leaner cut of his jaw, revealed that his frantic compulsion had set into a frigid determination fed by every cell in his mind and body.

"To start with," continued Stratton, "I got a job in the Nashold Mill up at Breckenridge. What I learned there about the amalgamation process of treating ores taught me how ignorant I am. So here I am. I tell you, Joe, when I finally hit it I'm going to know it — and what to do about it!"

Rogier nodded, remembering Siegerfries.

Like everyone else, the two men talked about the growing political issue of the time — silver. The Bland-Allison Act, authorizing the purchase of up to $4,000,000 worth of silver for coinage into dollars, had been insufficient. The production of silver was so great that the price kept declining. Throughout all the country demands by silver exponents increased. A Colorado Silver Alliance was formed, followed by a National Silver Convention in St. Louis. The result was the passage of the Sherman Act which provided for the purchase of 4,500,000 ounces of silver per month by the government. The price of silver had jumped to over a dollar an ounce, wildly acclaimed by almost two hundred silver clubs in

Colorado. But now the price was falling again.

"Figure it out for yourself," asserted Rogier. "There seems to be no end to the silver in these mountains. It's flooding the whole country. These Sherman purchases are just priming the economic pump. They can't go on — not as long as this country, and the rest of the world, is on the gold standard. Something's bound to happen."

"What?" demanded Stratton.

"I'm not a soothsayer, or a politician either," Rogier said bluntly.

Stratton looked at him a long time with a strange glint in his smoke-gray eyes. "I'm not pinning my hopes on silver any more. I'm going to find out about gold and every other ore the earth holds. That's why I'm going to Professor Lamb."

"Yes, gold," said Rogier quietly. "The sun of life in the earth."

They looked at each other without speaking, each thinking how strange it was that chance had not put him in the other's shoes. Then Stratton abruptly as usual rose and walked out.

If Stratton had been a little discomfited but not wholly surprised at Rogier's strange last remark, Rogier thought nothing about it. It reflected the texture of his thoughts as he spent night after night meditating on his books. They were strange books of which Mrs. Rogier and indeed few people in town would have approved, shipped directly to his office where he could study them without fear of detection and disturbance. Solid philosophy, Masonic ritual, medieval alchemy, the esoteric religions of the East, and treatises on what was becoming known as New Thought. What he first had hoped to find in them, as an uneducated man, was a simple explanation of the mystery that made him feel an exile on his earth. Whatever the mystery was, it was not simple. His loneliness had increased despite his prosperous business, his large family, and his horses. And so had his secret mounting need to find out who he was, and his relationship to this new wild earth to which he had been so unaccountably and irresistibly drawn by that high Peak which, year by year, focused all his hopes and his despair.

He found his own feelings duplicated by the reverence accorded other sacred mountains in the world — Popocatepetl in Mexico, Cotopaxi and Capac Urcu in the Andes of South America, Kilimanjaro of Africa, Fujiyama in Japan, Olympus in Greece, colossal upthrusts of the Himalayas in Asia. From time immemorial the root races of every continent, the black, the brown, the yellow, the red, and the white, had made pilgrimages to these great sacred mountains, as had the Indians to Pike's Peak, with votive offerings, prayer, song, and dance. Rogier had come to believe it was a matter of rhythm. For the inherent spirit-of-place of each continent, each land, vibrated to a different, indigenous rhythm. And only by attuning himself to this vibratory quality of his motherland could man release the dammed up power of creation within him. He had felt this years ago when he first heard the beat of Indian drums and the stamp of moccasined feet upon the earth. In the mountains you felt it best. They were like the swells of the sea, rising in wave after wave to crest in great peaks upthrust against the horizon — not immobile, as they might appear, but subtly vibrating as great repositories of power whose emanantions formed a magnetic field that could be felt for miles. This, Rogier was convinced, was what had drawn him here to this majestic Peak as it had drawn for centuries so many Indian tribes from the Great Plains and lesser forested ranges. It was alive as the whole earth was alive, each living stone, every breathing plant. And through the years he had come to recognize it as a homogenous entity, this androgenous mother of mountains which embraced the dual aspects of all creation. Yes, it was a living body like his own, the rock strata of its skeleton fleshed with earth, its veins watered by spring and stream, and in whose deep and hidden heart glowed the golden sun of life.

These reflections, which Rogier did not consider at all religious in nature as he was not a religious man, bore little resemblance to the tenets of the Shouting Methodists who perfervidly proclaimed the reality of harp-playing angels in Heaven and pitchfork-wielding devils in Hell. They did not coincide with the economic views of Free Silver advocates or the thousands of greedy white miners raping an inanimate earth of its natural resources. Nor, for that matter, would they have been acceptable to Little London businessmen and members of the Gentlemen's Driving and Pleasure Association. So Rogier kept them to himself. And if sometimes they seemed a little extravagant and frightening even to himself, he was again drawn back to them by his ever-growing need. And late at night, poring over his books, he would encounter a phrase, a thought, that swung open still another door to his intuition. There was something strange in him that knew what he did not know. It was as if it had known all this long before.

6

To Ona the days had become like beads on a string, separate yet indistinguishable, unending in their weary circle. No young man came to call on her; she was fast approaching the time when she would be regarded as an old maid. Without an interest, she seldom went out except for a walk uptown or a drive on Sunday afternoon. Once again she took up the lonely vigils of Sister Molly. On summer afternoons sitting alone under the elm or under the front window in the shade of the lilac; and in the winter rocking in the dark front room. Less than all the members of the family for being wholly theirs, she was a personality formed by the experience of their lives, out of the substance provided her by her own inheritance. Brooding alone through the months, she gradually assumed the placid, hard aspect of an idol cut in stone. Not with the unbroken repose of tranquility, but with the stillness of despair.

It became obvious to all the family that something had to be done about her, but it remained for Mrs. White to suggest what.

"That theah girl is jus' decayin' away. She ain't done nothin' but raise kids since she was eight yeahs old. You wouldn't wuk a horse that hahd, Joe. She needs a new pasture fo' awhile."

Rogier and Mrs. Rogier did not reply. Mrs. White continued. "I don' see why Ona can't go down to the Reservation and bring back Boné. He didn't come home with the Vrain Girls last yeah and he ain't writin' none. Like killin' two buhds with one stone."

"We'll think about it," said Rogier.

"A heap of thinkin' you need, with all the money youah makin' and horses eatin' it up by the bale. Ona's nevah had nothin'. I reckon you bettah be doin' that heap of thinkin' mighty fast!"

Rogier did, and wondered why he hadn't done it before.

Two weeks later the family saw her off on the Denver and Rio Grande for Durango, where the Girls were to meet her. She had a shiny new suitcase packed with new taffeta dresses, and a fifty-dollar bill pinned to her corset for an emergency.

The train finally pulled out; and when the Peak and the Devil's Horn were gone from sight, she leaned her head back and closed her eyes. For the first time in her life she was away from the family; a new world swung toward her as though the click of the wheels on the rails were the grind of subterranean machinery moving strange landscapes into view. Ona took no notice of them at all. She was utterly worn out. After a time she opened the little surprise packages given her by Sally Lee and Mary Ann, and put the trinkets away. She dozed, ate sparingly of the fried chicken in her lunch basket, and dozed again. Pueblo, Canyon City, the rushing Arkansas, and the frightening Royal Gorge it had carved, and always more mountains. The "Dirty, Ragged, and Greasy" little narrow-gauge kept climbing over them, going around and between them, heaving and jolting like a boat in a sea of tumultuous waves. The coach was crowded. Miners and prospectors. A sporting woman in a lace-trimmed hat. A group of Ute squaws huddled on the floor of the filthy aisle, blankets drawn up over their heads. Two drunken cowboys quarreling in the seat behind her. At dark the sputtering, hanging lamps were lit. Then when the spring night grew cold, the brakeman lighted a wood fire in the stove up front. Ona could not sleep for the clickety-clack of the wheels beneath her, the shrill whistle from the quill. Smoke was pouring from the straight-stacker now, seeping in every crack of the window. The patter of cinders on the roof sounded like rain. How horrible it was, alone and lost in a heaving sea of mountains in this frail and smelly toy train that never seemed to get anywhere at all.

But it did, late in the evening after a two-hour delay caused by a rock slide. Matie was waiting at the little wooden depot with a slim young Mexican. "Lew's off on a trip and so's Boné — they'll be back when we get home," she explained. "So Tony Lucero here drove me up in his wagon."

Lucero showed his teeth in what Ona supposed was meant to be a smile, and they got into a light spring wagon. "We'd better eat and sleep, then get an early start in the morning," said Matie decisively. Ona was disappointed in the appearance of Durango. The town was not yet ten years old and looked it: wooden buildings and shacks clustered around the yellow-painted railroad depot that had called it into being. There was no need to get out her new taffeta dresses when they arrived at the hotel. It looked more tawdry than Mrs. White's former boarding house. For a girl who had come from the celebrated and fashionable Saratoga of the West, everything looked raw and new. She chewed at an enormous steak and then went to bed on a hard and narrow mattress.

How different it was in the morning when they drove southward and downward toward the high plains of New Mexico! The very quality of the sunlight changed, mellowed and yellowed as if by time. Matie talked about her work at Farmington with the Women's Home Missionary Society. "How wonderful they are, '*The* People,' as they call themselves! Proud and arrogant, but so eager to learn!"

"Who are they?" asked Ona.

"The Navajos. The *Dineh*, '*The* People.' They're the ones we work with mostly. But we have others. Utes from the north, and Jicarilla Apaches from the east. It's all Indian country, Ona."

"And they're not wild Indians?" asked Ona, remembering from childhood the Arapahoes and Cheyennes who had burned her bottom against the stove.

"Oh, there was a little trouble of sorts three or four years ago when Largo Pete — that means Big Pete — went on a rampage and troops from Fort Lewis were called out. But that's nothing to speak of."

Tony Lucero talked about the Stockton Gang of outlaws that hung around Bloomfield, twelve miles east of Farmington. "Port Stockton, Senorita, was the leader. He was killed, unfortunately, Senorita. But the Gang still prospers. It steals cattle from the white *rancheros* and sheep from the Navajos. That was their steak you ate last night, no? They run a butcher shop in Durango."

Indians, Mexicans, outlaws! Ona let herself be driven all day without protest down to a high, treeless plain where converged from the Colorado mountains three great rivers: the San Juan, La Plata, and Las Animas. Farmington. The main street was two blocks long. But a shady street, lined with fruit trees. It was filled with Utes, Apaches, and Navajos, Indian traders, cowboys, and cattle rustlers. A few miles away, along the San Juan that gleamed silver in the dusk, Lucero drew up beside a low and long trading post. Behind it stood an adobe in which Lew and Matie lived with the trader, Bert Bruce. Lucero unloaded their baggage and drove away.

"He works for Bert and lives with his wife down the road," explained Matie shortly, "He's a Mexican, but he speaks Navajo fluently and knows wool and hides." Without more ado she flung open the door of the adobe and pushed Ona inside.

There was Lew, small, sharp, and dark, giving her a hug; and the trader, Bruce, a taciturn man who didn't even rise when she was introduced, but whose swift appraising eyes stripped her bare, flung her on the scales, and calculated her intrinsic worth in one look. Yet it was the room itself that wrapped comfortingly about her. There was none of the stiff formality of the front room at home and other parlors in Little London. It was just a big mud hut, but it broke upon her with a burst of color mellowed by lamplight. Brilliant Navajo rugs covering the rude plank floor, beautiful weaving on the stiff chairs and wooden table, Indian rattles and silver bridles hanging on the walls, shelves of pottery. Ona felt at home immediately and after supper went to her small room to sleep dreamlessly at peace.

"Where's Boné?" she kept asking next morning. "Hasn't he come back yet?"

"Oh, he's off on another horseback trip. Maybe to Hon-Not-Klee, maybe to those old Aztec ruins. He likes to putter around, you know," answered Matie. "Why don't you walk down the trail to his room and see if he came in last night? It used to be Bert's rug room — where he stored his blankets, you know. But Boné fixed it up for his studio as he calls it."

Down the trail it stood, another adobe, stout-walled, with iron-barred windows. Ona hesitated, then lifted the latch and entered. With her first glance she recognized the room as Boné's all right. An old upright piano stood against the far wall. On the bench lay the scattered pages of a Kayser. Like the other house, it was full of Navajo rugs and weavings, pottery, and artifacts; and a handful of turquoise stones lay strewn over the top of a deal table, with a stack of loose music and a coffee cup full of cigarette stubs. But how untidy it was! A pair of denim trousers dangled from the back of a chair. Three socks were spread across a heap of firewood; and in the dry ashes of the fireplace lay a tumbled coffee pot. From a row of nails hung a dejected string of clothes. A colorful, untidy room whose inmate kept nothing he did not have a use for, and who kept it where his hand or eye could find it easiest.

With a sigh, Ona cleaned and straightened the room, made up the couch with fresh sheets. Then tired out, she lay down to rest. As she stared out the window a bluejay shot from a piñon like a burst of smoke. She closed her eyes as if anticipating the sound of a report. There was nothing but the deep yellow silence, and the sense of the infinite dryness of the barren plain stretching across the muddy San Juan.

She was awakened by the click of the latch. The door flung back and Boné stood in the doorway. "Ona! — Ona!" he cried joyously.

She jumped to her feet, conscious of his tall lean form and dark face, and was caught in his arms. Before she realized it, Boné had kissed her on the lips. She could have counted on her fingers the times she had been kissed by the undemonstrative Rogiers, and she too drew slightly away at this outward display of affection.

"Ona! Aren't you glad to see me!" shouted Boné, shaking her by the shoulders.

She stood with slightly misted eyes absorbing the sight of his rangy body, half a head taller than she. His cheap gray shirt was open at the throat, revealing a tan dark as the color of his face. An old pair of blue denim trousers clung tightly to his slim hips, and around his waist dangled a wide belt studded with silver conchos. There was about him a curious sense of freedom, a wildness almost.

"Why, Boné!" she murmured softly. "You've grown into a man."

He laughed as he sat down. "Now tell me quick: are the Kadles still creeping up steps every night?"

"Yes!"

"And is Uncle Joe all right?"

"Yes."

"Well then, you better start right down the list with Aunt Martha. I can't stand her a minute and I love her just the same, and if I live to be as old as Mrs. Black Kettle down the wash she'll still be able to make me jump!"

"Boné!"

"Oh, I know. Filial respect and all, but it doesn't mean we can't see them with our own eyes."

The same Boné of old, free from others' opinions, with the priceless faculty of never denying the truth of his own intuition.

"They're all fine, Bone, and want you home again. I have some presents for you from them. Now tell me what you've been doing."

"Working, Ona! Every minute! Look!" He strode to a packing crate behind the piano and began to lift out manuscript after manuscript, spreading them on the bench and table.

"Oh. Music scores!"

He sat down at the piano, rattled off a score, flung it aside. "A man nearby has been helping me with composition, orchestration, fingering, everything. Gene Lockhardt. A wonderful man. A great musician. He's coming over tonight to meet you."

Jumping up, he reached for an Indian rattle hanging on the wall. Giving it a shake, he said, "I've been learning to dance too." Humming softly he began to circle the room. Ona smiled at his serious face, the way he lifted his knees high and stuck out his behind. Suddenly catching his boot on a rug, Boné tripped and fell sprawling on the floor.

Ona laughed until the tears ran down her cheeks. Boné sat sheepishly on the floor, rubbing his elbow. "Right on the funny-bone," he muttered, standing up. "We'd better be going down to the house. We're giving you a party tonight."

Late that evening after the trading post had been locked and bolted against stragglers, they all gathered for supper in the house. Everybody: Bert Bruce, Tony Lucero and his fat pleasant wife, the two Vrain Girls, Boné and Ona, and Gene Lockhardt, the musician. They were simple people and they ate a hearty simple dinner and talked of simple things: a wagonload of supplies freighted down from

Durango, the Navajo sheep clip, and of neighbors named Spotted Horse and Mrs. Black Kettle. Only Lockhardt seemed out of place in this remote frontier region.

A middle-aged man, tall and gaunt with two telltale pink spots in his white cheeks, he had come in wearing a foreign-looking worsted coat over a fresh white shirt and blue brocaded tie. When introduced to Ona he murmured, "Pleased, I'm sure," and bowed. The gesture was so gracefully natural that she felt big and clumsy as an ox despite her new taffeta dress, the first occasion she'd had to wear it. All during dinner she kept staring at the immense diamond solitaire ring hanging loosely on his finger. He had the big knuckled, regular shaped hands of a pianist, and a sensitive face.

She had learned that afternoon Lockhardt was an Englishman, a somewhat famous pianist, who for many years had lived in San Francisco. He was an invalid — a consumptive or lunger as they were called in Little London — of course, and had moved way out here for his health. "But why here of all places?" she had asked. Bruce the trader had been the one to gruffly answer. "Bloomfield, that other straggle of buildings down the road, was settled by an Englishman named William B. Haines. I suppose Lockhardt learned about it through him or his folks." Still Ona kept wondering what kept such an immaculate, strange bird of passage here.

"Are you going to be here long Mr. Lockhardt?" she asked without thinking, wishing she had bitten off her tongue instead.

Lockhardt looked up with a blank stare. "Quite. You'll find me the next time you come out in the desert if the coyotes haven't dug me up. Or haven't you heard I came here to die? I assure you it's my only object."

She caught a glimpse of Boné's face. There was a look in his eyes no one save Lockhardt had the right to see. Ona was glad when supper was over and Tony and his wife left.

"Now," cried Boné, "we're all going to my studio for a party!"

Crowded in the one big room, sitting on the couch and on the floor, they watched Boné get out a pair of beautiful silver candlesticks which he lit and ceremoniously placed on the piano. Then, a little formally, he said in a hushed tone, "Gene's going to play for us." Lockhardt got up, grumbling, sat down at the piano. With his first touch on the keys Ona knew he was not only a pianist, but a musician. He played like an angel, a devil, a madman, a madonna. Lordy, how he could play! Why, Lily Force could never have imagined anybody could get so much out of an old piano.

Yet gradually Ona began to feel disturbed. Boné did not sit down with the rest of them. He stood or sat beside Lockhardt in a position of alert attendance and humble adoration; his eyes fixed on the pianist glowed in the candlelight with feverish devotion. Of course, Ona thought, he owed the older man the admiration of a novice for a master. But somehow it seemed more than that. She did not know what; it was something a woman feels about a man without knowing why. Lockhardt seemed oblivious to all but the magic he was conjuring. He was like a different man, alive, self-confident, joyous and sad and moody by turns. Nevertheless Ona began to mistrust him — this lonely, ill man who had come here to die. Suddenly he got up after a crashing crescendo, and bowed to Boné And now it was Boné playing, but not with the same concentration. No matter how well he played — and his execution was far beyond Ona's expectations — he seemed to be showing off. Showing off to Lockhardt, flashing him intimate looks of understanding after difficult passages.

At last Bruce rose. It was over. Ona went out feeling a little ashamed of her queer thoughts. But just the same she felt she knew what was keeping Boné here along the San Juan, if she didn't know what was keeping Lockhardt.

7

Day after day as summer drew on Ona could feel the strength rising within her. It was if she were recovering from a long illness, this joyful resurgence of interest in everything. Laughing deep inside her, she looked into the mirror surprised that she hadn't grown. Her broad square face with its firm set jaw and ample brow had lost its whiteness and was colored a creamy cinnamon. How cheerful and healthy it looked!

She loved to sit in the trading post watching Bruce or Lucero waiting on the Indians: weighing wool and sheep pelts, appraising silver and turquoise jewelry they brought to pawn, measuring out pinto beans, lard, or yards of velveteen and gingham. One day as she was sitting quietly behind the long counter, Bruce poked her in the side with his thumb. "Get off that stiff corset and them high button shoes! Here. Be comfortable." He flung her a purple velveteen blouse decorated with silver buttons and ten-cent coins, a bolt of flowered gingham to make a squaw skirt out of, and a pair of fawn-brown moccasins. Another time when she picked out a bracelet to take back home to Sally Lee, he grumbled, "Hell no, not that! Don't buy anything until you learn what it is." So she began to learn the values of shape, weight, and design of Najavo silver with its chunk turquoise.

Often she went to Matie's missionary headquarters in town. It was a ramshackle frame house with a bell hung over the door. Here Matie and another woman conducted both school and Methodist services for the Navajo families who drove in. Afterwards they distributed groceries and clothing as a reward for their attendance.

Her trips with Lew across the San Juan and into the Reservation were something else. How immense it was! A flat, treeless plain of 25,000 square miles without a town, a house, or a road except for the wagon wheel tracks winding through the dusty sage. Only Lew knew how to find her way to an isolated hut of logs and mud — a hogan — in which a Navajo family lived while grazing its flock of sheep for miles around.

Nominally Lew was a government agent entrusted to pick out the smartest children and to induce their families to let them be sent off to a government school. Acutally she did everything else. She was a good doctor, able to set a bone and break a fever. An excellent judge of sheep and wool; an expert on silver and turquoise, and Navajo blanket weaving and design. She could speak Navajo fluently and, more important, knew how to keep her mouth shut. Like the sparse traders in this immense empty wilderness, she was in effect one of the few human bridges between this proud, independent tribe and the alien race encroaching upon it. Lew justified their trust. Thin, taciturn, burnt brown, she looked and acted like one of The People themselves.

Often they stopped overnight at Hon-Not-Klee, Shallow Water, where Bruce maintained his most important trading post. The one near town he regarded as but a country store for the convenience of stray Utes, Apaches, Navajos, and whites alike. This one stood isolated in the sage, a great L-shaped adobe fortress with iron-barred windows and iron-studded doors. One wing, inside, was the immense trading room. It contained everything possible to supply the needs of The People. And in turn it held in a locked room a fortune in their fine blankets and pawned jewelry. The other wing was used as living quarters, and here Lew and Ona stayed.

It was here at Hon-Not-Klee that Ona saw The People as they were. Not the ragged town-loving Navajos nor the destitute families

Matie's missionary quarters tried to succor. But the hordes of Navajos riding in from the empty wilderness on quick-stepping ponies or in springless wagons. The men slim and erect, with bright headbands holding back their uncut hair. The women sitting fat and shapeless with their children in the wagonboxes, dressed in brilliant velveteen blouses and voluminous gingham skirts. And in all their dark Mongolian faces the same proud arrogance, the same wildness and nobility of the earth itself. All day they would hang around the post, slithering in to trade and bargain with soft voices and quick poetic hands. Ona could not keep her eyes off them. There came back to her again the memory of the band of Plains Indians which had surrounded the house when she was young. The face of the tall young brave who had burned her bottom against the hot stove. And once more she felt the strange admixture of pain and ecstasy and the mellow glow in her crotch creeping down the inner side of her leg in a warm trickle. She had forgotten it all; few people in Little London went over to the Ute encampment, it was so unfashionable to associate with Indians. But here it was different. This was Indian country; and she realized that strange as they were, they held her with a queer attraction.

Boné worked every morning at the piano in his studio, and usually in the evening rode horseback over to Lockhardt's house. Sometimes he stayed all night or for several days. Orchestrating the tunes he had composed, of course. At first this worried Ona, but gradually she accepted it like Bruce and the Vrain Girls.

The two men were always going on trips in a light wagon and they took Ona with them. To the lofty butte called Shiprock. To a vast complex of ruins said to have been anciently built by the Aztecs. To El Huerfano, a sheer peak rising out of the flat plain, sacred to the Navajos who allowed no one to climb it. And then, in the middle of the blistering summer, all the way to the Hopi Indian villages in Arizona. Lew and Matie went along too, so Lew who spoke Navajo could inquire the way and keep them out of trouble. Bruce gave them a team to pull the light wagon heavily loaded with camping equipment, and two riding horses on which they could take turns to save the team.

How wonderful it was! The tawny desert forever spreading out under a brassy sky. The clear sharp flicker of the stars above as they slept at night. And always, as if out of the empty earth itself, a Navajo appearing to lead them to his *hogan* for mutton ribs, fried bread, and cheap Arbuckle coffee sweetened with too much sugar. What a wonderful woman Lew was! They could not have done without her.

Eventually they reached the Hopi mesas. Three of them in the middle of the Navajo Reservation. With nine stone villages or pueblos perched on their lofty summits like eagle eyries, almost indistinguishable from the rock cliffs. What they had come to see, explained Boné, was a *kachina* dance — a dance of masked men representing Hopi gods. There was a spring to camp by on one of the mesas; and while they waited for the day of the dance, they visited the pueblo where it was to be held. Ona was surprised that it looked no different than the ancient ruins she'd seen save that it was swarming with people. Rock and mud rising in terraces, one big honeycomb of tiny rooms.

"A thousand years old!" muttered Lockhardt. "And the people are still primitive as ever!"

Maybe so, thought Ona, but they looked so pleasant, these short, docile Hopis with their broad-faced, smiling faces. So different from the nomadic Navajos following their sheep from one waterhole to another.

The dance began at sunrise and lasted till sunset. They sat all day on a crowded housetop in the broiling sun, looking down into an archaic world populated only by dancing gods. Strange, anthropomorphic figures in their masks, part man, part beast, part bird, abstractly stylized as if they embodied the invisible powers of earth and sky. A long line of them, the *kachinas,* stretching across the cleared plaza. Curving into a circle, then forming into two lines with an old gray-headed priest between. Shaking their gourd rattles. Singing in deep voices that sounded like the wind through the spruce branches they carried. And always dancing, rhythmically, powerfully, calling up the potencies of the earth below and calling down the potencies of the brassy sky above. Ona stared hour after hour, mesmerized. It all seemed to exist in an invisible dimension her senses could not pierce.

Lockhardt broke the silence. "Ever see San Francisco, Boné? The most metropolitan city in the world. And the most beautiful.

The finest cuisine of every race. Opera. Symphonies, Music, boy! My apartment's on the Hill. Sitting at my Baby Grand I can look down upon the bay. The Golden Gate!"

No one answered, not even Boné. He sat as if he had not heard Lockhardt, staring down into that well-like plaza filled with sounds and sights old when the world was new. With one brown finger he was almost imperceptibly tapping out the rhythm.

The ride home was so long, so tedious! The feeling engendered by the mysterious ritual dance she had seen still lingered, but it began to be dissipated when she noticed that Boné and Lockhardt weren't as cosily familiar, as intimate, as usual. Nothing Ona could put her finger on, really, but it bothered her just the same.

When they arrived at Farmington, Boné remained at the post and in his own studio. A week wore on, and still he did not go over to Lockhardt's. Then again they resumed their companionship as if nothing had happened.

Late in September they evidently had another fuss, for Boné stayed home again. This time it was Lockhardt who came to make amends. He arrived in the evening as they were finishing supper and sat down to a cup of coffee. He had never looked so immaculate and distinguished, dressed in his loose, dark worsted jacket, white shirt, and flowing tie. But his gaunt pale face wore spots of deeper pink. When he emptied his cup he rose and said casually, "Well we must be off to Boné's room for a little work." The two men strolled up the trail.

Boné flung open the door of his studio and lit the lamp on the table. Lockhardt pulled out of his pocket a pint of whisky, the huge diamond solitaire on his finger sparkling as he opened the bottle. Taking a big swig, still standing, he resumed the conversation that had been broken off ten days before.

"Sweet mother nature — the great American foible! Look at Europe, its green meadows, its fertile fields, its peaceful rolling hills. Now look out there!" He waved a hand toward the window. "The American landscape. Jagged hills, monstrous mountains on every horizon. Or else a barren sun-struck desert without trees, without water. A devilish twist to every face it shows. It doesn't inspire me! I haven't been brought up to suckle a coyote's teat, and declare a holiday whenever it rains. This earth is malevolent, opposed and fatal to the white man. Every American hates it beneath his show-off sentimentality. There's so damned much of it here in America, heaped two miles or more high, that it exerts a gravity that drags one down. Like it has degraded the Indian and is still doing so. You can't argue against it, even with music."

Lockhardt took another hearty swig and when Boné did not answer, continued, "You're at the turn of your road, my dear boy. Get out of this primitive backwash into civilization. Absorb the rich culture of Europe, develop the traditions of classical music. Not tunes from the pipes of Pan!"

He hesitated, took another drink. "Rhythm, melody, symphonic orchestration. In that order. Those are the steps to the altar of art. But you must have a heart. Do you hear me? A heart! Like this!" He flung himself down on the piano bench. "Where's a light?"

Boné lit the silver candlesticks Lockhardt had given him, blew out the lamp, and sank upon the couch. The Englishman set the whiskey bottle on the floor beside him, closed his eyes. He brought both hands down, preluded brilliantly, then bent down to the keys. Wagner — Yes, *Tistan*. The music filled the dusky room, shook Boné like an ague. An hour passed. One of the candles, jarred loose in its holder, was dripping tallow down the long silver stick and building up slowly like a small stalagmite in the cavernous gloom. The other was out. Lockhardt kept on. At every momentary pause he reached for the bottle on the floor. Then he began again, reciting the different parts in a fervent, not unmusical voice. The moon rose, casting a tangent beam across his pale face. Keyed up by whiskey and drunk with emotion, almost ready to collapse, he began Isolde's Love-Death with shaking hands. It was almost more than Boné could bear.

That great mounting consumation, like surge after surge of moon-swung waves pounding against the sea-wall of man's resisting consciousness only to be flung back, to rise, and roll in once more. The most emotional music ever written but sexual surely, rising from the depths of instinct, of wildly passionate longing, that refused all sublimation and brooked no opposition. It would not let him still his heart nor catch his breath. And the angry tides kept pounding in, to triumphantly rise and crest and break at last in one great orgiastic climax of love and death.

"Gene!" The old man had collapsed over the keys. Boné ran to him, gathered the frail body in his arms, and laid him on the couch. Lighting the lamp on the table, he knelt beside him, watching him slowly come to with a gesture of one hand to the bottle on the floor. There was a drink left; and with it down, Lockhardt began to be himself.

"Oh, Gene! That's what I want! To write good music, big scores!"

Lockhardt, looking very old, turned on him a weary and shrewd look. "I don't know whether it's in you, dear boy. It takes more than I ever had. I rather believe you have more of a talent for lighter work." He was just drunk enough to be bluntly honest.

Boné flinched.

"Still you need to get to more congenial surroundings for professional work, Boné."

"Gene, I can't leave you! I need your help!" He leaned down and put his arms around the musician, staring imploringly into his eyes.

It was at this moment that Ona opened the door. Hearing the click of the latch and feeling the draft of cold air. Boné looked up defiantly.

All the Rogier undemonstrativeness in her rose to meet it. "Excuse me, Boné. I should have knocked. I only wanted to tell you the driver of the supply wagon brought me a letter. It's from Daddy. He's coming to take us back home."

Boné gave her an angry look. "Tell him I'm not going home!"

"Tell him yourself, Boné," she said quietly, and closed the door behind her.

8

The first sight of her father's heavy, powerful body and calm
square face with its steady eyes and sandy mustache reminded Ona
instantly of the mountains he had left behind. Rogier looked her over
from head to toe, then turned to Bruce. "Been trying to make a
squaw out of her, eh?" The trader did not crack a smile. "She'll
make a good one for the right Indian."

"And what've you folks done to the boy all this time?"

"Boy? There's no boy around here," the trader replied just as
gruffly. "There's a talented young man who might be dropping in."

"Maybe so. Maybe so."

Ona could tell they liked each other right off.

Rogier's reunion at supper with Ona, Boné, and the two Vrain
Girls was warm and exciting. There was so much to talk about, what
had happened here and back home. But it was Boné her father's eyes
followed: every gesture, every emotion flitting across his sensitive
face. "I reckon you have grown up, Boné," he admitted. "Have a
cigar?"

"Not enough for that black a weed," cheerfully replied Boné
rolling a cigarette.

All the trips they had taken that summer came up, and during the conversation Boné happened to mention another he was going to take next month—to see some   remarkable cliff-dwellings   just discovered on Mesa Verde by two cowboys hunting lost cattle.

"I thought you were coming home with Ona and me," Rogier said calmly.

"No sir." There was a stubborn defiance in Boné's voice that indicated he had not outgrown Rogier's hold upon him. His cheerful manner vanished instantly.

Rogier ignored the answer as if he had not heard it. It was consistent with Rogier's aloofness that he could not bear to discuss a personal or family affair in the presence of any outsider, even friends as old as the Vrain Girls.

After an awkward silence Matie suggested, "Boné, aren't you going to play for Joe and show him what a fine musician you've become in the last couple of years?"

They all filed up the trail to Boné's studio. Boné rather sullenly slumped upon the piano bench. "Give us a Southern tune or so, if you've a mind to," Rogier said as he used to say to Lily Force. The boy threw him a dark look of refutation and plunged instead into a difficult movement from Bach. Rogier had no developed ear for fine music, but at the boy's seemingly careless display of undeniable virtuosity his jaw dropped. "Dom! Sounds like you and that piano have got on more than speaking terms!"

"That lad's a born musician, Mr. Rogier," asserted Bruce. "You'll never make anything else out of him."

Rogier lit his cigar and leaned back for an hour's concert. Ona sat cracking pinon nuts between her teeth. The spectacle of Boné oppising Rogier with music, too proud and stubborn to confess openly the reason for his desire to stay and to ask Rogier's permission and aid, grew painful. Without Lockhardt at his elbow to criticize his slightest mistouch, determined to impress Rogier, and infused with excitement, Boné slurred a run, skipped a rest, and kept playing. The music rang out with an exultant challenge, with courageous sincerity, like a demand from Boné himself. If only her father would understand and avoid a quarrel!

Boné flung around. "What's the matter—don't you like my music?"

"It's getting late, Boné, and Daddy's had a long, hard ride," said Ona, getting up with Bruce and the Vrain Girls.

Rogier stamped around on one stiff leg, then sat down again. "You folks go on to bed. I'm going to listen to him out."

"That young fella's all right," Bruce whispered. "Just leave him alone. It'll work off like a dose of physic."

"The young jackass!"

Ona left with the others, but as she walked down the trail she couldn't hear any more playing.

Rogier stayed only a few days at the post. Lew had found an Indian boy to drive them to Durango, and he wanted to be off.

"I'll escort you by horseback to the top of the hill," said Boné.

The remark was Ona's first indication that Boné was not going home with them. She knew Rogier had talked to Lockhardt, Bruce, and the Vrain Girls about him, but still her curiosity prompted her to draw Boné aside. "Boné—I've got to know! Did you and Daddy really quarrel the other night about your not coming with us?"

"No, Ona. I've been ashamed ever since, the wonderful way he talked to me. He understands a lot more than he lets on, you know. And he's going to keep on sending me an allowance — a bigger one!"

The sudden realization that she had lost him as she had lost Hiney and Bob — he, this funny little boy whom she had loved best of all! — struck her like a blow. Tears leapt to her eyes. "Boné! You're one of us. You can't ever get clear away. Don't forget me, Boné!"

"Shoot, Ona. You'd know if I needed you if I were lost in Patagonia!"

Two mornings later at sun-up Rogier and Ona climbed on the wagon seat beside the Indian boy. Boné mounted his broomtail beside them. Lew and Matie came out with a going-away gift — a large and exquisitely woven Two-Gray-Hills blanket to throw over their laps. "Hold on!" cried Bruce, running up with a scooping handful of jewelry to thrust at Ona. A fortune in silver rings and bracelets set with chunk turquoise, a squash-blossom necklace, and a prize concho belt she had admired for six months! She began to weep, and Rogier drove off without a word.

Boné too jogged along in silence. What was there to say?

Perhaps all three of them were thinking of the jist of Rogier's talk to Boné that night. Rogier at least knew only too well to what a task the boy had set his hand with an urge as powerful as silver-madness. Like Tom, he was consecrating himself to the folly of extracting his meaning of life from a gangue that might not contain the silver ore of his dreams. But instead of force and luck, Boné was using a different approach: an elusive persuasiveness, more intangible, more heart-rendingly difficult, because there was no way to measure his success or failure. Rogier saw not the ready acclaim awarded to so few and lost so quickly, the deserved and final success attained perhaps by one man in his time, but only the toil and despair of the sincere who realize at the last the modicum they have been able to add to the work of those who have gone before. Never, after listening to Boné play, could he doubt his sincerity; but he could not measure whether the boy's strength would prove adequate to the task he had set himself.

At the top of the hill the wagon stopped. Boné dismounted, kissed Ona and squeezed Rogier's hand. Remounting, he trotted the old bay fifty feet into the trackless sage. Then standing in his stirrups, he raised his right arm aloft. The melodramatic, graceful gesture, as if unconsciously copied from a lurid print that hung on the kitchen door at home, brought a blur to Ona's eyes. Before she could wave, Boné turned back to his lifelong, lonely journey.

The wagon rolled on. Rogier settled himself on the seat, and with a face like flint, raised his eyes to the high steel-blue mountains before them.

Men, mere men, both of them, oblivious of the grandeur of their folly, blind to the futility of evoking an answer from an earth which but echoed back their questions in a voice hollow yet profound, and couched in terms neither could recognize for his own.

To Ona their long trip home was a miserable finale concluding a symphonic summer. It had seemed unusual that Rogier, busy as he was, had come merely to take her and Boné back. Now the real reason came out. Rogier wanted to look over some of the rich silver mines and boom towns. So now, following the Animas River north from Durango, they crept into the blue-ribbed Uncompahgre, San Juan, and Saguache ranges of the great male Rockies on the little D & RG narrow-gauge, by wagon, and by horseback. Silverton,

Ouray, Telluride, Ophir, Lake City — they all looked the same to Ona. Crude little towns and camps set in deep canyons or small mountain meadows. Squat one-story buildings with their false high "Leadville fronts." Miners with burros and pack horses crowding the narrow streets and thumping along the patches of wooden sidewalks. The sharp air was odorific with fresh-sawed pine and bar whisky. The noise of blasting echoed from the hills, picking up the clatter of a mechanical piano in a tinny minor melody.

Most of the time Ona stayed in the inevitable ramshackle hotel. She did not dare to walk about the streets in one of her still-new taffeta dresses for fear of being taken for a sporting woman; and her pride forbade that she go about in gingham or calico, ungloved. So she sat in her room, wondering if Tom had ever been here and why they'd never heard from him. Wondering too what had got into her father.

All day Rogier roamed mountainside and canyon, wherever there was a notable mine. In the evenings he talked in front of the stove in the hotel lobby, on the streets, and in the saloons, with mine-owners and workers. At night he sat in his room bending over maps and drawings in the light of a lamp.

Occasionally she visited mines with him. The difficult walks or horseback rides, with Rogier swinging along the trail ahead seemingly oblivious of her presence, tired her out completely. More exasperating were the hours she sat at the portal of a tunnel waiting for him to come up. When at last he did emerge, blinking at the sunlight, it was only to stand around talking, rapping his knuckles against the timbers. Or else he would pick at a piece of ore with his knife, and perhaps carry it into the assayer's office for another long palaver. Slow, methodical, never verbosely enthusiastic, he was not to be hurried.

"What's got into you, Daddy?" she asked bluntly. "You're not going into mining after all these years, are you?"

"Nothing like that at all!" he replied just as brusquely. "My trade's building — a process of addition, you might call it. Mining's subtraction, taking away. I just thought my education wouldn't be complete till I balanced the equation."

She looked at him sharply; he had a habit of speaking jocularly in such parables. "Why are you so interested in the composition of ore, then?"

"This is gangue! The country rock in which is imbedded mineral matter!" He thrust the specimen under her nose. "Dom it, Ona! A man ought to know what makes up the ground he walks on!"

It was October. Patches of aspen were turning deep yellow and pink among the forested blue mountainsides. The air was sharp with frost. An early snow might close the passes any night. But Rogier was not yet ready to head for home. They crept over Slumgullion Pass and turned south toward the headwaters of the Rio Grande where a fabulous new silver strike had been made.

Rogier recounted the details. The year before, a prospector named Nicholas C. Creede and his partner George Smith had worked north from Del Norte through Wagon Wheel Gap to the head of Willow Creek. Here they found float and sank a shaft. At the end of the day's work, Creede, examining the yellow quartz, had yelled, "Holy Moses!" thus naming the Holy Moses Mine.

The rush began. Two butchers at Wagon Wheel Gap, Granger and Buddenbock, grubstaked two prospectors, Haas and Renninger, who located the Last Chance. Creede, seeing the specimens, located another mine, the Amethyst. Shortly thereafter, Haas was bought off for $10,000 and returned to Germany. Renninger and Buddenbock each sold their shares for $70,000. Granger was offered and refused $100,000, and the Last Chance was now producing $180,000 per month. Creede had raked in $1,000,000 from the Holy Moses and Amethyst. And by the end of the first year the district around the camp of Creede had yielded $6,000,000.

Willow Gulch, when Rogier and Ona arrived, was jammed with people. For six miles up the creek every foot of ground had been staked out. Tents and shacks and cabins were crowded against the towering cliff walls between which crawled a corkscrew street barely wide enough for a wagon. There were a dozen hotels; one of them, a fresh pine shanty containing twenty cots in its single room, was named The Palace. Rogier finally obtained a room in another, the Cochetopa, for forty dollars a day. Here Ona huddled for three days, afraid to set foot outside, while Rogier prowled around.

Créede was red-hot and chaotic. Its patron saints were Chance and Luck; its shrines the Keno, Little Delmonico, and the Holy Moses Saloon. Day and night the tortuous winding street below swarmed with prospectors and miners, speculators, gamblers, and dancehall girls. Ona could hear the sound of saws and hammers, the tinkle of pianos, the clink of silver on the gambling table below, the sharp bark of a six-shooter up the gulch. Years later it all came back to her in the words of the homey poet, Cy Warman:

> Here the meek-eyed burros
> On mineral mountains feed.
> It's day all day in the daytime,
> And there's no night in Creede.

What held Rogier here Ona did not know. A Rogier herself and peculiarly sensitive to her father, she sensed a vibrant excitement emanating from him that his air of deliberate unconcern, his steady voice, could not hide. The queer impending change in him was accentuated rather than subdued by his calm demeanor. The feeling carried her back to those terrible days of the Leadville boom when, high above the trail with Sister Molly, she had watched Tom ascending Ute Pass. And as if with an ear to the ground, she seemed to feel a subterranean tremor within him, the faintest rumble of a movement betokening a growing unrest that would uproot him from his ordered life. She was relieved no end when at last they turned toward home.

Mile after mile it all slid behind her: the months in Indian Country with Bruce, the Vrain Girls, and Boné; the weeks in the Rockies with Rogier. What did it all mean? Although she did not realize it, it was the gangue that imbedded for all of them the pay streaks of their future lives.

But she never forgot Creede. It was 1890 and Creede was the last of the great Colorado silver strikes. The silver moon was setting, and above the mountain-rimmed horizon the golden sun was rising.

PART III

GOLD

1

The following spring Rogier became fifty years old. Wide-shouldered, of medium height, with an easy swing to his gait, he looked solid as the hills. He had the accentuated upper-level forehead of a reflective thinker, the square firm jaw of a man who stood behind his decisions, and deep-sunk penetrative gray eyes. And his hands — big, strong, coarsened with early years of carpenter work, yet with fingers peculiarly sensitive — confirmed the impression of his face.

Aloof and reticent to an unwarranted degree, Rogier would have been amazed that even the Little Londoners in the North End regarded him with a respect tinged by a spot of fear. A respect inspired by his hard-earned success as a builder and his enviable possession of land and buildings throughout town. The fear a growing bewilderment because he did not flaunt them, never made a conciliatory move toward their society, and remained down in the ungainly house on Shook's Run — an attitude rightly judged as suspicious because he was different.

While he had been away unfavorable news had come of Hiney. Between theatrical engagements, he had taken the job of night watchman at the Brown Palace Hotel. One night he was caught crawling through the transom of a room. The guest was out, leaving money and some jeweled studs on the dresser, but Hiney had taken nothing. The next morning when he was questioned at the jail, Hiney could remember nothing. In desperation he sent his only friend, a girl named Margaret with whom he was in love, home to Rogier. And Rogier was away.

Rogier listened impatiently to Mrs. Rogier and Mrs. White. He could well imagine Martha receiving the girl with doubt and lifted eyebrows. Hiney, for all his upbringing, had strayed from the path of righteousness.

"Never mind," said Rogier. "What did you do?"

"I give that sweetheart of his some money to get him out of jail," answered Mrs. White. "She was done taken up with that boy, ridin' all night on the train to get back to Denver."

Mrs. Rogier sat upright, unsmiling. She too loved Hiney but she feared the Lord's wrath more, believing that forgiveness should be the fruit of repentance and not, like Atlanta's apples, tossed indiscriminately before swift feet racing to destruction.

Rogier and Mrs. White exchanged a quick, secret glance. They were the only ones who knew that Hiney was subject to lapses of memory. "I wouldn't worry none," finished Mrs. White. "That theah Mahgret of his sent us a postcard about his gettin' along fuhst rate now."

Pet's new colt, Silver Heels, looked as if she might be faster than Dorothy, her first. To break and train them both, Rogier moved them to Denman's ranch a few miles east of town. Denman was a fine old man whose only love and interest were horses. He had few of his own and made his living handling those given to his care. One afternoon his stable boy galloped furiously down to the Rogier house, then up to Rogier's office with the alarming news that Silver Heels was sick. Rogier rushed to the ranch and spent the night with Denman in the colt's stable. There was nothing either of them could do; Silver Heels died of a punctured bowel.

A few months later Rogier sent to Maryland for the papers of a filly he had been interested in for a long time. Finally he sent for her. Never in this life had any horse so aroused that inward glow, the tingle up the spine, which Rogier felt when he first saw her. A keepee was a sleek little thing, dark bay, with a white diamond on her forehead and white stockings on the near front and hind feet. Even the family doted upon her. Stabled in back of the house, Akeepee was kind and gentle as a kitten, neighing across the fence, nosing all hands for a lump of sugar. Yet there was never any doubt what she was bred for, as she hardened and filled out.

Eventually Rogier took her to Judge Colton's excellent establishment near the track north of town. Not that he mistrusted Denman because of Silver Heel's unfortunate death, but he wanted Akeepee to have the best. The very best! "She's got the blood lines, the confirmation of a fine pacer," he kept insisting. "I want a horse that can run!"

A strange new passion for speed. None of the family could account for it.

There were a number of fine animals being trained at Colton's that winter. Even as early as March considerable excitement prevailed over the racing meeting to be held in the summer, and wagers were being made as to which of the horses would prove the fastest. Akeepee was considered one of the best. Her only rivals, in many an opinion, were Colton's big gray mare and a dun horse named Toller. Late one afternoon after Rogier had left, an impromptu race was held. Three starters dropped out halfaway around the course, leaving Akeepee and Toller running neck to neck. Cooped up inside for weeks waiting for the snow to clear from the track, neither was in the best of condition. And yet at the end of the mile they were whipped on for another stretch. Streaming wet, almost exhausted, their breaths enveloping them with frosty steam, the horses were led back to stable.

Whether Judge Colton was too drunk to care, or whether he did it to further the chances of his own gray mare, now warm and blanketed inside her box, no one ever knew. But Akeepee was left unblanketed and without being rubbed down. Providentially, an old handler who favored Akeepee sent for Rogier. With Sally Lee, Rogier hurried out in the buckboard and walked Akeepee home to his own stalls. A veterinary was waiting. All night he, Rogier, and Sally Lee worked her over with witch hazel and alcohol, drying her and wrapping her in blankets, then walking her around the yard. Akeepee almost died; it took weeks to get her back in shape; and from then on no one save Denman, Sally Lee, and Rogier touched her. No one ever knew what happened between Rogier and Judge Colton. Sally Lee insisted that Rogier horsewhipped him — perhaps a great exaggeration. But the incident drove Rogier away from the Gentleman's Pleasure and Driving Association he had finally joined; he didn't bother to submit a letter of withdrawal.

Soon afterward he bought a new Frazier sulky. Every evening as dusk clotted the prairie track, he sat in the low seat, legs outspread, leaning forward until his face was whipped with her silky tail, skimming the ground behind Akeepee. When she was warmed up he turned her into the straight-away, nose pointing at that lofty white Peak never even now out of his thoughts.

"See her, old girl?" he would ask in a rising voice. "Slam into her! Bust her wide open! Let's see what's inside!" And with a flick of his whip above her she would burst forward, leveling her stride into the path of projectile aimed at his heart's desire.

Embryonic in that high southern slope of Pike's Peak where the Pisgah excitement had ended in a miserable fiasco, a few disregarded but auspicious events were outcropping to surface. "Crazy Bob" Womack, the cowboy on the Broken Box Ranch, was still insisting there was gold along Cripple Creek. Having neglected to record his claim, the Chance, for six years, he finally relocated it as the El Paso. The samples he kept showing in town were ignored by everyone except a furniture store owner, E. M. de la Vergne, and his store manager, F. F. Frisbee. That January they had packed up to the Broken Box and staked claims. Not an experienced prospector in the area believed that gold could be found on that barren, high cow pasture on the slope of Pike's Peak. Yet by spring a hundred more tenderfeet and alfalfa miners were digging up the range along the meandering creek.

Bennett and Myers, the two Denver real estate men who owned the Broken Box, began to plat a townsite of eighty acres on the ranch, offering lots for fifty dollars apiece. The town was named Cripple Creek for mere convenience; the first purchasers of lots for cabin sites agreed to leave their timber to be used for patching fences after the town was abandoned.

In April Rogier met Stratton on the street. "Hunting for a job?"

he asked.

"Not this time, Joe I've already raised a grubstake. You know that plasterer, Leslie Popejoy? He's outfitting me. Maybe I'll take along another partner, Billy Fernay, so Popejoy can stay home and make more money."

Rogier did not reply. Billy Fernay was not too highly regarded in town. He seldom worked and was often carried home drunk on an ironing board which two friends kept handy for the purpose. The prognosis of success for the carpenter, plasterer, and town drunk was not too good, but Stratton seemed to know what he was after.

"Cryolite, Joe. Not well known but valuable. It's a fluoride used in making aluminum. I think there's a deposit somewhere near St. Peter's Dome or up Beaver Creek."

A few days later Rogier saw him and Fernay trying to pack their two burros in front of Stratton's boarding house. It was an unpleasant spectacle. The boarding house was near the corner of Pike's Peak Avenue and Cascade — almost directly in view of the luxurious Antlers Hotel, on whose porch laughed a group of ladies and gentlemen. Swiftly a crowd gathered around the prospectors. Rogier noticed that one of the Rocky Mountain Canaries had been cut on the back by barbed wire. The instant the pack touched the scab, the burro brayed and lashed out with both heels. Fernay stood back and swore. Stratton, with his quick temper, whacked the burro with a pick handle. Blood began to pour from the wound. A woman screamed, running to bring someone from the Humane Society. Hotel guests tittered. The crowd roared. Fernay finally wrapped a blanket over the burro's head and Stratton flung the pack on its back. As they ambled down the street the pack came off, spilling flour and beans. The two men did not wait to scrape up their supplies, but flinging the pack back on the beast, fled down the street.

Early in July the report came out that Stratton had struck a gold lode in Cripple Creek. Professor Lamb at the college had made the assays of the samples. They ran $380 to the ton! Most of the people in town were stunned. It seemed impossible to believe that a gold strike had been made scarcely twenty miles, as the crow flies, from the plush lobby of the Antlers Hotel. Why, the place was within picnic-distance of the Saratoga of the West! Moreover it had been passed over by prospectors since '58 — for thirty-three years! Self-important North Enders took it more seriously. They spoke of their duty to pronounce the fraud and nip the boom in the bud before the mining industry of Colorado was blackened with dishonor. Still something of a rush began — a slow, increasing influx into the region of men not wildly excited but taking no chances on losing out on a fortune.

Rogier was one of the many who kept his head. The secret nervousness, the repressed excitement, the sense of foreboding that had possessed him during the Leadville and Creede strikes, and all those between, did not trouble him now. It was as if all his life he had been preparing to meet the thing before him now. Sitting tight, he waited for the rumors to quiet down.

Late in the summer Stratton stopped in his office. He was dressed up, his mustache freshly trimmed, looking like a different man — a man who after seventeen years of fruitless searching had found what he sought. "It *was* a dream, Joe! Everything's settled now. I'll tell you about it."

For two months he and Fernay had hunted without finding any trace of the cryolite of which he had heard. They had then packed into the Cripple Creek district and prospected for another month. The region did not have the appearance of a mining country. Ordinarily veins of gold jutted boldly above the surface in outcrops known in Australia as reefs and in California as ledges. But here, except for a ledge of reddish granite at the foot of Battle Mountain which every prospector had passed by, the region was barren save for its innumerable hills. On the evening of July 3, on their way to make camp, he and Billy Fernay also passed this ledge.

Sitting at his campfire that night, listening to Fernay snore, Stratton remembered a scrap of geology Professor Lamb had taught him. The whole area once had been a monstrously huge volcano of which only Pike's Peak was now left. The country rock which composed it was granite of a pinkish tint that was now known as Pike's Peak Granite. Ages ago there had been a mighty eruption during which a complex of volcanic rock had burst through the granite. It was a purplish rock generally called porphyry: a name evolved from the Greek "porphyra" for purple, used to designate rock which the Romans had obtained from the quarries of Gebel

Dokhan on the shores of the Red Sea.

That night Stratton dreamed that there at that ledge where the granite and the porphyry met lay a vast deposit of mineral. "I could see a mine there, Joe. Right in that tangled briar patch on the slope of Battle Mountain, among the big boulders. A dream of gold on Pike's Peak! Just like the one I'd been carrying all these years!"

"And what did you do?" asked Rogier quietly.

"I woke up and rushed back there just as the sun was coming up. Some men far off were shooting off guns to celebrate the day — the Fourth of July. So I staked out a full lode claim on the spot and another beside it. Both named in honor of the holiday. The Independence and the Washington."

Three days later, Stratton went on, he had staked out two more claims, the Black Diamond and one named for Professor Lamb. There had followed the usual trouble: buying out Popejoy and Fernay, trying to develop all four claims. At last in desperation he had broken open the great boulders, some of them weighing over ten tons. Full of gold, they brought him $60,000 — enough money to sink a shaft on the site of the Independence.

"Then I hit it!" said Stratton. "That ore chute led directly into the main vein. Why, I never saw anything like it! Gold threads snarling up granite, porphyry, country rock, and grass roots, ore good enough to eat. Nine feet wide I figured and a hundred feet deep — $3,000,000 worth to start with, and more below!"

There he sat: forty-three years old, thin, stooped, and white-haired already, a lonely recluse. But a man who had found his dream. Winfield Scott Stratton, Colorado's new Gold King. He got up and the two men shook hands warmly.

"I've lost a good carpenter," said Rogier, grinning.

"I hope you're as lucky as I was," replied Stratton. "Don't wait too long."

2

During the few months of its first year the district produced $200,000 worth of gold. "Cripple Creek — the $200,000 Cow Pasture!"

Despite the general distrust of the district, the camp kept growing as a horde of tenderfoot Little Londoners, store clerks, bakers, and butchers scrambled up the Peak. Near as it was, the camp was difficult of access. Men had to pack up the mile-high Cheyenne Mountain trail; ride the Colorado Midland railroad train up Ute Pass to Florissant and thence eighteen miles south by stage or horseback; or leave the Denver and Rio Grande at Florence and ride thirty miles north in Concord stages drawn by six horses.

With the melting of the winter snows Rogier, never in a hurry, went up for a look around. Riding the Midland to the junction, he managed to get a seat in the stage. With the driver's whip cracking like pistol shots at the ears of the sixes, the boisterous shouts of the men inside, the dull thud of hoofs on the snowy road, the stage swung off into the thick gray silence of the hills.

Cripple Creek bore a distinct resemblance to the Broken Box which had given its name to the ranch on which the town had been built. Cabins, shacks, and lean-tos stood everywhere like the remnants of a wooden box. The town, built on the side of a steep hill, was divided by two streets: Bennett Avenue, trying to look something like a business street; and Myers Avenue, a block south, already being lined with false-front saloons, dancehalls, and cribs. Nearly 400 people crowded the camp. Water was selling for a nickel a bucket. Speculators were standing on the corners selling shares of stock in Frisbee's Gold King, the first mine to ship pay ore, and in the Buena Vista, the first mine on Bull Hill. Rogier waved them away. The town didn't interest him a whit. Nor did the reports of still more unbelievably true strikes.

His old druggist, A.D. Jones, had come up on his Sunday day-off. "I don't know anything about mining, boys!" he had shouted "Where'll I dig?"

"She's all good! Just throw your hat in the air!" they answered.

Jones without hesitation flung his hat in the air and dug where it fell, locating the Pharmacist, the second mine to ship ore in quantity.

The locator of the Elkton went broke and gave half-interest in it to pay off a grocery bill of $36.50. The two grocers let in a schoolteacher who during his vacation struck a vein that began producing $13,000,000. The Anaconda had been offered for $400; now the owners were considering $2,000,000 for a controlling interest. The first assay from the Rose Maud ran $2,800 to the ton.

Stopping in a saloon, Rogier listened to a bartender from Leadville who summed up the stories. "Hell! The tenderfeet are taking out gold where it is, and the miners are looking for it where it ought to be!" He mentioned a farmer from Missouri, A.G. White, who had laboriously dug through surface rock with no indication of mineral into a big ore chute that had yielded the Vindicator company $750,000. Professor Kimball was making gold discoveries by walking around with a willow branch. Another wizard, John Barbee, he claimed had located the vein of the El Paso with a forked stick.

Cy Warman, the home-spun poet, had arrived from Creede to inspect the Cripple Creek rush. His comparison was not entirely favorable: "People are rushing to Creede by the hundreds, and crawling to Cripple Creek by twos and fours."

To this he added the observation that "on the summit of Globe Hill in the camp of Cripple Creek they are prospecting with plows, mining with road-scrapers, and actually shipping the scenery." No man could deny it. The surface dirt on Globe Hill, specifically designated as that from the grass roots down six feet, was being contracted for by the wagon load.

Rogier, unlike the horde of hopefuls around him, did not feel bound to stake out a claim foolishly. He was not sure he wanted to stake one out at all. If he wanted anything, it was simply to know the district thoroughly. Learning it not only until its physiography was familiar to him at close hand, but geologically; and more than all, to feel out the indefinable strength of its will. It was like meeting a man for the first time. Rogier would have said he had to "size him up" before knowing how to deal with him.

The next morning after an uncomfortable night dozing on a chair in a saloon, he stretched his stiff legs in their stout boots, buttoned his overcoat, and holding a map in his gloved hands for ready reference, started out to encompass the district. Turning southeast past Poverty Gulch, he looked back at Mount Pisgah. It, like the town, was blurred in the gray mist. He walked on briskly, warming to his stride. Gradually the hills took shape around him, some bearing names consistent with the original cow pasture: Big Bull, Cow, Calf, Bull Cliffs, and Grassy Gulch. Others had sprouted newer names: Gold, Globe, Tenderfoot, Carbonate, Crystal, Mineral and Galena Hills, Beacon, Battle, Squaw and Straub Mountains. A maze of lumpish hills forested with spruce and pine and thin groves of aspens; and drained by Arequa, Squaw, and Eclipse gulches, crisscrossed with burro trails and the ruts of heavy wagons. A 10,000-foot-high shelf, as it seemed, on the south slope of that 14,000-foot Peak rising above him, aboe timberline, to stand nakedly white above the lifting mist. And silent with a queer silence that had in it the timelessness of an earth upthrust forever above the faintest murmur of the vast monotone of human misery far below.

Almost every hill bore signs of digging, open shafts, glory holes, new mines. In every gulch clustered a huddle of cabins and shanties already taking on names: Independence, Winfield, Strattonia, Anaconda, Goldfield, Arequa. Walking steadily southeast, Rogier began to notice that most of the new mines were not located in Poverty Gulch and around Cripple Creek to the west, but six miles east and southeast near the new camp of Victor. This was natural; Stratton's great strike on Battle Mountain had been made there. But still Rogier, constantly referring to his map, was inclined to believe that near here somewhere had occured the main eruption of porphyry through the granite walls of the now extinct volcano. How big was its diameter? Whatever was taking shape in his mind was too nebulous to see clearly, but he kept looking for it in the pinkish country rock and an occasional speck of purplish poryphry. There was little to see; a thin layer of snow still covered the ground.

Victor was a tawdry array of cabins, shacks, and tents. Men were cutting down trees to make way for streets: the pines for building and the aspens for firewood. Lots were being sold for $25 apiece. If a man did not have the cash he was asked merely to sign a paper as a future resident of the town, the signatures to be used in securing a postoffice.

Worn out, he turned back toward another sleepless night in Cripple Creek. Fortunately he met George Carr, the former foreman of the Broken Box Ranch and now being talked of for Cripple Creek's first mayor, who offered him a bed. That evening, dozing in front of the hot stove, Rogier learned of another strike on top of Battle Mountain that had been kept quiet.

"You know Jimmie Doyle, the carpenter, and Jimmie Burns, the plumber, down in town? They made it three months ago," began Carr.

"A carpenter and a plasterer, and now a carpenter and a plumber! Yes, I know them both."

"They filed a little claim of only one-sixth of an acre 700 feet above Stratton's full lode claim of ten acres, but didn't find much. So they took in another Irishman, Johnny Harnan, who had worked for Stratton. He hit it — thirty-two ounces to the ton!" Carr paused, then continued. "You can guess the trouble, even if they did lug out the ore on their backs by night. They couldn't follow their vein from its apex on top the mountain without running into the properties of other mines between them and the Independence, and vice versa. That meant lawsuits. The news got out and all the other mines went to court."

"I haven't heard anything about all this," commented Rogier.

"You will!" asserted Carr. "Stratton's no fool and he's learned how to keep his mouth shut. The case hasn't been settled, but he's given the Irishmen money to hire lawyers and to buy up the conflicting claims in exchange for stock. They'll win, all right! And when they do that little one-sixth of an acre will be forty acres big and Queen of the District controlled by and combined with Stratton's Independence as King of the District!"

Rogier went to sleep thinking how shrcwd Stratton was, and how immensely rich and powerful he was becoming. But more than anything else of the importance of that eastern edge of the district around Victor.

He had encompassed the whole district, an area about ten miles square that contained every strike of note. He had looked at mines, shallow diggings, and prospects, talked with men of every age and type. The only mine he had not visited was the Independence; a stiff-necked pride had restrained him from looking up Stratton without an invitation.

Walking down the street in search of a geologist he wanted to talk with, Rogier reached for a cigar then suddenly stopped. He went through all his pockets. Their emptiness apprised him of the fact that he was also out of money. He looked down at his boots, hardly distinguishable in a pool of muddy water. His trousers too were splashed and torn at the cuffs. A queer looking customer to approach a consulting geologist without a cent! Abruptly he swung across the street to a general merchandise store and accosted the man behind the counter. "You're up from the Springs, aren't you?"

"Yes sir. On Huerfano Street. I sold out and moved my stock up here this spring.

"I thought I'd seen you down there. I'm out of cash. I want you to give me a hundred dollars. You can draw on me for that amount the next time you send down for supplies or I'll send you a draft. My name's Rogier."

The man met his steady gaze. "Why, I think I can let you have that much, Mr. Rogier." He went to the safe and came back with a wad of bills.

Rogier counted the notes carefully. "That's fine of you. I'll see you don't lose out."

As he walked out the door one of the men at the stove set up a guffaw. "God Almighty! Who's he think he is to come strollin' in and walk out with a hundred dollars?"

"I ain't worryin' none," the storekeeper replied quietly. "That there Mr. Rogier's name is as good as his bond. And if he gets to doin' anything up here this store's goin' to get a lot of hundreds rollin' in it wouldn't have got."

A chair overturned as one of the loungers leaped for the door. "Hey, Colonel!"

The shout stopped Rogier in the middle of the road. The man caught up with him, nervously heaving a deep breath. "Reynolds the name, Colonel. I'm plumb busted myself. Thirty dollars would grubstake me long enough to put down a ten-foot hole on a likely property I got my eyes set on."

Rogier's gaze went through him but the man did not flinch. Rogier drew out a ten-dollar bill. "The storekeeper will know you just got this from me. Tell him to give you twenty dollars more worth of goods on my account."

Reynolds grabbed his arm as he strode away. "What'll I call her, Colonel?"

"The 'Silver Heels' might do if you don't think of a better name," he said quietly and walked away.

When he finally arrived home, Mrs. Rogier and all the girls rushed into the hall to greet him.

"Daddy! Did you find a gold mine?" shouted Mary Ann. When he did not reply, she added, "Mr. Jones found one on his Sunday off — the Pharmacist he calls it!"

"No," Rogier answered good humoredly. "The hills were so full of holes I couldn't find enough solid ground to stand on to dig another."

"You look dirty enough to have dug out a dozen," Mrs. Rogier said testily, amazed that he of all men hadn't found a gold mine richer than any yet. "Look at those shoes! And you've probably ruined your good overcoat. The mud will never come out. I hope no one saw you walking from the depot."

"Well, draw me a hot bath and I'll get out of them. Mary Ann, find me a cigar. I haven't had a good smoke in a week!"

3

That year saw the turn. With the presidential re-election of Grover Cleveland, openly declaring himself a gold advocate, the free silver question came to a head. What could dam the flood of moonlit metal poring from the mountains — now $11,000,000 worth a year from Leadville alone? Eastern capitalists feared that the heavy purchases of silver under the Sherman Act would result in the replacement of the gold dollar by a depreciated silver dollar. Business tightened, commerical houses began to fail. A rush to redeem securities in gold brought down the national gold reserve to the danger point, $100,000,000. Then it dropped to $70,000,000.

Alarm spread throughout the world. Foreign governments stopped buying silver. The mints in far off India closed to silver. Within four days the price of silver plunged to sixty-two cents an ounce — less than half its set price — and then dropped to fifty cents. And when the Congress repealed the Sherman Act, Colorado's silver days were over. In Leadville, Creede, every silver camp in the Rockies, mines and smelters closed. Loose stones rattled down the dumps. Water filled the levels. The wind began to rip off planks from abandoned tool shanties and shaft houses. Silver Dollar

Tabor, multimillionaire and silver king, was toppled from his throne. All his vast holdings, his wild millions were swept away, leaving him a friendless, penniless man wandering the streets of Denver.

The silver reign was over; gold had come into its own; and the whole metallic West began to acclaim Stratton who had stepped upon Tabor's throne. "The King is dead! Long live the King!" And the thousands of men who were thrown out of work in the deserted silver camps swarmed to Cripple Creek to dig for gold. But prices were down, labor was cheap, and there were three men for every job. In the Mush and Milk House, the English Kitchen, and Monaco Buffet, at the bars of the Gold Dollar, Blue Bell, Becker and Nolan's, the Manitou Exchange, men tossed down their whisky straight and muttered surlily of shorter hours, more money, and a job for every man.

. . . Yet all this was but one facet of the problem confronting Rogier. There were other facts to be considered besides these of economics and politics, of climate and altitude, less discernible but subtly influencing the shape of his thought. Facts of geology, ore structure, and mine development. Facts of men, banking and finance. And of course there were his family, his horses, and his growing business.

"Ona," he asked one evening, drawing her aside, "how would you like a job? I'm so busy I never have time to make head or tail of those ledgers of mine. I can't stand to have Mooney or any other time-keeper messing in my business. Why don't you go down to the office every day and tend to them?"

"Why, all right, Daddy."

"I'll pay you a salary, of course. And you ought to have something to occupy your time," he added kindly.

Thereafter, with Ona trying to read his illegible great ledgers bursting with contracts and old check stubs, answering his mail, and keeping his accounts, Rogier went up to Cripple Creek more often. The family supposed he was prospecting for gold like everybody else. Rogier did not botner to deny it. A discovery was necessary to fulfill his purpose; that resolve born from his sense of alienation and directed against the implacable mystery of the Peak.

For the time at least he seemed like two different men. Day by day one of them went quietly, surely, about his work, visiting briefly with his family, pacing Akeepee in the evening; a man contemptuously indifferent to the craze for gold, the mad dreams of the riches and fame it might bring. The other sat alone in his office by night, his topographical maps and geological reports spread out on the drafting board, fingering a piece of ore. No one could have discerned if and where the two men fused. Yet at that contact between the logical, analytical man of his time, and that tormented spirit which knew no turning of the road to what he sought, but only the enigma formless and timeless that towered above him, might have been glimpsed the disturbing image at the end of his quest.

There was no hurry, none at all. He was as set to his course as a ship with rudder and sails lashed tight, waiting for the tide. Cripple Creek was having its share of labor troubles. Coxey's army was marching on Washington and 300 men from Cripple Creek commandeered a locomotive and a string of railroad cars to join them. The Strong Mine, just west of the Independence, was blown up. Fights and riots, and then a general strike called up the state militia.

Despite the strike — by which the miners won an eight-hour day — the production of the $200,000 Cow Pasture increased to $2,010,400 for the year, with the unheard-of average of more than three ounces of gold in every ton of rock shipped. Two railroads raced into Cripple Creek: the Midland Terminal connecting with the Colorado Midland at Divide to the north and the Florence and Cripple Creek connecting with the Denver and Rio Grande at Canyon City to the south. Dozens of mining companies were renting offices on Tejon Street in Little London. Every real-estator and land agent in town turned himself into a mining broker, and with hundreds of speculators and promoters stood along the sunny curbs of Pike's Peak Avenue in front of Rogier's office selling shares. The first thirty thousand shares of Virginia M were offered at ten cents each and sold out within an hour, Ona and Rogier hearing through the window the shouted announcement that the certificates hadn't been printed yet but would be as soon as possible. And men other than brokers swayed the price of shares as with a single wave of their hands, the stock of the Mutual instantly jumping from ten to twenty cents with the announcement that the noted wizard, Professor Kimball, had located the ore body. All day long Rogier and Ona were pestered with offerings until Rogier slammed the door behind a salesman and turned the key in the lock.

"But Daddy!" remonstrated Ona. "That was a nice young man with Anaconda stock. Yesterday when he came it was only a dime. Today it was thirty cents. Why — "

"Nonsense! Paper profits!" interrupted Rogier. "Keep those men out of here, Ona, or I'll throw you down the stairs with the next one who comes in here with a gold certificate!"

Shortly a Board of Trade and Colorado Springs Mining Stock Exchange was formed, with offices in his block, and was soon trading more shares than any other mining exchange in the world. This was more than Rogier could stand. "Ona, I won't have this business going on under my nose. If a man can't sit in peace in his own office he'd better get out!" He jammed his hat on his head and strutted out.

Ona sat staring at the closed door in shocked amazement; she had never known her father to betray such angry annoyance.

Rogier was as good as his word. Moving all his running horses to Denman's, he brought home a crew to wreck their stalls and build a huge two-story wooden shop in the barnyard. The upper story, with wide swing doors opening in back, was a loft for storing and seasoning green timber for use on his building jobs. The lower story, also one great room, served as a shop for his carpenters and cabinet makers. Along one side extended a work bench fitted with vises of all sizes, and supplemented with cabinets and racks to hold a vast collection of tools of all kinds. The north end, facing the house, he fitted up without a partition as his own office. The whole front was inset with glass panes slanted so there would be no glare. In front of this from wall to wall he constructed a high drafting table fully equipped with drawing boards, triangles, T-squares, scales, pencil racks, and blueprint cabinets. To the right were built his book-shelves, with a wood-stove near the corner for heat. Here was everything he needed: winches, reels, and concrete mixers stored under the wagon shed in the yard outside, spare lumber in the loft above, room for his carpenters and cabinet makers to work at the bench and a draftsman at the drafting table — and in the corner, close to his voluminous library, a private retreat where at night, undisturbed by the world outside, he could study his ore speci-mens, topographical maps, and geological reports of Pike's

Peak.

On the morning it was ready he went uptown to his office to make sure Ona knew how to instruct the packers and movers when they arrived. In silence he surveyed the room he had occupied for twenty years. From the window he had watched a frontier settlement grow into the famous Saratoga of the West with building after building of his own: Cutler Hall of The Colorado College, the Colorado Deaf and Blind School, the Elk Hotel, the downtown Gazette and Durkee buildings, churches, every school, houses galore. Down the wide, dirt avenue below he had watched covered wagons gathering to make up the trains which had crawled up Ute Pass on their way to Leadville. Here Sister Molly had come to him with a bunch of bluebells and worry about Tom; in the same chair, long afterward, Tom had sat in sullen defiance breathing whiskey fumes before vanishing forever from their sight. He remembered the boy Boné, white and shaking, but refusing obstinately to return to school; Mrs. White stopping by from Haekel's Boarding House; Bob coming to pay token installments on the Pest House; his own children playing with his pencils at the drafting board. This was the room in which he had heard the news of the Mount Pisgah Fiasco; the office young Stratton had given up to participate in the Yreteba Silver Lode bust, and to which he had returned seventeen years later with news of his discovery on Pike's Peak of the most fabulous gold mine in America. From his methodical, dedicated, simple work here he had fed a nest of hungry mouths — Martha and their three girls, Molly and Tom and their two boys, Mrs. White and Boné, to say nothing of Lida Peck, Lily Force, and his crews of workmen. A hundred trivial incidents leaped at him from the room, all impregnated with the smell of his innumerable cigars and with the one cloying dream that had held him there by night. To move away was like closing a door of his life behind him.

"Don't you hate to leave, Daddy, you've been here so long?" asked Ona.

"Places wear out like old clothes!" he answered brusquely. "Now be sure and have those movers pack those books carefully. I've had to send to Europe and India for some of them. Hear?"

"Daddy?"

"Yes?"

"Maybe I oughtn't to tell you now, but have you heard who's taking over your lease on this office? It's Mr. Stratton."

Rogier carefully bit the end off a cigar and lit it. "Sentimental nonsense, Ona! Haven't I just told you a man can't go back to old clothes he's outworn!" He turned on his heel and left without a backward look.

That night after everything had been unpacked and arranged to his satisfaction, Rogier settled down in what thereafter the family called "The Shop." It was indeed a workshop, an office, a *sanctum sanctorum*. But it was more than that. It was the cabin of a sea captain who from the charts on its wall piloted the course of his ship through an unknown sea. It was the tent of an army commander who laid out the strategy and tactics of a battle that was to be joined on a 10,000-foot-high field of a cloth of gold. And it was the dark interior of an unknown continent in which no explorer could find a trail marked by the milestones of the past. It was only by facing the infinite emptiness of the heavens above, and pinning his unshaken trust to that one star which in his despairing solitude he had chosen as his own, that a man could lay his path toward the destiny which was his alone. There could be no turning. And though he chose a star which glimmered and was gone, if it be lost behind the peak which undid his strength, still it remained for him to know that he had done what he had done — that his star had gleamed and faded, and rest in peace.

The lights in the house went out. Still Rogier sat there unstirring, staring at that massive granite-clothed adversary taking his measure in the darkness by timeless time. At last, curiously light-headed, he blew out the lamp and went in to bed.

4

Hiney, ever since he had moved to Denver, came down occasionally to favor the family with his engaging presence. A tall, handsome Beau Brummel, he dressed nattily, spoke largely, and always carried crumbs of Sen-Sen in his pocket. In addition to moving stage props behind the curtain in the theater, it was understood that on due occasions he performed in front of it. His talents were many. He could mimic any noted actor, keep three balls in the air with one hand, and in the bathroom sang "She's Only a Bird in a Gilded Cage" to everyone's delight. Also in front of Nigger Bill, Rogier's stableman, he could dance with abandon — tap, soft shoe, and buck-and-wing. There was an air about him no one could deny.

He was a great favorite with Mary Ann, of course. In her teens and crazy after boys, she had learned how to overcome Mrs. Rogier's objections to her preposterous behavior. She had only to mention that a particular young man was a close friend of the well-known So-and-so in the North End, to secure permission to walk with him to church and to sit with him in the parlor that night till Mrs. Rogier's cough sounded from the head of the steps at ten o'clock. To the boys she alluded casually to "Colonel" Rogier, vaguely of a gold mine that was soon to erupt a fortune into the family's lap, and more specifically of cold chicken and a surreptitious drink of sherry after the family had gone to bed.

Ona could hardly blame either her or Sally Lee for catching at any straw that floated past the somber house on Shook's Run. They had been reared in that creaking structure as if it had been a house of glass through which any North Ender could observe their every move. Mrs. Rogier had watched over them like a hawk. There was no playing with ambiguous children down along the creek. They were too dirty, too illiterate, or just too "common" for a Rogier to be contaminated by their mere human frailities. Just what being a Rogier implied the girls never found out. It always enveloped them in a mysterious aura which they hardly dared to disturb with even a sudden sneeze. Restrained from participating in most school parties, they acted self-consciously their roles of lonely and miserable but perfect little snobs. Sometime the world would unfold to them like a flower, ripen into a fruit to be plucked only by her who was a Rogier and could prove it to high heaven with a pair of twin toes.

It seemed quite natural to Mary Ann then, giddy as she was, that Hiney wanted her to visit him for a few days. She was to come right away, tomorrow! His letter she did not read. It had been addressed to Rogier, as a matter of fact; but as he was up at Cripple Creek it had seemed appropriate for Mrs. Rogier and Ona to open it. The message was brief. Hiney was in trouble. He asked Rogier to send him a bank draft immediately, not by mail but by Mary Ann, in a sealed envelope. The two women debated the mystery at length. Mrs. Rogier was not one to send an innocent girl alone on her first train trip to a large city; Rogier could settle the matter when he returned.

"But Mother, Hiney can't wait. He's in trouble!" argued Ona.

"We have no money," wailed Mrs. Rogier.

"Get her ready," said Ona decisively. "I attend to Daddy's payroll and I'll make out the draft."

The next morning after breakfast Mrs. Rogier checked the contents of Mary Ann's suitcase, looked her over carefully to see that even her handkerchief was folded in place, and then mysteriously crooked her finger as she went upstairs. Mary Ann followed her into the bathroom and watched her mother lock the door.

Whenever Mrs. Rogier desired to lecture or impart important news to any member of the family, it was the bathroom that offered sanctuary. These "bathroom talks" were an institution holy and ceremonious as a talk with the pastor of the church or a meeting of a board of directors, and one emerged from them an enlightened and chastened spirit. Finally the door was unlocked and Mary Ann came out, a sealed envelope pinned to her underwear, like a messenger entrusted with all the secrets of state. Ona took her to the depot and put her on the train.

Had Mary Ann's been a mature mind able to look back through Hiney's life to his childhood fall from a horse, her reflections would have overshadowed every mile of the journey to Denver. But she had never heard of his queer lapses of memory, and was as blissfully ignorant of his last escapade as the rest of the family.

It had happened a couple of years before. Hiney and several of his cronies had emerged one night from the bar next to the Opera House. Strutting under silk top hats and holding themselves up with light Malacca canes, they hailed a cab. They were all quite drunk.

As he stepped into the cab, Hiney felt the thing happen as it had happened a dozen times before. His life, his whole past, seemed instantly obliterated. Sometimes a drink seemed to do the trick, a sudden jar, or more often nothing. It was as if an unseen hand reached into his head and jerked the switch that controlled his memory. He would find himself on a street car, in a barber's chair, or walking down a street not knowing who he was or where he was going. There was nothing to do but slink into a hotel and wait until time and mind again began to tick within him.

Now, adjusting the silk muffler around his throat, he hic-coughed and looked at the faces of his companions as if he had never seen them before. Beyond Hop Alley the cab drew up with a sudden halt as one of the men yelled and opened the door. A woman was crossing the road under the arc-light with a big bundle of washing. The men gathered around her, arguing who should carry the bundle home for her. The lot fell to Hiney. Heaving the bundle to his shoulder and leading the washwoman by the hand, Hiney set off with his companions shouting and trouping behind. Like a decrepit hearse the cab brought up the rear, the horse's hoofs breaking the spasmodic silence with steady clicks.

The woman lived in a wooden shack overflowing with children.

Once the lamp was lit, the gentlemen, hearts touched by the squalor, began another argument. Which one of them would oblige and become the widow washwomen's husband?" "Wantcher sh'd marry the lady?" queried Hiney, wavering on his long thin legs. "Sure, b'glad to!"

His companions howled approbation. "A perfect gemmleman — s'wat ch'ar Hiney!" The lady, nothing loath to secure a husband in a silk top-hat at a moment's notice in the dead of night, agreed heartily. The cab was dispatched for a preacher as fast as the horse could travel. In an hour Hiney was a married man. He was almost out; the men laid him on the bed with two small children, covering that miraculously grown family with a rag rug. It had been a perfect evening and they left singing an imperfect bridal chorus.

After spending two days in his bride's shack Hiney's memory returned. Neither he nor his companions had a single doubt that the marriage would be annulled the minute Hiney raised enough money to pay a lawyer's fee. The annulment was refused. Hiney was horrified. The girl Margaret who had got him out of jail after the Brown Palace episode was heartbroken; they had been planning to get married.

The washwoman was one of those queer oddities of human nature that could not be explained. Despite two grown sons who never worked and a small girl, she had a mania for adopting babies. When they had grown to be seven or eight years old she left them at an orphan's home or thrust them out upon the street. There were always two or three new ones in the squalorous shanty and for them she washed late into the nights. She was obdurate to Hiney's appeals for a divorce and had taken a six months' old baby to court, swearing that Hiney was its father and insisting on his support. She got it. For two years Hiney lived in a hell of despair, moving from one rooming house to another as fast as the family or the court learned his whereabouts. The woman's two grown sons followed him relentlessly. It took all the money Hiney earned to satisfy their insatiable demands. One night when he came home from his work at the theater he found that they had broken into his room. The next morning, after talking with Margaret, he had sent a letter home asking for a bank draft and Mary Ann.

This was the Beau Brummel Hiney with Sen-Sen in his pockets and "She Was Only a Bird in a Gilded Cage" on his lips Mary Ann was on her way to visit.

When she got off the train Hiney was not waiting on the platform. Instead, a woman came up to her smiling, and placing an arm across her shoulders, said, "I just know you're Mary Ann! My name's Margaret and I'm a friend of Hiney's. He's waiting for us across town."

Taking a street car, they rode to an ugly little street and went in an ugly little house. On the top floor Margaret got out a key and unlocked a door. The room was ugly too: it had a chipped iron bed and old dresser, even a hole in a threadbare carpet. "I've got to hurry to work now, but Hiney will be here in fifteen minutes," Margaret told her. "Tonight we're all going to the Opera House and eat supper in a fine restaurant. You're a big girl. You'll understand what Hiney tells you, I can see that. You're not afraid to wait here a little bit, are you?"

Mary Ann rubbed her new shoes together and nodded; a lump in her throat prevented her from speaking. For an hour after Margaret had gone she sat stiffly on the bed, thinking of the pretty dresses in her suitcase, listening for steps coming up the dark stairway, for a voice to tell her she was dreaming a tawdry dream.

At last it came: the clatter of a key in the lock, the bang of the opened door. It was Hiney all right — all dressed up like a Thanksgiving turkey, with a wide grin and a red flower in his buttonhole. "How-d'doodle!" he yelled, jumping on the bed to kiss her. Mary Ann felt better. They talked about the family, then she asked about Margaret and why they were here instead of in a nice big hotel like she expected. Hiney rose to draw down the window shades a bit more. Then suddenly he jumped up in the air and clicked the heels of his yellow shoes together three times before landing. It was a trick he had learned from actors in the theater, he said laughing fit to kill.

"You didn't think I lived in this dirty old house, did you? With this raggedy old carpet? Land sakes alive — look here!" He yanked open all the drawers in the tarnished dresser. "Empty, every one of them! Why? Because we're going to act parts in a mystery play all the time you're here. What do you think of that?" He paused dramatically. "No use of your coming up here just to sit and talk. That would be dull as Little London! The fun of it's the mystery. You can't ask questions. Just play your part."

"But what do I have to do, Hiney?"

"Practically nothing," he assured her, pulling a key out of his pocket with a tag on which was written the address of the rooming house they sat in. "Just suppose we're walking down the street and all of a sudden I run off and leave you. Or something like that. You just take this key, ask a man what streetcar to take and the conductor to let you off. Then you come here and unlock the door."

"What'll I do then?"

Hiney was suddenly very serious. "You brought something for me?"

"It's in an envelope pinned to my underwear, Hiney."

"The bathroom's down the hall. Take it out and bring it back to me."

When she came back he locked the door behind her and put his finger to his lips. "Here's the big secret!" He pulled back the covers on the bed, lifted the mattress. Underneath was a fat manilla envelope to which he added the envelope Mary Ann had brought. "Probably I won't ever come here again. But one of these times, when Margaret or I send you, you come here the way I told you and bring back these envelopes, both of them. Understand?" His face set in a hard gray mask as his eyes bored into her. "You'll remember? Don't say a word to anyone about it. And don't lose that key!"

Mary Ann was suddenly frightened. "It's all too mysterious and scary, Hiney. I brought my Sunday dress and new shoes, and I'd rather go to the Opera House and eat supper at a restaurant and all that."

Immediately he put his arms around her. "You little goose! Afraid to have a single adventure without Ona holding you by the hand!"

"I'm not either, Hiney!"

Lying on the bed together, they talked about Akeepee and the gold mine Rogier was going to find while Hiney blew smoke rings from his cigarette. Then the room began to get dark and it was time to go after Margaret.

All her life Mary Ann was to remember every detail of her strange visit to Hiney. The first night was a glorious celebration of her arrival. They had supper in the Manhattan Restaurant on Larimer Street where Hiney ordered her a lobster which she had never tasted before and everything else she wanted. Margaret was dressed up her prettiest in white, wearing long amethyst earrings, watching every man who came in through the frosted glass doors. "I wonder if we've been wise to come here tonight," she asked quietly. Hiney patted her hand. "Of course. They'd never expect me here of all places. And we may never see it again."

In the Tabor Grand afterward they sat way back in a box where Hiney could tell Mary Ann about the actors and actresses, all of whom he knew by their first names. Walking out, Hiney stopped short as if he saw a ghost in the lobby. Immediately they turned around, going backstage where he introduced Mary Ann to the actors in their dressing rooms. Then they slipped out into the alley and up the street to Mary Ann's hotel room. It was a wonderful room with pictures of stage people, wine lists and menus tacked on the walls. Hiney's clothes were in it, but a few minutes after Margaret left he went to sleep somewhere else. It was a glorious nght, but it was not repeated.

The following two nights Hiney put her in different hotels as Margaret insisted. "I wish I could have her with me, but we can't take chances," she told Hiney. "We've got to make it Saturday morning."

In the daytime Hiney took her to a matinee or out to the park, or Margaret to stores and museums. But never together. And each one of them was always nervously watching everyone around them. The nights alone made her nervous too. She thought longingly of her bed at home. The squeaky steps of the Kadles would never seem mysterious after Hiney's and Margaret's queer behavior: taking her to a different hotel every night and suddenly leaving her as they walked along the street, only to show up later without a word.

Mary Ann was relieved when on Saturday morning Hiney took her to the depot. He carried two suitcases besides her own. It was long before train time, but he was on pins and needles and kept looking at his watch so often Mary Ann was afraid he'd wear it out. At last a woman in a big hat and veil sat down beside them. Hiney without a word got up and left.

"Don't be nervous and don't turn around," the woman said after a time, raising her veil a trifle. Mary Ann recognized Margaret's voice. "That big man in a derby hat is looking for Hiney," she went on. "Now do just as I say. Ride on the street car to that rooming house I first took you to. Remember the big secret? You have the key to the room. Get the envelopes under the mattress and hurry back. If we don't happen to be here, take the train and give the envelopes to your father at home. Are you sure you understand? Sure, Mary Ann? Now get up and buy a package of chewing gum. And then walk out very slowly. And don't say a word to anyone till you get back. Go on now, dear!"

Mary Ann did as she was told. On the street car she sat looking from the tag on her key to every street she passed. She had not returned to that tawdry rooming house since, and was afraid she had taken the wrong car. Finally the conductor called out the street. A few doors from the corner she recognized the house. Running up the stairs she opened the door to the barren room. Queerly frightened, she lifted the mattress, took out the fat and slim manilla envelopes, and hid them in her dress. Then she ran out of the room and down the steps.

On the street car a new fear attacked her — Hiney and Margaret wouldn't be at the depot and her train would go off without her. When she arrived in the big waiting room, a man was calling out her train and Margaret was standing at the gate. "Did you get it?" she asked anxiously.

"Yes," said Mary Ann, pulling the envelopes out from her bosom and giving them to her.

Margaret let out a sigh. "Oh, if Hiney only comes in time!"

A minute later he sauntered up. His sleeve was torn and he had a bruise on his cheek, but he was grinning like a cat. "How do you do, folks! Taking a little train ride this morning?"

"Thank God!" breathed Margaret. "Mary Ann got the money and the papers. How lucky you showed her where they were. Neither one of us could have got back for them."

The conductor was yelling "All aboard!" now. Hiney and Margaret took her to the train and boosted her suitcase to the vestibule, but they kept standing there with the other suitcases Hiney had brought. He kissed her. "Remember me, Mary Ann. I'll thank you all my life. And give this letter to your father. He'll understand."

There were tears in Margaret's eyes as she kissed her too. "I love you too, Mary Ann. Almost as much as Hiney."

As the train pulled out Mary Ann could see them crossing the platform to another train. Where it went she never knew.

5

Hiney's strange disappearance or elopement with Margaret was a mystery to the family, compounded by Mary Ann's exorbitant and melodramatic tales. Still he was one of the family even if he were a little strange, and Ona missed him. Not as much as she missed Boné who had gone to San Francisco with Lockhardt. She thought of Lockhardt impeccably dressed in his white shirt and dark worsted jacket, the yellow candlelight striking white fire from the big diamond on his finger as he pounded the piano keys so forcibly that it set atremble the tumbler of whisky above his bent head. Now he had left Indian Country despite his health, as he had to; for in the end we reject everything we are unsuited to assimilate, however much we may admire it. Back to sit at his Baby Grand, looking down at the misty gray bay, eating the best euisine of every race in the world, and attending operas and symphonies. But what was Boné doing with him? Writing music that Lockhardt was going to have published. Still Ona worried about him as she did not worry about Hiney.

Rooted in the passionless stability of the big house and the irritating confusion of Rogier's business records, Ona often looked back with nostalgia to her stay on the Reservation. Shadows of clouds in the sunshine, distant jutting mesas flaming red at dawn, dark faces and soft voices, the sound of drums across the San Juan — it all came back to her with that remote and inconsequential trading post maintained in austere dignity by Bruce and the Vrain Girls.

She was reminded of it, curiously, by her first sight of the family's new roomer. Or rather Sally Lee's, for she had persuaded Rogier to let her rent her room when he had refused to increase her allowance. The new roomer had moved in last night, and Mrs. Rogier had invited him for supper this evening. Both Sally Lee and Mary Ann were in the kitchen helping Lida when Ona came in from the shop. In the dining room they had set the table, lit candles and lamps. How exciting it was! A new man in the house! Ona walked on out to the front porch and sat down beside ailing Mrs. White.

"Has the roomer come home yet?" she asked.

"Reckon not or Marthy would be buzzin' around him like a fly over a sorghum barrel."

"You don't like him?"

"Humph. One look was enough to tell me he's a Jew or a foreigner of some kind. Different."

In a few moments Mrs. Rogier came out and seated herself primly. "I do hope Mr. Cable comes soon and that Daddy's not late again. Baked ham dries out fast, and I allowed Lida to use brandy in the cider."

The sun had dropped behind Pike's Peak and dusk was blurring the branches of the lilac. Down along Shook's Run the crickets were beginning a faint but strident chorus only to be interrupted by the sound of soft footsteps coming down the walk. "Here he comes," murmured Mrs. Rogier.

Ona turned her head to see the figure of Jonathan Cable turning in the yard. What struck her immediately, before she could clearly distinguish his face, was the sinuous litheness of his walk. An inch under six feet, his slender body gave out the impression of a soft sensuousness wrapped in iron nerves. Before she could rise, his foot was on the step and she was looking up at a pair of large brown eyes and an arching Roman nose set into a high-cheekboned swarthy face.

For fifteen minutes Mrs. Rogier kept him on the porch. She had put on her Sunday dress of gray and black and chatted aimlessly. Cable was pleasant but silent, and Ona was relieved when they went in to table. In the light she was impressed by the red-brown color of his face, a swarthiness deeper than weather exposure. Even his wrists showed an even sepia whenever his starched white cuffs crawled up his coat sleeves. From his big nose one might admit Mrs. White's implication of Jewish blood. But to Ona his hair, every separate strand, gave him away. It was Indian, straight and black, without kink or sheen, as heavy and coarse as a horse's mane.

Rogier strode in and sat down. "Hello Cable! How did the first night go in your new room?"

"It's going to be fine, I'm sure," replied Cable cheerfully.

"I just wondered if the Kadles walking around all night kept you awake." Rogier grinned at the girls, avoiding Mrs. Rogier's face.

"I did hear someone walking up and down the stairs. I hope none of you was sick." He looked from face to face as a restrained titter ran around the table.

"No indeed," went on Rogier, ignoring Mrs. Rogier's pinch under the table. "It was just a couple of white-bearded old fellows who have been dead for fifteen years or so, but who had to investigate the new occupant of your room. The girls will tell you about them. They're old friends by now."

Cable's face had set darkly as if he were being made fun of, but with the girls' giggling explanations he grinned humorously.

"And how was Little Man, Daddy?" asked Mrs. Rogier, watching him slice the ham. "Do you think he'll ever beat his mother's time of — wasn't it three minutes?"

"Three minutes!" ejaculated Sally Lee with horrified amazement. "Why, Akeepee could pull that old lumber wagon of Daddy's around the track in less than three minutes! Two-sixteen for the mile is more like it!"

Mrs. Rogier smiled apologetically at Cable. "We have so many lovely race horses I just can't remember all the times they make."

"Maybe you can give me some information about Cripple Creek, Mr. Rogier?" asked Cable. "I hear you're a mine owner."

"I'm not," Rogier answered curtly," but tomorrow I'll give you what information I have. Is that what brought you here?"

"I've got a third interest in a claim on Big Bull."

Mary Ann exploded a giggle into her napkin.

"Mary Ann! The very idea! Get up this minute!" ordered Mrs. Rogier.

Mary Ann, shamefacedly rising, confessed the plausible cause of her guilt. "The very minute Mr. Cable mentioned Bull Hill, why Bull Hill pinched me on the leg!" She stooped and lifted up a puppy.

"Well, you just take him out of here and don't come back till you can sit up in your chair quiet like a lady!" Turning to Cable, Mrs. Rogier explained with profuse apologies. "You see, Daddy found that little puppy near Bull Hill and brought him home. That's why we named him Bull Hill. Once Daddy brought the children down a fawn — when everybody had a pet fawn in the yard."

Rogier interrupted. "Big Bull and Bull Hill aren't the same at all. I can't say I'm too impressed with the showings around you, Cable, however highly they're touted. But I'm no mining man."

Cable spread his hands and smiled. "The claim's only a ten-foot hole yet. I hope there's something in it or I'll be stone broke."

The almost childish simplicity and outspoken honesty of this dark and stern looking man nonplussed every Rogier around the table, yet instantly drew them to him.

"You have no experience in mining?" asked Rogier with a sympathetic grin.

"None. A bit of Indian blood has always kept me out on the long grass plains and prairies. I know nothing about these mountains."

This confirmation of her intuition aroused in Ona a quick glow of satisfaction. It was broken by Mrs. White who flung down her napkin and pushed back her chair.

"Mother! Wait for dessert," remonstrated Mrs. Rogier. "It's tapioca and pineapple with whipped cream."

"It's always tapioca!" With a sharp look at Cable, she left the room.

The two men, with Ona listening beside them, continued to sit over their coffee long after the others had left the table. Mrs. Rogier, peering from the china closet, was infuriated by the sight of Rogier, left arm resting on the table where he had pushed back his dishes, calmly smoking his cigar, and holding Cable like a fly in a web. Mining was all very well if it would bring a gold mine into the family, but to hear talk of it night and day, at every meal, was more than she could stand.

In a few minutes Ona silently left the two men and went out on the porch. Cable's glance followed her as she left the room, and after awhile he followed her. In the darkness her white dress was a pale splotch on the front steps. The scratch of a match and its quick yellow flare illumining his face as he lit his pipe aroused her. "Oh, hello. Sit down if you want to."

"Don't you want me to bring you a wrap? This mountain air gets cold the minute the sun goes down. Maybe I should have said 'fetch'. All the family says that."

Ona laughed. "Well, go fetch my scarf then if that makes you feel better!" How observant and sensitive was this man who looked so sharp and stubborn!

Cable returned, sprawling down on the steps beside her.

"What do you think of our town by now?" she asked.

Cable inclined his head toward the pale splotch of Pike's Peak's snowy cone against the sky. "Can't get used to these mountains sticking up like a wall. I like open country. Prairie country with the grass bending in the wind as far as you can see. Makes me feel free."

How much Indian blood he had, what tribe it had come from, and how, he did not say. But it was there: in his appearance, his small feet which she now noticed for the first time, his reactions — and his reticence. He had been born in a large family which lived on a wooded quarter-section of land on the Iowa-Missouri border. Poor farmers, none of them had obtained much of an education. Cable had made the most of his opportunities in the small village nearby. Beginning work after school as a printer's devil on the weekly newspaper, he had learned with stubborn thoroughness to set type, write simple accounts of the happenings for miles around, and to balance the books — a literacy, interest in people, and rudimentary business education he could not have obtained had he remained in school. When his step-father died Cable struck out on his own, falling in with an Indian trader on the Great Plains. Here he came into his own. Chivington's massacre had broken the power of the two tribes which had claimed by right of treaty most of the plains west of the Rockies. Sent to a Reservation in Oklahoma, bands of them still kept coming back to hunt, trade, and conduct their ceremonies — the same bands, thought Ona, that she had seen as a child. From the trader, Cable learned to speak Cheyenne fluently and Arapaho haltingly, and often stayed in their encampment of tepees. If something in his nature rose up to meet them, it also set him apart from the increasing settlers and homesteaders who still held that the only good Indian was a dead Indian. As the bands stopped coming, Cable and a man named Grimes opened a general merchandising store on the Colorado-Kansas line. It was here that the Cripple Creek tide had caught him up. Grimes' brother had staked a claim on Big Bull, but needed a stake to develop it. So Cable and his partner had sold their store and come to work the mine with him.

"It looks like mining will be an expensive business," ended Cable. "We're thinking of opening a store here in town so we can take turns running it while the other two work the mine."

"What kind of a store?" asked Ona.

"My partners want a men's clothing store."

Ona could not imagine Cable selling neckties behind a counter. "Well, Little London's an unusual town. You should learn what it's like before you make up your mind."

Cable puffed silently at his pipe before answering. "I wonder — if I get a horse and rig from uptown will you drive around with me sometime?"

"Some afternoon when I don't have too much work I will." In the darkness she smiled. With a stable of horses out at Denman's, she was going in a rented rig. What would her mother think of that?

As she went upstairs to bed, she met Mrs. White in the hall wearing a sulky frown. "What's the trouble?" Ona asked.

"A red niggah in the house!"

Ona shrugged and went into her room. How old and cantankerous her grandmother was getting!

A few days later Ona went on a drive with Cable. She enjoyed it; she had not realized how Little London had blossomed under the influx of Cripple Creek gold. The electric street cars which had replaced the horse cars ran in all directions and were crowded with people. "Fifteen thousand people in town now," Ona told him "and three railroad lines bringing more every day. The widest streets of any town in the country. Here. Turn up Cascade." The wide avenue was lovely, lined with shade trees on each side, and another double line flanking the bridle path in the center. Big brownstone houses stood on each side, set back in wide lawns smooth as velvet. A block west, beginning at the campus of The Colorado College and running north, ran Millionaires' Row.

"It's called that because here's where all the Cripple Creek millionaires are building their mansions. Its real name is Wood Avenue. I suppose it's named for somebody in the Woods family — the three Woods brothers who've got control of about sixty mines in the district, established the town of Victor, and now are building a big hotel in the middle of it. Now stop a minute!" Cable obediently pulled back his reins. "Here you are," went on Ona. "The show-place of all the mansions: 1315 Wood Avenue. That's all you have to say in town. Everybody knows it belongs to James Burns the plumber, one of the three men who discovered the Portland, the Queen of the district, just above the Independence, the King. Stratton helped them settle twenty-seven lawsuits and consolidated all the thirty-seven mines into one company. Lordy knows how many millions it'll produce!"

"I don't know that a big mansion like this can come out of the little hole we've got," said Cable dubiously, turning back.

Ona laughed. "You can see how foolish Mother is for wanting a house up here in the North End. Poor thing! She just doesn't realize how much money it would cost. So we just let her talk."

They drove west to the mesa and up to the mouth of Queen's Canyon where Ona pointed out the solitary munificence of Palmer's castle, Glen Eyrie. "General Palmer, the one who founded Little London and built the Denver and Rio Grande Railroad. Just to show you a man can become rich on something besides Cripple Creek gold. But nobody envies him. His wife left him and he lives there all alone — always riding around on his horse in an English tweed jacket and boots. A stone man on a stone horse."

Cable and his two partners found a likely space on Tejon Street for their new store, which Cable showed to Ona. The location, she thought, was good; but the narrow room seemed too small, squeezed between two office buildings. Nevertheless Cable, with the help of two carpenters, was busy at work putting up a partition between a salesroom and a storeroom. Often after work in the late fall afternoons he took Ona for more drives.

One afternoon they drove to the lower slopes of Cheyenne Mountain southwest of town. Here in front of Cheyenne Lake rose an elegantly beautiful, three-storied building with long verandas flanked by gracious white pillars. "The Broadmoore Casino!" explained Ona proudly. "Built by Count Pourtales of Prussia. They say the dining rooms are elegant and the French chef who prepares the meals was brought from Delmonico's in New York. I've seen Rosner's Band which plays there. Hungarians and Austrians dressed up in gorgeous uniforms — white trousers and blue coats trimmed with gold. Up till a few years ago one out of every ten people here was a Britisher. But now Little London's becoming a cosmopolitan spa, the Saratoga of the West, with Cripple Creek just around the corner!"

"And a mile straight up!" Cable reminded her, glancing up at the wall of mountains rising above them.

How pleasant it was to drive in a rented rig with this dark, silent, and unaffected man. Over to the mineral springs in Manitou, through the queerly eroded red sandstone and white limestone area known as the Garden of the Gods, and up North and South Cheyenne Canyon along winding carriage roads beside tumbling white-water streams.

Early in December, Cable showed Ona the new haberdashery shop. The partition between storeroom and salesroom had been erected. Furnishings and display cases had been installed and sales goods were coming in.

"We've opened the New Moon in Cripple Creek," he explained. "It's not much shakes as a curb mine and our stake is exhausted. But its first showings are good. Let's hope the shop will carry the mine through the winter."

Then, without telling Ona where he was going, he swung over the mesa to the encampment of the Utes who were still permitted to pitch their lodges here for a few months each year. Leaving the rig, they walked slowly into the ring of smoke-gray tepees. How tawdry it seemed after Glen Eyrie, the Broadmoore Casino, and Burns' mansion. Old men with faces of dark wrinkled leather were squatting silently in front of their lodges. Half-naked children crawled about in the dirt. Boys were trying to mount shaggy, broomtailed ponies and being pitched to the ground. An old woman was hacking at a fresh red carcass covered with flies. The whole place seemed permeated with a smell compounded of smoke, refuse, and urine-soaked earth.

Cable seemed not to mind at all. In his derby hat and halfboots, always carefully polished although he sometimes neglected his well-worn suit, he was walking down the lanes thoroughly enjoying himself. Abruptly he halted. An old Ute woman with a maimed arm had burst out of a tepee rubbing the tears out of her smoke-filled eyes. Cable, without a word, walked around to the side. Ona was casually familiar with these lodges or tepees, simply skins stretched over a conical framework of poles with an opening at the high, pointed apex for the smoke to escape. She had never noticed on the outside an inclined pole attached at the top to a protruding, triangular wing or fin. As she watched him, Cable jerked loose the bottom end of the pole imbedded in the ground and moved it several feet around the circular edge. As he did so, the triangular wing swung with him like a rudder. For a moment he stood looking up at it, testing the wind. Then he imbedded the end of the pole firmly in the ground again.

The actions of this white man in a derby and shined boots drew the lounging Utes around him. Cable got up, dusted his knees, and looked through the doorway. Ona and the old woman peeked in beside him. The smoke from the open fire was rising in an unbroken column through the opening at the top. All the Utes were now jabbering and gesticulating, talking to Cable. Unable to understand them, he simply grinned and with the forefinger and middle finger of his right hand made the rapid gesture of slashing the inside of his left wrist. The old men's leathery faces broke into grins of surprise and approbation. The woman patted him with her maimed arm.

In a few minutes Cable took Ona by the arm and they walked back to the rig. "That dew-flap had to be adjusted to catch the draft," he said casually.

"What did that funny movement of your hand mean?"

"Oh, just Cheyenne in sign language."

His casual, terse comments, the whole incident, momentarily

confused her. She had got so used to him she had forgotten how different he was. And now suddenly he had slipped away from her, like a cake of soap, into a different world.

"You know, I don't think I'd mention to grandmother tonight that we drove out to see those Utes. She — "

Instantly she wished she'd bitten off her tongue instead. But Cable did not reply. As they drove into town he said quietly, "I'm leaving for the mountains tomorrow. I've been lucky, staying here to work on the shop so long. But now it's my turn to work in the mine for awhile."

"Be sure to come down for Christmas," replied Ona warmly. "There'll be room for you here, though not for the Grimes."

Cable, a few weeks before, had brought his two partners to meet the family. They were big men, gruff and hearty and good-natured, but somehow they did not seem to fit into the household. Although neither requested it, Ona rather suspected that they wanted to occupy Cable's room during their turns of work in Little London. Logical as was her assumption, Mrs. Rogier scotched the idea the minute they walked out the door. "I do hope they don't think we're running a boarding house for every Tom, Dick, and Harry. Jonathan is all right, but — "

"No, of course," answered Cable. "As a matter of fact they have a good friend in Colorado City who's going to bunk them whenever they're in town. I'm the lucky one. Both your mother and Sally Lee said they'd save my room so I'd have a place to come back to anytime."

Ona felt relieved, a little glad really.

6

Two miles above tidewater in its amphitheater of innumerable hills, Cripple Creek blinked through the snow-flecked dusk of a late December storm.

Since early morning the gaunt ridges had lain beclouded in gloom as if the wind had snuffed out the lighted taper behind the leaden skies. Dropping heavily, filling the canyons with a warm wet mist, and trailing albuminous streamers through the somber pine slopes, the clouds just past noon had snagged upon the rocks. At first slowly fluttering to earth like the feathers of a wild goose, the snow fell faster until the skies were driving white. The dark forested ridges, the bare mountain tops were enwrapped steadily until all the hills were as anonymous as a group of women in white furs. And still the storm rushed slantwise, smothering the earth with snow. Seen from one of the hills at dusk the yellow lights along Bennett Avenue looked like a row of portholes in a ship laboring through a heavy sea. The whole town wallowed in a trough of drifts. For a moment the storm subsided, and the windows of Becker and Nolan's, the Gold Dollar, and other saloons glowed steamy yellow behind the frosted spume sticking to the panes. Then the wind began again, and like a ship resuming its crawl between the foamy crests of two waves, the town appeared to move forward through its white drifts as if uneasy of coming to grief on Pike's Peak's granite reefs.

Near ten o'clock the wind let up. Within an hour the skies were drained of snow. A silver moon polished smooth as ivory by the storm wore through the sky above Gold Hill. In the luminescence of a new white world Cripple Creek stirred and unbuttoned. Men got busy and shoveled their way to freedom — at least to the nearest saloon. The Pueblo House, the Red Elk, and the Palace Hotel, the English Kitchen and the Mush and Milk House, every store opened its doors.

Towards midnight the skies hardened to the ashy gray of new-cut steel. The night grew so clear and cold a man could hear across town the squeak of his partner's boots in the snow. A mile down on the plains it was still snowing. But here above timberline and close to the gritty brilliant stars, men felt the stir of a new day as the world clicked on its hinges. In a ravine on Crystal Hill a wolf howled waveringly. A group of men, tipsy on the walk, yowled back before turning into the Mint Saloon. Inside, the bar was wild with shouts. It was twelve o'clock, December 31, and Cripple Creek had finished, was beginning, another year.

That area of barren hills which had jumped upon the map in a scant six months as a $200,000 Cow Pasture, had increased its production of gold tenfold to $2,010,400, tripled this, and then doubled it until in the year just ended the production had reached the colossal amount of $12,000,000. And that was nothing compared to what it would do! Sir Morton Frewer, the English bimetallist, said so in an article in the *Great Divide*. He stated that in 1887 when gold was discovered in Johannesburg, South Africa, London experts reported that the formation at the Witwatersrandt gold field was unfavorable for gold production. The Rothschilds refused to pay £20,000 sterling for the Randt gold quartz reef. Yet its production had increased from 13,000 ounces of gold per month in 1887 to 140,000 ounces per month in 1894 — in six years placing the Dutch republic at the head of the gold producing countries of the world. But at the rate Cripple Creek was developing, Sir Frewer believed it would catch up and surpass the record of Johannesburg.

"Hell, yes!" the talk ran in the saloons. "The Independence is already the marvel of the mining world. It's not a mine. It's a blooming bank. You heard about that chamber Stratton hit and called the Bull Pen? The stuff assayed as high as $100 a pound. Why, the ore they're shipping out of it without sorting returns $450 to the ton. And that mineral bank is yielding over $120,000 a month!"

A mile below, Rogier sat in his shop in Little London. There was some kind of a New Year's Eve party going on in the house, with Ona and Cable chaperoning the girls and their guests. Every light in the house was on, the whole place vibrated with noise. To escape the confusion Rogier had fled to his shop out in back. Here, seated at the long drafting table with his back to the hot stove, he bent over his maps and reports of the Cripple Creek district.

There had been another one of those unbelievable strikes that was spreading the fame of the Pike's Peak district. The three Woods brothers who had laid out the new town of Victor, east of Cripple Creek, had drawn elaborate plans for their Victor Hotel to be located in the center of town. Contracts were let and excavations were being made for the foundations when a curious assayer scooped up a few samples of loose dirt. They assayed rich in gold. The blueprints for the hotel were jubilantly town up and a large shaft house was erected on the spot instead, the gallows frame being sixty-five feet high on a stone base. Below it the vein, eight feet wide and averaging $46 to the ton, ran under the town itself. Victor was no longer merely a town of 6,000 people, but the surface of an immense mine with a mile of underground workings already, and beginning its average production of $1,000,000 a year. The Gold Coin!

Its location pleased Rogier. For months on end he had been patiently marking on his map the locations of new mines as they were reported. It was a large map thumbtacked to a soft pine drawing board propped up before him. Embracing the area from the western edge of Long Hungry Gulch to Cow Mountain on the east, and from Tenderfoot Hill southward to Big Bull, it topographically outlined with their elevations every hill, gulch, and stream. The map had become fly-specked with dots which, scrutinized more closely, resolved into fine inked squares which located shafts, triangular wedges which designated tunnels, and tiny bars with vertical cross-cuts to mark the locations of steam hoists. With this map before him, and remembering the topography of the district more clearly than any face in his family, Rogier was beginning to arrive at the conclusion on which he was to base his secret plans.

The Cripple Creek gold belt, as it was first known, comprised an area about eleven miles square. Gradually the thousands of men prospecting the hills and gulches drew in to a section roughly seven by eight miles in extent. Then it became evident that most of the gold deposits lay in a small area of some six square miles. Nothing like it had ever been known: an area so small and so confoundingly rich. Geologists could explain it only by the theory that the district occupied the floor of an extinct volcano whose superstructure had been removed by erosion, leaving Pike's Peak as its culminating point. The basic country rock was Pike's Peak Granite whose pinkish color was imparted to it by feldspar, and which was assumed to have formed the bed of an ancient sea which received the sediments now composing the sandstones of the Garden of the Gods a mile below.

During the great eruption a mass of volcanic material had burst through the granite in an aqueo-igneous condition. Cooling, solidi-fication, and contraction followed, resulting in the formation of fissures. Hot water ascended with great velocity from the depths of the volcano, and nearing the surface spread slowly through the fissures. As it stagnated, deposition and chemical action changed the composition of the solution and gold ore was precipitated. The principal volcanic rock was andesite breccia, more commonly known as porphyry from its deep purple color.

The ore itself was something of an enigma. As Rogier remem-bered, one of the first carloads which Stratton had shipped to a Denver smelter had been held as waste, the officials believing a load of ballast had been sent by mistake. The ores were tellurides, calaverite, and sylvanite, which had been found in Transylvania but which were little known in America — the reason, of course, why prospectors had passed over the district for so many years without recognizing it.

This deposition theory, held by the most noted Geological Survey engineers and generally accepted, had bothered Rogier. It maintained that precipitation had taken place abundantly near the surface but very sparsely at depth. Free gold, the engineers asserted, did not occur except when set free by oxidation; and this zone of oxidation did not exceed a depth of 1,000 feet, the depth to which oxygen could penetrate in water or through fissures. The extremely large number of surface strikes first made by tenderfoot and alfalfa miners, especially on Globe and Gold Hill, bore out this assumption. Indeed, half of the sixty most important pay chutes were still less than 500 feet down.

It was this that for so long had held Rogier back. Only to the extent and depth that the layer of porphyry with its interlaced veins of gold held out would Cripple Creek exist — a short-lived grass roots mining district.

Then gold had been found in the granite. All over the gold-bearing area the underlying granite showed evidence of disturbance. It was penetrated and traversed by vertical sheets of phonolite called dikes — a dike being easily seen where the softer rock had scored away. During the vein deposition the phonolite had been disintegrated and replaced by equivalent volumes of ore in fissure veins carried up by hot waters and heated gases. These fissure veins were vertical or inclined, varying in width from a few inches to several feet. The one fact that stood out clearly in Rogier's mind at last was that the deposition of gold had taken place in fissures after the eruption and solidification of the volcanic breccia, and was not restricted to its confines. Gold could be found in the granite depths of the Peak!

Now, hunched over his midnight lamp, he began to mark his map in a peculiar way: tracing the brecciation in the three central hills, Gold, Raven, and Bull Hill; then from Tenderfoot Hill south to Squaw Mountain; and down the eastern boundary from Trachyte Mountain to Big Bull, where the phonolite capped the granite hills. There were five general ore zones, trending from south to north. In these zones he plotted the trends of the veins of their most important mines. The Lillie-Vindicator zone system on the east swung to the northwest; the Independence-Portland system had a northward trend as had the Gold Coin zone; the Elkton vein swung to the northeast; while the two westerly zones, the Raven and the Mary McKinney-Anaconda, swung to the northeast. Sticking out on the map like the rude outline of a pear, the blue-penciled lines disclosed that the ore-producing area was broad at the south and narrow at the north. A bulbous pear-shaped region of mineralization, as if the veins had risen from the depths of the earth at the southern base of the pear and run together toward the north — into the very summit of the Peak itself.

Other men, he knew, had been studying the district assiduously. Like Stratton, who believed Gold and Globe Hills were the primal sources of mineralization, and who was buying up all the patented claims he could get.

The lights up front had gone out. The house was dark and still. Rogier was unaware of it. Profoundly disturbed, he sat staring at his map. He could see the Peak as clearly as if its hills and gulches stood before him. It was like that legendary lodestone imbedded in a sea-girt cliff against whose pull ancient mariners fought their ships, but which drew out even the iron bolts from the planks. Through the long years of his exile he had sought the key that would unlock the secret of its hold upon him and free him from its bondage. And now, having marked the course of its veins upon his map, he saw with revealing clarity the way to his fulfillment. He knew now where to search for the bloodstream of its living flesh, where to sink a shaft to tap that great arterial fountain whose viscous veins ran through pulsing stone. Life! And yet it was also death. A gate and a tomb. The final oubliette.

The fire in the stove behind him had gone out. Shuddering with the cold, he turned over the page of the calendar on the desk. Then blowing out the lamp, he went into the house and up the creaking stairs to bed.

7

A family is a peculiar entity. Its members are like islands in the
same archipelago. Sometimes the constantly changing stream of life
tears a new channel through the group. Internal ruptures break away
reefs. Old atolls sink and new ones rise from the placid blue depths.
The eternal palingenesis goes on, but the island group remains a
whole. Far down in the impenetrable bloodstream they remain fixed
together, adjusted to the same internal vibration, knowing one
communion in the deep unseen currents that wash between them.

So it was with Ona and Rogier. The indecencies of family
"heart-to-heart" exposures were not, thank God, vices of the Rogiers. Yet a silent understanding always had held them together.
Now, as she worked daily on his books and papers, she began to see
him not only as her father but as man whom no one had ever known
before.

The job of looking after his affairs while he was in the mountains was the worst Ona had ever attempted. She would have
preferred the Herculean task of cleaning up the barny third floor in
the house to spending the day puzzling over Rogier's ledgers. There
were a dozen of the big volumes crammed with old letters and

scrawled in his handwriting, records of every job he had figured on, copies of bids he had submitted with their detailed supporting data, and periodic records as the construction progressed, together with monthly bills for material used and deposit slips for money deposited in the bank to his various expense accounts. Rogier always wrote in his ledgers with ink but seldom bothered to use a blotter. Many pages looked as if he had closed the book with a bang, imprisoning ink like a crushed fly.

It seemed paradoxical that he could be so methodical, sure, and accurate in his work, and so sloppy even with his time sheets and payrolls. Mooney the timekeeper sent him impeccable records each week, and Rogier invariably spoiled the neat rows of figures with scrawled comments. He knew every man who worked for him. Ona had often seen him on the job talking to a stonemason, holding a plumb line for a bricklayer, or looking over a mule with a teamster. He could take off his coat and square a timber with any carpenter on the job; one who worked for him more than once had to be jim-dandy at his trade. He was hardly ever in the shanty that served as a field office, and Ona could see the results of his observations — a random comment on a laborer and a note on Diston saws, but interspersed with a statement that Akeepee needed more grain.

But when she balanced his books and bank accounts she was stunned. All the pasture land along Shook's Run he had not sold had been subdivided into lots which were selling at nice prices indeed. He owned houses on Wahsatch, and several pieces of valuable property and store buildings in the business district uptown. Receiving the evaluation on each that he had requested, together with statements from the banks, and making an approximate conversion evaluation of his construction machinery, winches, cement mixers, drays and work teams, tools, timber, finished lumber, and supplies, Ona stared open-mouthed at the sum of her father's holdings. Why, he was rich as a North Ender!

Naturally he had made money on contracts that ran as high as $80,000. But it was necessary to post big bonds and expend a great deal before the job was entirely paid for. Still he was a peculiar man. There were many things he did not tell her or entrust to his records. He might walk in and mention a piece of property he had owned for years that none of the family had ever heard of, or give her a check on an account for which she had never seen the pass book. Some time ago a man from Cripple Creek had called, telling her he had come for $120. While they were talking Rogier walked in.

"Why, of course, Ona, write out a check." The two men shook hands. "I hope you haven't been put out any."

Then one day a tacky man named Reynolds came in to see Rogier. For an hour they talked quietly in the corner. "I tell you, Colonel, this here Silver Heels is goin' to pan out. The assay says so."

Ona pricked up her ears at the name, and heard the rustle of Rogier's big map. "Open her up then. But not until you take a hard look where I told you. Up the gulch, Reynolds. Up, not down. And mind you, keep my name out of it if you have to sign any papers. Use your own."

When Reynolds was ready to leave, Rogier directed Ona to walk up town with him and draw for him from the bank $1,000 in currency.

"Silver Heels—isn't that nice to remember her! Have you got a gold mine, Daddy?"

"I wouldn't call it that," he answered tersely.

"It will be, Ma'am, and we're partners," spoke up Reynolds.

Rogier didn't try to dodge out of it. "Your wife's in town, isn't she? Bring her down for supper tonight." Then turning to Ona he ordered, "On your way through the house tell your mother and Lida to cook up a good one. If a man's my partner he's got a place at my table."

The news that Daddy had a gold mine and his partner and wife were coming to dinner threw Mrs. Rogier into a turmoil of excitement that was transmitted to the whole family. Out came the Sunday china, on went party clothes, in went a huge turkey to brown. What she expected, of course, was a prosperous mine-owner cut to the cloth of Millionaire Row. Reynolds, however, had come down from his shack in the gulch dressed in an old suit covered with fly specks and moth holes. His lady did better, this first time in town for nearly a year. Her get-up was astonishing from her red and purple petticoats to her enormous fruit-and-flower-trimmed hat, large as the bottom of a hogshead, which she refused to take off at the table. Rogier alone seemed to enjoy the occasion. Overlooking

Mrs. Rogier's shocked amazement and the girls' sly smiles, he kept refilling Reynolds' plate until he had to unbutton his vest and stretch out his legs sideways.

Speculating on how their first million dollars from the Silver Heels was to be spent, Reynolds suddenly slapped his lady on the knee and said lustily, "And Old Girl, we'll get us married too! We'll ride to church behind a team of big gray horses wearin' red plumes, and have a little tike throwin' red roses along the aisle!"

The lady snorted. "It's just like my Old Man to be throwin' away good money fer nothin'! With them front teeth of his'n out, I ain't afraid of any other female gettin' him even if we ain't hitched!"

Mrs. Rogier stiffened and became polite as a cold oyster. Rogier had forgotten to mention that no marriage certificate had ever been drawn up between these two faithful weather-beaten cronies of thirty years. Rogier looked at her with sudden admiration. Not the devil nor the prospect of Cripple Creek gold could quench the fire of her righteous indignation.

Yet now, with a gold mine in the family, there was no reason why she shouldn't have at last her mansion in the North End among the divine gentility of Little London. During her evening drives with Sally Lee or Jonathan Cable when he was in town, she would stare longingly at the great houses set back in their close-cropped lawns as if fearful of contact with the vulgar stream of life, peering over a wall or through the iron grillwork of a huge gate. Sometimes as a door opened there would be a momentary glimpse of a marble Apollo or a plaster cast of Venus de Milo behind a liveried servant. But even through the orange-lit windows her penetrating eyes seemed able to discern those ornate manifestations of wealth and culture destined to be hers someday. She knew every house; the driveway that boasted a Park Four or a spike team of three grays; whether this lawn had a circular fountain or that one a cast iron deer peering toward the shrubbery surrounding the summer pavilion; and on every vacant lot she recreated those parts of each that she meant to fuse into the Rogier mansion.

"Not yet, Martha," Rogier said decisively. "I'm too poor and too busy to throw up one of those big barns. You'll just have to wait. What's wrong with this place, anyway?"

It did look comfortable enough and very tidy, now that the big.

pasture had been cut through with shady streets and houses were going up, and a new bridge had been thrown over Shook's Run. The driveway of the house had been graveled, and in front stood as a hitching post a little cast iron nigger boy whose riding silks were painted red, yellow and blue. A large open porch had been added in back. The walk leading to the shop was flanked on each side with purple flags, the garden filled with currant bushes.

"It's all in your name, Martha," Rogier assured her again. "I can never touch it for any reason."

A few weeks later Rogier had another caller. Working with Ona in the shop, he saw him coming down the walk from the house.

"Stratton! Mr. Stratton, my daughter Ona! I'm glad to see you again!"

The Croesus of Cripple Creek, the Midas of the Rockies, with an income of $3,000 a day, more than $1,000,000 a year, resembled little the $3-a-day carpenter of a few years ago. He was dressed neatly in a gray tailored suit and handmade boots, and wore an air of importance and authority. Yet his tall thin body was frail and stooped, his hair thin and white as silk. He looked like a man bent under a burden too heavy to bear. There was little the town did not know about his peculiarities. Instead of building a mansion on Millionaire Row he had moved into a house on Weber Street, a few blocks from the Rogier's; a simple, two-story frame house he once had worked on as a carpenter. Aloof and lonely, he ignored Little London society in a futile effort to spend the wealth remorselessly pouring into his lap. Not only was he buying up hundreds of claims in Cripple Creek, smelters and stock control of other companies, but business blocks in downtown Denver. In Little London he had acquired his old office building which he converted into a modern Mining Exchange Building, the electric streetcar system which he extended to the Stratton Park he was establishing, and downtown corners which he was donating as sites for a new post office, city hall, and courthouse. His generosity was already legendary: money to ruined Tabor and to penniless Bob Womack who first had discovered gold in Cripple Creek, meal tickets to the hungry, donations right and left. All this was not enough to assuage the nameless hunger gnawing at his mind and bowels. Tales of his Satanic revels, of his Bluebeard stable of kept women, enraged every housewife in town. And he had begun to drink heavily, a quart of whiskey a day. A man from whom seventeen years of privation and despair were now taking their frightful toll.

What had brought him here Rogier could not imagine. Nor did Stratton have a chance to tell him. For down the walk behind him came Mrs. Rogier, head up, eyes blazing. Sweeping in the door, she thrust a handful of gold coins into Stratton's lap. "What do you mean giving my girls and maid these, Mr. Stratton? I will have you distinctly understand we do not need your charity!"

Ona jumped to her feet. "A gold piece from Mr. Stratton's a souvenir anybody'd be glad to have! And I've heard about your giving a bicycle to every laundry girl in town so she wouldn't have to walk to work. That's kind of you, Mr. Stratton!"

Mrs. Rogier took her by the hand and marched out the door.

"Damned women! I hate them all!" Stratton shouted after them.

Rogier shrugged his heavy shoulders. "They're a queer breed, Stratton. I can never make them out."

Stratton stalked out the back door.

Never again did he come to the house, but a few days later and several times thereafter he came down the alley and through the back door of the shop. Each time he came Rogier sent Ona into the house, ostensibly to avoid any more scenes. The purpose of Stratton's calls was simple.

"You haven't been up to the Independence," he said. "Strange for an old friend and a man who's getting interested in the district."

"You're bothered too much and I'm busy myself."

"You must be. I hear you've leased the Garnet and Fleur-de-Lis."

How astute he was! He knew everything going on up there, and this arrangement had been kept quiet. Two businessmen, Diggs and Handel, had been working the Garnet profitably until a horse in the vein had cut down their returns. Indications were that the main chute would be picked up again on the adjacent claim, the Fleur-de-Lis, and they proposed that Rogier go into partnership with them to open up the new mine. Rogier, despite abhorring partnerships, had agreed.

The properties were no good, insisted Stratton. They lay just outside the rim of that great porphry-filled granite bowl in which sat the Independence and the Portland. He proposed instead that Rogier develop for him a new property, the American Eagles, as he felt ill and was going away to recuperate.

Rogier declined; he had a different opinion of the Garnet and Fleur-de-Lis location.

"It's no good, whatever it is!" angrily declaimed Stratton. "And Diggs and Handel are no better!" But he made another offer. If Rogier would develop the American Eagles, Stratton for a share would guarantee to develop the Fleur-de-Lis to the extent of Rogier's one-third interest, insuring him against total loss of his investment.

Rogier gladly accepted. Both men agreed no contract should be drawn as Stratton wanted to avoid publicity and they were old, trusted friends. "Come up to the Independence on Monday and I'll show you through. Then we can look over the Eagles," said Stratton. The two men shook hands on the agreement, and Stratton left by the alley door.

Not only Rogier was amazed at the Independence. An investigating committee comprised of members from the Colorado Scientific Society, American Institute of Mechanical Engineers, the United States Department of Mining, and several other civil and mining engineers, had reported it to be the most noteworthy gold mine in the Western Hemisphere if not in the world. It now embraced fourteen claims covering more than a hundred acres. The main shaft was down 415 feet and its underground workings aggregated more than six miles. The principal veins were so rich that they had been named like other complete mines: the Independence, Bobtail, and Emerson. "Now I'll show you the Bull Pen," said Stratton, signalling for the third level. The gold depository was a chamber from eight to thirty feet wide of sylvanite that ran from hundreds to thousands of dollars a ton. "I don't mine it," explained Stratton. "I just dip in it, like a bank, when I need ready cash. I'm trying to curtail the Independence production to $120,000 a month." Turning to Rogier with one of his rare smiles, he added, "You know, gold is worth more in the ground than out of it."

Shooting up to surface the two men climbed up to the American Eagles which when opened up for production would be the highest mine in the district. "The showing is good and I want no expense spared," ordered Stratton. "I've got two good mining men to lay out the levels, drifts, and crosscuts as we follow the vein. What I want you for is to sink the shaft and put in the surface plant. And manage the men. I don't want any labor troubles." He paused. "Stop fooling around with those rat holes like the Silver Heels. And don't waste your money on that Fleur-de-Lis. They're no good!"

"I'll do your job," Rogier answered quietly. "But don't you interfere with my affairs. I've got my own ideas."

"You're a fool!" Nevertheless he stuck out his hand before turning back down the slope.

8

The news came out, of course, that Rogier had thrown in his
resources with Diggs and Handel to develop their sister mines, the
Garnet and Fleur-de-Lis. It not only raised the sagging price of the
stock on the exchange and reestablished the two men on a footing
with their bankers and neighbors, but it briefly focused attention on
the aloof and retiring contractor. Rogier was invited to a banquet
given by the mine owners of Cripple Creek. Swearing that it was
nothing but a back-slapping orgy, he protested against going until
Mrs. Rogier cornered him for one of her bathroom talks.

"They've invited you, Daddy! Your place at the table is marked
with 'Colonel Rogier.' The *Gazette* said so. You've got to go!"

With the three girls she got him ready in his broadcloth suit and
starched white shirts. Then another argument started. He wouldn't
wear a tie. Always he wore a stiff collar fastened by his only piece of
jewelry, a diamond collar button. This was the way he finally went
despite their protestations. Yet when he stepped out to the carriage
waiting with Nigger Bill in the front seat, the fine texture of his coat
revealing his wide muscular shoulders, his graying hair gleaming
above the diamond at his throat, none of the family but admitted

that, however he detested the false appellation, he was indeed Little London's Colonel Rogier.

To Ona there was no doubt left that Rogier was committed to Cripple Creek. He was letting his work slide, neglecting to bid on several promising jobs. For days on end he would be up in the district. She was stunned by the checks she made out, the money he so casually commanded. Just what he was doing up there she did not know, but it often seemed to her that his interests and money were being expended on something besides the Fleur-de-Lis and the Silver Heels.

It was his ledgers that gave him away. Stuck in one of the dusty volumes she happened by chance to find a cryptic note scrawled on a scrap of crumpled paper. Spreading out the paper to decipher the cramped writing, she felt leap out at her those terse phrases oddly turned of wording and impulsively expressing an inner thought of the writer, sublime and yet pathetic, that was not meant to be read by any man. Abashed like any Rogier by the candor of a heart that had so forgotten itself to reveal without repression its most secret treasure, Ona tore the page across and dropped the fragments into the waste basket. For the first time she had an intimation of what Rogier might be seeking in Cripple Creek.

A few weeks later she drove up to the district in the family buggy with Jonathan Cable; next day Rogier would drive her back. The Cheyenne Mountain Trail had been widened to a four-horse stage road to give shorter access into the district, and it was beautiful: climbing up through deep canyons thickly forested with pine and spruce, and winding through high mountain meadows ablaze with wildflowers. It was always good to be with Cable. Despite his absences this Red Niggah, as her cantankerous grandmother still called him, had come to be accepted as part of the family.

They talked little all day as he drove her around the district. Victor, the City of Mines, was booming above the Gold Coin. Cripple Creek she did not recognize. Jennie Larue, a dancehall girl in a den of vice, and her lover had knocked over a gasoline stove while quarreling, and the ensuing fire had wiped out most of the wooden buildings of the camp. Now it was being rebuilt into a modern city with stone and red brick buildings glowing on the dull gray granite hillsides. A town of 10,000 people without a tree. Everywhere they drove stood other huddles of shacks growing into more new towns. Everywhere she looked, she could see the gallows frames of great mines, gaping holes blasted out of the hillsides, shanties and tool houses, litters of machinery, swarms of toiling men. And rising above them all the pyramidal bare summit of the Peak itself.

The Silver Heels was not up to her expectations. A dark vertical shaft surmounted by a hoist house and nearby, Reynolds' squat board shanty. His wife had taken off her hat, Ona thought grimly, and was dishing up beans and salt pork to Reynolds.

"Where's father?" she asked.

"Oh, he's over the hill and up the gulch, Miss Ona." He thumbed toward the Peak. "I wouldn't go up there, he's mighty touchy — if you could get up there in them nice clothes."

Glad as he was to see them, he seemed reluctant to answer questions and Ona left them to their cold beans.

"Now I want to see your mine, Jonathan. That's what I came up here for."

Cable grinned as he drove her to Big Bull Mountain. "The New Moon's not the sliver it was," he said humorously, "but it doesn't seem to fill out too fast. But we're getting along."

The best that could be said of it was that it was a working mine like hundreds of others in the district. The three partners now had a crew of three more men, and Cable showed her the inclined tunnel down which they went to work. They were underground now, hacking away and filling a little metal cart with ore which from time to time a burro pulled out. There was a large log cabin with tiers of bunks in which they slept, and an adjoining plank kitchen in which they took turns cooking. It all looked very dull to Ona and she was glad to go out on the dump to sit in the late afternoon sunlight. Picking up a grayish, damp piece of rock, she asked, "So this is ore, gangue, whatever you call it?"

He nodded. "Calaverite, a telluride. We had a hard time at first. Ore containing less than an ounce of gold to the ton didn't leave us much profit. But now we're shipping to a new mill in Florence that uses cynanide instead of chlorine as a solvent, we're making money even on half-ounce ore."

"You mean to say all these hundreds of mines and thousands of men have to blast and dig out a ton of rock to get a tiny ounce or less of gold!"

"Doesn't the place look dug up enough to produce $19,000,000 worth a year?" There was a somber tone to his voice and a far-away look in his eyes as she followed his gaze across the gutted hillsides and torn up gulches. This was not a man, with his love for open prairies, to devote himself to mining. Yet tomorrow he would be down there in the clammy blackness, hacking away with the rest of them.

Not too surprisingly Rogier drove up in a buckboard. "I've been expecting you. Reynolds said you were here." He flung a quick look around. "Still at the grass roots, eh Cable? You've got to get down, way down!"

They all drove to Cripple Creek and had dinner at the National Hotel where Ona was to stay that night. Rogier was no more talkative than Cable, but Ona detected in him a nervous excitement, a keyed up expectancy, that he had never betrayed during his work in Little London. Cable was a reassuring presence; a simple man, sensitive to his surroundings, without a driving ambition perhaps, but living fully in the moment.

"Did you register for a room?" Rogier asked her. "Make it for two nights, I can't drive you back tomorrow. But I'll show you some of the big mines."

"No," she answered decisively. "I'll take the Midland back tonight. I want to see the new resorts at Cascade and Green Mountain Falls. This is no place for women — or trees."

Rogier gave her a sharp look but did not answer.

When he returned to town, Ona gave him the clippings of statistics she had been saving for him. He thumbed through them rapidly, then reached for his big steel square. "Humm. That's interesting. The district producing almost $20,000,000, Colorado $26,000,000, the United States $70,000,000, and the world about $300,000,000. That means Cripple Creek is accounting for four-fifths of the annual gold production in Colorado, nearly a third of the country's, and one-fifteenth of the gold mined in the world. Already! And most of that is coming from a little block of six square miles. Now figure that per square foot and you'll see — "

"I hate figures! Copying them all day long!"

Holding the square on his knee, he said quietly, "You don't dislike figures as much as you think you do. What marks the time you get up in the morning and every second of the day? Figures. Why, astrologers claim that the moment you're born is no more than an astronomical juxtaposition of universal figures which determine your future, and that your life vibrates to one primary number just as a thin wine-glass vibrates to a certain pitch. Your mother will tell you from her Bible that even the hairs of your head are numbered. But she won't be able to tell you why the Book of Revelation is composed almost entirely of numbers whose significance is unknown. What locates a ship on the boundless seas but figures!"

"But Daddy!" She wanted to ask him how he expected her to balance his own figures when he was spending more than his income — and without knowing where it all went. But Rogier could not be stopped.

"How good is Little Man? Only figures can tell us. Jot them down — 5,280 feet in a mile, and you can figure a good horse can pace it in 2:15. That's 135 seconds — say forty feet a second. How long is a horse's body, Ona? Say six feet. A good trotter or pacer to do that time will have to move forward about six times the length of his body every second." Taking the scratch pad from her, he went on. "But how does he do it? You've got to breed a good horse for spirit, feed him for stamina, and work him for wind. Then you've got to train him. Every stride just so long to give him the most drive forward for what he's got. Stretch him out! Every hair in place, by Jove! Just to get him ahead six lengths every second. But it's the horse — and his mammy and his sire, and his mammy before that — who has to win his own race. Breeding, evolution, the time comes when every living soul has to run his race against the past!"

Ona quietly put away her pencil and paper, closed her ledgers. "It's getting late. You'll be wanting to see Little Man before suppertime."

Not even Cripple Creek had lessened Rogier's love for his horses; a love, fascination, queer in a man so slow and methodical, of seeing the speed he could get out of them. There had been so many of them: Lady-Lou, Pet and her fillies Dorothy and Silver Heels, old blind Colonel, and that great Maryland lady, Akeepee, each a little faster than the others. He had been sure that Akeepee, a pacer, would fulfill his hopes. But Judge Colton had ruined her, and he had let her foal two colts, first Little Man and then Aralee, still a spindling brat.

Rogier rode out with Ona and Sally Lee to visit Little Man at the ranch. This horse had taken the cake for orneryness from the day he was foaled. Nigger Bill said he was brimmin' with hell-fire. And after the only occasion he was sent out on the streets with a buggy, the *Gazette* reported he had tried to climb the telegraph poles. He was not high-spirited; he was a long-legged devil in a smooth satin skin, a chicken-killer who delighted in nipping any arm or leg within his reach. Fearless and excellent a hand with horses as she was, Sally Lee could never acquire Rogier's persuasive touch. Little Man was no exception. Whenever anyone approached, he would rear up on hind feet, pawing with his forefeet. Denman could handle him with care, but only for Rogier would he stretch out his muzzle with a rumble of welcome.

Arriving at Denman's ranch, Rogier wandered from stall to stall, having a look at every horse. He greeted them as old friends; scrutinized them like delicately chiseled stone statues; went over them like a physician. By this time the handlers had made ready his sulky and brought out Little Man. Rogier settled himself firmly in the low seat, legs outspread, and drove slowly to the track. The sun, settling in its crotch in the blue mountain wall, flooded the prairie with a light coppery sheen. Cut into the dry level expanse of buffalo grass and tumbleweed, the circular track looked black, fresh, and inviting. Waiting on the course until the men were ready at their posts and the girls had come up, he held Little Man while Denman inspected his leg wrappings for the last time and then stepped back with his watch. Then suddenly they were away, Little Man lunging viciously into his stride and Rogier settling down to his one invigorating relaxation.

The wind streaked past whining softly, but too weak to extinguish the blur of dust that followed him like the smoke of a burning fuse. He could hear the rhythmic concatenation of the hoofs before him and glimpse the twinkle of the white wrappings, could watch Little Man's breathing as his sides swelled and receded regularly against the trembling shafts. Timing his pace, he watched for the first man's hand to fall exactly as he passed the two-furlong mark. Alive to every stride, it was as if his own self had died and had been born anew. His worries and troubles dropped from him and were trampled into the fine dry dust. An elixir electric as a current swept through his veins. The track curved northward in its turn; Little Man was a length behind at the half-mile. Rogier leaned forward, let out the reins. Little Man ran smoothly, every stride in time. Slowly the high blue mountains swung across the course like a dark and menacing wall of rock. And far down the track, like a pigmy at its foot, Denman stood with his arm upraised as with solemn warning. Rogier compressed his lips as he took a tighter hold of the reins. Always that Peak forbiddingly blocking his path! But sensing the splendid power leaping into his fingers and flowing up his arms, he felt that with one plunge he might hurtle over it into the waiting blood-red sun. With a quick slap he threw out the reins, and Little Man lunged forward.

Everybody was shouting and grinning when he eased Little Man back. "Man. I was sho you was goin' to jump that theah chah'iot ovah the sun and moon!" yelled Nigger Bill. "He's the one, Daddy!" cried Sally Lee, eyes shining. "You *have* entered him in the meeting, haven't you?"

"Maybe so, maybe so. We'll see," replied Rogier.

Comparing observations and the time of each quarter-mile, Rogier and Denman walked back to the ranch with the girls while the men followed with Little Man. That evening at home Rogier made up his mind to enter him in the race meeting. "You better," said Mrs. White, old and poorly as she was. "What you keepin' all them horses for if it ain't to race? Buyin' enough hay and grain every month to feed us a year! If you're doin' it jes for an evenin' ride, it's better you tuk Akeepee out in the buggy!"

The meeting was a great event to which every member of the family went. Cable was along, and so was Lida Peck who wanted to see how her former barnyard enemy, the chicken killer, would behave in company. There were five harness events, trotting, pacing, a free-for-all, a six furlong running event, and the last a mile pace for which Rogier had registered. During all the races the rest of the family kept their eyes on Rogier talking quietly to Denman and Nigger Bill as if he had no concern at all. When the last race was called, Cable walked Ona and Sally Lee down to the finishing line, leaving the rest of the family in the coach fronting the track.

Mrs. Rogier swelled with pride when Rogier drove up to the starting line, his sulky polished until its frail outline reflected the sun. Little Man was too docile for words, arching his neck and glancing demurely at the crowd.

"That chicken killer!" spat out Lida under another new hat. "He's actin' too good to be true. Showin' off!"

Mrs. Rogier sat back, folding her hands. "Blood will tell, Lida. He knows when to be on his good behavior."

Almost before they knew it the horses were off, streaking for the inside. It was a fair field, and two entries beside Rogier bunched at the turn with the others strung out obliquely behind. Little Man held his stride beautifully, running smoothly as if he were alone at dusk on Denman's track. At the half-mile he was leading by half a length with a young black gelding just behind and a little sorrel mare coming up fast. Rogier paid no attention to the black but glanced back once at the sorrel. He was running Little Man at the pace agreed upon with Denman, but it was obvious his race was with the little mare. At the fifth furlong the gelding burst ahead, lost his stride and began to drop behind. In an instant the little sorrel took her position beside Rogier. Then she and Little Man went at it neck to neck. Rogier never took his eyes from the finish line.

Quick as a wink it happened. The sorrel lengthened her stride and was a good head beyond Little Man when that beautifully behaving colt saw her at the corner of his blinders. He twisted his head, let out a squeal. Before Rogier could pull him back Little Man bared his teeth and made a grab for the mare's ear. The two sulkies met with a bump that almost overturned them both. Then Little Man stretched out his nose, broke away, and streaked for the finish. Running wild, his stride broken and ragged, he finished four lengths in front of the field.

The fiasco set the crowd wild, whooping and hollering for the horse from Shook's Run. Lida sat screaming, "Chicken killer! Look at that ornery horse run!" Mrs. Rogier did not answer. She sat stiff as a corpse, feeling her ears slowly burning off.

Little Man was disqualified and the purse awarded the sorrel mare. As it had been a selling race, Little Man was offered for sale according to the rules and Rogier had to buy him back for three hundred dollars. It was the last straw Mrs. Rogier's dignity could uphold. She drove home in a silent coach.

Rogier was put out at Little Man's action, particularly because the colt had shown up so well in training. Speed and power were no good without complete control. He let Nigger Bill blanket and walk the horse home alone. That evening he drove out to Denman's ranch. It was dusk when he approached the stable. The door was open, and Little Man unhaltered heard him talking to Denman. At the sound of a squeal Rogier looked up. There was Little Man uprisen on his hind legs, pawing the air as he walked toward them. Then he dropped to all four feet, whisked his tail mischievously, and stretched out his muzzle toward Rogier. Suddenly Rogier grinned. "You ornery colt, you!" he said, putting out both hands.

Little Man should have had twin toes.

9

Rogier was up at the Silver Heels when the results of the assays came in. "It's a strike, Colonel," Reynolds said solemnly. "Sixty dollars to the ton." He acted little like a man who had hit his mark after years of toil and privation.

Nor did Rogier betray any elation. "I've told you before to stop calling me 'Colonel!' Have you hit a defined vein or is it still grass roots gangue?"

"Three ounces a ton at a hundred feet's good enough for me, Colonel! When can we start shipping?"

Mrs. Reynolds was in town for groceries. They sat down to a cup of muddy coffee undisturbed. Reynolds was a born miner. He knew the earth as a bookbinder knows a book. The strata unfolding beneath him, leaf after leaf; its type the hieroglyphic marks of fossil and geological change; its bindings the tunnels, shafts, and gallows frames that rose about him. Rogier trusted him completely. And yet — what was the meaning of the text?

The argument began — a queer time for an argument! Rogier of course would bring in machinery, men, and supplies. But only on the condition that if the vein pinched out, or could not be found,

Reynolds would move with the equipment to a new working he had in mind.

Reynolds looked at him as if he were staring at a mad man. "Colonel! We've made the strike we been after! We're goin' to get rich! And here you're talkin' about leavin' it for a no-account prospect already."

Rogier appeared unconvinced. "Reynolds, the Silver Heels is a step in the right direction, that's all. We're going after something better!"

"But Colonel!" Reynolds grasped at a last straw. "What are you going to use for money, buyin' all that machinery for the Fleur-de-Lis, bringin' more here, payin' all the crews? You got to get the gold right here in the Silver Heels to keep you goin'! I'm your partner, Colonel! I'll sink or swim with you. But haven't I hit it for you like I said I would?"

Rogier got up, flung his arm around him in a hearty hug. "Get some muckers up here! I'll move in some machinery. Let's go down!"

"Hooray!" shouted Reynolds. "Wait'll the Old Girl hears of this!"

Now at sunset Rogier sat on a spur of that high saddle between Bull Hill and Bull Cliffs where perched a conglomeration of shacks growing into the highest incorporated town in the world and named after another lucky carpenter, Sam Altman; sitting alone in a rock cleft, letting its full meaning sink into his mind and heart. He had drawn blood at last! And just where he'd known he would — at the mouth of that grassy gulch running northward like a heart line directly up into the bare snowy summit of the Peak itself. Sitting 11,000 feet high, he could see it looming another three thousand feet above him. Like a great snow-goose halted a split instant in flight for his arrow to strike home, like an uprisen saurian beast baring its heart, like a monstrous fish breaking water — like nothing but that massive anthropomorphous Peak of heart's desire itself. The showing in the Silver Heels was not a vein, merely a capillary indication of its living flesh that confirmed the truth of his aim. When it petered out he would move up the gulch and sink deeper at a location he already had staked out. And with the gold shipped from it he would ascend the steadily narrowing cut to its last granite crack and at last strike deep into that hot beating heart within the stone of all stones, the self of all selves.

It was a pear-shaped pattern of conquest that had formed on his maps and in his mind long ago, a strategy he had followed in taking a job on the American Eagles on top of Bull Hill and developing the Garnet and Fleur-de-Lis on the Altman saddle. They were all in line with the arrow course of his secret hope. But not until he had drawn blood from the Silver Heels had he realized how close his triumph was. And it was Reynolds, that profane and ratty miner, who had jerked him down to earth. Dom! How much money it would take, all he could raise! Rogier rose, his mind clear, to begin the tactics of his campaign.

With the first shipment of ore from the Silver Heels, Reynolds and his wife went on a spree that rocked Myers Avenue on its own silver and gold heels. Rogier gave his share from the first carloads to Mrs. Rogier. It was enough pin money to go around handsomely for new frocks and to justify all the time he spent in Cripple Creek. Even Nigger Bill's little son, George Washington, age seven, came in for a brand new suit — candy-striped red, blue and white just like the cast-iron blackamore hitching post in front. The whole family blossomed out like an anemone breaking through the snow. Daddy, doing no more than what everyone expected of him, finally had discovered a gold mine.

Mrs. Rogier, thin and electric, was a Frenchwoman from her sharp aristocratic nose, upraised to cut the air before her. In church she obeyed the divine necessity of maintaining an irreproachable front. Devoutly conscious of the eyes upon her—with her solid entrenchment in that House of the Lord whose pillar she had been longer than most of the congregation could remember—and of the full weight of that carload of ore from the Silver Heels, she sat like a stone carved from pride into an image of humility.

There was much to be proud of. Boné from San Francisco had sent the first copy of his Indian Suite "Manitou" for which Lockhardt had found a publisher, and all the clippings about it. The four songs were catching on. During the evening concerts in Acacia Park, even at the Broadmoore Casino, his "Song of the Corn," "The Wolf Song," "Fire Dance," and "Song of the Willows" were played. With a composer in the family — despite it — Mrs. Rogier felt it incumbent to produce at least one member of the household who could perform gracefully at the piano.

Ona was too old and dull. Mary Ann too young and giddy, and thought only of eating. Perhaps because she had a new beau, whose father owned a delicatessen store catering to the North End trade. To impress him and the young gentlemen who called with him, she jumped to the telephone a half-dozen times a day to call for special dainties. And to placate Rogier in case he might notice the growing bills she ordered oysters and mackerel shipped all the way from his beloved Maryland.

Only Sally Lee could do. Horsey as she was, she had a good ear and a deep rich contralto that enabled her to sing "The Dawn" by D'Hardelot, Stuart's "Bandolero," "L'Esclave" by Lalo, and a group of selected nursery songs of Geibel, Neidlinger, and Riley whenever called upon. To develop her, Rogier obtained Professor Albert E. Dearson. He was a talented man of German and Russian extraction who once had conducted an orchestra in Leipzig, and was now in Colorado for his health. For awhile he was in great demand in the North End. Then the man militated against the musician. He went around in brown leather leggings, neglected to trim his stubble of reddish gray whiskers, and never accepted an invitation to a social function as an unpaid guest. Above all, he had a violent temper. Soon, with one accord, the whole North End raised hands and exclaimed over teacups, "The Master of Musicians, but — !"

Even Rogier met his match the day Professor Dearson came down to audition Sally Lee. The big sliding doors were pulled shut upon professor and pupil, her father and mother. There was not a word spoken until she had finished. "Well," asked Rogier, "do you want to take her?"

Professor Dearson was as blunt. "What! With that old box! It sounds like a street organ!"

"Appears to me it's not the shoes that count but the man who fills them" Rogier answered calmly.

Nevertheless a new piano was installed before Professor Dearson returned. Despite his social setback it was a feather in one's cap to have captured him, and Mrs. Rogier made the most of the opportunity. With Sally Lee driving up to his house with a hundred dollars every whip-stitch, it behooved her to see that Sally Lee learned her lessons. The sanctimonious hours when she was entombed to practice were very well, but let her give vent to her predeliction for the new ragtime and Mrs. Rogier was on her before you could say "Jack Robinson!" The first bar of the "Yama Yama Man" or the "Black Hand Rag" was sufficient to start a row. Still, in due time Sally Lee was admitted into the Musical Club, and even Professor Dearson appeared satisfied that he had wrung the last ounce of gold out of the ore given him to refine.

By summer Cable's position in the house was secure. For weeks he would be away, working up in Cripple Creek. Then he would come down to work in the haberdashery store, sliding into his room and niche in the Rogier household as if he'd never been away. The New Moon apparently had hit a good pocket. "None of us think it's more than that," admitted Cable. "But it has enabled us to lay in a stock of the most fashionable cravats and waistcoats in town. The sale of these should carry us through the summer and give me more time in town."

Everyone of the Rogiers liked the Red Niggah, except Mrs. White; and, as the only man in the house while Rogier was away, he was relied on more and more. Sally Lee and Mary Ann conjectured privately when Ona would marry him. Their conjectures were without the warmth of conviction, however, for there was no sign of romance between them. Besides, they were too old: Ona, an old maid of thirty, and Cable nearing forty.

For Ona herself Cable's friendly companionship seemed quite sufficient. Big-boned and resolute as Rogier, she too repressed within her granite shell any indication of volcanic porphyry within. Cable made no attempt to draw her out. Fluid as he was, sensitive and responsive, Ona felt within him a hard and secret quality that frightened her a little. She no longer thought of his Indian blood, but sometimes she was aware of a peculiar difference in him that for an instant set him apart from everyone else. For one thing, his small feet for a man his size and the care he took to keep them well shod. Shoes were his one extravagance; he always had them handmade from his last at the bootmaker. And the way he walked in them, so softly and lithely that you never heard him coming until he was up to you!

That midsummer evening they drove Akeepee to a place unusual for them both, the Broadmoore Casino. It was still early. Cheyenne Mountain, blue, soft, and benign, loomed up like a backdrop to a prairie stage of flaming Indian paintbrush, bluebells, and wild onions screaming patriotically with vivid colors.

"Isn't the Casino extravagantly expensive?" asked Ona. "Are you celebrating something?"

"Oh, nothing special. But things look pretty good all the way around. The New Moon and the haberdashery shop are each paying their own way, though we're not making much money. And my partners would rather work in the mine than down there, which is good for me."

"And good for me too, Jonathan!" she replied warmly. Nevertheless Ona could not repress her qualms. If she could not envision Cable mucking underground in Cripple Creek with the two husky Grimes, her every glimpse of him in the haberdashery shop showing cravats and waistcoats to genteel New Londoners was more foreboding. A strange dark man whom she could never quite place in his proper setting.

Slapping out the reins, Cable shook Akeepee into a smooth, fast pace. The wind flapped the ends of Ona's scarf about her head and brought the blood to her cheeks, as they flew up the mesa and rounded the curve toward a blazing diamond set in an emerald park.

The long two-storied temple of pleasure, girdled by broad piazzas, its gabled roof upheld by four high, spotless white pillars, was as elegant inside as out. Bar and game and reading rooms were crowded; in the ladies' salon Ona could hear the discreet murmur of Rosner's Hungarian Orchestra reflected from the polished floor of the immense ballroom. A table in the great dining room was reserved for them and Ona sat down with some trepidation among the fashionable, distinguished, and wealthy guests. She would have been distinctly uncomfortable had Mrs. Rogier been present with that air of superiority which masked a lack of the cultural and financial habiliments she had not yet attained. Cable was not impressed. He was not a drinking man, as Mrs. Rogier said, but he loved wine; and he was not too proud to ask for advice in the selection of something appropriate to their taste. He ate hungrily, enjoying the novelty of the food and surroundings. Sitting there he had something of a foreign look about him, with his dark face and Roman nose, his straight black hair, and sensitive brown hands protruding from his starched white cuffs. A simple unaffected man, he knew exactly what he was. Ona was reassured by his presence.

After dinner they rowed across the lake to sit in the little pavilion, staring at the reflection of the Casino lights in the water and listening to the strains of the Hungarian orchestra.

"Why, that's Boné's 'Song of the Willows'," she said suddenly.

"They're all good tunes, that suite of his," Cable replied casually, "but there's nothing Indian about them. They all seem to come from the nose and not the belly."

This extremely acute observation mentioned with such casualness struck her with singular force. She too had been a little disappointed with Boné's Indian suite, expecting something more serious and with a fuller texture than these light melodies. At times she secretly suspected Lockhardt's touch, for had he not prophesied one that Boné's future lay in lighter work?

"You can't very well put a belly-drum in the middle of a piano score," she said defensively. "And of all his songs I like this one best." It was indeed the only one heard often of late. It reminded her not of summer's lush weeping willows drooping over the stream, but of those stark bare branches glowing pink and red against the snow.

Returning to the Casino they watched the dancing in the ballroom awhile, then drove slowly back home in the moonlight. It had been a perfect evening; she felt relaxed and content. Cable acted so too. She could hear him talking to Akeepee as he put her in the stall next to the carriage house, and whistling lowly to the pigeons in their loft.

She was not aware when he came out, so quiet were his steps. Then abruptly, without warning, she felt caught in his arms. It was as if a brutal, engulfing passion had leapt upon her from a darkness where it long had been lurking. Everything struck her at once. The peculiar odor of his body as he bent over her; his hot breath in the instant he kissed her full upon the mouth; the pressure of his knee between her thighs. And suddenly it all came back to her from childhood: that other dark aquiline face with the steady fixed stare of its black eyes into her own, the sharp pain of her burned behind creeping down like a slow mellow glow to her crotch, and the feeling of a warm wet trickle down the inner side of one leg. Here it was again, all of it — the pain and the ecstasy, the fright and sweetness and strange familiarity, all blended together in one incomprehensible whole.

At her cry he released her at once, stepping back into the shadow like an animal withdrawing from its prey. "What's the matter?" he asked in a far-off, strange voice.

And she could hear herself answering in a tremulous voice not her own. "Nothing! Oh Jonathan! Just kiss me again! Now!"

They were married a month later, on a late Sunday morning, in the front room of the house. Only the family and friends were present, yet there was quite a crowd: Professor Dearson, Cable's two partners and the Reynolds couple from Cripple Creek, Denman, Lida of course, Nigger Bill who was to drive them to the depot to catch the train to Denver where they were going to honeymoon in the Brown Palace, and close neighbors.

The news had been calmly accepted in the family. Mrs. Rogier had proposed at once they live in the big master bedroom on the second floor. Ona was delighted with the prospect.

"No!" Cable replied firmly. "We'll have our own home!"

"Not too far away for her to walk here every day. I need her to look after my affairs," Rogier cautioned him.

Now again, as the couple was ready to go out to the waiting carriage, Rogier said gruffly, "Now look, Cable, don't you be staying too long up in Denver. Ona's got a lot of thinking to do about all the work I need done."

Cable's dark face set. "She won't do a bit of thinking about all that if I can help it."

There was a look in Ona's eyes as she ran out to the carriage that remained stamped on all the hearts of the family long after the wheels had rolled away. The look of a woman from whom the curse of an eldest daughter had been suddenly lifted and who at last had found her heart's home. It wasn't as if she had been the family drudge. Hadn't Lida been hired to do most of the work, and didn't the younger girls do their share of chores? But still into the suddenly gaping vacuum created by her absence rushed memories of the quiet, capable, and generally ignored girl who from childhood had borne uncomplainingly the brunt of their pain and worry; who had helped to raise Sally Lee and Mary Ann, Bob, Hiney, and Boné;

who had shared the fatal burden of Sister Molly; who had endured
the foibles of Mrs. Rogier and Mrs. White; whom Rogier now
depended upon to look after his affairs; this simple, untalented girl
who had never had time to finish school, had never been kissed.
Ona!

A long keening cry burst from Mrs. Rogier. And suddenly,
unaccountably, they all broke into tears. Behind them in the dining
room, table and buffet were loaded with everything appropriate to
the occasion: the meats and sweets, pickles and pastries, the rolls
and hot biscuits and honey, the wine and raw whiskey, a box of
Rogier's cigars. No one noticed the spread. They sat weeping
because Ona had got married.

Rogier brushed a furtive tear out of his eye with his fist. "Well, I
hope she stays as long as she has a mind to!" Then he strode out to
sit alone in his shop.

10

These were the days they all remembered! Days lengthening and shortening with the seasons like the rhythmic strokes of Time's accordion. Everywhere, high in the mountains, wide upon the plains, the wine of life rose brimming in its cup; the days shone bright with promise; and ever the song ran on.

In its first decade Cripple Creek had produced $100,000,000 worth of gold. With the closing of the Transvaal mines during the South African War it was leading the world in gold production, and had enabled the United States to acquire $118,435,562 of the world's $255,954,654 worth of gold. The population of Little London, a mile below this greatest gold camp on earth, had increased to 35,000. In the North End there were forty millionaires; on Tejon Street more than 400 mining company offices. No one in the family cared about these statistics — or about those other phenomenal figures on the monthly bills which Rogier casually tossed to Ona to pay. Like a shield bright against the day, tempered to withstand the world, the family stood waiting to receive the heraldic crest of its own Cripple Creek gold. Rogier, as a matter of fact, had given Cable as a wedding token a set of shirt studs fashioned by the jeweler from

Silver Heels gold in the shape of small acorns in which was set a tiny pearl.

Not that Cable had frequent occasions to wear them, selling haberdashery in his and his partners' store the months he was in town, and mucking ore in Cripple Creek the rest of the time. Ona was busy too. They had moved into a little frame house along the creek, just past the Santa Fe Railroad underpass; close enough to walk to the shop every day where she worked for Rogier.

What did it matter? These were the days they all remembered! Days woven into a tapestry of bright promise with threads of Cripple Creek gold.

September came; and as if to end that Indian Summer of a glorious decade with a pageant of praise, Little London held its Sunflower Carnival. No expense was spared to make it the greatest festival the mountains and plains had evern witnessed. All the Utes had come down to their annual encampment to hold their Shan Kive: Chief Ouray, for whom a mountain, town, and county had been named; his wife, the venerated sage, Chipeta; the lesser chiefs, Colorow, Red Shirt, and Little Mound; and little Dripping Spring and Charley Horse. Day and night the drums beat while onlookers, forgetting their prejudices, clapped and yelled. Charley Horse rode a pony to death before a crowd that laughed at the boy's indomitable pride and cold brutality. At a free Cowboy Barbecue booted cooks handed out steaming chunks of beef from a pit six feet wide and thirty feet long. Manitou Day and Pike's Peak Day were tooted in and out with the Colorado Midland Band, the Cowboy Band from Pueblo, and the Rough Riders Band of Colorado City, Past, present, and future paraded by in an endless procession of feathered Utes, cowboys, miners, covered wagons, ore wagons, buckboards, carriages and a horseless Locomobile steam carriage spouting black smoke.

Then came the Flower Parade, arranged by the flower of Little London's aristocracy. From the roof of Cable's store the Rogiers watched the gorgeous display of pride and wealth. Pony traps, spiders, four-wheelers, surreys, tandems, and four-in-hands followed each other down the wide avenues. There was a trap of clematis and oak leaves, another trimmed with holly and evergreen, a spider phaeton smothered in chrysanthemums. Behind this a liveried groom sat enthroned on a seat covered with light blue hollyhocks, proudly driving a chestnut stallion decorated with blue ribbons. Then came Donaldson's brake drawn by a spike team of three grays. Mrs. Rogier gasped. Four thousand! — as the *Gazette* said — 4,000 Jacquinot roses bordered by kinnikinnick! Only to be followed by a team of white mares sporting white snowballs and white silver-willow branches. And still another all red and black: red and black poppies, black horses with red satin blankets, and with harness and hoofs painted red.

The celebrations were climaxed with a four-day meeting of the racing association which had reorganized with an eye toward membership in the Grand Western Circuit. The meeting was held north of town at the new Roswell track built and donated by Stratton. Restrictions were imposed on local horses and no expense was spared to bring for show the finest horseflesh in the West. Ensconced in a grandstand box, the whole Rogier family watched the first day's exhibitions. Lena N who had come within a second of the track record of 2:14 showed off beautifully as did Asbrook's high stepper Jean Valjean and Roberts' trotter Trilby with a record of 2:13½. A sulky was displayed weighing only twenty-four pounds. Drawn by Star Pointer when he made a world record of 1:59¼, it was the only sulky drawn by a harness horse in less than two minutes.

Sally Lee sat disconsolately, chin in hand. "Daddy, I'm just sick you haven't entered Aralee! Why not?"

"A green horse that's never run? In company like this? You must be crazy!"

There were thirteen harness events with $7,500 for purses, running races with $250 purses, and innumerable heats. Monday passed and Tuesday, each complete with thrills. The crowd was settling down. Elimination heats had weeded out many entries and the time was beginning to drop. Ariel in the 2:16 trotting class made 2:22. Torsion in 1:03½ ran the three-quarter mile with lots to spare.

Rogier had begun to look tense and moody. Quitting the grandstand, he spent his time with Denman in the paddock. In the evenings he did not come home for supper, but stayed at Denman's ranch. There he went over Aralee as though she were a fragile piece of amber glass. Aralee, following Little Man, was Akeepee's second colt. A liver-colored chestnut with the same markings — a diamond in her forehead, and white stockings on her near fore and off hind feet, she was in appearance, size, and temperament exactly like her mother. An inch under fifteen hands high, with long sloping shoulders, hocks well down, Aralee showed in her breeding Akeepee's Maryland blue-blood. Just three years old, she paced like a veteran. Gentle and unexcitable as her mother, she ran as if she were alone in all the world. Another Akeepee with the strength of youth, a dream come true at last!

Darkness settled. The stars popped out. Out on the prairies a coyote yapped. "Well, what do you think? It's a terrible chance to take," said Rogier.

Denman lit his pipe. "Damn that Judge! Did you really horsewhip him that time?"

"I said what do you think?"

Denman gave him a curious look. "There never was a horse any righter."

"Then take her down tonight. Late. And be careful." He turned, and walked away.

At breakfast on the last day of the meeting Rogier announced curtly, "Everybody be at the track today! I want you to see what a good horse can do!"

"Which one? Taffy Lass?" Sally Lee asked morosely.

"Keep the bit between your teeth and you'll find out."

The big race of the day was a mile for three-year-olds and up, the winners of the previous elimination heats. The four leaders were Priam, a big gray from the North End; Cheyenne Annie, a Wyoming horse; a beautiful bay mare Ilena II, from Denver; and a nervous little buckskin from New Mexico called Mazie. To compete against these winners the Association had brought one of the finest pacers on the Grand Western Circuit, a foreign chestnut named Taffy Lass, the much touted favorite. Just before the horses were led out, Rogier left the family's box and walked down to the track. They could see his wide shoulders holding back the crowd, legs wide apart, a wisp of smoke from his cigar ruffling in the wind which was to prevent fast time. Denman and Nigger Bill were not in sight.

The long string filed out, followed by the chestnut, fashionably late but not enough to irk the waiting judges. The crowd set up a yell. Taffy Lass, the favorite! The liver-colored chestnut stood in a tremble hardly visible, head down like a thoroughbred in a pasture, wholly unconcerned over the noise, the flutter of ribbons, and the trouble in keeping Mazie still.

"What's the matter with Taffy Lass today?" asked Sally Lee. "Every time she's showed off she keeps arching her neck like she was taking a bow." She kept intently staring at Taffy Lass. "Seems to me she had white stockings on one forefoot and both hindfeet. Do you remember?"

"It's the wrappings. I can't tell," answered Cable.

Then Taffy Lass turned around, stretching out her long neck. Sally Lee caught her breath. The line of those long sloping shoulders, the white diamond on her forehead! Abruptly they broke away, lunged forward, and were off. Sally Lee jumped to her feet. "Aralee! Aralee! It's Aralee!" she kept screaming. A hundred times she had watched that awkward first plunge as the mare settled into her gait, the level head, nose forward, the deceptive long stride. "Aralee! Watch our Aralee!"

The gray beat her at the start, the nervous Mazie jerking at the reins and setting up the dust beside her; but Sally Lee's gaze hung on Aralee. She couldn't tell who was driving, but it wasn't Denman. Ilena II broke from the field with Cheyenne Annie close behind. At the first turn six sulkies were spread out across the track. The little buckskin was too eager and lost her place to the big gray. Ilena II kept her stride like a lady and fought it out with Cheyenne Annie for second place. A length behind, Aralee drew away from the field and slowly crept up on the leaders. With her long even stride she seemed to be moving slowly but unconcernedly, nose out and slightly up, running without effort. Sally Lee shifted her gaze to the man in the sulky. "Oh, if only he doesn't give her her head! I hope Daddy told him what to do till the half!"

As the field swept into the far turn, Sally Lee glanced from the track to steal a look at Rogier down at the finish line. He had thrown away his cigar and stood as if alone and lonely, twisting the hat in his hands. Denman in overalls stood silently beside him. In the box with her, Mrs. Rogier was shrilly screaming at old Mrs. White, wrapped in blankets. Lida Peck and Cable sat with wide eyes, watching a lady of the family run her race. Ona breathed deeply as if at the end of a silent prayer and clasped her hands. And only that great seamed face of Pike's Peak rising majestic and unmoved above the cottonwoods along the creek, stared down at the crowd clamoring for Taffy Lass to lead into the stretch.

It was very close. Aralee and Ilena II, both ladies, were neck and neck with their respective partners, Mazie and Cheyenne Annie. Priam, the gray Beau Brummel, was back with the field. The little buckskin, still nervous, shied at the fluttering ribbons ahead of her at the finish just enough to let Aralee cut ahead into the stretch. Cheyenne Annie who, unharnessed, might have run the legs off any horse on open prairie, gave way to Ilena II. The two ladies swept evenly into the long straight stretch.

Ilena II was fighting beautifully, reins limp on her back, every tremendous stride seeming likely to tear apart her slender body. But Aralee! — in the sunlight she was dark with sweat, her nostrils flaming pink, and still she ran smoothly true in every paced stride, like a machine whirring in perfect time. She had her head and kept her course like an arrow.

Sally Lee jumped up, a flood of tears bursting from her eyes until she could hardly see. Aralee's driver had lifted his whip. "Goddamim" she screamed through her tears. "Don't let him whip her, God! Now now!"

But he did. Yet of Sally Lee, Denman clawing his lower lip, immobile Rogier, of all the crowd, Aralee was the only one who did not seem to notice the whiplash laid on her flank.

Sally Lee let out a single, sobbing scream. "Akeepee!" It was the one perfect tribute. Aralee swept in a nose ahead.

The crowd went wild. Much as it would have liked to see its own horse win, a champion and a favorite had demonstrated her right to their acclaim. The Rogiers stood watching people pouring down from the stands, filling the winning sulky with flowers, and throwing a garland upon a liver-colored chestnut dark with sweat. A few days ago they had stood on the street, a mere family up from Shook's Run, marveling at all the gorgeous flowers displayed by the North End. And now look! Look at those same flowers being thrown at a horse raised in their own back yard, a spindling colt begging cookies at the kitchen door. Aralee! Not Taffy Lass, but Aralee!

Rogier, down on the track, had his hands full pushing back the crowd while Denman hurriedly blanketed Aralee and Nigger Bill unhitched her from the sulky, so they could lead her to the tents. A man in a top hat walked up with the judges. "A beautiful run, Rogier. We just can't thank you. You'll be in your office tomorrow?" Shaking Rogier's hand, he helped to keep back the crowd.

In a dusky stall in the big tent they were alone now. Rogier removed the garland from Aralee's long wet neck. Unobtrusively he tore out a rose and thrust it into his coat pocket. Then he stood at her head, swabbing her nostrils with a wet sponge while Denman and Nigger Bill rubbed her down. Two stalls down, some hostlers were dousing Taffy Lass with warm water to stain her coat darker. Finally Denman and Nigger Bill blanketed Aralee and fastened the straps.

"Is she all right?" asked Rogier.

Denman grinned back. "All right? There never was a horse any righter!"

Rogier thrust a roll of bills into Nigger Bill's hand.

"No, suh!" remonstrated Nigger Bill. "Ah put mah wad on huh nose! I'se all fixed good!"

"Well it won't hurt none if George Washington collects his little bet too, will it?"

They slapped each other on the back, then Rogier turned to Denman. "When it gets dark hitch her to the buckboard and walk her back slowly. I'll see you later."

As he drove down Bijou Hill on his way home, Rogier could see the house ablaze with lights. He pushed open the door, crossed the hall into the dining room. The table was set with a fancy lace cloth and the buffet was stacked with china and polished silver. In the front room all the family were waiting in their Sunday best. Mrs. Rogier was wearing her black silk dress, at her breast a silver brooch given her by Hiney who had lifted it from the boudoir of a famous actress.

"Daddy! I knew she could do it!" yelled Sally Lee.

"I reckon she did come in first," Rogier said shyly.

"I'm just dying to have it!" began Mrs. Rogier. "We could see it from the stand. Isn't it lovely? It'll hang right over the mantel. Then we'll save it in the trunk with the Confederate flag."

"What's that, Martha?" he asked.

Switching around on her chair like a duchess assuming imperial sway, she stuck out her foot for Rogier to tie a black ribbon shoe-lace. While he knelt awkwardly before her, she went on. "That big horseshoe of roses they put over Aralee's head. And that sulky-full of flowers. Why, we'll have enough to smell up the whole house! I told Mary Ann I'd give her a switching if she didn't fill every vase in the house with water. And you better hurry to get fixed up before they come, too!"

Rogier rose slowly and backed against the fireplace. "Who's that coming, you say?"

Mrs. Rogier got up and stamped her foot. "Why, the men with the flowers if you didn't fetch them! And all the people who'll be coming down to congratulate us now they know it was Aralee instead of Taffy Lass. We're all ready to give them wine and coffee. And Mary Ann had some of Durgess' finest cakes sent down." Something in Rogier's face kindled her to sudden anger. "Of course they will! Even the North Enders aren't that stuck up! Why, if Aralee was a nigger's horse you know we'd go down to congratulate him!"

Rogier looked hard and grim. "Sit down and keep quiet. And you, Mary Ann, bring Lida in here too. I've got something to say to all of you that's not to be repeated outside of this house."

He stated the facts briefly and methodically. He and Judge Colton, as they remembered, had had a little trouble after the Judge had ruined Akeepee. That's why he had walked out of the Gentlemen's Driving Association, but without submitting his resignation. All these years the Judge had nursed his grudge, and he had finally got even by not allowing Rogier to enter Aralee. Maybe he was right. By Rogier's failure to submit his resignation, he had been carried on the books as a member who had never paid his dues and was therefore ineligible to enter a horse as a member of the new racing association formed from it. Nor could Rogier enter Aralee as a visiting horse.

But as the meeting got under way, something happened. Taffy Lass had been brought at great expense in order to insure the racing association's admittance into the Grand Western Circuit. She had been exhibited the first day with state-wide publicity, drawing a great crowd to see her run. But the next morning after a workout she had come in weak and trembling like a foaled colt. Off her feed, the altitude, nobody knew what. The owners refused to let her run lest she be injured irreparably. Think what happened to Akeepee. In this devil of a fix the officials themselves had appealed to Rogier to benefit the association, the great crowd, the town itself with a harmless subterfuge. Aralee, an unknown horse, was the same size, color, and build as Taffy Lass, and her clocking on Denman's track warranted her substitution for Taffy Lass. Who could tell the difference in the excitement? In return for this favor, Rogier would be reinstated as a member of the racing association, permitting him to run Aralee under her own name thereafter. What would be the harm? Rogier had been undecided. But Denman had swung him over with a single remark. "Let's see her run. We've waited and worked long enough, Joe." Didn't he owe Denman that, and Nigger Bill, and Akeepee herself? So he assented.

"Poppycock! Monkey business! They've pulled the wool over your eyes!" Mrs. Rogier stood up, her frail body shaking until the black beads trembled on her throat. "Aralee won! That's all there is to it! And me and the girls will see to it everybody in town knows it, if we have to go door to door!"

"Nobody would believe you, Martha. Taffy Lass' name is posted on the records. Not even her owners could do anything about it now. Everybody would think you were just bragging."

There was a deathly silence in the room. Word by word he had stripped away every possibility of flowers, of congratulatory guests, of even confiding the secret to neighbors. Now after twenty years of raising horses, the betrayal of Akeepee, and Little Man's disgrace, Aralee had justified their faith only to have Rogier reduce their one great triumph to the taste of ashes on every tongue.

Sally Lee flung over on the sofa, head down, hands clenched, and began to sob. Rogier walked over to her. "Don't take it like that, girl," he said in a low, halting voice. "When the *Gazette* comes out with a picture of Aralee and Taffy Lass's name under it, let's just sit back and chuckle. It's not the talk and the flowers that count. Akeepee's finally run her race, and Aralee. So've all of us too, I reckon. We all know that, and it's enough." His hand suddenly encountered the crushed rose in his coat pocket. He brought it out and bashfully entwined its stem in Sally Lee's hair. "Dom! It was just a horse race, wasn't it?"

11

The track meeting with Aralee was the straw that indicated how the wind was shifting. Rogier was in trouble in Cripple Creek.

The dip of the original Garnet vein ran northwest and the working shaft had been sunk in a parallel incline in the footwall in order to obtain minimum cost and maximum stability. Diggs and Handel had come to grief at a fault in the vein. It appeared to have been displaced some distance westward, then continuing at the same angle into the leased Fleur-de-Lis property. At this time Rogier, becoming a partner, took over the development. In order to avoid excessive drifting and long tramming by cars to the chutes, it was decided that it would be cheaper to sink another shaft westward at a site suitable for the surface plant. Accordingly Rogier sank a vertical shaft cutting the inclined vein at the second level — two hundred feet. It was continued another hundred feet and the levels connected by a winze, an interior shaft driven at an angle downward in the ore body from a drift and used for ventilation. A new shaft house and boiler room were built, and a small electric light plant installed. Then again the vein had faulted just before the lease was up. Rogier had wired Diggs and Handel to come up on the noon train and was now waiting for them.

It was early fall and the air was chill. Across the gulch he could see a few hirsute aspens quaking in the breeze. A muffled sound as of blasting rolled in upon him, immediately dispelled by the shrill scream of a whistle. It was one o'clock; and exactly on time, like men who thought little of keeping their word but who kept their working hours punctiliously as slaves, Diggs and Handel walked in the door.

Diggs with his bald head, sharp nose, and chamois gloves reminded Rogier of a Thanksgiving turkey. Handel had small feral eyes and a dead white face so smoothly shaven that the bluish tint of his whiskers underneath made his fleshy cheeks appear bloated and decomposed.

Rogier stated the conditions tersely. The assays had been decreasing alarmingly; again the vein had faulted; the lease on the Fleur-de-Lis was almost up. If it were not renewed all the development expense would be lost. If it were renewed there was no guarantee they would not be throwing good money after bad. However he believed that with a crosscut they would pick up the vein again; the Fleur-de-Lis was within the curve of the prophyry limits. He wanted their concurrence and money to proceed.

The two men settled back, Diggs drawing his chamois gloves between his fingers; Handel, poker-faced, eyeing him steadily across the table. They had already discussed the matter, Diggs said, and were ready to abandon the disappointing venture. They both hoped the partnership could be dissolved amicably, and that next time with better luck — his voice spun out into silence.

Something in their ready acquiescence to defeat sounded a warning Rogier could not ignore. "All right. We have only to balance the books and allocate your shares of the cost of the development to you for payment. Also the whole of last month's running expenses which I've paid without holding things up to locate you."

The two men droned their rebuttal in oily tones, Handel murmuring apologetically about poor business in their trucking business, the unpaid loans at the bank. Diggs finally came to the point, explaining that the two mines were not separated specifically in the partnership agreement, and that as he and Handel had done their share on the Garnet, it had been up to Rogier to develop the Fleur-de-Lis.

"Preposterous!" Rogier said gruffly. "The Garnet was your own sole venture long before I came in. The development of the Fleur-de-Lis was undertaken by the three of us as partners, bearing equal shares of the cost!"

"As I say, the agreement does not separate the two interlocked mines. We've had it carefully gone over by legal counsel."

"Poppycock, and you know it!" snorted Rogier. "Personally I believe enough in the Fleur-de-Lis to renew the lease by myself if you're backing out."

"But the lease is in our three names. It can't be renewed by one separately," answered Diggs softly.

"All I want from you now is the statement you're through! Are you or aren't you?"

The now heated conference ended fifteen minutes before train-time with the verbal agreement that Diggs and Handel, through their lawyer who had drawn up the partnership agreement, would renew the lease in all their names for another six months, and that operations should be continued. They shook hands formally, and the two men rushed for their train.

The months dragged by. Rogier's suspicions increased. The noncommittal lawyer, Nicholas, who had drawn up the original agreement, stated he had received no instructions to draw up an extension of the lease. Diggs and Handel could not be found; whenever Rogier called at their office, they were out of town. Rogier accepted this as plausible, for they owned a trucking business that covered a large area. Curtailing expenses was not enough; Rogier was running short of cash with the heavy drain upon him. Reason and suspicion counseled him to shut down the working and sit tight. Yet some perverse compulsion kept him driving down the shaft.

Then he happened to think of Stratton who had agreed to guarantee him against loss in return for a one-sixth share of the Fleur-de-Lis if Rogier would develop his American Eagles.

This Rogier had done. The American Eagle No. 1 and Number 2 on top of Bull Hill were great mines in the Stratton tradition and with Stratton's millions behind them to provide a great shaft house containing the best surface plant money could buy, deep shafts, tunnels well timbered with seasoned pine stulls and props, and a triple expansion pumping engine with a capacity of one thousand gallons a minute. The work had been little trouble, and Rogier had taken the precaution of installing change rooms to prevent high-grading.

The practice was becoming profitable in the district. Selected high-grade ore worth from $10 to $30 a pound could be slipped out by miners wearing high-graders' belts under their clothes. Change rooms prevented these thefts. The arrangement provided two rooms, one for working clothes and the other for street clothes, miners being obliged to walk naked between them so that concealed ore could be detected.

Stratton meanwhile had sailed to Europe in an effort to recuperate from the strain of worry over his mounting millions, and his excessive drinking. None of the spas did him any good — Aix-les-Bains in southern France, Constance in Switzerland, Carlsbad, Vienna, Brighton on the south coast of England. Suddenly from London came the electrifying news that in a fit of despair he had sold his Independence for $10,000,000.

Now, in the midst of Rogier's worries, he returned home and shortly walked down the alley to Rogier's shop. Rogier was frightened at the change in him. Frail and wasted, moody and irritable, Stratton had begun to die. He seemed pleased enough with the work done at the American Eagles, but with his hands twitching he demanded abruptly why Rogier had fired a man called Bert Jensen.

"He's a high-grader and an agitator. I kicked him out the minute I recognized him," Rogier replied.

Stratton's gray-blue eyes chilled. "You're working for me now and don't you forget it! When I send a man up to work for me he stays!"

They faced each other for the last time: Rogier who first had worked for Stratton, Stratton who then worked for Rogier, and now Rogier who again had worked for Stratton.

"Not with me around, Stratton!"

Stratton flew into a rage. "This is the last time I'll have any dealing with you! I'm through with you for good!" He yanked out his check book. "I'm going to pay you off for everything! How much?"

Rogier was about to mention the large sum representing Stratton's private one-sixth share in the Fleur-de-Lis and for which he was now in debt. Before he could speak, Stratton, who perhaps had forgotten the matter, resumed his tirade while scribbling his name on a blank check. "Everybody I know is trying to get something out of me, trumping up verbal promises, filing fake lawsuits, foisting off on me dry holes! Here! Fill out the amount yourself and be damned to you!"

Rogier looked at the check after Stratton had stalked out the alley door. It had been signed, but the amount left blank. How shrewd his old carpenter had become! Had he really trusted his old friend to fill out a modest amount? Or was he already on his way to the bank to stop payment? Or was this merely a grand gesture to shame him? Angry himself, Rogier thrust the check in a book on the shelf.

The agonizing months wore on. Distrusting lawyers whom he had never used as an honest builder, and trying to conceal his affairs from Ona, he depended on himself to weather the storm: borrowing money from the bank, transferring his accounts back and forth, selling one of his downtown store buildings. When this was not sufficient, he bid on two new construction jobs — one for rebuilding the Broadmoore Casino which had burned down, a lucrative job which he lost; and the other a four-story addition to one of the town's hotels which was awarded to him. With this to supervise as well as the Silver Heels and Fleur-de-Lis, he was seldom in the shop.

"What's this bill for pumping equipment marked Gloriana?" Ona asked him one day when he came in. "Don't tell me you've opened another new working, Daddy?"

"Pay it and forget it! I know what I'm doing if you don't!"

It was soon evident that he didn't. He was too frantically busy, in fact, to follow the rumors of Stratton's activities until the official reports made front-page news. The Midas of the Rockies, Colorado's Count of Monte Cristo, the Croesus of Cripple Creek was dying of a cirrhotic liver and diabetes, and drinking more than ever. But the other fatal disease he had contracted years before was spreading at a more alarming pace. Through his veins raced liquid gold; from his inflamed mind rose fantasies of greater wealth — no less than all the gold in Cripple Creek. To obtain it he already had bought hundreds of claims and acres, one-fifth of all the gold producing area, and was still buying every mine and working he could get his hands on. Nor was this enough. The Klondike gold rush in Alaska was under way; and Stratton, outfitting an expedition, had sent two boats, the *W.S. Stratton* and the *Florence,* up the Yukon to Dawson.

If this tragic display of the last ravages of gold fever shocked Rogier, he was stunned by the impertinent assumption on which Stratton had based his Cripple Creek purchases. Why, he believed that the convergence of all the veins and ore chutes criss-crossing the district was somewhere in the triangle marked by Gold, Globe and Ironclad Hill. What a monstrous fantasy!

Rogier's own intuition had guided him slowly and surely up into the neck of that heart-like, pear-shaped, porphyritic area of mineralization; over the Altman saddle; up the narrowing gulch beyond the Silver Heels to the root-stem of the fruit — that deep crack high on the slope of the Peak itself into which he would strike into its golden heart. But to prove it, he would have to strike a showing in the Fleur-de-Lis; and Stratton's announced assumption only committed him further to the folly of pouring down its shaft all the profits from his job in town.

The assays increased in value, but pay ore had not been reached and the renewed lease ran out. Rogier knew he had reached the end of his rope. He dismissed the crew, closed the mine, and notified Diggs and Handel he was through. This time they were in their office with Nicholas when he arrived for the meeting.

"I'm sorry we were not advised of your action in closing the mine," said Diggs. "Handel and I had just persuaded Mr. Nicholas here to extend the lease again. Now you have made it worthless. But as long as termination papers have drawn, you might as well sign your release so we can wind things up legally."

Rogier gave each of the three men a look of unutterable scorn. "You heard what I said, didn't you? I'm through!" He turned and walked out the door with the same ingrained integrity and foolish pride with which his father before him had relinquished his rice plantation.

In despair he went to one of the best mining lawyers in town in an effort to obtain reimbursement of expenses for his development of the working. The lawyer, Brooks, listened to him carefully. "Leave your papers with me, Mr. Rogier, and come back a week from today. My secretary will give you an appointment."

A week later Brooks received him with a dour face. "I have reviewed your matter fully, Mr. Rogier. I find this agreement highly irregular. May I be presumptious enough to ask why, before entering into such a partnership and spending such considerable sums of money, you did not come to me or another reputable mining attorney?"

"Diggs and Handel assured me that Nicholas would handle the matter to all our best interests."

"Mr. Nicholas is retained to look after the best interest of Mr. Diggs and Mr. Handel and their freight truckage business. Apparently he has done so."

"I'm not in the habit of questioning any man's integrity! My own word's as good as my bond. Ask any man!"

"I have," replied Brooks softly. Then after looking at Rogier a long time he said sternly, "Mr. Rogier. Business is growing more and more complicated. Each type has its own peculiarities. That's why there are professional attorneys in every field. No one should hesitate to take advantage of them." He drummed on the table with his fingers. "You might take the case to court, but I couldn't handle it. There are holes in this agreement you could drive an elephant through."

Rogier jumped up from his chair. "You're trying to tell me I've been hoodwinked and hornswaggled by those mountebanks, thieves, and downright crooks!"

Brooks' only reply was to open his hands emptily.

Ona, entering the shop a short time later, saw Rogier bending over a roaring fire in the stove. "What are you burning on such a warm morning, Daddy?"

Rogier snorted. "All that stock in the Garnet and Fleur-de-Lis I bought out of courtesy to those two mountebanks!"

Ona looked at him a long time. Then she said quietly, "That stock went up this morning seventeen points on the announcement that Diggs and Handel had sold the properties to Stratton."

The look in his eyes was frightening. She went back to the house.

Diggs and Handel had sold out just in time. That September Stratton died — just over ten years since he, as an obscure carpenter and penniless prospector, had discovered the Independence and opened up the greatest gold camp on earth.

The fame and the glory of success, the thunderous roar of world acclaim, the glowing wealth of Cripple Creek gold — what did it matter to a man who like Silver Dollar Tabor before him now lay entombed in pinkish Pike's Peak granite, while down a hundred gulches the sparse aspens quaked in the breeze, and wisps of clouds gathered languidly above the Peak to presage the first snowfall?

Rogier released the end of his T-square to slap decisively on the drafting table and stared out the window. The sun was rising but a few stars still shone brightly in the sky. Once again it loomed before him as it had the first time he had glimpsed it a quarter of a century ago; like something risen from the depths of dreamless sleep to the horizon of wakeful consciousness, without clear outline yet embodying the substance of a hope and meaning that seemed as vaguely familiar as it was ineffable. The clouds lifted. Shadows, seams, and wrinkles smoothed out. Under the rising sun it lifted a face, serene, majectic, and suffused a glowing pink, yet wearing a look benign, compassionate, and divine that he had never recognized before. Oh great mother of mountains, womb of all creation, Self of all selves, how he had misjudged her! She was not an adversary but an ally in his quest. Men had lived and died, never knowing what they sought while she had waited to clasp them to her granite breast, to take them into the prophyric womb from which they had been born, and to welcome them home again into the one vast golden heart of which they had been a single beat. There she stood as she had stood for aeons immeasurable and would still stand, rearing solidly aloft until the stars themselves were pulled from their sockets by the hand of Time. But he himself was Time! He could feel the ages born within him hardening his bones as they had hardened the sharks' teeth imbedded in the limestone cliffs, running through his veins with their ebbs and tides, evolving the brain cells that had envisioned the image of the goal now clear before him. Time! Eternity would give him all the time he needed to achieve it.

Mrs. Rogier pushed open the door. "Daddy! Haven't you been to bed all night! You wanted to catch the first train to Cripple Creek, so I came down."

He patted her clumsily on the back. Good women, like bright blades, shine best in adversity. "Just doing a little figuring, Martha. That's all."

"It's going to snow up there. I've laid out your winter coat and packed your bag. You better get ready. Ona and Jonathon will be coming after you."

"I'm ready, Martha! Been ready a long time!" he answered cheerfully.